Praise for the novels of Christy Yorke

"Peopled with sympathetic characters, adding to the charm of this often ethereal exploration of the complications of love."

—*Publishers Weekly* (starred review)

"Fabulous, delightfully unique. The real spell is cast by Christy Yorke's lyrical voice and stunning characterizations. Haunting and evocative, it will hold the reader spellbound until the very last page."

—Kristin Hannah

"Wise, warm, and lyrical. Christy Yorke writes with the brilliance of a fine poet and the kind heart of a true believer."

—Deborah Smith

Song of the Seals

CHRISTY YORKE

BERKLEY BOOKS, NEW YORK

A Berkley Book
Published by The Berkley Publishing Group
A division of Penguin Putnam Inc.
375 Hudson Street
New York, New York 10014

This is a work of fiction. Names, characters, places, and incidents either are the product of the author's imagination or are used fictitiously, and any resemblance to actual persons, living or dead, business establishments, events, or locales is entirely coincidental.

Book design by Tiffany Kukec
Cover design by Rita Frangie
Cover illustration by Maggie Taylor

PRINTING HISTORY
Berkley trade paperback edition / February 2003

Visit our website at
www.penguinputnam.com

Library of Congress Cataloging-in-Publication Data

Yorke, Christy.
Song of the seals / Christy Yorke.—Berkley trade pbk. ed.
p. cm.
ISBN 0-425-18824-8
1. Women—California, Northern—Fiction. 2. California, Northern—Fiction. 3. Loss (Psychology)—Fiction. 4. Foster home care—Fiction. 5. Foster parents—Fiction. I. Title.
PS3575.O634 S66 2003
813'.54—dc21 2002026127

PRINTED IN THE UNITED STATES OF AMERICA

10 9 8 7 6 5 4 3 2 1

For my brothers,
James and David,
who were the first ones I called

. . . my soul is full of longing
for the secrets of the sea,
And the heart of the great ocean
Sends a thrilling pulse through me.

—HENRY WADSWORTH LONGFELLOW

Acknowledgments

Writing a passable novel is a difficult and lonely experience. Writing one to be proud of is a collaborative effort. First and foremost, I want to thank my husband, Robert Cohen, for being the one part of my life I've never doubted, and the one person who has never doubted the value of my writing. I'm also blessed to spend my days with my two joyful, imaginative children, Claire and Dean, who keep me abreast of wonder.

This book is dedicated to my brothers, David and James, inveterate sympathizers and loyal friends. Fellow artists, they've deflected a good portion of Mom's dismay and offered personal adventures too wild to put into print. When all else has failed, they've given splendid advice on gardening and feng shui.

I'm lucky enough to have four parents to call when great and sad things happen, and two wonderful in-laws who have warmly embraced me and generously financed my writing time. Thank you, June and Steve Young, Rocky and Pat Yorke, and Shelly and Leona Cohen.

Other people's books helped enormously. *The Bird in the Waterfall* by Jerry Dennis makes the story of water an engrossing read. *Folklore and the Sea* by Horace Beck is an invaluable resource for oceanic mythology. I read dozens of books about the sometimes thrilling, usually habit-forming lives of fishermen, and the one that stands out is *Their Fathers' Work* by William McCloskey, a fascinating and thorough descent into choppy fishermen's waters. Nothing took as much courage to read or proved as ultimately satisfying as Lois Gold's *The Sacred Wound*, the spellbinding story of the author's devastating loss and eventual healing from the death of her only child. Her words caught and held me from the first sentence as few books have.

Freelance editor Lesley Kellas Payne had the guts to tell me all the things I didn't want to hear. She was right. And Leona Nevler, my new editor from heaven, did more than treat me and my work with professionalism and respect. She restored my faith in myself and in the simple joy of writing.

Finally, I cannot overstate how positive a force my agent, Natasha Kern, has been to my career, my growth as a person and a novelist, and my peace of mind. Her unswerving loyalty, relentless faith, and keen editorial eye are as much a part of this novel as my words.

Song of the Seals

— 1 —

Fog

When she began to live again, she craved, of all things, fog. The thicker the better, fog soupy enough to ground planes and send the Santa Monica sunbathers scurrying inland. Slick and silky fog, like whale skin, rising and falling in long, sinuous arcs. She wanted to feel it around her neck like a cool, silver necklace or coating her throat like that first evening cocktail. Only then would the difficulty she normally had taking a deep breath turn suddenly to relief, as if the fog flushed her system, prying loose the impediments deep in her lungs.

Mist curled her hair and smoothed her complexion. Freckles, she'd come to believe, faded with every gray day. Dark days seemed a gift, someone's stab at recompense—she'd have the beach to herself, would not have to suffer the smell of cocoa butter or the jarring beat of a radio tuned to rap.

So it was little wonder that when the baiting began, it began with the clearing. The fog, which had been clinging to the sand

and sea for days, rose up like a giant white bird and flew northward. The sun came on like a spotlight, and Kate Vegas blinked a time or two, feeling ambushed, suddenly exposed. Near the pier, the same old man swung a metal detector, and the Zamboni-like machines the Santa Monica City Council had splurged on groomed the sand into snake tracks. It was setting up to be a typical southern California October day—warm, dry, heartbreakingly clear—and though Kate still had a little more packing to do, when she pined after the fog, she knew she was already gone.

She turned toward the narrow street that, two blocks away, dead-ended at her apartment. An apartment she had already sublet. Two steps toward home, she got a whiff of something awful. Rotting seaweed. Perhaps that Long Beach oil spill oozing in with the tide. She shielded the sun with her hand, looked up the beach. Then she saw him.

Ray Vegas leaned against the waist-high concrete wall, his hands in the pockets of his faded blue jeans, black boots toe deep in the sand. He was thinner than she remembered, shorter, as if he'd spent the last eighteen years shrinking. All that black hair she'd once run her fingers through was streaked with white, uncombed.

She felt a familiar stabbing sensation below her heart, a pain that until this moment she'd thought she'd blanked out, like the agony of childbirth. She recalled the last time she'd seen him, the inhuman sounds she'd made. She felt so nauseated, she did not believe she could stand there and withstand the memory. She even said out loud, "I am going to fall."

But she did not. She squared her shoulders, calculated the time it would take to run home, into the arms of her father. Before she had a number, before she even moved, she decided the notion was silly and, worse, weak. She had long since stopped believing in the power of Ray Vegas, though the sight of him standing there, lighting a cigarette, then holding it between his thumb and forefinger, reignited some long-buried instinct, her most primal, murderous urge.

Her legs moved with an energy she hadn't exhibited since she'd begun taking in the children, since she'd learned the depths of exhaustion a mother of unhappy, cynical, and even criminal teenagers can feel. She realized the peace she had struggled for was like an old scar—functional but ugly, something that shouldn't have been there, if everything had gone well. Now it began to ache.

She ran across the sand just as she might have eighteen years ago, looking for some kind of weapon—broken glass or jagged rock—anything to cut out his diseased heart. In the beginning, she'd imagined this moment a thousand times, and it usually ended splendidly in her killing him with a slow-acting poison that began innocuously enough with a little foaming of the mouth, perhaps some queasiness, then accelerated rapidly into agonizing abdominal pain, paralysis, death.

She'd lived on that fantasy, digested it like food, but now it started making her a little sick. The sand snared her ankles, reduced her to slow-motion. She looked at the wall and he was no closer. She looked again and he was gone.

She fell to her knees on the sand. The parking lot on the corner was empty, the whitewashed condominiums on this stretch of clean beach lifeless. She spotted one tentacle of fog still clinging to the shoreline, then that too disappeared before her eyes.

She breathed deeply, but already the air was too light to capture, dry and speckled with sand. The grains stuck in her throat. She forced herself to laugh. She had conjured a ghost and that in itself might be optimistic, a sign that she valued life still. It was merely the wrong spirit. The only ghosts she believed in were the ones kept alive by devotion. The only psychic she'd put any stock in was Savannah Dawson, a tarot card reader with a blind spot for bad fortunes. Kate had driven to San Francisco a dozen times to let the woman read the palms of each of her children, to hear the confident promises of true love, long lives, and wealth.

She'd imagined Ray because of the move. She'd once sworn she would never leave Los Angeles, never budge from the place where she could be found. But over time she suffered the same fate as couples who've been married forever: She began to wonder what her life would have been like if she'd made no vows, if she'd learned, earlier on, to be less sentimental. She began to appreciate the value of change.

When her seventeen-year-old foster son, Wayne, pleaded with her to move north, to a fishing town he'd read about, she had actually had to fan the grief. This morning, she had walked not to say good-bye to Los Angeles, a town so spread out and disjointed she had lost what she loved best inside it, but to hide her guilty excitement beneath the fog, to run like a sprinter so no one got a good glimpse of the light in her eyes. She had dredged up tears, one last, long shudder, now that these were the only things she had left.

That shudder might have summoned the devil, if she was prone to that kind of dramatic thinking. But she was not. She started back toward her apartment at a brisk pace, did not turn around once. She believed in heaven but not in hell, in fate instead of in God. If the answers were in church, she would not find them. She'd stopped going when she began to question not only the doctrine but also the intentions of the pastor, the sincerity of the choir. When she no longer believed a single word that was said.

Wayne had already piled his meager belongings on the curb. Her father, Gerald, had popped the hood on her car and was swiping the dip stick. A rogue breeze caught her shoulder-length hair and slapped it hard into her eyes, drawing tears.

"Hey, sweetheart," her father said. "Some morning, huh? Fog's clearing out quick."

She smelled cut grass, her neighbor's jasmine. The Dooleys on the second floor blared hip hop. Mrs. Crandall, who played a conniving nurse on *General Hospital,* sat on the stoop practicing lines. It was amazing really, extraordinarily lucky, to have accumulated next to nothing all these years—a few boxes of clothes, her paints and canvases stacked in the trunk of her car, no friends who would mourn her for long, no child she could keep. She could leave, follow the fog, start over. She could paint anywhere; the only thing tying her to Los Angeles was memory and a pinprick of hope she could hardly acknowledge, if she wanted to make *this* boy happy. She and her father had talked about going to Miami after this, but really, she had no idea where she'd end up. This secretly delighted her in a way her paintings and her children could not. Sorrow had once seemed lodged in a loftier atmosphere than anger and even joy, but over time she had realized it was no different. As with anything, it snapped like a frayed cable if you put too much weight on it, if you hung your whole life on its thread.

"You sure you're okay with this?" Kate asked. "Just leaving?"

Her father replaced the stick and moved on to the various liquids her car required. "You realize I've never been north of San Francisco? Lived in California all my life and never been north of the Golden Gate." He shook his head as if this galled him, as if it was the disappointment of his life.

"I don't know about you, but I feel like a teenager," Kate said.

"Just heading out without even a hotel lined up, let alone a place to live. I feel made of air."

Her father stuck a funnel in the hole she could never find and added a quart of oil. In the last twenty years, his hair had gradually fallen out. She had told time by his slow slide into baldness, his switch from slacks and wing tips to sweat pants and sneakers, each purple spot that rose up on the hands he had once used as weapons. He had put on more weight, especially after her mother, Patti, died. Thirty, maybe forty pounds. It was all around his middle, hard as stone. Sometimes she imagined he'd gone through the house after her mother had died swallowing the things she'd loved best—her silver jewelry, paperback novels, the porcelain Lladrós they'd bought her every Mother's Day. He didn't move right anymore. He'd been fierce once, a Los Angeles detective. Now he grimaced when he sat down, sometimes cried out when turning too fast, as if too many things were clanking around inside him.

"I'm ready for a little adventure myself," he said.

She toyed with the idea of telling him she'd seen her husband, but it was only melodrama. She'd already grouped the mirage with the other things she would leave behind—a bulky armoire, a dozen old paperbacks on the shelf in the closet, a bottle of champagne she'd bought on some New Year's Eve and never drunk. Her father had suffered enough on her behalf. Seventeen years ago, he and her mother had passed on a trip to Europe, afraid to leave her, worried about what she might do with that bottle of Valium the doctor had prescribed. They'd manned the hotline, cooked her dinner for the better part of a year. Then her mother had gotten sick, and worse than that, the complications from MS took their sweet time killing her. After the funeral, her father could have moved to Miami—his dream—but he'd stayed in the same tiny house in Santa Monica so he could watch over Kate, keep on top of the investigation, hold her during the sobbing jags after everyone else grew frustrated with her relentless crying. He'd taken up woodworking, making rocking horses for other people's grandchildren.

He wouldn't leave as long as he thought he might be needed. For as long as she could remember, he'd passed up poker Fridays and fishing trips on the off chance he'd be required during the night. Obviously he'd never forgotten the night she'd stood on the roof of her six-story apartment building and climbed out onto the ledge. She'd heard the rattle of traffic below her, but she was so alone wind didn't touch her; it bounced off her nose and headed right back to sea. Her father had found her, but he'd been on the force long enough to know to keep his distance, to feign calm.

He'd stayed by the door, but when he spoke, his usually gruff voice was wobbly, like a little boy's. "Honey?" he'd said. "Honey. Come on back now. Come here, sweetheart."

Three years since her baby had been stolen from her, and she hadn't willed herself dead yet. Three years when she should have succumbed to despair, but her body had betrayed her and continued to work. She'd been to forty states following leads, but the more telling fact was that she had gotten up every morning breathing. Even on the morning after William had been taken, she'd eaten half a bowl of Raisin Bran. *That* was the most hideous betrayal, that living, those hunger pangs, the unrelenting urge to go to the bathroom. Even worse, she reached a point when she woke up some mornings and didn't think of the baby first thing, when she didn't want to think of him, when she betrayed him all over again by waking up all right.

"Look at the ocean out there," her father had said. "So beautiful I can hardly stand it. God's got a soft spot, that's for sure."

"God does not exist."

She heard the shuffle of his tennis shoes, the nervous swallows he hid with a dry cough. Of course he didn't understand. He survived as a detective for the LAPD—pulling sheets over babies, shooting heart-high in order not to be shot—for one simple reason: He was on the right side. He believed in justice, and any man who did so in this day and age had to know when to play blind. He had to have a share and a half of faith.

If God was there, he would have noticed she could no longer curl her arm into a cradle and form a pillow of soft skin beneath her shoulder. If God was there, he would have given her the courage to jump. Instead, by the time her father reached her, her legs were numb and she knew she was going to close down the hotline. She allowed her father to take her arm, then she rose on tiptoes, as close to heaven as she could get, and spit at it. She never looked up again. Even years later, when the children started coming, when they told their first jokes and she laughed, she kept that one vow. She made her peace with everyone but Ray and God. Both, in her opinion, were unforgivable.

Now, she squeezed her father's arm, kept her phantoms to herself. "Start packing," she said. "Wayne's been up since dawn. I'll bring down the last of the bags and we'll go."

She walked into the building, remembered to check the mail one last time before the stop was put on tomorrow. She took out a stack of catalogs and bills, started to climb the stairs. She made it only to the second floor when she spotted the pink envelope with no return address. Years ago, she'd gotten all kinds of letters from strangers—tips, leads, sympathy notes. She'd found, in the first few weeks after it happened, that there was an almost mystical reciprocity of affection between her and strangers. She was more generous with people than she'd ever been—forgiving impatient drivers, putting an arm around teenagers with no respect—while strangers hugged her without warning, with no knowledge of her situation except for the horror-struck look in her eyes and the precarious way she stood, always leaning. A woman she'd never seen before had shown up on her doorstep with an afghan she'd been knitting for her grandson—a boy who had died of leukemia before she could finish the last stitch. Kate still had that blanket; it was packed in a suitcase with one precious photo album and the only infant-sized dressing gown that had been left behind.

But it had been years since she'd gotten a note. She sat down, ran a finger over the wavery script, checked the postmark. Cambridge, Massachusetts. She worked a fingernail under the seal, pried it open. She saw the tip of a photograph.

She leaned back, caught her breath. She heard Wayne thundering down the stairs. He bypassed the last two steps, leapt to the second-floor landing, a laundry bag stuffed with his clothes in hand.

"This is awesome, Kate," he said. "This is so rad."

She laughed, tried to grab hold of him but he was too quick. He flew by, was down to the ground floor in a second. "I don't want you to get too excited," she called after him. "I know that article said they need fishermen, but we have no idea if they'll take you on. We really don't know anything. We're taking such a risk."

Wayne turned back, his free hand tapping his jeans, the whites of his eyes cleared of the last fuzzy traces of marijuana. She knew this for a fact, thanks to court-ordered drug tests. His smile was brilliant. "It's no risk when you're doing what makes you happy. I know all I need to. Seal Bay is where I'm staying. This is it."

He launched himself out of the building, tossed his bag in the back of the car. Her father started the engine.

She looked down at the envelope. The corner of the photo was blurry—dark blue, perhaps the edge of a table, a lace curtain beyond. Her heart had begun to pound, rattling her chest, sending pulses up her neck to the soft skin behind her ear. She pressed a finger against the pulse, came away with a bead of sweat. She traced the white border of the photo, slid it back inside the envelope. She looked out the door, watched Wayne, who, for once, was talking too much for her father to get a word in edgewise. Wayne, who had spent twenty-two days in her house before saying hello.

"Silly," she said to herself, then she slid out the photograph. She stared at it a good ten seconds before the world went dark. She knew the picture well; she had taken it herself. William was two weeks old, still with white speckles on his nose and cheeks, his fist curled up under his chin, his eyes squeezed shut and glistening at the corners. He had an uneven thatch of black hair and wore the light blue dressing gown she'd picked out herself, on a shopping spree Ray had told her they couldn't afford.

Something emerged from her throat, a cry, perhaps a scream. Something loud and raw enough to draw her father and Wayne, to bring them running. The alarm on her father's face was bad enough, but it was Wayne's resignation that steadied her. He walked in the building with arms crossed, expecting to be denied. He'd anticipated nothing less than total disappointment for weeks, since she'd told him they could move to Seal Bay. Every time he'd dropped a fork or been told to turn down the television, he'd closed down his expression, uncoiled his body as if he'd already been steamrolled.

She stood, slipped the photograph back into the envelope before either of them saw it. The worst possible thing had already happened. What more did she have to fear? It was a prank, and not a very good one. Only one person could have done it. Ray had taken this photo with him the day he'd stolen his own son, and she wasn't about to listen to another thing Ray Vegas had to say. She wasn't about to believe in him.

"I slipped," she said. "Turned my ankle. It's fine now."

She walked down the stairs, ignoring her father's steady gaze. She took Wayne's arm, felt him stiffen. "No more dawdling," she said and watched his shoulders rise up despite his attempts at cynicism, watched him sway to the balls of his feet. "Go get the last of the bags. We're following the fog north."

— 2 —

The Merrows

Kate Vegas had read about the hundred-year-old California laurel tree that stood guard over Seal Bay, but the picture in Wayne's newspaper clipping did not do it justice. She stopped the car at the top of Fahrenheit Hill and rolled down the window. The tree on the knoll above her was easily fifty feet high, twice as wide, with meandering trunks and gargantuan roots pushing up through the soil like dinosaur bones. Apparently, not even mealybugs and whiteflies bothered the tree; the leaves were the size of softballs.

"You know what they say about it," Wayne said. He sat beside her, his hands spread out on the dashboard. "They say when it gets a cut and weeps, a man goes to sea and doesn't return."

Kate glanced at him, saw that he was smiling, delighted. Apparently, he couldn't ask for more than the chance to succumb to legend. She shook her head, looked for help from her father, who had been dozing against the boxes in the backseat for the last few hours. He came awake slowly, probably from the growing stink.

"Oh," Kate said, and reached for one of the peppermints she kept in the glove compartment. She popped one in her mouth, rolled up the window, but the noxious odor had already filled the car. It smelled like gasoline, and she felt a prickle along her neck that intensified when she noticed the demise of the bees. They seemed to swoon in mid-flight above the tree, falling into what might be tombs of oozing amber sap.

"It's ridiculous," she said, but Wayne laughed.

"Oh, yeah? The first time it was Crazy Mary's husband. That's what they called him in the newspaper. Caught his hand on a hook and went overboard as extra bait."

The newspaper Wayne had shown her featured a grainy picture of this spot, the damp inhabitants of Seal Bay picnicking beneath the sheltering limbs of the laurel tree. They'd sat in the laps of roots, eaten ham sandwiches with their backs to what appeared to be a fine, flat ocean. Dressed in their finest, wide-brimmed hats, lace collars against their chins, they had seemed oblivious to the viscous fog creeping up the hill behind them, to the fact that, possibly within seconds, they would lose each other.

An unsettling photograph, but what had unnerved Kate more were the paragraphs beneath it. The tale of the two times the tree wept, and the men went to sea and did not return.

Crazy Mary's husband Wally Felder was indeed the first casualty. He'd gone out longlining, just like he'd gone out longlining for twenty-five of his forty-one years, but this time the bait hooks snagged him and pulled him overboard. By the time the crew untangled his nibbled body from the net and stood in front of Mary's door, hats in hands, the gash in the laurel tree had scarred over. The tree went on to grow to gargantuan heights, producing lovely, sassafras-like leaves, but after that no one curled up in its granite-hard branches or steeped its leaves for tea. Only daring teenagers and the loveless scrubbed the mildew from its trunk and took a skiff into the harbor, just to see what might happen.

Twenty years after that first drowning, they got their answer. The tree wept again and three men out on a pleasure cruise on a perfectly sunny August afternoon were never heard from again. A rogue wave, people said, but they also took a can of black sealant up Fahrenheit Hill and painted over the tree's wound.

Kate started up the car, unimpressed. Even if the superstition was true, which she doubted, death wasn't much of an accomplishment. A real feat would have been to bring those fishermen home and make them happy. To take a boy like Wayne, a boy who expected nothing, and give him everything he wanted.

She blasted the fan, drove past a startling Victorian-style house painted in copper and bloodred. Farther down the hill, most of the buildings looked as if they had once been as bright. They were all the more forlorn for having faded, the years of relentless fog and sea spray chipping away at emerald banisters, dimming magenta siding to a disconcerting shade of flesh. The porches on most establishments were mildewy and sagging, even the grass had been overrun with moss. A woman coming out of the Mercantile wore rubber boots and a khaki-colored rain jacket, though it wasn't raining, and turned at the hum of the unfamiliar car.

The fog sat a hundred yards out on the bay, like a curtain hiding what came next. Tepid sunlight hit a rusted metal arch on the street to the docks, Pier 27 it said, though Kate saw only the one pier. There were a dozen boats in the harbor, each weathered to the same shade of gray. A few were occupied by large, silent men restringing nets or repairing trolling poles.

Despite the L-shaped breakwater, fashioned out of hard, basalt rock, the harbor was plagued by whitecaps, and two-foot waves slowly ate away at the dock pilings. Seal Rock marked the entrance to the harbor, with thousands of bellowing elephant seals lounging on its rough cliffs.

Wayne stared at the curlicues of whitecaps, the ever-changing fog, and sucked in his breath. "Man," he said. "Look at it. Didn't I tell you? The elephant seals out there on the rock? The breakwater? Nothing beyond that but sea and fishing boats. Didn't that reporter get it just right?"

"It's picturesque," Kate said. "That's for sure."

"It's more than that," Wayne said. "It's perfect."

Kate drove to the small beach near the docks and cut the engine. Wayne leapt out, reached the water in a few strides. Kate helped her father out of the backseat, both wrinkling their noses at the smell.

"Fish guts," Gerald said.

Kate stepped onto the sand, stooped to pick up a handful. The grains were coarse and cool to the touch. The sun barely heated the boardwalk. The few trees along the path were stunted, bent inland.

"This is awesome," Wayne called over to them. He was halfway to the docks, to boats he already knew by name. The *Sarah Jane*, the *Kathy Ann*, the *Jeannie*. In every way that mattered, he'd been living in this town for a month now, since he'd first seen the article in the *Los Angeles Times*.

There'd been a picture of this very harbor on the front page of the Travel section, a headline that read MEN OF THE PACIFIC. Wayne, who had dropped out of school in the tenth grade because, as he'd said, his teachers kept expecting him to read, had devoured every word.

He'd come into Kate's room late that night, something he had never done before, and for a moment he got sidetracked by the photographs covering the walls. Twenty-two children stared back at him, including himself. Girls with haunted eyes, boys with smiles of bravado. She'd taken his picture while he'd been standing outside her apartment, squinting up at the six-story building as if it were a bully he'd have to outsmart. He'd held up his bandaged hand to block the sun, and in his brown eyes was a look only teenagers managed, an unnerving blend of fury and hope.

He turned away from the photos and sat on the edge of her bed, ran his hand over the lace coverlet as if he'd never seen anything like it. He'd been living with her for eight months, since the latest drug charge, since his mother kicked him out, and he'd yet to look her straight in the eye.

But that night he did.

"I've always had this dream," he said. Beneath the comforter, she felt the pressure of his hand on her leg. She didn't move. She wondered how long it would take him to notice he was touching her. "Not a wish, but an actual dream I'm a fisherman. No one to answer to, nothing too solid beneath my feet. Night after night, I dream it's just me out there after a storm passes and a million stars come out. All I hear is the ocean breathing beneath me."

Kate had not touched him yet. There was always a waiting period. With eleven-year-old Daphne, whose parents had slipped out in the middle of the night, taking all their furniture with them, it had been three days. With Kevin, who'd been molested, it was nearly the entire year he'd stayed. When she'd started fostering, she'd mistakenly believed it would be the way to get her arms around a child. What it turned out to be instead was a brutal lesson in self-restraint. Night after night, she'd lain awake, listening to other mothers' children sobbing in the next room, or feigning sleep if she peeked in. Night after night, she'd hugged herself, no one the slightest bit comforted.

She slid her hand across the covers, brushed Wayne's fingers. He was her last, she'd told herself. He was nearly eighteen, the oldest she'd taken. When she'd picked him up that first time, he'd made it clear she was an insult; he could have done without her just fine. "You may be right," she'd told him, "but perhaps I need you." He'd looked at her with such skepticism she'd marveled at the efficacy of time, her own often unwanted resiliency. She had never gotten her old life back; it was gone, snuffed out in an instant. She'd literally spent the first four months in her bedroom—her parents had brought her food on a tray; she'd never gone farther than the bathroom. She had, like her friends, insisted she would not survive. But that was melodrama, that was what she would have preferred.

Ultimately, she'd been drawn out by the birds. One morning, she could no longer stand the racket and lifted the blinds. She spotted two obnoxious magpies in the tree outside her window, bickering over a rock. Her limbs had tingled. She got the most unlikely urge to climb that tree, to stake a claim between them, take that rock for her own. She thought, *I would like to go to the movies.* She reached a point where she had no choice but to try to fill the unfillable.

The only demon left was forgetting. She had written down all she could—the luxuriousness of baby hair, like silk against her skin, and the way William had calmed when she stood but not when she sat. The heat a tiny head gave off. How tightly he'd kept his eyes shut from the light, how long his fingernails had been at birth.

He was a baby still.

Wayne suffered her touch for a moment, then slid his hand away.

"What does the article say?" she asked him.

He turned to her so quickly, with such fire in his eyes, she knew right then she had to help him become a fisherman. But she drew it out. She had to satisfy the caseworkers. She had to make believe she was the responsible, stern parent, when inside she plotted ways to give the children whatever they wanted.

"It's about this town," he said.

A mere month later, Wayne launched himself onto Seal Bay's only pier while Kate watched a young boy scale the dunes, sandy shovel in hand. He raced to a tidy pink house on the bluff, called out, "Mom! Come *on*! This time I found treasure for sure. A couple quarters to start. Mom!" Kate dropped the sand, stood straight, held herself remarkably still. When the boy's mother came out, distracted, her hands wringing out a soiled gray dish towel, her long hair escaping its ponytail, Kate knew in many ways she'd been saved a great deal of pain. She'd had her heart ripped out, so she'd never had to watch it pinch off day by day, chore by chore, until she couldn't even stand beside her son on a sparkling autumn afternoon and revel in his excitement, his fifty-cent bounty, the absolute miracle of his *living*. She'd never reached the point when all he was to her was another task, along with the baby who was crying in a crib inside, another thing to tend.

"Wayne!"

His foot was halfway onto one of the fishing boats. He pulled back reluctantly, shoved his hands in his pockets.

"Let him be," her father said.

A man emerged from the cabin and Kate wasn't sure if she was more alarmed by his giant proportions, six feet seven or more, or his frizzy, red hair, which appeared to have been taken off a rag doll and stitched haphazardly onto his mammoth head. Wayne had to roll back on his heels to meet the man's eyes.

She hurried past her father and climbed onto the pier. Wayne had already started running back to her, his sneakers slamming onto the weathered planks. He was muscular and dark-haired; from a distance, he could have been mistaken for her son. But up close, his complexion was too dark and there was a bump on the crest of his nose that never ceased to disappoint her.

"Ben Dodson's the owner of the fleet," Wayne said quickly. "He's out trolling. That guy? Dominic? He said Dodson'll be back in the next couple hours. He invited me on his boat to look around. I'm going, all right? I'll just hang out there until Dodson comes in."

"Did you see the size of that man?"

Wayne laughed. "Come on. He's a fishermen. They all look like that."

Kate opened her mouth to argue, but her father came up behind her and took her arm. "That's fine, son," he said. "Remember that diner we saw? Trudy's Kitchen? We'll be there."

He steered Kate away without allowing her another word. By the time he opened the car door for her, Wayne had disappeared onto the giant's boat.

"You don't have to manhandle me," she said. "I know when to let go."

She stared at him when she said this, daring him to refute her, but of course he couldn't. No one—when it came to the topic of children—had the guts to say a single word to her.

* * *

Kate and her father walked into Trudy's Kitchen and were immediately assaulted by the heavenly odor of charbroiled hamburgers and deep-fried onion rings. They were glanced at briefly, then, probably because of her Birkenstocks and her father's Venice Beach T-shirt, dismissed as tourists. The entire waiting area was a shallow puddle, silver flecks of something Kate didn't want to know about skimming the top. Finally, a waitress led them across a floor that curled up in the corners; before it had taken on the cast of dishwater, it might have been orange. The counter, on the other hand, was a brilliant shade of magenta, the acoustic tile ceiling painted blue. Where squares had fallen out, stars had been painted in.

There were only six tables, though the counter was long and every stool along it taken. The waitress seated them in the corner. The lines around her eyes and mouth suggested a woman of sixty, but her hair was dyed a young starlet's shade of blond. Her name tag, *Trudy,* was hand-painted with purple ink and elaborate curlicues. A cigarette dangled from the corner of her brightly painted mouth. She poured them both coffee without asking.

"Larry makes a mean batch of onion rings," she said, gesturing to the young, stocky man in the kitchen.

Kate nodded. "All right. Those and an egg salad sandwich."

"What kind of fish you got?" her father asked.

The waitress took the cigarette from her mouth. "I don't even glance at the albacore Ben Dodson brings in," she said. "It's bad enough I've got to smell it all day. Sorry, handsome, but if you want a tuna sandwich, you'll have to drive clear down to San Francisco."

Gerald placed his hands flat on the table, did not bother with the menu. "Well," he said. "BLT then. Heavy on the bacon."

The waitress crushed her cigarette into the ashtray on their table and smiled, and Kate thought perhaps she had been wrong about her age. Despite the cigarettes, her teeth were white and charmingly crooked, as if she were an awkward teenager still in need of braces.

She left to put in their orders, but was back within seconds to refill their coffee. Later, she repositioned the sugar packets, filled up the ketchup dispenser, and each time her lipstick was a little brighter. By the time she delivered iceberg salads, on the house, she gave off the scent of Obsession perfume.

"Looks like you've got a girlfriend," Kate said.

Her father grumbled, but a minute later he moistened his fingers, combed out the few remaining hairs on his head.

Kate turned to hide her smile and watched a large group of fishermen come in, their wet boots and coats adding to the puddle by the door, flecks of fish still clinging to their oilskins. They claimed all the booths around them, and by their muscled arms and strong, deep voices, she judged them mostly young men. What peeked out of their hooded sweatshirts, though, were middle-aged faces, ruddy-skinned, wrinkled, eyes permanently squinted.

"It's going down monthly now," one of the men said. "Forget about the record albacore. That's a fluke. We pulled up, what, five thousand a day in September? I'm down to two now. I'm telling you, it's nearly over. You'd better start brushing up your typing skills."

"Nah," another said. "We just need some luck is all. Get Bill over there to stop whistling on deck."

The one they called Bill lowered his head sheepishly. "Can't help it," he said. "My dad was a Rodgers and Hammerstein fanatic. I keep getting these tunes in my head."

"My brother says Moss Landing is full of salmon," another said. "My brother says—"

"Your brother's full of shit. Wasn't he the one who said to head to Cedros Island for mackerel? Goddamn desert out there."

"You hear about Henry Zeele over at Morro? Three-hundred-pound guy, a champion wrestler, then someone says pig on the *Ruby Lane,* and he's out of there before anyone can blink. Someone saw him at his house later, burying his nose in his wife's hair. Same time the *Ruby Lane* hit that reef and went down."

They were all quiet, then someone said, "Luck will save you one day just to kill you the next."

Trudy came to take their orders. One of the men took her hand, pleaded with her to ignore the existence of his girlfriend and marry him. "I'll make only two trips a week," the man said. "No farther than Ghost Island. Be back for supper each night, guaranteed."

Trudy scoffed, extricated her hand. She did not use a memo pad, though there were a dozen fishermen now, all ordering various soups and sandwiches. "You're a liar," she said. "I've coached the girls on you, Lyle. If there's a diamond solitaire in your pocket, ten to one you're too drunk to know what to do with it."

"Ah, Trudy. You're not giving me a chance."

"Heard Jamie telling Gwen you're out of chances," another man said. "Said she dragged you in dead drunk with the garbage cans last night."

They all laughed. Trudy returned to Kate's table, refilled their coffee though their cups were nearly full. "I've told the girls to stay sober and hum loudly enough to drown out sweet talk," she told them. "Lyle's a good fishermen. At sea, he knows how easy it is to die, but on land he's as careless as the rest of them. Mean, drunk, and lazy. Even more frightening, now and then he figures out a way to be charming."

Trudy got the men their drinks, ignored their flirtations. Lyle, a lean, dark-haired man with a poorly healed scar beneath his right eye, would not give up. "Thought I saw you out on the water, Trudy," he called after her. "One of the merrows. Had to curl up in my bunk to keep from jumping in after you."

"The problem with you, Lyle, is that after a while *everything* begins to take on the shape of a woman. A seal from thirty yards out is the spitting image of Sharon Stone."

The men laughed. Trudy stepped behind the counter, lit another cigarette. "The merrows drown their lovers, you know," she went on with a smile. "Give them pig faces. Maybe that's why you're not supposed to say pig on board."

Kate was the only one who laughed. Conversation at the tables around her stopped abruptly. Heads swung toward the door.

An old woman wearing a black skirt and blouse tapped a cane in front of her. No one got up to guide her to a table. Trudy glared from the counter. Bill the fisherman started whistling a wobbly rendition of "Hello, Young Lovers," and Kate got a funny feeling in her stomach. Nevertheless, she and her father got up.

"Can we help you?" Kate asked.

The woman smiled, her startlingly blue eyes floating right and left. The men started talking again, quietly. The temperature in the room seemed to have dropped ten degrees.

"Scaredy-cats," the woman said, craning her head to the right, where the fishermen hid behind their menus. There was nowhere left to sit, so Kate led the woman to their table.

"I'm Kate Vegas," she said, sliding onto the bench beside her father. "This is my father, Gerald Frankins."

"Mary Lemming," the woman said, resting her cane on her knees. "Crazy Mary. The town witch."

The men on either side of them had been listening, but now

they rearranged their silverware. Kate's gaze fell on the end of the woman's cane, an owl carved out of mahogany, one eye open, one closed. Trudy came reluctantly to their table.

"Mary, you're spooking the regulars." She glanced at Gerald apologetically as she said this. "You'll drive me out of business."

Mary laughed. She was missing two teeth on the bottom, and the gums there were pure black. "George Eaton's driving you out of business, not me," she said. She looked Kate's way, though her gaze fell on a point over her shoulder, then drifted aimlessly, as if it was caught in a breeze. "Trudy opened her diner the same year George Eaton started up Eaton's Bar and, from day one, Trudy's Kitchen smelled of bacon and cigarettes while Eaton's smelled of cash."

"The men don't like to eat when you're here," Trudy said.

Mary shrugged. "They're big, strong fishermen, aren't they? What can a little old lady like me do?"

She smacked her lips, practically cackled. One of the men tossed his menu on the table and left.

"You could take a butter knife to the undersides of their boats," Trudy said. "You could scratch up the laurel tree."

Mary laughed. "Is that the best you can do, Trudy? Bring up ancient history? Bring me some of that blueberry pie. I can smell it from here. And hot tea. Don't dawdle like you usually do."

Trudy glared at her, but she went to fill their orders. Mary Lemming still smiled. Her lips disappeared in an avalanche of wrinkles. Only her cheekbones protruded, covered by a strained expanse of translucent skin. Yet her eyes were the blue of a robin's egg. The blueberry pie came, along with their sandwiches. Mary breathed in deeply, reached around the table until she found a fork. She stuck a large piece of pie in her mouth.

The three of them ate in silence while the men in the booths around them shoveled in their food, then left far too much money on the table, not wanting to wait around for the right change. They raced through the door and shook themselves, then headed toward the docks.

"I sunk their boat," Mary said, her gums stained blue. "My husband was out with them that day and I was mad at him. I was always mad at Sam. But I didn't kill anybody. They all got in the dinghy. I don't see the big deal."

Kate glanced at her father, but he was leaning back, smiling. He'd been a successful detective not only because of his ability to solve cases, but because he'd never gotten through a single interrogation without laughing. People weren't bad, he'd always told her, so much as extraordinarily weird.

An unsettling itch started at the base of Kate's neck, though the tiny woman looked completely harmless. She looked like she couldn't hurt a fly.

"So he wasn't the one who died in that fishing accident?" she asked. "I read in the newspaper—"

Mary cackled, reached around for her tea. It was steaming hot, but she drank it without scalding herself. "Oh, no. That was Wally, my first husband. Sam had more elaborate plans than a straightforward death at sea."

"How'd you sink his boat?"

Mary shook her head, smiled. "That's a house secret."

Kate dug into the onion rings. They were marvelous, decadently greasy and sweet. "You'd have to be pretty mad to sink your husband's ship," she said, licking her fingers, although she was fairly certain the old woman was insane.

Mary wrapped her fingers around her cane and held on tight. "If you stood my husbands side by side, you'd pick Sam in a heartbeat. He was the handsome one. The charming one. Wally used to get a little mean when he was drunk. But here's the secret of marriage, Kate Vegas: It can stand anything except indifference."

Kate looked away. She always looked away rather than tell someone who meant well that they didn't know what they were talking about. Indifference was hard on a marriage, sure, but what about treason? What about a man slipping out in the middle of the night with what you loved best?

Trudy brought their checks and slapped them on the table. Kate picked up both, fished money out of her wallet.

"You're not from around here," Mary said, sniffing.

"No. L.A."

"Ah," Mary said, wrinkling her nose. "Hollywood."

"I saw the Surfside Motel up the road," she said. "Do you know if they have long-term rates?"

Mary fixed her with that unsettling, blind stare. "Why?"

Kate decided right then that she liked her. She liked a woman who could look her in the eye without bursting into tears. Without thinking, immediately, of her deepest fear.

"My son—my foster son—is looking for a job. We saw this article—"

Mary's laugh cut her off. The old woman laughed so hard, the men still braving the counter did not move. They appeared to think their hearts might stop beating. Even Kate's father looked suddenly ill.

"Jack Evanston's article? The 'Men of the Pacific'?"

"Yes. Wayne saw it. He wanted to move up here and try his hand at fishing."

"Oh," Mary said, laughing again. Her blue eyes bobbed in their sockets while she shook with delight. "Oh, my. That's a good one. We've had tourists flocking up here left and right since that article came out, but you're the first who wants to stay. That's lovely."

"Look. The article said Mr. Dodson is looking for—"

"The article's hogwash," Mary said. She dried her eyes, chuckled once more. She curled a shrunken, pockmarked hand under her chin. "What did he call this place? Picturesque? The foggy side of heaven? My dear, look around you. Can't you tell when something's going to pieces?"

Kate sat back. Her father reached over and took her hand from her lap, held it firmly between both his own.

"That may be, Mrs. Lemming," he said. "But we're here now. Our Wayne's got it into his head he wants to be a fisherman, and we're going to support that. He deserves someone's support."

Mary fixed her blind eyes on him, inhaled deeply, and the lines around her mouth softened.

"Of course she worried about you," she said, "but she must have loved you, too. Women will put up with a lot for a good man. Believe me."

Her father dropped her hand. "I beg your pardon?"

"Your wife." Mary folded her napkin, sat back with an unnerving smile. "I read thoughts. Well, maybe just a stray idea or two now. I used to be able to look in a girl's eyes and scrape out her deepest, darkest secret, but I'm getting old. Can't hardly pick up my own thoughts now." She cackled again, then squinted at Kate. "You believe in magic, Kate."

Kate laid the money on the table. The fog over the bay was swirling, casting sweaty, white tentacles toward the houses closest to shore. It was not a question, but Kate answered anyway. "For some people. To a point."

Mary nodded. "Yes. That's right. To a point. Magic can't cure despair. That's true."

Trudy paced behind the counter, and Kate was beginning to understand why. The itch she'd felt earlier turned to a tickling along the underside of her skull, as if someone were poking around.

"Look, how did you know—" Gerald began, but Mary cut him off.

"That article. Your boy needs to know it's not like that. The men of the Pacific. Hah! They work sixteen-hour days, come back drunk and stinking of fish. They board in my house and leave girls crying in my kitchen. Mr. Evanston came here on the one sunny day in June. He had no idea what he was talking about."

Kate stared at the old woman. "Wayne is seventeen. There's no talking him out of adventure."

Mary nodded. "My husbands' minds were filled with adventure, too. I could hardly stand to listen in to all those battles with storm waves and cold-blooded beasts. Those fishermen back there? They think they're heroes, but they really stink of fear. They're just less afraid of drowning than they are of doing anything else. They don't care what it does to the women. They'll fish these waters until they're empty, then they'll go into some dark room and cry."

"I don't think—"

"Now, you," Mary said, twitching her nose and leaning back in the booth. "You—"

"Look," Kate said. "I've paid the bills. Thanks for the company. We've got to find a motel."

"Well, now, that's what I was going to say. I'm not getting much from you, Kate Vegas, except fog. Secrets. Hidden things."

"Her pictures," her father said suddenly, and Kate glared at him. "She paints those three-dimensional posters that have images hidden inside them. You've got to stare at them just right to see what's underneath. Psychiatrists like to put them up in their offices. Teenagers love them."

"Hmmm," Mary said. "Sounds like a lot of work for art."

"As a matter of fact—"

"But that's not it," Mary went on, sniffing. "You're stashing something. Or no. Looking for something. Yes, that's it. You're looking for more than a hidden picture. You're looking for a lot more than that."

"This isn't about me." Kate stood, nudging her father until he got up after her.

The old woman smiled. Behind them, the door opened and Wayne walked into the restaurant. "He wouldn't hire me," he said, stuffing his hands in his pockets. "Can you believe that? That whole article about how badly he needs fishermen, then he goes and says I'm too young. I'm, like, inexperienced."

The first thing the social worker had told Kate was that the night Children's Protection Services had been called by a neighbor, Wayne's mother had been holding his hand over a flame. She'd been getting screams out of him, but not what she'd been after, which were the first tears of his life. By the time the case worker had packed Wayne's clothes and gotten him into the car, the mother had been sitting on the front porch, her head in her hands. She'd been crying enough for both of them.

Wayne was not close to crying now, either, but Kate swore tears leached out of him through the sweat on his forehead. His arms were too slick to hold.

"Honey," she said.

He jerked away. Mary Lemming got up and clicked her cane in front of her. She leaned toward Wayne and breathed in.

"You want to know about fishing?" she said. "It's backbreaking work coupled with days and days of total boredom. You'll load a thousand pounds of ice, another thousand of bait, then spend two days sitting on your bottom, dreaming of a girl who'll never have you if she's got her wits about her. Then suddenly the captain will haul you up before dawn and you'll spend the next thirty-six hours straight hauling in deep-sea sole and rockcod. You'll come home exhausted and ugly, and that girl you love will laugh in your face. That what you want, boy?"

Wayne just looked at her. His sweating had subsided. In fact, at some point during her speech, he'd begun to smile. "Yes."

Mary shook her head, then leaned over to Kate. "Don't let him go out on Friday the thirteenth. Throw out every red shirt he owns; they attract sharks."

"Aren't you listening?" Wayne said. "He doesn't want me. He said—"

"You think people are that certain? That they stick to what they say?" Mary snorted. She turned to Kate, fixed her blind eyes on her face. "You think it matters if you're here or there? People will find you, if they're looking."

Kate stepped back. She had the clearest thought she would have for the next three months: She should grab her son and run. A sane person, a woman who had truly let go, would not grasp at a faint, illogical hope, would not start the whole thing all over again.

Yet somehow the shameful secret seeped through her, rose to the surface of her skin where a crazy, mind-reading old woman could read it: She believed the fog hid wonders. She still woke up each morning believing this was the day when justice would be served.

"People?" her father said. "What people?"

Mary lifted her bony hand and Kate realized she knew exactly where to place it, on the turn of her elbow.

"It's all over you," she said. "His face, that great big thatch of black hair. I can see him as well as if I had eyes."

"Katie?" her father said, coming toward her. "Did you hear something? Why didn't you—"

"It's a hoax," Kate said, but her voice was thin. She slid her purse gently under her arm, the photograph tucked carefully inside. "I've made my peace."

"Oh, no," Mary said. "I don't think so. You need to follow the signs. They led you to me, didn't they?"

"We were just hungry. Wayne needed some time—"

"They led you to me," Mary said, "and now you find out I've taken in boarders for years."

"We'll just find a motel for now."

"After that," Mary went on as if Kate hadn't spoken, "you'll need to keep talking to Ben Dodson until you convince him to take on your boy. You've just got to make the right point. You've got to find his soft spot, though God knows he's done a good job of covering them all up."

"I don't know what I could say to him," Kate said. "Frankly, I don't know about any of this."

Mary sniffed again, before Kate could step back and steer clear of her. "Sure, you do. You know something's started. You know that, deep down."

Kate looked at her, felt an uncomfortable stirring in her gut, a rush of adrenaline she didn't want, couldn't bear to feel again. A motor somewhere inside her, clicking on. "No," she whispered.

"Kate," her father said. "What's going on?"

Kate turned to her father, forced a smile. "Nothing. I got a photograph is all. From Ray. He's baiting me. After all these years, he's grown bored."

"Kate—"

"I'm all right. I'm not falling for it. Wayne is what matters now." She turned to her son, whose eyes were half closed and guarded, his hands still in the pockets of his jeans so he couldn't be accused of begging for anything. He had heard the story of William as all her children had. She'd made a point of telling them everything so there could be no recriminations later, no claims that disaster homed in only on them. "Let's go to the Surfside Motel and see if—"

"Trust me," Mary said. "You don't want to stay there. They've got problems with crabs in the bathtubs."

Kate began tapping her foot, that motor revving up, a spark traveling across her skin, raising one hair after the other. She felt the sensation of falling, though of course she was on stable ground. She even reached for Wayne, held him around the wrist whether he wanted her to or not. "What do you suggest?"

Mary smiled, and her whole face scrunched up until it resembled a dried-out, puckery apricot, a fruit a less hungry soul would have tossed away. "What I suggested in the beginning, dear. Follow the signs. Follow me." She took Kate's arm and held on tightly. "Let's take a look at my house."

— 3 —

Fahrenheit Hill

According to Jack Evanston's article, one hundred years ago, Fahrenheit Hill was more ominous. Shaped like a volcano, its sandstone cone tip was almost always lost in fog, its flanks dotted with sickly-looking cypress trees that had managed to take root in poor shale soil.

Then a tuna boat captain pulled into the bay on an unusually balmy December day and got the crazy idea that Fahrenheit Hill was the most beautiful place on earth. He bought the property and dynamited the top third flat, but before he could nail the first board on his Georgian mansion, he was shot dead by a discontented deckhand and buried where his bedroom would have been.

For whatever reason, no cypress trees had grown since. The laurel tree sprouted from windblown seed and grew voraciously, the ground around it turned slick with a particularly invasive strain of wild moss. Mary Lemming bought a half acre lot downwind from the tree, and in the years since, the street to her house had fallen apart. The gravel had turned to mush and the concrete brought in to replace it was undermined by shoddy workmanship and a fetid spring. It buckled in some places, turned squishy near the gutters, and by Mary Lemming's driveway dissolved entirely into a spongy, gray soup.

From sea level to the laurel tree was a gain of nine hundred feet, and Kate had the feeling only fitness fanatics and teenagers on Halloween night dared to walk it. The air on top of the hill seemed thicker, to an open mind even clumpy. In a deep fog, she might not know what she was running into, tree branch or ghost.

She slowed in a lumpy patch to let Mary Lemming catch her breath. Hunched over, the old woman was no more than four feet high, thin as splintered wood.

"You should have let me drive," Kate said.

Mary breathed in and out with a rumbly cough. "I need the exercise. Besides, I might have a heart attack at James Galley's front door."

Kate looked down the hill that was quickly being swallowed in fog. Trudy's Kitchen was already gone, the downhill side of Jim's Tackle obliterated. A light post there, then gone, a Volkswagen being eaten from the fender up.

Kate was not surprised to discover Mary Lemming's house was the copper Victorian she'd seen on the drive in. The porch columns had been painted jade, the front door bloodred, though both had faded beneath the onslaught of sea salt and sand. Cracked over time, the house looked like a giant, unpolished gem.

The front door squeaked when Mary opened it, spooking the roosting crows who took flight from the laurel tree. Kate's father and Wayne came up behind them, laughing loudly until they entered a dark parlor eerily devoid of furniture. The bare floor was old pine planking, scratched clear to subfloor from chairs and old boots. Two small windows on either side of the room were wavy single panes. Beyond them the dim sun was winking out behind a wall of fog.

"Oh," Wayne said, the empty room playing tricks, turning his baritone into a boy's uneasy squeak.

"I moved everything upstairs years ago," Mary said. "After Sam died. This was his office. He converted the garage out back into a warehouse. Ran a mail-order fishing supply company when he wasn't out to sea."

Kate walked across the room, her footsteps vibrating through the thin wood. For some reason she pictured Mary sliding across the room in a pair of fuzzy socks.

She walked to the window and laid a hand on the moist sill. She could see nothing outside now, not the gaudy purple Emporium down the hill, not a single speck of sky. She tapped her fingers, imagined the fog lifting sometime during the night and everything beneath it emerging transformed—houses restored, walls repainted, a rose garden thriving where only weeds had been before.

"Wayne," she said.

Wayne had already crossed the room and found the kitchen. They followed him into a small room dominated by dark walnut cabinets and a huge cast-iron sink. Mary must have been cooking sugared sausages. A thin line of smoke still snaked along the ceiling; the decadent smell of burnt sugar, sweet pork, and fat made Kate's mouth water.

Mary walked past them, expertly making her way around furniture and a half-finished quilt to another door at the rear. She opened it and stepped through.

"Gerald can have this room," she said. "The boy can have the guest room upstairs. Smells of fish. There's no getting around it."

Wayne was already halfway to the stairs when Kate grabbed his arm. "Honey," she said. "Just hold on. I wonder if . . ."

She stopped when she saw his eyes. Deep blue, almost gray, with lashes that swept clear to his lids. The eyes always undermined her convictions. She'd been more stern with her girls, religiously enforcing curfews, forbidding tattoos and makeup before the age of fifteen. But the boys were another story. Kate didn't care what the news said about school shootings and young sociopaths, the teenage boys she had raised were almost too beautiful to bear. Their shoulders hunched not from meanness or spite, but from unrequited love, from a bravely stashed sorrow that would not be matched until their last years, when everyone they cared about was gone. They admitted to nothing, held their breath when confronted with anger or love, only laughed genuinely with each other. A pack of boys breathed like the ocean, in synchronous, swelling arcs.

"I'll end up here, one way or another," Wayne said quietly. "You can stay with me or not."

She touched his cheek. He was so foolish sometimes, threatening her with leaving when she had already resigned herself to letting go. Twenty-two times she had packed bags full of photographs, bubblegum, and the portraits she'd painted. Twenty-two times she had cried until she hurt all over. Just like any mother who had to say good-bye, she'd told herself, which was the only thing that eased the pain. Whether you have a year or a boy's whole youth, you do not have enough time.

Wayne's skin was already scratchy and wind-chapped. The few whiskers he'd sprouted had multiplied and she thought to herself, with only the barest sting now, *My boy would be like that. He'd have whiskers by now.*

"I wouldn't mind staying here for a while," her father said, walking out of the back bedroom.

Kate glanced into the room. It was no more than ten by ten—a double bed covered with a white eyelet comforter took up most of the space. Wedged in the corner was a small pine bureau with two of the chrome handles missing. Yellowed lace curtains hung limply against the only window. The room smelled moist, and when she stepped forward, the hardwood floor gave a little.

"I think—"

"Have you got a place for Kate?" her father interrupted.

Wayne had managed to extricate himself and was already upstairs, thumping around the room that smelled of fish. Mary walked out the back door. Her father laughed, nudged Kate after her. When she stepped out into the thick fog, she felt dizzy, almost upended. She could not see where her next step would take her, could not tell ground from sky.

She reached for the house, waited until the dizziness faded. She felt the flagstone beneath her feet. She squinted and thought she caught a glimpse, through the fog, of Mary's black dress, an open door, a light flipped on. She followed the old woman cautiously. Beyond a small brick patio covered in moss was a one-story converted garage, painted sky blue. Mary had already gone inside and Kate had every intention of drawing the line there, of not even crossing the threshold. Then she looked inside.

The concrete floor had been painted hot pink, the walls lemon yellow. Two Queen Anne chairs faced off in one corner, a four-poster bed stood across the way, a large, shaggy rug softened the floor. It was charming and somehow otherworldly, flooded with dim blue light.

"My bed and breakfast," Mary said. "After that article, I posted an ad at Trudy's. You would not believe how many people were willing to pay eighty dollars a night for a hard bed and pancakes."

Kate stepped into the room. Dew had beaded on the sills, and in the distance she heard a foghorn, an answering signal from a boat. She thought the price was actually a little low. The yellow walls glowed, as if they were tucked away inside a locket. Counting the walls, the fog, the hill, the ocean, there were four layers to get through just to reach them. Four layers no one would have the energy to breach.

"This is a wonderful room," she said.

Mary smiled. "So they tell me. I took a stab in the dark with the paint."

"Oh, you did great. The light . . . I'm a painter. I'd really like to get my canvases in here. I could—"

"Seven-fifty a month, for the three of you," Mary said. "That'll include dinner, but if your boy gets a job with Ben, he won't be around much for that."

Kate stopped in the process of running her hand up the yellow walls. She tried to bring back that sense of unease she'd felt just a moment ago, but in that room, it was impossible. A hum rose up the back of her throat, an unlikely giggle threatened to erupt. She reached into her pocket, took out a peppermint. She was crazy, surely, packing up her belongings, betting everything on the fickle dreams of a seventeen-year-old, but at forty, after all she'd been through, she popped the candy in her mouth and reveled in the sweetness of her own optimism.

"We'll take it."

There was supposed to be a half-moon that evening, but it never rose. The sky rested low and firm as black velvet. The seagulls didn't even try to fly against it, but curled up atop the mussels on Seal Rock, their gray wings over their beaks. The wind that almost always skimmed in over the ocean, sucking up salt and spray and depositing it on mossy windows and decaying roofs, was still, the air dense with stalled water. Walking down the road from Mary's, Kate had to turn sideways to slice through the clingy atmosphere. If she had turned to look, she would have seen a cloud of pink phosphorescence behind her.

But she didn't turn; the advantage of crossing forty was that she had stopped worrying whether or not she left something beautiful behind.

She passed the purple Emporium, two emerald green houses, the shuddering blue walls of Eaton's Bar. She looked through the windows of Trudy's Kitchen. A dozen men slouched over the counter, watching a Sunday night football game on ESPN. She followed Mary's directions through the winding streets and finally took the turn onto Pacifica Lane.

As soon as she stepped onto the street, she was broadsided by the roar of the surf. This was the first street beyond the protective arm of the breakwater, and the waves pounded the cliffs below at full strength. At low tide, there might have been a narrow band of rough beach, but it was submerged now beneath a foaming, black surf. Sea caves and blow holes had been hollowed out by the blasts, and there were faded warning signs on the cliffs proclaiming the dangers of being trapped at high tide. After spending all her life near a smooth, patrolled beach in Santa Monica, this shoreline seemed something else entirely, more sea than land, relentless and even mean.

She turned her back to the ocean and checked the house numbers, spotting Ben Dodson's Victorian one house down. The slender lath siding was painted a dim turquoise, the trim faded lavender, and the whole thing, if she was not mistaken, was sloping to the right. She cocked her head, thinking she was seeing things, but no, the foundation on the south side had settled a good six inches deeper than the north. Endless sea spray followed a creek across the roof, gurgled down a rusted gutter.

She took a deep breath and walked up the gray concrete path. She raised her hand to knock, but before she could do it, the wind blew open the door. Or so she thought. She blinked and a girl stood right in front of her. About fifteen and frizzy-haired, dressed in flared jeans and a big, ratty sweatshirt.

"Hi," Kate said. "I'm looking for Ben Dodson."

The girl looked her over, pausing once when her gaze reached her waist, then again at her mouth. She closed the door halfway. "He's kind of busy," she said.

She started to close the door, but Kate managed to get a hand on it. "This won't take long. It's about my son."

The girl's shoulders relaxed visibly. She stepped backward into the gloom of the house. "I'll see if he can come out."

Kate stepped back to the porch railing, listened to the relentless surf. *Grrrr-wooosh, grrrr-wooosh, grrrr-wooosh.* Not a soothing sound at all, but one that suggested erosion, a ravenous sea nibbling at the toes of houses, sweeping whole beaches away in the dead of night. She expected a siren or distress call to go up at any moment, but instead the door opened behind her.

A man in jeans and a chambray shirt stepped out, his short, spiky hair still wet from a shower. His hands were a textbook of scabs in various stages of infection and healing, the rest of him solid as stone. A handsome man, if not for his eyes. They were a kind of green gone flat, like dried kelp, and she wondered if she'd just solved the riddle of all the paint in town. The glare off the ocean had made everyone color-blind. Despite gardens of Oriental poppies and gallons of fluorescent paint, everything still looked gray.

"I'm Ben Dodson," he said. "Can I help you?"

A shadow passed the front window. The lace curtain fluttered, then whoever had dropped it retreated into the house.

"I hope so. I'm Kate Vegas. My son, Wayne, came to see you today. About a job."

Ben Dodson just stared at her. His skin was sunburnt and brittle; she wondered if it hurt him just to smile, something he hadn't done yet. He stood over six feet, but he crouched a bit. Those torn-up hands curled slightly, as if he were holding imaginary rope.

"He's a good boy, Wayne," she went on. "He's had some trouble, but we've worked through it. This is his dream. To fish."

Ben took another step onto the porch, and the screen door slammed shut behind him. "I'm not in the habit of hiring boys," he said.

"I understand. But he—"

"He read the article, right?"

"Yes."

Ben shook his head. "More fishermen die, per capita, than men in any other profession in the world. And if they live, their wives tend to leave them."

Kate's gaze was drawn to the vulnerable part of his neck, the last smooth hollow, an even pulse. "Why on earth do you do it then?"

The shadow passed the window again, a pale finger around the curtain, a flash of pale hair through the panes. Not the girl she'd seen before.

"They say a fisherman learns to drink sea water," Ben Dodson said, "and he only gets seasick when standing on solid ground."

For a moment, there was no sound but the beating of Kate's own heart. Then she heard the surf start up again.

Ben crossed the porch to stand beside her. "He wants to be a fisherman?" he asked. "Or does he want to play George Clooney's part in an adventure movie?"

She was surprised he didn't smell of the sea, but of soap and aftershave. "He wants to belong somewhere."

"We all want that, but there's usually a way to do it without killing ourselves."

"Look—"

"You staying at Mary's?"

Kate stepped back, tucked her hair behind her ear. The last few years, she'd kept her dark hair in the same style—cut all one length at her shoulders, so she could pull it into a ponytail while she painted. But in this climate, in fog, it had started to curl. Already, a few strands were twisting free, twirling.

"Yes."

"Your husband think this is a good idea?"

She had a split-second image of black hair and blue jeans, a flash of smile that could have belonged to the devil himself. She touched Ben Dodson's arm to bring herself back.

The surf seemed to rest for a moment, because she heard him swallow. She heard the swish of curtain near the window, and she dropped her hand and stepped back.

"I'm here with Wayne and my dad," she said. "And I've long since stopped caring what anybody thinks. I just want to make Wayne happy. Surely you can understand that."

Ben stared at her, and that hum in the back of her throat pushed all the way through. She startled them both with the whisper of an old Louis Armstrong tune.

Ben smiled, then looked away. "I'll give him the most menial jobs to start," he said. "Loading ice. Scrubbing out the hold. He'll hate me before I'm through."

He stood awkwardly, she thought, one foot slightly forward, on guard. She imagined the things that might have been different if he hadn't chosen to work at sea. Smoother skin, certainly, a straight spine, soft fingers a woman would not flinch from. She imagined the life she would pick for Wayne if she had the choice, all the things he'd probably hate—a dependable job, a safe, boxy car, a loyal wife and children.

"Thank you," she said.

He took a deep breath before he walked back to the door. "Tell him we start at dawn."

He walked inside, and a light came on. For an instant, Kate got a clear view of the figure by the window. Blond hair, a tight pink sweater, feral green eyes. Then the curtains slammed against the glass, and Kate wondered at the sudden speed of her heart.

Kate would have left Los Angeles anyway. She'd run out of things to paint there.

She set up her easel on Mary's driveway and decided to paint the laurel tree that stood watch over the hill. It was another foggy day, giving off something akin to northern light, which was good to paint by. She used olive greens and grays, and for four hours felt as though there was nothing in the world but mist and muted color, the play of dim light on leaves.

The next day, when the image was dry, she used her digital camera to take a series of snapshots of it, then downloaded them into the laptop she'd set up in Mary's garage. The rest was less artistry than computer design. Software covered the image with swirls of blue and black. Only after the eye relaxed into the picture could it see the tree beneath.

She emailed the photo to a printer in Santa Monica, who would turn it into a laminated poster retailed at $19.99. After she called her buyer and got a tally of this month's orders, she was free to take up the real challenge. She set the painting back on the driveway and began to paint over it with a mixture of white and gray oils. She had no buyers for these; no one, apparently, could see through the oils. They thought it a child's finger painting, a portrait a less sentimental person would have thrown out. But she wasn't sentimental; she simply could see the tree beneath the layers of fog she painted over it.

Her father came up behind her. "That's a good one," he said.

"Can you see it?"

He stared for a long time. "A dolphin?"

Kate stared at the tree, front and center, a string of bay leaves swirling down to the ground. "Don't worry about it."

She'd taken up painting fifteen years before, on the advice of her counselor. She'd started in watercolors, mostly for the quickness with which she could jump from one picture to another, and brought in stacks of crinkled paper for analysis. For fifty minutes, Dr. Weatherby had sat in his leather chair and told her all that black in the corner was her anger, the excessive use of red a symbol of her blood and soul leaking out. Perhaps he'd been right, but she'd had a simpler theory. The paintings meant she was not dead inside. Every time her body failed her and she retreated to bed, she started to dream in color. In the mornings, she would pick up a paintbrush and some exotic flower would erupt from her fingers, as if her hands and eyes had been sneaking out at night.

The paintings, and the career she began to eke out in commercial art, had also meant she would not have to go back to sociology, the field she'd been studying when her life fell apart. Strangers often assumed she'd been planning this life all along, that she'd meant to be here.

"I called Roger last night," she told her father. "He's already got sixty orders. That'll keep us for a while. Pay the rent, at least."

Her father stared down the hill, though there was nothing to see. The bay was gone, even the sounds from the harbor had been muffled by the fog. "I've still got my pension coming in. And once we get Wayne settled, I'm taking you to Miami. You'll love it once you get there. I'll take up my woodworking again. We'll be fine, Katie."

Kate smiled at him. "I heard Wayne shuffling around last night. At first light, he was out the door, despite the fact that Ben Dodson's got him loading ice eight hours a day. This is the boy who complained when I asked him to vacuum beneath his bed."

"He's decided to be another person. He ditched himself on the road up from L.A."

Kate dropped her brushes in a jar of turpentine. "And you? Who did you become?"

Her father drew himself up, gave her his best leading-man smile. "Clint Eastwood, with a little extra around the middle. I'm telling you, Kate, I've suddenly developed a taste for whiskey. I'm gonna see if I can get me a girl."

Kate reached for her father's hands. "I hope you're serious," she said.

"Remember what your mother used to say?"

In the last days, her mother had sat in her wheelchair in the garden, eyes a little wide from the pain though she never would have admitted this out loud. Kate could no longer remember her face without a photograph, but she had a clear vision of her mother's fingers—the last to fail—sorting rose petals for her potpourris.

"Joy is in pursuit of us all," Kate whispered.

He kissed her cheek, whistled as he set off for Trudy's. He was a regular already; at nine in the morning, he claimed a stool at the counter with the old-timers, demanded black coffee and warm blueberry pie. Kate picked up her canvas. The tree was so obvious and lifelike, she swore she could see sap running down its trunk. She took it back into the garage to dry, then found Mary in her kitchen, tearing a shirt to shreds.

Kate had noticed the unfinished quilt in the corner of the kitchen, an ugly conglomeration of gray and brown flannel. Mary felt for the quilt now, reached into her sewing box and came out with a needle and thread.

The old woman moistened the end of the thread and slipped it through the eye of the needle on her second try. She slapped a shred of the shirt over the corner of the quilt and began to sew.

Kate sat down opposite her. "When I was at Ben Dodson's, there was someone in the window. Someone stunning. I assumed it was—"

"Jenny," Mary said.

"His wife?"

"No. His oldest daughter."

Kate sat back. She was still certain he was married. He had that extra weight about him all husbands had, right around the middle or down in the soles of their feet. Good husbands lived with one foot stuck to the ground, rarely ever getting carried away.

"She was peeking around the curtains."

Mary sewed in every direction, her stitches half an inch one way, two inches another. "Jenny doesn't peek. She plots. If she was looking at you, you'd better watch out."

"How old is she?"

"Eighteen in body, eighty in spirit. Ever since her mother died."

Kate went still, pressed her hands flat on the table.

"You were right, though," Mary went on. "Ben's married. Ask any man whose wife killed herself and he'll tell you how hard it is to get a divorce."

"God," she said.

"No. God had nothing to do with it. God was not around when it happened."

Kate stiffened. She'd walked around Seal Bay, past the four churches in four corners, one to combat each bar, perhaps. She'd lingered longest in front of the Church of Sea, Sky, and Salvation, where the stained glass did not portray salvation at all, but a particularly heartbroken and downcast Jesus, not bothering to look up to heaven.

"When did this happen?"

"Hmmm. A year ago January, as I recall. Almost two years now. On the forty-seventh-straight day of fog. It lifted the morning of her funeral. Got up to ninety that day, in fact. Her name was Jeanne."

"Was it depression?"

Mary shrugged. "Hard to say. Depression is a lot like normal life in a fishing town. Too much drinking and sleeping, a future so grim it's a wonder any of us finds a reason to get out of bed. But the paint in town was Jeanne's doing. A long time ago. She grew up here. Most of us grew up here and learned how to deal with it, but Jeanne did a dumb thing. She went away to college."

Kate watched Mary work the needle. The old woman poked her finger twice, didn't even blink.

"UNLV," Mary went on. "Can you believe that? Las Vegas. Neon city. She studied nursing. I have no idea why. She studied to be an RN, then came back here, where there isn't a hospital in sight."

"She married Ben."

"Well, yes. Everyone knew they would. Their fathers fished together. They were high school sweethearts. But Jeanne had this crazy notion everything was going to change. She ignored the fact that Ben had started fishing for pay when he was eleven. His dad, Patrick, sent him out longlining when he was only fifteen. And he had a knack for it, for sure. Came back two weeks later with more deep sole than any of them had ever seen."

"He owns the fleet now?"

Mary nodded. "Patrick retired a few years back, but he's still out on the bay every morning. Takes his newspaper and coffee out in that skiff, won't come back until dinner. Patrick was always lost. But Ben . . . Well, maybe Jeanne wasn't the only crazy one. We all dreamed of different things for Ben. Better things."

She went quiet. Her stitches got more uneven, one traveling a good six inches, puckering the gray fabric in half.

"It must have been awful for him," Kate said. "Being left on purpose."

Mary dropped her hands in her lap. "For a while there, he wouldn't admit it. We loved him, so we'd refer to it as that terrible accident, although it was plain as day, sixty sleeping pills at one time was no fluke."

"Was she on antidepressants?"

Mary shrugged. "Maybe. Maybe not. Ben didn't talk about it. I don't think it would have mattered with Jeanne. She came back from that neon town and you could tell she'd taken some kind of stand with Ben. He took her into San Francisco for dinner dates and movies. She walked around town in her nurse's shoes. They tell me she didn't even unpack all her bags. She was that certain she could get Ben Dodson to move inland."

"You can't change anyone," Kate said.

Mary's blue eyes stared through her, prickling the hairs on Kate's neck once again. "They were taking bets up at Eaton's," Mary said. "The men have always prided themselves on the strangest things. How much they can drink, how much pain they can stand. How stoically they refuse their wives' pleas. Some of them won't even go south of town, like it's some kind of trap the women have set for them. They put their money on Ben Dodson, and it worked out that way. One day Jeanne unpacked her bags and put on her mud boots. They got married and bought that house out on Pacifica. She took a part-time job for our local lawyer. For a while, maybe, it was all right."

"She could have worked in a doctor's office," Kate said. "Carved out a niche for herself. It's so beautiful here. The sea . . ."

Mary laughed. "Just wait. Everything is beautiful the first time you see it. But try waking up to the same thing, or the same person, day after day and you'll see how hard it is to keep your spirits up. The women put up with a lot here. The danger, the drinking, the waiting. But it's the fog that eventually drives them insane. Some take to drinking as much as the men. Others get a little mean. And some, like Jeanne, go into their bedrooms and refuse to come out."

Mary spread her quilt over her knees, tried to smooth out the wrinkles she'd sewn in. "Anyway," she went on, "after they got married, Jeanne painted her house sky blue and lavender, then she wouldn't stop until everyone had repainted theirs as well. She'd stand on the sidewalk and cry if your siding was anything less than fire-truck red. The men thought she was crazy, but the women, well, they had enough to do to stop their own tears. They just couldn't listen to her anymore. I had the boys at Mr. Fix-It Hardware do mine. Told them I wanted the colors to clash. What the hell do I care?"

"I like the colors."

Mary nodded. "It took us all by surprise, how right Jeanne turned out to be. How good it felt to shock the men. But you can see we haven't kept it up. It's gorgeous when the color goes up, but that kind of intensity takes work, constant attention. Some of the young women have still got the fire in them. Lisa Stottenmeir, for one. She's got that pink house overlooking the bay. You'll catch her out some days, adding lime trim and crimson stencils while that colicky baby of hers fusses, and her boy chops up the beach, looking for buried treasure. When her husband, Ron, puts in, you can hear his shouts clear up here."

"It's so sad, the way everything has faded. We need—"

"When Jeanne's girls were small, you'd catch her out there, too," Mary interrupted, her eyes closed now, a sad smile on her lips. "Then we started noticing chips in her trim, dust on the siding. After she quit her job, all her rosebushes died. Once Jenny, her oldest, hit high school, she stopped coming out of the house entirely. Jeanne adored Jenny, treated her like a little princess, but it was the youngest, Nicole, who gave up her friends, who stopped going out for a while, afraid her mother would do something drastic while she was gone. And it turned out that way. Poor baby. She was the one who found her."

Kate thought of that sloping house, how that family must have felt watching the roof slowly cave in on them. "That's horrifying."

"Is it? Some human beings fail, plain and simple. They're not meant to survive, and they don't."

Kate sat back. Harsh words didn't take into account what the suicide of a parent would do to Jeanne's girls, what the guilt of not finding a way to prevent his wife's death would do to a good man like Ben Dodson.

"Don't," Mary said.

Kate turned to her. "Excuse me?"

"I said don't. The girls are Ben's responsibility. He knows this. He knows it so well he can hardly stand straight anymore. He won't tolerate their slightest unhappiness, he's so afraid it will turn into something worse. Don't start thinking about him. Jeanne might be dead, but she can haunt him. He's off-limits. He knows he is."

"I wasn't thinking about him."

Mary returned to her sewing. "He took her to San Francisco for treatment. Never let a man say a single word about her. He got saner over the years. Took up the slack, so to speak. Never let himself get out of control, never drank with his crew, never laughed too hard, for fear Jeanne would hear him. Shut himself down, secured the hold, like a boat he couldn't abandon. He was loyal till the end, though that's got nothing to do with the things he was thinking. I heard some things . . . Believe me, I don't blame him. He was due whatever he thought. She *did* ruin their lives, she probably *did* want to hurt him, but I can tell you, by the end, she wasn't thinking about any of them. Not Ben or the girls. Nothing but herself."

"Those poor girls."

Mary snorted. "Don't torment yourself over Jenny. She's not about to turn sappy just because she's got a dead mother. The youngest, Nicole, is the one I worry about. A good girl, so she's been sucked down. You can see her every afternoon, walking home from school along the water, walking so slowly the crabs beat her home. She's taken up the responsibility for her father's happiness, and even I can see she's going to be supremely disappointed."

Mary took a deep breath, made three perfect stitches in a row.

"Are you really blind?" Kate asked suddenly.

Mary cackled. "Macular degeneration. Started in my late thirties. There was bleeding in the retina, then scar tissue. I can't see too well in the center, but I catch things out of the corners of my eyes. I can see color, surprisingly. I like those bright skirts you've got."

Kate looked down at her purple skirt and smiled.

"Don't you tell anybody," Mary went on. "It's my business, what I can and can't see. You should have been there when I took Sam's car down to Trudy's. Never saw people move so fast in all my life."

Kate watched her sew awhile, then walked out onto the front porch. She inhaled the sea air and leaned back into a shoulder of white mist. A strand of her hair was now a perfect ringlet over her eye.

She stared in the general direction of Ben Dodson's house. Frighteningly, she understood his wife completely: Everything outside her front door had scared her to death. Night was a monster, daylight showed too clearly the things she couldn't bear to see. The house had been her comfort, her bed like a bodyguard. But it was the depression itself that turned out to be the most seductive, like a lover luring her farther and farther inside. Kate understood all of this, so she was surprised at how little sympathy she felt.

You had daughters, she kept thinking. *What right did you have to your own misery?* She paced the brilliant but faded porch, tried to imagine Jeanne peering out her window, unable to take another step. But what came to her mind instead was Ben. She'd thought the sound of the surf was deafening, but now she remembered what else she'd heard on Pacifica Lane: The deep breath Ben Dodson had taken right before he'd opened his own front door.

— 4 —

Fishermen Souls

The deepest part of the ocean is the Challenger Deep in the Marianas Trench. From top to bottom, the walls plummet 36,200 feet, nearly seven miles. An awesome spectacle, no doubt, but by the time a man got to the bottom, his body would be pulverized by eight tons of pressure; he'd be nothing more than flakes of bone and salt.

Ben Dodson thought of this sometimes, the weight of the sea, when he was riding effortlessly on top of it. Miles from land, a thin piece of fiberglass separating them from an excruciatingly slow death by drowning, most fishermen had the same grim thoughts. But when they spoke aloud, they complained about the weather, lied about tangled nets and empty seas. It was impossible to tell anything by the way fishermen spoke.

Today, Ben Dodson spoke of the lingcod running near the rocky islands north of the bay. He instructed his new hire, Wayne Furrow, on how to gill-net with the tides. Fish were travelers, he told him, moving with the incoming tide, and the best sets were right after the tide turned to flood.

They'd reeled in the 1800-foot net twice by the time the sun cleared Mt. George, bringing in close to a hundred lingcod a set. Wayne Furrow plucked the fish off the net silently and quickly, his hands already raw and bleeding, the set of his mouth suggesting it was harder work than a scantily researched article had implied.

Ben studied the satellite photo, located a pocket of overlapping currents near Ghost Island, one warm, one cold, where the fish might gather. When they reached the spot, they idled over a rare glassy ocean and let out the net again.

Ben handed Wayne a cup of coffee. The kid was seventeen, dark-haired, and desperate to fish. It was obvious from the careless way he leaned overboard and the unfiltered cigarettes he smoked that he'd already given up on everything on land. He had no idea how lucky he was to have an alternative. Unlike the boys who'd been born in Seal Bay, he saw fishing as a way out.

Ben had agreed to take him on not because of the freckles across Kate Vegas's nose, or the unlikely and somehow alluring scent of peppermint on her skin, but because a boy like Wayne needed to see a fifty-foot rogue wave coming at him. He needed to learn that sometimes the worst thing that can happen to you is to get what you want.

"There's talk of sea monsters," Wayne said.

Ben shook his head, squinted into the thickening fog. On solid ground, men let their imaginations run wild. When walking past the docks at night, even he thought he saw otherworldly heads bobbing up past the breakwater—heads that in daylight turned out to be six sperm whales, riding end to end. But at sea, a man had to take things seriously. Storms swallowed ships and a slight change in the wind meant catastrophe. The earth was mostly seawater, and Ben thought he knew why. Because men could not live in it, drink it, or use it for irrigation. Because otherwise people would have thought the whole planet was theirs for the taking when, truly, they could only go so far.

Ben did not believe in sea serpents, but he did know the ocean was alive. Like skin holding a man's blood and bones in place, the sea was knitted together by surface tension. Beneath that thin veneer, it was not silent at all. Put an ear to it and you could hear catfish barking, sea bass beating their gill covers against their heads, pistol shrimp snapping their claws like firecrackers, stunning their prey. And in an upwelling current, the life is so rich, the ocean breathes. Ben bent his knees slightly as the *Sarah Jane* rose to the crest of an inhalation then plummeted along a trough of salty breath.

"More than eighty percent of the earth's biomass is found in the oceans," he said to Wayne. "Most of that is single-celled algae. There's little chance we've missed something as unique as a sea serpent."

Wayne still had land legs, was occasionally sick over the side, but he'd already learned to bend his knees with the swells. "Still," he said, "I'd like to think there's something down there. Something I can't imagine."

Ben watched the net. "You're seventeen. You'll change your mind about surprises soon enough."

They stayed out until six, the fishing tapering off after flood tide. It was a mediocre harvest, and the sale would be even worse. Lately, local buyers had been taking on only half a catch; the rest Ben would have to transport on ice clear down to San Pedro, where he'd get just $900 a ton.

He headed into the harbor, past the fog light on Seal Rock and the seals lounging below it, their thick skins impervious to barnacles. Wayne stood on the bow and watched the littlest ones whimpering and crying like human babies. Ben had studied the creatures long enough to know they shed tears and suckled at their mothers' breasts. They had to be taught to swim.

The fog settled in hard as they idled across the bay; at one point, it thickened to the consistency of cotton, which Ben could cup in the palm of his hand. Nothing pierced it except a single orange glow off the starboard bow. Ben came astern of a lone skiff, within it a huddled, old fisherman, his face the color and texture of peeling birch. Ben cut the engine and walked out on the bow, the wind slapping his cheeks hard enough to leave marks.

"Go home, Dad," Ben shouted over to him.

Patrick Dodson waved him off, started reeling in nothing. A hand of sea fog reached toward the *Sarah Jane* and though Ben considered most of Mary Lemming's superstitions dubious at best, he instinctively drew back. Mary's theory was that the souls of drowned sailors hid in low-lying fogs and plunged down the throats of men unlucky enough to breathe them in. One inhalation and you swallowed your last chance at ever being happy on land.

Ben admitted this was a good story, but it was an even better excuse for men to get drunk and not try for anything more. It wasn't fishermen souls that made his crews pass up opportunities for real jobs with their distant, upstanding cousins. It was the fact that fishing held an irresistible lure: Unless you were luckless, it was very hard to mess it up.

"Bah," Patrick said and recast.

Since Ben's mother had died and Patrick had retired from the fleet he'd built up from one boat to three, the old man had mapped every inch of the bay, looking to reel in his supper and perhaps a few choice albacore he could sell to the Merc or to tourists from the back of his boat. He could have moved to a mobile home in Salinas, the way he'd always talked about, fattened up on strawberries and artichokes. Instead, last year he bought a new fiberglass skiff and started eating three meals at sea.

"Baja was a bust," Ben said to him. "We'll head back the first of January."

Patrick nodded. He'd retired after they'd dropped the quotas so low, a man could fish out in two days. He still talked about the years when Monterey had a decent sardine run, and the salmon were so thick, the sea turned the color of coral.

"Albacore's hot," his father said. "Down in Morro."

Ben dreamed of water, but he'd always known it wasn't a good idea to talk fish too much. He'd made sure to ask Jeanne about her garden, the girls, for a short time her work as a receptionist for Lou Griffith, the town's only lawyer. He rarely brought up the latest quotas, empty holds, or killer hauls, but Jeanne had still gotten quieter and quieter. She'd started to cry no matter what he said. A woman could hate you for what you didn't say, for the weary tone that crept into your voice every time you soothed her, no matter how gentle and patient you were.

"See you, Dad," Ben said, and his father waved him off. Probably thought he'd been spooking the fish.

They tied up at the docks, and Ben instructed Andy Gullet, his office manager, to call the buyer down to the *Sarah Jane.* Wayne leapt off the boat. He stunk of fish and his hands were bloodied, but when he looked at Ben, he laughed. "That was awesome."

Ben smiled. He didn't have to spoil the secret then; Wayne already knew. Children demanded your attention and women wanted you to talk. All the sea asked was that you survive. Anything more than that, and you came home a hero.

He led Wayne toward the office, and his old dog, Lucky, came bounding out from the alley around back. The dog was a weird combination of Labrador, collie, and Rottweiler. He shook his tail furiously, or as furiously as he could manage. Ben had no idea of Lucky's age; seven years ago, he'd picked him out of the shelter full-grown, thinking Jeanne might like the company. But there was no need to be specific; Lucky was old. Deaf, incontinent, arthritic, and triumphantly lingering on. He never took to Jeanne at all; in fact, he wouldn't sleep in the same room with her. He whimpered whenever she cried. She usually forgot to feed him and, by the time Ben came back from a three-day trip, the dog would be curled up on the kitchen floor, too weak to do anything but look up at him with accusing eyes. Ben started taking him on his long hauls, continued to do so even after Lucky could no longer manage the leap on board and had to be carried. He did little more than sleep in the wheelhouse, kicking his paws in dreams.

Ben scratched the dog behind the ears, then saw Kate Vegas watching him from the door of his office. She shivered beneath a light blue sweatshirt, her hands in the pockets of her blue jeans.

"Your mom's here," Ben said.

Wayne stiffened. His smile vanished. "She's not my mom," he said. "My mom won't have a drug addict in her house."

Ben massaged Lucky's arthritic hips, pressed deeply until the dog moaned. He could sniff out drug users a mile away and never hired them. Addicts could not be trusted to survive. Most of his men were drinkers, satisfied with killing themselves slowly. Wayne might have done drugs in the past, but his eyes were clean, his temperament even. He didn't look to be much of a drinker either. He was too quick and limber, too pleased with the current state of his life.

Kate started toward them. As usual, the fog seemed colder on land, but Ben still felt a flush around his neck, an almost uncomfortable stirring in his groin. She was too beautiful for this place. Tall, thin, too frail for a good Pacific tempest, too fair for the rare but effective sting of the sun. Jeanne had been that beautiful once. All the women had.

He heard the clacking of sandals behind him, turned to find his oldest daughter, Jenny, walking up the pier. She was dressed in a miniskirt and short-cropped sweater, exposing an alarming amount of creamy white abdomen. She'd pulled her hair back tightly, the result stunning rather than severe. Jenny knew how pretty she was. She had high cheekbones and porcelain skin, the kind of features that dropped boys to their knees with longing, that had robbed her of most of her friends.

If this bothered her, Jenny didn't let on. She sashayed right up to them, her smile turning sly when Wayne's mouth parted a bit. She didn't hug Ben, nor did he make a move to put an arm around her. All that had stopped even before Jeanne died, when Jenny's slim body had turned womanly and she'd started walking with a sway to her hips that, frankly, embarrassed him. It stopped when he found a shred of Polo-scented T-shirt on the trellis outside her window and his crews started talking about her, only to shut up when they saw him coming.

Ben still heard things—about the translucence of her wheat-colored hair and the things she'd been known to do when the fog was thick and she was drunk. He did not know how other men survived fatherhood, but his strategy was to doubt every word that was said about his daughter. When Jeanne had stopped going out of the house altogether, he'd taken Jenny to the doctor for birth control pills. He was not *that* blind. But no one would convince him his daughter would do anything on a dare. Her ancestors had fished the sea, and while they'd never been creative or particularly happy, they had known one thing for certain: Life is too precarious to waste it being stupid on land.

She looked past him to Wayne, smiled that smile of hers, the one that had sucked in every boy in town. But Wayne, who only a moment ago had obviously had to stuff his hands in his pockets to keep from snatching the loose hairs on her sweater, now studied her with a scrutiny fishermen usually reserved for three-eyed fish.

"Jenny, this is Wayne Furrow," Ben said. "He's new on the crew. And this is his mother, Kate Vegas. This is my Jenny."

Kate's hand started toward Wayne, but she dropped it well before she touched him. He'd turned a shoulder to her, focused all his attention on Jenny.

"Nice to meet you," Kate said. "I've heard a lot about you."

Jenny narrowed her eyes. "All bad, no doubt."

Kate smiled. "No. Not all bad. You're even more beautiful than people say."

Jenny tilted her head slightly, used to compliments. Kate turned to Wayne. "How did it go?"

Wayne shrugged, took a step away from her. Kate hardly reacted to the rebuff, merely wrapped her arms around herself, but it hit Ben the way the girls' sorrow did, like the lack of sea birds, a particularly ominous sign. When he couldn't sleep, he counted the ways a woman could be comforted, a hundred ways he'd never tried. With jokes, chocolates, by suddenly bursting into bad song. Ordering in dinner or surprising her one morning by not going to work at all.

He touched Kate's arm. Perhaps she smiled; he noticed little except the jolt through his body, an actual charge that realigned something, because afterward his shoulder no longer pained him, the ache in his knees was gone. She had eyes the color of dark chocolate, and he knew, suddenly, the mistake had not been hiring the boy but standing this close to a woman who smelled like candy.

"We had a good run," he said. "Wayne's got a way with the net. I didn't want to let him fish right off the bat, but he changed my mind."

Perhaps she knew, just from looking at him, that he usually didn't talk so much. He dropped his hand, marveled at the unexpected tingle along the tips of his fingers.

"Well," she said. "Good."

Wayne had moved beside Jenny. He had yet to say a single word, which might have explained why she suddenly snapped at him.

"Do you have a problem?"

"Jenny," Ben said, but Wayne only smiled.

"I was just wondering if it's really possible for you to look that good."

Jenny sucked in her breath, something Ben did all the time. When she declared her boredom or, worse, her unhappiness, it was as if she were a weight on his lungs, a stone pushing on the weaker side of his heart.

"Why don't you give Wayne a tour of the town?"

"Oh, please," Jenny said. "Like there's anything to see."

Ben looked at her, and she rolled her eyes. Wayne hadn't moved from her side.

"Oh, all right," she said. She held her hand out listlessly to the side. "Dock," she said. "Pier over there."

Wayne laughed as she led him up the hill. Ben took a deep breath, but not enough clear air got through to keep him from making mistake number two, and three, and four. He turned to face Kate Vegas. He smiled. He said, "Can I walk you home?"

* * *

The fog in Seal Bay was a scapegoat, blamed for everything from depression to shipwrecks, the destruction of brand-new permanents to turning uncollected mail to soup. There was almost always a pocket of it in Sea Lion Cove, ready to chill the desire of teenagers who had nowhere else to make out. The most common nightmare, apparently, was running blindly past monsters who couldn't be seen.

Yet as Kate walked up Fahrenheit Hill beside Ben Dodson, she welcomed the tenacity of the fog, the way it clung to her back and shoulders like threads of white silk. On a clear day, she might have looked ridiculous, a woman of her age walking with her hands jammed in the pockets of her jeans, taking no chances she might brush the brittle man beside her.

He told her about the parade the town had put on for the grand opening of the Mercantile, the only grocery store in town, and she thought, *You don't get over a wife killing herself.* He pointed out Gwen Marmosett's Emporium, which sold toiletries and driftwood furniture, and she thought, *He could never be mine.*

And then, surprisingly, she felt a little better. She knew about the things she couldn't have. She knew how to cope with that.

"She's beautiful," she said suddenly.

He stopped in front of the Emporium. Even through the fog, she realized she'd been mistaken about the color of his eyes. They weren't dull green at all, but merely muted by other colors, a dozen flecks of yellow and brown.

When he said nothing, she went on. "Jenny, I mean."

He nodded. "Yes. She takes after her mother."

They stood in silence, until Kate began to hum again. This time "Route 66." Ben looked startled a moment, then began to smile. They started up the last rise toward Mary Lemming's copper house. They reached the front porch out of breath, and Ben leaned against the post. His dog, Lucky, ran up to the laurel tree and just as quickly came sprinting back down, whining.

"I heard—"

"It started fifteen years ago," Ben said, "right after Nicole was born. We thought it was postpartum depression, but a year or two later, it still hadn't gone away. By the second psychiatrist, Jeanne had been convinced the black moods stemmed from her childhood, the way her mother ran off and left their father to raise them. After they beat that theory to death, they finally got around to me, how I wasn't available enough. How she did not trust me to stay. Apparently, I wasn't open with my feelings."

"Ben . . ." Kate did not know what else to say. She'd lost her interest in a career in psychiatry during therapy. When she'd recounted every second of that awful day, of the endless days and nights that followed, Dr. Weatherby's gaze had often drifted to the photograph on his desk of his young sons. Unwittingly, he'd crumpled a sheet of paper in his hand, as if pleading with her to be quiet, to just sit for a while and be still.

Sorrow was contagious.

"Anyway," Ben went on, "eventually they ran out of theories and got around to the possibility that it was biological. I tended to agree with that, but none of their fancy drugs worked. We tried Prozac and shock treatments, but one day she just stopped at the front door and said, 'No more.' And I had to respect that. I kept her here, after all."

Kate hesitated, then touched his arm. He was surprisingly warm for a man of the sea. Her fingers fit into the dark groove inside his elbow. "I'm sorry."

His gaze brushed her face; he pressed his hand on top of hers. She didn't breathe for a moment as he slid his fingers between hers. Then suddenly he released her, and her breath came out in a rush.

"It was good of you to bring him," he said. "To give him this."

Kate looked out over the bay. "He'd have come anyway. It's dangerous."

"It is. I'll watch over him as best I can."

"I just want to see him settled," she said, and she must have sounded a little panicky because he leaned closer. "I mean, as settled as a boy can be. He's nearly eighteen. His birthday is in three weeks, in November. The court will officially release him from my custody. I wanted to set him down in his world."

Ben moved so close he suddenly came clear through the fog. She could make out the gray around his temples, a scar that had healed into the shape of a comma beneath his left eye.

"Then you'll go back to yours?"

There might have even been a fleck or two of lilac in his eyes. She could spend an hour just counting colors and, for a moment, she let herself imagine it. A full hour staring into eyes like that. "My world is wherever my art is," she said. "I'll be moving to Florida with my dad."

He blinked, then turned away. "I hope not."

There was no uncharged word left in her vocabulary, not a single sentence that wouldn't sound like she was asking him for something. And what she'd really like to do was ask nothing, stun him with the power of a woman who can take care of herself.

But his words made her smile. In fact, her lips lifted to a level they hadn't reached in years.

"I should go," he said, but he didn't leave. The fog slithered through the openings between them, hooked his arm, strung the belt loop of her jeans. They heard Mary humming in the house behind them, her father out back, running a saw.

"What about your daughters?" she asked. "How did they . . . how do they cope with what happened?"

"Not well. None of us has done particularly well. Jenny . . . Jenny was Jeanne's daughter. They used to look at themselves in the mirror, marvel at the similarity of their faces. On her better days, Jeanne took her shopping. They were the same size, they'd wear the same things."

Kate shivered, the fog tunneling down beneath her collar.

"As Jeanne got worse, Jenny got angrier. To her mind, I think, Jeanne could have controlled it. I have to admit, there were times when I felt the same thing. I wanted her to get over it. Just knock it off. Jenny was always a self-preservationist. She started to distance herself. She wouldn't come to her mother's room, and by then Jeanne had stopped coming out. My daughter had no mercy, and maybe that's the best way to deal with someone you can't change."

The saw wound up, sputtered, then went still. They listened to Kate's father cursing.

"And Nicole? I met her that night I came to your house."

Ben smiled, and Kate wondered if Nicole had any idea she produced that look in him, that level of devotion. "Nicole was always interested in fishing. The tomboy, I guess you'd say. Mine. Yet she was the one who looked after Jeanne, who worried the most about what might happen. She begged me not to leave on that trip, but I told her her mother was her mother, and we all had to go on even if Jeanne had stopped moving forward. That's what I said, exactly, then I loaded my crew and set out. Jeanne took the pills that night."

"Ben—"

"One foggy day after the other. Men fish and women go crazy."

"No," Kate said, shaking her head. "No. You can't stereotype people that way. Tragedy isn't like that. It strikes uniquely. It heals in its own way."

Ben stared at her. "I knew Nicole was right. I knew it, but I left."

"Maybe what you knew was that you couldn't save her. That she didn't want to be saved."

They were silent. Kate's father, apparently, had given up. She looked up at the ugly limbs of the laurel tree. "I've had girls like your Jenny," she said. "Foster kids. They won't let you hold them. They'd eat dirt before they'd let you see them cry."

"What did you do?"

She saw the intensity in his eyes, two creases of panic that ran from his lashes to his ears. It had been easier for her; she'd been trying to salvage her kids for someone else, help heal them so they could go home or move on. She had never expected to get something back, to rediscover a child she'd once known. "I don't know. I tried to find common ground. One thing we could do together. I didn't go out much, in case they needed to talk."

"I'm gone every day. Sometimes for days or weeks at a time. My father watches them. Or Gwen Marmosett comes down."

"Why didn't you leave? Take Jeanne somewhere sunny. You might have . . ."

Ben straightened. The energy between them snapped. Kate actually heard it, like a twig snapping, then she felt the weight of the fog, the cold seeping into her skin.

"Believe me, alternate endings run through my head every night," he said. "I blame myself for everything, but someone had to remain sane."

"I didn't mean—"

"Good night."

He walked back down the hill, Lucky hobbling after him, and in a way Kate was thankful for the sudden rift. She was thankful for the cold of her skin, the way her head cleared. She had chosen a man with demons before.

She glanced at the lights trying to break through the fog below her, wondered how Ben's girls got themselves to sleep. Perhaps with loud music to drown out their thoughts, or with the help of contraband liquor. One of them—Jenny, she thought—might hardly sleep at all, three to four hours at best. Kate remembered what that had been like. At two in the morning, her skin had seemed to crackle with electricity. She'd scraped her socks along the carpet and walked around the apartment causing shocks, testing how much pain she could stand.

And when Jenny did sleep, when she dreamed her mother back, healthy, Kate knew exactly what it felt like to wake up—a punch in the stomach, a painful breathlessness as she lost her all over again.

She didn't know those girls from Adam, but that didn't keep her from imagining herself in their bedrooms, turning down the lights, tucking in blankets, sitting in a corner until she was certain they were asleep. Perhaps staying there all night.

She walked to her studio, put her hand on the door but didn't turn it. The smell of rot was back. A tingle climbed her back, like a spider navigating the crevice of her spine, plotting to spin webs through her hair.

She looked up toward the laurel tree and saw Ray there, leaning lazily against the twisted trunk. She thought of Jeanne Dodson, of what Ben had said about the women going crazy. She stilled her breathing, would not be one of them.

She blinked until he disappeared, then forced herself up to the laurel tree, passed right through the space where he'd been. She laughed shakily when she saw nothing but the shadow of a crooked limb. She found nothing—no footprints, no lingering scent.

She walked back down the hill and opened the door to the studio. She flipped on the light, saw the pink envelope that had been slipped under the door with such force, it had scooted clear to the legs of the Queen Anne chair. For the first time in years, she began to cry.

She sat down in the chair, pulled her knees to her chest, and wept like a little girl. But even then she was aware of her father, who didn't need to hear this, just outside the thin walls, and how her body revolted against the hysteria with a decidedly middle-aged stomachache, and a craving for tea, and time being wasted. She glared at the envelope, got into a pair of sweatpants and a threadbare Dodgers T-shirt, set a kettle on the hot plate. When the tea was ready, she took the cup to the window, let the steam mist the glass. Then she snatched the envelope off the floor.

She studied her name on the front. It had been two decades since she'd seen Ray's scrawl, but this wasn't even close. The *K* in her name had been swirled, the diagonals looped. The *V* in Vegas was more like a calligraphic *U*. Ray was not a man to take care with anything. He had never been a man of fluff.

The envelope had no postmark, no identifying marks. It read:

Kate Vegas
Witch's house—Fahrenheit Hill

She used a fingernail to slice it open, pulled out the wallet-size photograph. "Oh," she said, and she sunk onto the bed, curled forward. She thought, *This is not a hoax,* then formed an oval, head to toe, the picture cradled on her thighs.

He would have been one, she figured. His chunky legs poked out of a white coverall. He was barefoot, on a lawn with no discernible characteristics, smiling impishly with a chocolate-covered face, the remains of pudding still seeping through his fingers.

"Oh, God," she said, the pain rearing up through her back, clumping in her neck and shoulders, around her heart. She stood, let the picture slide off, aimed for the bathroom. She'd eaten less than an hour ago, but she threw up only water. She flushed the toilet but couldn't move. She was still there, forehead against the cool enamel, when Mary Lemming came in.

"I smell ghosts," the old woman said.

Kate pushed herself to her feet, walked back to the bed. She handed the photo to Mary, who ran her hand over it, pausing at the tip of William's chocolatey fingers.

"You're a witch," Kate said. "Help me find him."

Mary handed the photo back. It was hard to tell if it was tears or mucus in her watery eyes. "This boy is long gone," she said.

Kate might have slapped her. Instead, she stuffed the picture in her shirt pocket and walked out. Halfway down Fahrenheit Hill, though she wore no coat, she no longer felt the cold. She stomped into Trudy's Kitchen, looking for Ray. She saw no one but Larry Salamano in the kitchen, a frail-looking middle-aged woman in the corner, sipping tea, two old fishermen. Trudy started over to her, but Kate turned and walked out.

She checked the bars next—Eaton's, Donnie's Ale Pub, the Sea Lion. She found all kinds of scruffy men, more than her share of hoodlums, but none with Ray's devil eyes. She went to the Sparrow last, on the docks, and for a moment the room was so dark she thought it was empty. Then she saw the red bar lights, two men at the counter, smoking, a green velvet pool table, scarred with cigarette burns, and one gray-haired man slipping out the back.

She ran after him, flung herself through the back door to the alley, saw the tail end of a raincoat as it disappeared beyond the docks. She ran full speed, but by the time she reached the wharf, it was deserted. She curled her fist, shrieked, then made her way back to the Sparrow. She approached the bartender, an enormous man in his twenties, with a pink scab where his left ear ought to have been.

"That man," she said. "The one who went out the back. Do you know him?"

The bartender shrugged. "Know most everyone around here."

She tried not to stare at the scar, but it was impossible. The skin was pink and shiny, like the moist inside of a mouth. The bartender smiled, ran a finger up over the disfigurement. "Hook got me. Took the ear clear off. Taped it up with a dishcloth and finished the trip. Biggest payout the *Sarah Jane* ever saw. But I lost my craving for it after that."

His smile faded. Kate noticed his eyes behind the layers of fat—crystal clear, almost gold. "The man?" she said.

"Funny," the bartender told her. "He's been in a couple times. Haven't seen him before. Doesn't say much. Sits in the corner. Drinks ginger ale."

Kate's chest tightened. When she went outside, she stood in the street for a good ten minutes, not knowing which way to go. Then her legs decided. She walked the few blocks to Ben Dodson's house, nearly stumbled over the girl she hadn't even noticed sitting on the steps.

Nicole Dodson wore black jeans and a sweatshirt that blended into the night. Much of her frizzy, light brown hair had wormed its way out of its ponytail. In the house behind her, rock music blared at a painful level, blasted out even the surf.

Kate sat beside her, and her heart began to calm. The girl inched away, but Kate could still smell her—lavender soap and potato chips. There were crumbs on her jeans.

"Remember me?" Kate shouted over the music. "My son's working for your dad."

Nicole said nothing. If anything, the music in the house got louder. It penetrated skin and bone, took over the rhythm of Kate's own heart.

"I hear you're a good student," Kate yelled. "That's something to be proud of. Keeping your grades up after your mom died."

The music stopped on the word *died*. Both Kate and Nicole jerked, then in the sudden absence of noise, they heard the slightest things—a girl stomping across the living room, clicking her fingernails along the wall as she climbed the stairs.

"Queen Jenny," Nicole said. "She'll open her closet door to a row of size-five clothes, and still not see a single thing she likes."

Kate noticed the girl's eyes, much like her father's. Brown at first, revealing their secrets and colors only after you'd invested a little time.

"I wish you'd leave Dad alone," Nicole said suddenly.

Kate sat back, slid her hands beneath her legs. "Why?"

"Because he doesn't need any more heartbreak, all right? Because he's sad enough."

Kate looked toward the ocean while Nicole swiped her tears, steadied herself. "I don't intend to hurt him. We've only just met."

"That's what I'm saying. Everyone else in town remembers him and Mom." Nicole curled up, brought her knees to her chest.

"You take good care of him," Kate said softly. "He couldn't ask for more."

Nicole shook her head. "He doesn't ask for anything."

They were silent, then Nicole finally stood. "Anyway, he's not here. He never comes home until late."

Kate shrugged. Maybe she'd been looking for Ben, and maybe she hadn't. All she knew for sure was that the photograph in her pocket seemed to weigh a hundred pounds.

"That's okay," she said. "I just . . . I needed to see a pretty face."

She smiled at Nicole, but the girl merely opened the door. "Then you'll want Jenny," she said.

"Nicole—"

But she was already gone, the screen door slamming behind her. The music came on again, softer this time, jazz instead of rock.

Kate didn't move. She had the feeling that if she stood she'd blow away. She'd be at the mercy of the wind and sea, like a child's blanket snatched from the sand by the tide. So she sat and listened to the girls play music and make themselves dinner. She listened to the clanking of dishes, their argument over who cleaned up—Nicole, finally. She listened as they watched a soap opera they must have taped, Jenny scoffing every time someone kissed, and finally put themselves to bed. She heard one of them pacing, another singing herself to sleep. She sat until Ben Dodson finally walked up the road near midnight, and she realized two alarming things. No one in Seal Bay expected to be happy, and everyone treated Ben Dodson with kid gloves.

"If you ask me," she said, standing, "they're not mourning the loss of their mother so much as the absence of you."

He walked past her, up the slanting stairs toward the porch. "This is not your business."

She didn't even blink. She had half a lifetime invested in other people's mishandled business. She could look Ben in the eye and tell him the family was not as sacred and inviolable as he'd like to believe. Mothers who abused their children then wanted them back, fathers who deserted their families and still expected loyalty lost their rights as far as she was concerned. They deserved nothing, didn't earn one ounce of her respect.

The weight of the photograph in her pocket was one thing, but the sound of those girls singing lullabies to themselves was much worse.

"You have daughters," she said. "You're lucky." She couldn't keep the tears from her eyes.

"Don't you think I know that?" he said. "Don't you think I *know*?"

Kate kissed him so quickly, it startled them both. His hands came around her before she could take it back or pretend it had only been sympathy. He smelled of the ocean, of fish and death and loneliness. Of things she didn't understand and could not respect. His whiskers scratched her cheeks.

He let go, finally. Stepped back, looked out toward the sea, though all that could be seen was a blacker black. The surf kept coming, *grrrr-wooosh, grrrr-wooosh, grrrr-wooosh.*

"Well," she said, "that's not what I was planning."

"No."

"It's just . . . those girls. They—"

"Please. Don't."

Kate crossed her arms. "If you don't have anything to say to them, they'll find someone else who can talk. Someone you probably won't want to know about. One day, you'll have to beg them just to visit you, and the whole time you'll know they'll be itching to leave."

She took a step down, before she tried to kiss away the despair in his eyes. He leaned against the post. "When I got the radio call, I wasn't surprised," he said. "In fact, I hadn't let the crew set the nets that day. I was waiting. And I didn't cry. Not until the funeral, and even then only because Nicole was so distraught. Because Jenny wouldn't let me hold her hand."

Kate took another step, landed on ground that must be nearly impossible to garden. Ground that was mostly sand, coated by salt, spawning moss. "You must hate her."

Ben stiffened, as she'd known he would. As men often did, when confronted with a nasty truth about themselves.

"You *must* hate her," she said again. "Leaving you like that. Leaving you with girls you hardly know."

"Kate—"

His voice broke, and she felt for him. She really did. But she felt for those girls more. She walked back up the steps, stood an inch from his face. She smelled his breath, just a hint of liquor, not enough to mitigate anything. "If you hate her, it's easy. You rip up her picture, go to her grave, and tell her she was weak. Then you come back here and cook those girls dinner. You promise to never leave."

"That would be a lie," he said softly.

Kate blinked, felt the picture in her pocket like a finger, poking her. Not only would she have promised never to leave, she would have insisted the world was a merciful place. She'd have told her son anything was possible, that he could become whatever he wanted. It was so obvious, she didn't know how Ben could question it.

"The best parents," she told him, "lie all the time."

— 5 —

The Weeping Tree

Nicole's bedroom was on the sinking side of the house, on the ocean side, where the wind blew in continuously and the rain pelted sideways. Her sheets never dried and, if tucked too tightly, hatched mold. The windows rattled, along with anything else not tied down—pens, bracelets, and she swore her own bones. On the stormiest nights, the bed shimmied to the window, dresses fell in a heap on the closet floor. Even on a good day, the room rumbled like a low-grade earthquake. Her mother had hated to come in, had held her hands over her ears and begged Nicole to make it stop. But when Nicole had turned up the two-way fishermen's radio, her mother had scoffed at Dominic Allen and Ron Stottenmeir trying to outdo each other with stories of empty lines and freak waves, despite the obvious sound of flapping fish on their decks. Jeanne Dodson had gone still at the sound of Nicole's father's voice declaring he'd have to stay out another day to fill the hold.

For days after her mother's funeral, Nicole couldn't bring herself to turn on the radio. But when Jenny started blasting her heavy metal, Nicole thought nothing could be more indecent in their hushed house than suicidal lyrics by The Anarchists. She turned the radio back on, didn't go to sleep until her father announced he'd cleared the breakwater and was heading south for tuna and halibut, or north for salmon and rockcod. Until she heard him say, as he always did, "Go to sleep now, Nikki. Daddy's all right."

The first thing she heard most mornings was Henry Zeele, captain of the *Kathy Ann,* insisting he hadn't snared a single albacore and probably never would. For the rest of the morning, the other captains would try to outdo him with lucklessness until, apparently, not one of them could afford a beer at the Sparrow.

This morning, she woke not to Henry Zeele, but to another man's distress call. Whoever he was, he managed to keep his voice level—all fishermen did, even in typhoons—but Nicole still heard it, the tiny rise at the end of every syllable, the stoical fisherman's plea.

She threw back the covers and turned up the volume. The man was captain of the *Lioness,* out of Morro Bay, and he couldn't get back into the harbor. The waves were eighteen feet against the breakwater. He'd rammed the rocks twice and was "taking on some water," which meant he was sinking fast. Morro Bay was one of the roughest harbors on the West Coast, closed forty days a year due to turbulent seas, and most fishermen didn't give a damn. They put out despite freakish skies and rechristened ships, trusting luck to bring them home.

Nicole walked down the hall, into the tiny bathroom clouded with Jenny's purple talcum powder and musk perfume. She threw open the window, waved her arms around the room to clear it. She brushed her teeth, tried to manhandle herself to the door, but as always, her own hands rebelled. She felt a rise in her stomach as she opened the medicine cabinet, a steady pressure against her lungs. She snatched a bottle of aspirin and another of Midol. She sat on the floor and pried open the caps. Though she knew exactly how many pills there were, she counted them anyway. When she passed sixty, she had trouble catching her breath and had to lean forward, press her head to her knees.

Forty-seven coated aspirin tablets. Nineteen extra-strength Midols. Jenny had taken only one since last Thursday. Nicole worried she'd dip below sixty, but if she did, she knew Trudy Casson kept bottles of Advil all over the diner. Her friend Angel's mother kept a stash of Valium in the back bathroom, and might not miss one or two. For a month, Gwen Marmosett had cleared the shelves at the Emporium of every last sleeping pill, but after some of the wives took to late-night karaoke singing at Donnie's Ale Pub, the men demanded she put them back.

Her mother had swallowed sixty sleeping pills, and Nicole obsessed on whether aspirin or Valium would have done the same trick. She remembered how she'd known, the second she opened the front door on that Thursday night, that it had happened. It had been so quiet, she'd sworn she'd heard her own blood whizzing past her ears, a noisy rumble rising from her toes that turned out to be the sound of relief. She'd hesitated, leaned against the doorjamb, and thought, *Now I don't have to worry anymore. Now it's over.*

When she'd found her, her mother had been lying in a pool of vomit, as if her stomach had tried to save her, but her will had been too strong. The relief Nicole had felt just a second before exploded in her head like machine-gun fire. They say she passed out for a while, didn't make any calls until eleven, even though she'd come home at eight-thirty. They say, when they arrived, she had adjusted her mother on the pillow, cleaned the vomit from the sheets. But she remembered little of those hours except that there were minutes within them for which she would never be forgiven. She remembered that was when her fear of Thursday began.

She heard Jenny downstairs, slamming cupboards, making the coffee double-strength. She put the tablets back, her stomach churning the way it always did on Thursdays, as if she'd swallowed enough pills to make her sick but not to kill her. She didn't want to kill herself, abhorred the thought of anyone killing themselves, but she was fascinated by how it could be done. Pills, carbon monoxide, rope, pistol. She tried not to look in the mirror when she put back the bottles. It was no longer her frizzy hair or baby fat that disgusted her, but the eyes of some kind of freak.

She waited until the front door slammed and Jenny had gone before emerging. She walked down the hall, paused in front of her mother's door. She knew her father slept in there, but she could not figure out how. By the end, her mother's hair had grown clear to her waist and was curiously cool and moist, as if it was coming out slightly liquefied, everything inside her breaking down. Nicole imagined that even now her father had not found all the strands, and while he slept one would coil itself around his arm, another slither along his shoulder blade until it attached itself to a bead of sweat. It was entirely possible he was being haunted, but he was gone too much for her to know for sure. He'd stayed home for a month straight after the funeral, weather-stripping all the windows, trying without success to re-create their mother's elderberry pancakes. He'd slept in a chair halfway between her room and Jenny's. He came running whenever they cried, something they quickly learned not to do after they saw the panic in his eyes. Once they realized his crying was worse. When he finally went back to fishing, Nicole was grateful the sea would have him. He was too rare, now, to pity.

She walked downstairs, grabbed her backpack off the counter. She cut through old man Engell's yard, zigzagging around his garden gnomes, and the empty lot where a liquor store had burned to the ground, twice, then finally up the hill toward Main Street. She passed three people who'd known her since the day she was born and none of them greeted her, but it wasn't until her sister walked right past her on the arm of the newest fisherman in town that she realized she had disappeared into the fog.

"Jenny," she said, and her sister stopped, let go of Wayne Furrow's arm. She looked right where Nicole was standing, then back down the hill.

"Nicole?" Jenny said, then narrowed her eyes. She stomped her tiny, perfect foot, reached into her pocket and took out a pack of Virginia Slims Lights. Wayne watched her with the same vapid, lovestruck look in his eyes as all the others, as if Jenny had sent some hatchling down his throat to take him over.

One week after their mother died, Nicole heard what she first thought was crying coming from Jenny's room but turned out to be Kevin Hardin getting what every boy wanted from Jenny, yet still saying her name like a plea. In the morning, Jenny brought out a bloodied sheet and washed it before their father got up. She looked Nicole in the eye and waited for her to say something, but Nicole couldn't think of a single word. After that, Jenny hardly looked at her at all, and the boys of Seal Bay High started to call.

Surprisingly, Jenny never got a reputation for being easy. The only boys she allowed to climb the trellis outside her window were dropouts, potential criminals, and the ones reckless enough to swim with her to Seal Rock and back, after tiger sharks had been spotted in the bay. This sounded risky, but in truth, no sharks came within ten feet of her. She'd bought a stun gun, but never had to use it, and this boiled her. "I swear to God," she told Nicole one night after flinging herself on the sofa, "nothing is ever going to happen to me."

Now Jenny searched the pockets of fog, didn't notice when Wayne suddenly shook himself clear of his love haze and realized Jenny had forgotten he was there. He left without even a perfunctory fight for her attention. Nicole waved her hands, made herself out clearly—arms that were too fleshy above the elbow, repulsive pockets of damp skin at her wrists. Her long skirt skimmed the pavement and was bright as daylight, but Jenny walked right past her, and stomped down Warren Lane.

"Come on out, you chicken," Jenny said.

Nicole took a step after her, and her heels clicked on the concrete. Jenny whirled around, finally spotted her in the fog. "Stop doing that."

Nicole shrugged. She wasn't doing anything. She couldn't help it if Jenny couldn't see what was right in front of her.

Jenny inhaled deeply on her cigarette. "Wayne?" she said, then spotted him clear down at the pier. She put a hand on her hip. Even if he felt the sting of her gaze, he didn't turn. He laughed at something Dominic Allen said and hopped on board.

"He got picked up for assault at fifteen," Jenny said. "Some fight over drugs."

Nicole shrugged. She could not see the attraction of a man with a compulsion for violence. She could not understand why, nearly two years after their mother's death, Jenny was just now beginning to throw herself away.

"So what?" Nicole said. "He's still a fisherman." She started down Warren Lane, but Jenny caught her by the arm.

"Come on. Ditch today. I'll drive you into San Francisco, buy you lunch at Union Square."

Nicole extricated her hand, shook her head vigorously. She would not be lured by the dark side.

"Goody-goody," Jenny said, blowing smoke in her eyes.

"Satan."

Jenny's mouth curled around her cigarette. "Go ahead then," she said. "Stay in this godforsaken place. Start drinking Eaton's Stout and maybe you'll see a sea monster in the bay."

Nicole smiled. She would like nothing better. She walked home from school so slowly not because she was afraid to enter an empty house, as many believed, but because she wanted a drunk like Keith Barnaby to be right.

Keith himself had no doubts. He was certain of what he saw, even after a case of Eaton's Stout. When he passed out in Sea Lion Cove and came to at four in the morning, something was dying a grisly death in the bay. Dizzy when he stood, unsure where he was, he was nonetheless absolutely certain that beyond the breakers was a mammoth beast, its jaws the size of an American car, clamping down on a diamond stingray. The last of the blue, poisonous tail quickly disappeared down its torture chamber of a throat.

The creature, he later told the stunned crowd at Eaton's Bar, was easily sixty feet long, with a blunt head, dinosaur tail, and strange looking wings along its flank. It rolled over, splashed the water with its green-spotted tail, then dove down and disappeared. A story he stuck to, despite the ribbing he took.

Keith was sixty-eight and called all women Angie, the name of his wife who'd been dead for fifteen years, but he still had eyes. Nicole was one of the few people who took him seriously. She made sure there were always sixty pills on hand but never took them, and if men drowned, then something wondrous had better rise up in their place. This wasn't naïveté, as Jenny might think, but common sense. There was just enough gravity to tie her to Earth but not enough to crush her, and if twelve hours of darkness always led to light, then why couldn't her mother have waited for morning? Why, if there was such a thing as fate, couldn't it always be good?

"You're a fool," Jenny said, then stomped down the hill.

Nicole turned toward school, but walked slowly. She had a biology test during first period she would ace. An essay to write on *The Scarlet Letter,* which she'd already begun in her head. *What is sin? Which is the worse evil—adultery or spite? If we . . .* She saw a shadow slip out the back door of Trudy's Kitchen, then dart up the hill. Gone so quickly, she made out only a gray coat, a beard, and long, scraggly hair. But something about the rushed, skittish movements set her heart racing. She ran after the shadow up Fahrenheit Hill.

She lost him in the fog, didn't catch another glimpse until she neared Crazy Mary's house. He stepped beneath the laurel tree and paused, touched his hand to a branch and drew back. He stared her way with eyes that, from a distance and with her imagination running wild, looked like empty sockets. He nodded as if he'd already made her acquaintance, then disappeared beyond the tree.

She wrapped an arm around her waist, couldn't find the courage to follow him any farther. She knew everyone in this town and he was no acquaintance of hers. He could be a mass murderer for all she knew, an ex-con only Jenny could love. She jumped when the wind chimes above the Emporium jingled, but it was only a middle-aged tourist opening the door, a woman so pale and frail-looking Gwen Marmosett had to help her inside. When the door closed behind them, Nicole realized she'd done something very few teenagers dared. She'd walked alone to Crazy Mary's house.

She glanced cautiously toward the bloodred door. Legend had it Mary Lemming sliced open the hearts of doves to do magic, she turned half human/half beast after midnight. If you kissed her, you'd turn into a beast yourself, you'd grow fangs and your blood would begin to boil, and soon it would pour out your ears.

Nicole dug her fingernails into her palms. She wasn't scared of witchcraft. What truly frightened her was the chance that Crazy Mary was faking it. That there was no magic at all.

She glanced at her watch, was already ten minutes late for school. If she lingered any longer, it would seem almost pointless to go at all. Maybe Jenny *had* lured her over to the dark side, or Crazy Mary had placed a spell around her house. Her thinking certainly got muddied, her feet would not budge. She got the ludicrous idea that if she broke the rules, she'd be able to run faster. Something would come loose inside her, an unnecessary bone that had merely been holding her back, thwarting speed.

When she noticed the pink envelope propped against Mary's door, she felt curiously calm, almost hypnotized. By the time she walked up to the porch to grab it, it didn't even matter that it was addressed to Kate Vegas.

She slid out the photo and note from within. The picture was of a boy, five or six, standing rigid and rosy-cheeked in a pile of snow. He had straight brown hair, parted on the left, and wore a puffy, orange snowsuit. The date in the corner was December 1989. The note, on pink paper, had only three words, scrawled sloppily.

He was happy.

Nicole jumped when the door opened. Crazy Mary tapped her cane against Nicole's toe.

"Did you ring?" the old woman asked.

"N-n-no," Nicole stammered. "I was . . ." She tucked the photo and note into her skirt pocket. She felt an awful thrill when she did it, and was amazed by the weight of the letter, the way it thudded against her hip like a stone. She could be quite illogical when it suited her, and this time she went clear to the absurd. Regardless of who it was addressed to, that letter had been for her. "I was hoping you could teach me some magic."

Mary narrowed her blind eyes, but she wouldn't spot a lie. It was the truth as soon as Nicole spoke it. Prone to invisibility, her talent might very well rest in things that could not be seen.

Mary stepped back and held open the door. Nicole entered the empty room, sniffed no blood or dove meat, just the scent of mold and damp wood. She stopped short when she walked into the kitchen and found Kate Vegas smiling at her from a chair.

"Well, hello," she said. "No school today?"

Nicole had been lifting her hand to her pocket, but had to stop halfway, feign an itch on her thigh. "Teacher conferences," she said.

"Nicole's come to learn magic," Mary said. "What do you want to know? Love spells? Charms to make your sister's hair fall out?"

Nicole squared her shoulders. "I want my mom to haunt me."

Kate slid her hands around her coffee cup. Mary eased herself down on the chair beside her. "Well."

Nicole walked to the window. "Everyone worries about me, thinks I can't get over it, but that's not it at all. I'm okay. I really am. I just . . . I can't tell if she's listening. I really wanted to see that movie. I hadn't seen a movie in so long. It had Russell Crowe in it. I *love* Russell Crowe. It was a Thursday, so I couldn't be out late anyway. And she seemed better, you know? You remember? She went to the bonfire, danced with my dad. She *laughed* that day. I mean, I only went to the movies. I'm not sitting around torturing myself about it. I was gone only two hours, and I ran all the way home. I swear, I ran as fast as I could."

They were silent, then Mary said, "I'd like to have a few words with your mother myself, but I can't conjure ghosts, Nicole."

Nicole pressed her palm against the window. "Can you read the future?"

Mary scooted back her chair and walked to the giant stove that dominated the room. She filled a pot with water, turned the burner on full, then closed all the doors to the room.

When the kettle whistled, she felt around the counter for a hot pad. She picked up the kettle, took it to the window, held the pot up to the glass. A few drops of boiling water spilled over her fingers, but Mary seemed oblivious.

"Now," she said. "Look at the glass. Pray for your heart's desire."

Both Nicole and Kate laughed, but it was short-lived. A figure instantly took shape in the mist. The steam drew back until a head came through—hair parted on the left, eyes placid and wide-set. A boy of about eighteen, probably. Kate leapt out of her chair.

But at fifteen, Nicole was faster. She smeared the vision with her free hand.

"No," Kate said. "I think that was my son."

Kate's arm shook so badly, she could hardly clasp the edge of the table. She might have started to cry, but by then Nicole had made a terrible discovery about herself: She was no longer willing to stick around for sorrow.

She ran out, more like Jenny than even her worst nightmares had suggested. She slammed her feet into the squishy pavement, decided then and there that the image in the glass was the same as the boy in the photograph, a decade or so later. Mary could read the future and her future was the boy in her pocket. *Her* heart's desire, whether or not this made Kate Vegas cry.

Kate set the two pictures in front of her father. He put on his glasses, studied the faces of the infant and the toddler. He fingered the postmark. "Cambridge is a big town," he said. "And if the last letter was hand-delivered, that implies he's no longer there."

Kate paced the kitchen floor, from table to stove. She hadn't slept last night, hadn't napped all day, had not closed her eyes since that face had risen up on Mary's window. She was afraid of what might appear in her dreams—William wholly formed, speaking her language but with a voice she didn't expect, a proper Bostonian accent. Or with blond hair instead of brown, with a mean streak. It was possible, she realized, that he had grown into someone she wouldn't even like.

"Are you sure Ray's doing this?" her father asked.

Kate stopped, turned. Her body rose an inch and froze there. "It could be William," she said. "Coming to find me."

"Maybe. But why these games?"

"I don't know, Dad."

She put on a jacket, sneakers, and went out into the cold October afternoon. She circled the town—a task that took less than two hours. The fog thickened, obscured the exact time of sunset. She kept to the woods as the sky turned black, listened to bird calls, crickets, a whistle, the sound of stone hitting stone.

She paused, tried to see through the cypress trees that gradually turned to pines. There were no lights, no signs of habitation. She'd walked this way before and had seen no cabin. She took a step in, the ground changing subtly from sand to richer dirt. She heard the grinding of rock, then silence. A whistle again, a man's grunt.

She walked a few paces and was quickly enveloped by pines. She gripped the bristly trunk of a tree, turned back to make sure she knew where she'd come from. All sounds stopped. She laid her head against the trunk, felt heavy with a sorrow that had nothing to do with the photographs. She hadn't seen Wayne for days. He fished all day, frequented Jenny Dodson's hangouts in the evenings, slept hard at night. Sometimes he seemed startled when she waited up for him, as if he'd forgotten her somewhere between Ghost Island and Seal Rock. As if he'd anticipated her just fading away.

She waited for another sound, heard nothing. She didn't know what she was looking for anyway. She left the woods, headed to the library though it was near closing time. The librarian gave her five minutes, and she hurried to the scanty selection of phone books. She found one for the Boston metro area, prayed it contained listings for Cambridge. She opened the pages to the Vs.

She found a column of Vegases. No Rays, but an R. Vegas, a G. and R. Vegas. She wrote down the numbers, long shots or not.

She saw Jenny Dodson on her way out, crouched over a book in the corner and reading so furiously her lips moved. Kate took a step toward her and Jenny looked up, slammed the book.

"They're closing," Kate said softly.

Jenny shrugged, moved the book sideways so Kate could not see the spine. She grabbed her purse, slung the strap over her shoulder.

"What are you reading?" Kate asked.

Jenny hid the book beneath her arm. "Not the latest Oprah pick. I can tell you that."

Kate followed her out the front door, stopped short at the

rain. It dripped from a saturated sky, had already coated everything. Jenny pulled a scarf over her head. "Goddammit," she said.

A woman came out behind them, her skin the same cloudy hue as the sky. She wrapped a thick man's coat around her shoulders, noticed them standing there.

"Jennifer," she said, "have you gotten *Last Light* in at the Aerie? You told me you ordered it three weeks ago."

Jenny rolled her eyes, a gesture she didn't hide. "Why don't you convince your book club to read the latest Nora Roberts novel? I swear to God, if I have to read one more twenty-year-old's take on how he was mentally abused as a child, I'm gonna do some damage myself."

Kate saw the hint of a smile on the woman's weathered face. "Consider us warned," she said. She held out her hand to Kate. "Gwen Marmosett. Owner of the Emporium. I've seen you at Mary's."

"Kate Vegas."

"Nice to meet you. Don't let Mary read your tea leaves."

"Why n—"

"She likes the drama of bad fortunes." She turned to Jenny. "Call me when you get the book in."

Jenny waited until Gwen had started up Fahrenheit Hill, then snorted. "I ordered her the latest Dave Barry book by mistake."

Kate smiled. "I think that's lovely."

Jenny headed out into the rain. She didn't aim for her house on Pacifica Lane, but down toward Sea Lion Cove. Kate started after her.

"I know my way," Jenny said, eyeing her. She picked up her pace.

"Sure. I'm just curious which way it leads."

Jenny hopped off the boardwalk. She kicked off her shoes, buried her toes in the icy sand. Kate did the same, though she winced at the cold. Jenny glanced up the hill, where Gwen Marmosett was now a slow-moving speck beneath the lamplight.

"Whenever I look at her," Jenny said, "all I can think is that she's over fifty and it shows. She won't even come to the New Year's bonfire anymore. Won't dance or drink, like she might—horror—do something she'll later regret."

"Is she married?"

"Not anymore. Her husband didn't even die like a fisherman. Slammed his car into a tree on a perfectly sunny day."

Kate looked up the hill, but Gwen had gone beyond the lamplight. "Sad. It's so sad here."

"You got that right. You know what she does? Gwen? She sells T-shirts with gargantuan elephant seals on the back. Peddles seashells in bags of white netting for $5.50 apiece. She arranges chartered fishing boats for tourists and bugs me about Oprah's latest, so she can discuss it at the ninnies book club at Wanda Finch's oppressive little house."

Kate stared at her. She thought Jeanne Dodson had been right about one thing: This town needed paint. Neon colors and geraniums and singing. If the men insisted on fishing, then the women needed a reason to stay.

"You want out," she said.

Jenny ripped off her scarf, threw it on the sand. She laid the book gently on top of it and wrapped it up. The rain intensified as she unzipped her jeans, climbed out of them, until it must have felt like pellets against her bare skin. She slid out of her panties and shirt and bra, then stood before Kate naked but not shivering, as if she were a Selkie immune to cold.

"I don't want out," she said. "Wanting just frustrates you. I'm leaving. Preparing. Taking steps."

"That's good. That's—"

"Gwen is everything wrong with this town," she said. "After her husband died, she could have taken up with some hunky bricklayer and moved inland, but instead she ordered another line of tacky shell wind chimes; she entrenched herself even further in her junky store. She walks in circles around this town every night, like she can't find her way out, when I could have told her the path is dead ahead of her. It's in the opposite direction of everything she knows."

She started toward the water. Kate fingered the paper in her pocket, those R.Vegases she would have to call later, after she saw Jenny safely home. After she waited up for Wayne. She peeled off her own clothes, stepped out naked and shivering. She reached the waves as Jenny dived over the last line of breakers.

Kate waded in, the water so cold her toes curled, her right leg spasmed. She cried out when a wave splashed her thighs, and Jenny laughed.

Kate took a deep breath and dove into the black surf. She came up gasping beyond the first line of breakers, miserable, so cold she might never get warm again. Jenny eyed her from a dozen yards away, treading water. "There's a sea monster, you know."

Kate couldn't speak. Her teeth chattered, she'd lost feeling in her toes. Jenny started swimming for Seal Rock, which seemed a mile away. A terrifying, glacial mile.

The numbness spread up her knees. She found it hard to tread water, so she started to swim. She followed Jenny's wake, found that after a few minutes, the cold was bearable, more like dull knives across her skin. Then merely a tingle. When she put her head down and swam the breaststroke, the style she'd competed in in high school, a shocking warmth crept along her arms and the backs of her thighs. She hadn't swam in the ocean in twenty years.

When she tired, she floated on her back, felt the current carrying her south. She imagined floating straight into San Francisco Bay, emerging naked and triumphant. She turned over again, saw Jenny at the base of Seal Rock, climbing its barnacle-encrusted cliffs, unafraid of affronted elephant seals. Apparently fearless.

Kate tried to swim after her, but the current was stronger now and her arms fatigued. Her jubilation turned to anxiety, then skirted the outskirts of panic. She looked back to shore, did not see how she could make it. She'd drifted far left of their starting point. With every stroke inland, the sea took her out two.

She heard Jenny singing as she put her head down and swam hard. She didn't look up until she was exhausted, then saw with relief that the first line of breakers was only a few yards ahead. She could hardly move her arms, but her legs were stronger. She kicked until she hit the first wave and rode it in. It pushed her to the bottom, crushed her cheek against the sand. She pushed off the shelf and broke to the surface. She realized she could stand now.

She crawled up on shore, exhausted but also jubilant. She no longer felt the cold, which was probably a dangerous state. She walked back along the beach; she'd drifted nearly a quarter mile. She could not see Seal Rock from here.

She finally made it to her clothes, put them on, and the shock of that little warmth brought on the shivering. She scanned the bay for Jenny, but couldn't see her. She trembled so badly, she could hardly walk, but she forced herself back to the water. She searched the waves, glimpsed something just beyond the line of breakers.

It was not Jenny. Long and slick, its back emerged from the water and kept coming. Blue-gray, with green spots, it looked like a gigantic eel. Except it had what appeared to be wings along its flank. It twisted, spiraled, turned onto its back, and splashed down to the depths. A whale, her logical voice told her. But her heart soared, and she felt a shiver unrelated to the cold down her spine.

A few minutes later, Jenny slashed through the breakers. She jogged out of the water, apparently ready for more. The current had not pulled her. She'd returned to the exact place she'd started.

Kate expected some harangue on her wimpy performance, but instead Jenny lightly touched her arm. "Not bad," she said, "for an old woman."

Wayne Furrow stepped off Mary Lemming's front porch and climbed the hill. He stepped over the first root of the laurel tree, which in the darkness and rain looked like a discarded body. He took out a cigarette, lit it, then held the match up to the tree. He saw no signs of old wounds, no evidence of sap. He glanced back toward the house, wondered if Mary was staring at him through her dark bedroom window. He had to be up in five hours to haul ice, the hardest, most menial job any fisherman could do, and he was looking forward to it. He had not been the same person since he'd gotten here. He'd been happy. He'd stopped wanting anything more.

He let the match go out and stepped up to the tree. His eyes adjusted to the darkness, and he made out the wrinkled bark, the twisted, coiled limbs. The tree smelled like gasoline and he didn't even mind. Jenny Dodson was unapproachable and mean, but he was already well on his way to loving her. Start getting what you want and apparently all the fire goes out of you. Find a place that suits you and you might never leave.

He lifted the cigarette to the tender V in the trunk, drew back, glanced toward the house again. His mother had wanted him to cry, but back then there'd been no reason to. He'd always had a taste for marijuana, had never gotten better than Cs at school. He'd been told all his life he had no future, so what did he care if he fucked everything up? He never lost anything, never had anything to lose.

Now he had something, too many things. He could die at sea or Jenny Dodson could tell him to go to hell. Ben Dodson might fire him, or he could wake up tomorrow morning with pneumonia and lose the strength to fish. Despair had been easy. It didn't ask anything of him. But this hopefulness was something else—demanding, energetic, relentless. It unnerved him, increased his craving for cigarettes, made him yearn for a dark room, a joint, even the routine tirade that came after, some equally hopeless person telling him he was ruining his life. He wanted to test the integrity of joy, know its boundaries, be prepared for the moment when everything would be lost.

He took a deep drag on the cigarette, watched the tip flare orange. He pressed it quickly to the trunk, held it there a good five minutes, until the wood began to smolder, until he could no longer stand the smell of smoke and gasoline. When he lifted it away, he saw that the wound had gone half an inch deep, that already the amber sap was oozing out to try to heal itself.

Then he sat in the lap of a giant root and cried.

— 6 —

Mermaids

For as long as Jenny Dodson could remember, people had been calling her beautiful, and for just as long, she'd stashed a nasty truth: Things were not always what they appeared. There were days when it took hours to steam the salt-air frizz from her hair, mornings when she woke with puffy eyes, two new pimples on her chin, and a stomachache that grew worse if she had to leave the house. There were nights when she peeled off her makeup and didn't find a single feature she liked underneath.

Nothing was as good or bad as it first appeared. Take Miles Stavers, who was renowned for knocking gentle Leonard Stein over the head with a bottle of Jack Daniels for no good reason. He was a punk, sure, the likely culprit of that liquor store robbery out on Highway 86 though no one could prove it, but that kind of suspicion merely put a little color in his bland, vanilla hair. He was capable of violence so his eyes danced a bit. But what really proved he was not worthless was his disgust with Seal

Bay. Like Jenny, he dreamed of L.A., Houston, Taos, anyplace the heat sapped your energy along with your unhappiness, where it was too dry and dusty to put up a fuss.

Since midnight, she and Miles had been smoking his thickly rolled joints, talking about how they'd do it, how they'd get away.

"I'm not doing manual labor," Miles said near dawn. He stretched out on the concrete floor of his shabby apartment, hands behind his neck. Oblivious or resigned to the cold. "No more working with my hands. I could take bets maybe. My uncle's a bookie in Queens. He's got some apartment over a Laundromat. I ever tell you that?"

Jenny walked to the window. She was not moving to Queens. She watched the sky turn from black to blue, as if in the process of healing. She had the same slim chances of employment he had, maybe worse. She imagined herself a writer, a poet, though she'd never written anything she'd let people read. She'd nearly failed high school English by concentrating too much on her own inept poems instead of paying attention to the Brontë sisters. She was unmoved by Rita Dove, confused by Plath. She didn't even understand what went into a good poem. She just liked words. Sliver. Sting. Rapture. Fecund. She *loved* fecund. Dirty and offensive-sounding, yet just the opposite. A hopeful word—prolific, fruitful, ripe.

"We can worry about that later," she said. "We've got to concentrate on the escape. We can take my car. How much money have you got?"

She turned in time to catch his wince. He'd promised to put together every penny he made loading ice for her father, from the odd jobs he scored in town, from his drug sales, but now she knew he hadn't saved a dime.

"Jen—"

"We're already into November and it's only going to get worse. The sudden chill of December always drives the elephant seals crazy. The males bellow all night. Stupid, fat pups chase you down just for the fun of it."

"I had to pay off those speakers. Pay Saul up-front for the pound. I'll make it back."

"January is cold and smells of fish guts," she went on, ignoring him. "February is miserly with sun. It isn't until March that the sand starts to heat up, when it doesn't feel like crushed ice beneath your toes, but the sky still looks like slate. April, May, and June are obliterated by fog, in July we might as well be living in an oven. Then in August there's the red-nosed tourists, snapping pictures of my dad like he's a relic. Only September is decent, but not until after Labor Day, when the crowds clear out. It doesn't matter though, because October is coming on fast, the month when you grow more depressed than ever, because you haven't got the nerve or the resources to leave before it starts all over again."

Miles had closed his eyes. Whether in pain at her words or because he was furious, she couldn't tell. Nor did she care. She'd used most of her savings to buy her Honda. She had only four hundred dollars left. Four hundred dollars that might get her to Los Angeles but wouldn't keep her there for long. She wouldn't leave until she could ensure she would never come back. Working full-time at the Aerie, that might take a year.

"You're more like your mother every day," Miles said softly.

Jenny stiffened, pressed her tongue against her teeth. She felt Miles smiling behind her. Mean again, now that the buzz had worn off.

"I don't have time for anyone who isn't serious," she said. "I don't have patience for talkers."

He ignored that, rose surprisingly quickly for a man who'd been in a stupor most of the night, for someone so dense. He was no longer pretty. A wad of his blond hair stuck to the corner of his eye, his bottom lip had a nasty cut. But when he grabbed her wrist, she smiled. She might look like her mother, but she was no weakling. The counselor her father had brought her to had loved statistics—thirty thousand suicides a year in the U.S., a tripled likelihood of a child of a suicide victim taking her life as well. Jenny had taken one look at his snazzy Sausalito office, his leather and chrome furniture that, in its own cool, pristine way, seemed like some kind of rebuke to mourning, and knew she would never come again. Did he think she was an idiot, that she didn't know what was in her own blood? Did he think she could, for one second, forgive her mother for what she'd done? That she wouldn't turn herself into an abomination before she'd let herself become another Jeanne?

She yanked her hand away, walked to the door. She took five steps, six, before Miles slung her around, slammed her shoulder into the door to pin her. The trouble with Miles was that he could jump off a cliff tomorrow and no one would care. And somehow he knew this. When he woke up on any given morning, he was capable of anything.

The poem came right then, perfectly formed and totally different than anything she'd written before. Another species entirely. When she'd been trying to compose poetry, she ought to have been striving for rock songs. She heard music in her head, the steady beat of a bass guitar, and she sang the words before she could stop them, or consider how foolish they might seem to a man who didn't value words at all.

I'd like to wish you well
But there's no way to tell
you're not pretty to me
anymore.

Ain't hard to say good-bye
Just turn my back and fly.
I'm no one's pretty girl
anymore.

It wasn't the blow she dodged, but the laughter. The sight of his ugly yellow teeth. At least when he slapped her with the back of his hand across her nose and cheek, she knew she would never be tempted to come back. It hurt more than she expected, then she felt the blood dripping from her nose.

"Shit," Miles said, going for a towel, but she was already gone. She was out the door and down to the sidewalk by the time Miles appeared in the doorway.

"Jen—"

"Don't hit women, Miles," she called back to him. "It's not nice."

"Jenny, please."

She walked toward home, trying to stop the blood with her palm. When the flow intensified, she turned instead toward Fahrenheit Hill. She tilted her head back, saw the stars for once, the Big Dipper, Orion's Belt. She might have even seen a flash of fiery Mars before a wisp of fog stamped it out.

She cursed the weather, the gloom, the mildew along the concrete that made walking in the dark treacherous. She skidded out twice, caught herself by gripping a lamppost, the hood of Abby Grange's scuffed pickup. She was halfway up the street when a stooped, middle-aged woman opened the door of the Surfside Motel, then caught herself on Jenny before she went sliding clear across the sidewalk. The woman's skin felt like leather, one eye was moist. She was dressed in a man's gray sweatsuit. When she tried to speak, she managed only a cough.

Jenny pressed a palm to her bloody nose, tried to walk past, but the woman held on. She coughed harder, something thick and crusty rising up.

"Sorry," the woman said, then coughed once more. She was gaunt, with sunken cheeks, circles under eyes. Jenny turned away. She'd seen that look before.

"Look, I'm kind of bleeding here."

The woman seemed to notice her face for the first time. She lifted her hand, stopped it just before she reached Jenny's cheek. "You need ice," she said.

"Okay."

"You shouldn't . . ." She trailed off, glanced up the hill. "You know that woman up there? The one staying with the witch?"

Jenny pictured Kate Vegas jumping into the ocean after her. She wasn't easily shocked, but that had stunned her. A woman of her age doing something so reckless. "Maybe."

The woman reached into her pocket, took out a pink envelope. "Give her this."

She pressed it into her hand, then finally released her. She trudged across the street, disappeared inside Trudy's. Jenny looked at the envelope, saw a line of phlegm across the corner. She might have tossed it if she hadn't been feeling so woozy and weak. She stuffed it in her pocket, forgot about it by the time she stood outside Crazy Mary's house. She picked up a rock and threw it at Wayne Furrow's window. She missed her first few tries, then finally hit the glass.

The light came on after a minute, the window slid up. Wayne poked his head out.

"I'm bleeding," Jenny said.

He studied her a moment, finally said, "I'll be right down."

He came out with ice wrapped in a washcloth. He hesitated before handing it to her, as if a nosebleed was contagious and whatever was ailing her might start attacking him, too.

"What happened?" he asked.

"Don't worry about it." She held the ice against her nose. "Just some jerk."

He narrowed his eyes, must have seen fingerprints on her cheek. "How's the pain?"

"Not too bad now."

"It doesn't look broken."

He led her to the bench outside Crazy Mary's kitchen door, sat down beside her. He took the ice from her, held it against her skin more gently than she had herself. He swabbed the cut, and in no time at all she'd stopped bleeding.

"Jennifer," he said. "You're too good for this."

She wished he had more gruffness to his voice. If he wasn't so goddamn nice, she might like him. It was impossible to go from a man like Miles to someone like Wayne. It was like eating potatoes after a can of hot chili; you couldn't even taste it.

"You don't know anything."

"No." He looked up the hill toward the laurel tree. "Maybe I don't."

"I'm not throwing myself away, as everyone likes to think. I'm just examining all my avenues out of here."

"Okay."

She glanced at him, knew that when he looked back, he didn't see her. Even with blood on her nose, he thought what they all thought—that as long as she was pretty, she was not required to be anything more.

"Listen to this," she said, then cleared her throat. She thought of ugly yellow teeth and panicked, stuffed her hands under her legs so he wouldn't see them shaking. *"I'd like to wish you well, but there's no way to tell you're not pretty to me anymore. Ain't hard to say good-bye. Just turn my back and fly. I'm no one's pretty girl anymore."*

She was no singer. Her voice shook and she dared him to laugh, wished he would laugh so she could go. So she wouldn't start thinking, as she already had, that because he was a stranger he might not know that Nicole was the one who was considered smart.

"What is that?" he said. "An old Joan Baez song? My mom had some of her albums."

She turned away, tilted her head back presumably to stop the flow of blood. "Look," she said, "I should probably get home."

She started to get up, but Wayne had dropped the ice, somehow gotten hold of her hand. With his other one, he swiped a hand through his dark hair. He looked just about perfect, already like someone's sweet husband, and Jenny couldn't meet his gaze.

"I put a hole in that tree," he said.

She looked past him to the laurel tree. She jerked back her hand, horrified and then incredulous. She laughed, didn't believe it for a second.

"I can't sleep anymore," he went on. "I don't know how people stand it, having so many things to lose. Wanting so much."

She studied him, waited for him to laugh so the pulsing down the back of her neck would subside. When he took out a cigarette, she hiked the hill to the laurel tree, ran her fingers over the bark until she found the wound. It was an inch wide, puddled with amber sap as it tried to heal itself. She smelled gasoline and brine, felt sick to her stomach and strangely impressed. He'd start living now. He'd have no choice.

She tried to wipe the sap off on her jeans, but it had already hardened on her fingertips. She walked back down the hill, standing instead of sitting beside him.

"It doesn't mean anything," she said. "People here just like to think about disaster."

"Yeah."

"But I wouldn't tell anyone if I were you."

He looked up. "Your dad is the first person who looks me in the eye not to see if I'm stoned, but to ask me what I think."

"You've got a funny way of showing gratitude."

Wayne dropped his head, pressed his hands between his knees. "You think I won't survive," he said. "You think I can't offer you anything but this." He glanced down Fahrenheit Hill, at the fading houses beneath it.

Jenny laughed at his conceit, the nerve of him thinking he knew what she thought. Then she felt tears prick her eyes. In the last two weeks, he'd shown up at the Aerie at the end of her shifts. He ignored her assurances that she didn't need a bodyguard and walked her home as if she'd been in danger all these years without him. Sometimes she let herself imagine touching him, then she smelled him. He reeked, as they all did, of slimy seaweed and rockcod, the two stenches that permeated everything in this town—bedrooms and soup pots, even newly laundered clothes. When she got out of here, she was going to soak in a perfumed bath for a week. She was never going to the beach or eating fish again.

"You know," she said, stilling her tears, "there are people who do something other than fish for a living. You could get a degree. Make something of yourself. You're a coward to stay."

She heard him breathing, deep and slow, then finally he said, "So what they say is true."

"And what's that?" She jutted out her chin, even though, at that moment, she didn't really want to know. Jenny Dodson, who could survive everything from seeing her doomed mother every time she looked in a mirror to swimming with sharks, was suddenly standing on very thin ice.

"They say you've got the looks of an angel," he said quietly, "but your heart's made of devil's ice."

Jenny blinked. She blinked five times, then was still. She was not crazy and she was not depressed. Of course she had a heart of ice, that was why she was still standing. She wasn't going to start falling for some soft-talking, drop-dead gorgeous fisherman. She was almost sure of it.

"They say I sold my soul to the devil, too," she said, "just to get skin like this. Just to drive you all crazy."

She expected him to laugh, or at least to turn and run, but all Wayne Furrow did was stand and look at her. She stared at his hands, the cuts across his knuckles. It was as if they'd been cut off someone else's arms and sewn onto his. They were hands no sane woman could bear to be touched by, for fear of getting scraped up.

"You don't scare me," he said.

"I don't know who you think you are," she said, because it was easier to say that than to cry, "but let me tell you something. I'm not going to—"

He put his hand on her cheek, turned her toward him. He kissed her before she said another word. She should have stopped him immediately, because after a few seconds, she lost all motivation for ever pulling away again. She lifted her arms, wondered just how much blood she had lost. Falling, she thought. *I'm falling so quickly.* There was nothing else to do but hold on to him.

Pickle juice was dribbling down Jeanne's chin when he saw her. She'd bought one of Abby Grange's enormous dills and taken it outside the Merc to eat. She sat on the old wood bench, tapped her nurse's shoes against the wood planking to some internal rhythm. She was lovelier than she'd been when she'd left for college—her pale hair longer, breasts more snug against an enticingly soft yellow sweater. Even so, he walked past her, did not succumb to that glistening chin, did not ask her about nursing school or remind her of the kisses they'd shared before she'd left. He hurried down to the docks before she could speak to him, call him back. He forgot his crew, hopped on board the *Kathy Ann,* took her farther north than he'd ever gone before. The typhoon came on suddenly, swells of forty feet. He struggled to keep the bow to the waves, though he knew it was pointless. He was lost either way.

Ben woke from the dream covered in sweat, achy and sore as if, during the night, his fingers had lengthened, his lungs had expanded to accommodate more air. Whatever the case, some elemental piece of him had altered. He woke with room for more.

To his surprise and satisfaction, the first thing in was lust. It slid through his bloodstream, covered every surface of his skin. He imagined walking up Fahrenheit Hill and pounding on Kate Vegas's door. He imagined the pleasure of her touching him first, wanting him, then making love to her beneath the laurel tree, vanquishing all curses.

He sat up in bed, looked to Jeanne's side. He ran his hand over the cool sheets, remembered how pleased he'd been with himself two decades ago, when he'd been the man to make Jeanne stay. How he had, in actuality, kissed that pickle juice from her chin, led her straight to her father, proposed then and there.

He lifted his hand, formed a fist. After lust, there was guilt, tenderness, gratitude for his life. He swayed between thinking Jeanne a victim and a murderer, yet how could he regret the day that led to all the others, to his girls? How could he consider one second of his life a mistake?

He put on his jeans and a sweatshirt, walked down the hall. He put his hand on Jenny's door, but didn't turn the knob. He had answers to everything, to why waves calmed when oil was poured on them and the secrets of underwater waves, but he did not have an answer for this: Why would Jenny date a man like Miles Stavers? When had she decided to be worthless, and why couldn't he prove her wrong?

He had prayed for daughters while Jeanne was pregnant. He'd grown up playing with boys who had more courage than common sense, boys who, on a dare, would dive headfirst into the ocean without bothering to first check the depth, who started fishing before they had a chance to come up with a more ingenious plan. The world did not need another fisherman, so when the girls came, he had a few months of bliss, followed by years of bewilderment and pure terror. What was he supposed to do with daughters? They shredded expensive oilskins into ribbons and cried when he chopped the heads off struggling fish. The air in his living room became permanently stained lavender, all his towels reeked of rose-scented shampoo. He fished more and more, grateful there were no poets or crybabies aboard the *Jeannie*—only men who could slice open the bellies of thrashing triggerfish and not feel a single thing.

Yet now he craved softness, giggling, elderberry pie. He wondered if all that seawater forced down his throat had amassed somewhere inside him, like a puddle of unshed tears. For once he ignored Jenny's request for privacy and turned the knob. He wanted to press his cheek to her forehead, find out if she still slept at a hundred degrees, the way she had as a baby and little girl.

Instead, he found the window open and her bed empty, the sheets crisp with frost. He was not surprised that she had sneaked out; what surprised him was that he had, until this moment, let her go. The only time he'd stayed close to home was after Jeanne died. He'd slept just outside their rooms, shushed their sorrows with badly sung Chubby Checker songs, shopping lists, plans that all of them knew would never materialize. He'd rejoiced when Nicole brought him her broken radio, drew the repair process out into an entire afternoon. He decided, however ridiculously, that no one had been eating enough vegetables. He rototilled the entire backyard, planted seeds in February, though he knew they'd be too cold to germinate. When Gwen Marmosett finally walked down from the Emporium, stepping right across his barren garden, he had never felt such relief. She showed Nicole and Jenny how to change a tire. Trudy Casson came a week later and explained to the girls how to access the life insurance money, should anything happen. They filled his living room with chatter and an even headier scent of lavender, sent him fishing again, and in his absence taught his daughters the trick to waiting for a man to come back: Be quiet, keep your hands busy, and start right in on loving him less, in order to be ready for the worst.

Ben turned and walked into Nicole's room. She was still sleeping, curled up, her radio tuned to the Coast Guard frequency. She was the child who took after him the most, who loved Seal Bay, admired the fortitude of its people. Men died at sea and, within a few years, their wives remarried their first mates. Instead of selling out and moving to Italy, the way she'd always dreamed, Trudy Casson kept her restaurant open daily until midnight and painted her ceiling to look like a Tuscan heaven. The cypress trees leaned precipitously inland and were stunted at ten feet, but nevertheless they stayed alive in a soil of pure sand. Nicole loved the New Year's bonfire, Lisa Stottenmeir's irises, the slightest, most hard-won signs of joy, so he prayed for something that might surprise her. He pressed his lips to her forehead and whispered, "Demand *more*."

It was not even dawn, yet he left the house and went door to door, looking for his oldest daughter. Every time a girl told him she hadn't seen Jenny, and in fact hardly talked to her at all anymore, he got colder, his left side sagged more. By the time he reached Fahrenheit Hill, he had difficulty walking uphill and, more than that, he hated his wife like crazy. What selfishness, what absolute gall, to create this mesmerizing, high-strung creature, then leave him alone to see her through.

He saw nothing but shadows, an unkempt man on a bench one minute, emptiness the next. A woman walking haltingly down to the wharf. He heard a distant airplane, a car warming up, a cough.

At last he spotted them, sitting on the bench outside Mary Lemming's kitchen, kissing.

He felt relief for the barest instant, then he knew he couldn't stand one more woman doing things he couldn't predict.

"I've been out searching for you," he shouted.

When Jenny stood, he saw the patch of dried blood beneath her nose, a swollen cheek. He stepped backward, realizing that whenever he ought to say something meaningful to his daughters, he was more afraid than he ever was at sea, even in the middle of a typhoon.

He turned to Wayne, who had stood up beside her, who now worked an arm protectively around her waist. "You want to tell me about this?"

Jenny laughed. "Right. Like he would hit anybody."

"Would you please tell me who would?"

Jenny went silent.

"Jenny."

"Don't worry about it," she said at last. "I can take care of myself."

He studied the mark, wondered how he would stop himself from walking up to Miles Stavers's apartment and beating the kid to a pulp. He wondered how he was supposed to assure his daughters' happiness when they kept outwitting him and messing it up.

"You sneak out of the house again and you're grounded."

Jenny threw back her hair, and her eyes, Jeanne's eyes, were incredulous. "You've got to be kidding. I'm eighteen. I don't have to sneak. I can do what I want. Where the hell have you been?"

He made a fist, let it go. He yearned for a stormy night at sea, bad weather, anything but this. "Underwater, obviously," he said. "All I know is I'm not going through a repeat of this morning ever again. If you can't follow my rules, you can pack your bags and leave."

His voice caught, but he didn't take back the words. Wayne squeezed her, but she didn't even glance at him. She stood still, as beautiful as Jeanne had been but a thousand times stronger, and he thought, *Tell her that.* But before he could find the words, she cut loose from Wayne, stomped up to him.

"I'll pack my things tonight."

"Jenny—" Wayne said, but she waved him off.

"I'll crash with friends."

She ran down the hill. Ben leaned slightly, realized he was holding his breath. He let it out slowly, almost reluctantly, as if it was possible that he could still lose more.

"Don't have daughters," he said.

Wayne laughed nervously, but he also drew himself up to his full height. "I'm going to have four, if Jenny will agree."

Ben looked him over carefully, wondered if he'd mistaken exuberance for recklessness. If he'd overlooked some obvious flaw.

"She looks exactly like her mother did at this age," Ben said.

"She's not her mother," Wayne said with the certainty of a boy who has yet to be disappointed in the girl he loves.

"No."

After Wayne returned to the house, Ben made his way to the laurel tree. He could no longer see Jenny, did not know which way she'd gone. He yearned to go after her, but forced himself to stay there, to settle for praying that she had a friend who would take her in, a plan in mind. If he feigned calm and pretended he could live without her, would she stop being so determinedly discontented and realize she was free? He thought it the worst irony of parenthood that sometimes you had to make your children hate you in order to prove your love.

He touched the tree, was about to go back down when he felt the sap. He searched for and found the gash in the tree, right in the center of the V. A slender line of amber sap slid down, and though he didn't believe in any of it—superstitions of weeping trees and men dead at sea—he felt chilled to the bone.

He heard footsteps, turned to find Kate Vegas coming up the hill. She wore baggy sweats and a large flannel shirt. Inside the huge clothes, she looked tiny.

"I heard you and Jenny," she said. "I'm sorry."

He didn't hesitate. He put his hand over hers and confronted, head on, the crux of the matter: The only problems you can fix are your own.

"Ben," she said, and he leaned down to kiss her. She tasted of peppermint, of something that, for too long, had been denied him. She drew back, laughing, and he thought he'd never been given so much. "I want to show you something," she went on. "Will you come with me today?"

At last, the answer was easy.

Kate drove inland until they outran the fog. They climbed into rolling hills, peppered with oak trees, lush green grass. She set up her easel under the oldest, widest tree she could find.

"You see," she said. "It's beautiful here, too."

She'd painted a mermaid a few days earlier, but didn't lift it from the trunk until Ben left for a hike. She painted over it not with swirls, but with Jenny's face—pink lips, green eyes, cream-colored skin.

Ben returned after the mermaid was hidden beneath his daughter. He said nothing while she filled in wisps of blond hair, emerald eyes that might have been cruel, but stopped just short of it. She heard him breathing, stumbling on a sigh.

"She'll be all right," she said as she set down the brushes, turned to smile at him. "I can always tell."

Ben looked at her, at the picture. He seemed to be trying to peer beneath it, but if he saw the mermaid, he didn't say. Gwen Marmosett had taken pity on her and agreed to market three of her oil paintings on consignment. Everyone, apparently, considered them modern art, one-dimensional, and they'd gone unsold.

Ben put his hand on her shoulder. There had been men, since Ray, but none she'd let watch her paint. Somehow that had been a relief, keeping at least one thing safe, chancing nothing.

He turned her toward him. He was something to look at—skin weathered, almost gray, his posture erect, as if he'd spent so many years standing up to gale-force winds, he could no longer bend an inch.

"People can leave you in any number of ways," she said. "You owe it to yourself to go on without them."

He took her face between his hands and kissed her. She found his upper lip and sucked the salt out of it, slid her mouth across the windburns on his nose. His hand on the side of her face trembled, and she reached up and covered it with her own.

"Kate," he said, and she stopped him with more kisses. He pulled her down on the grass, threading his fingers through hers, bringing them both under his shirt to his chest. His skin was cold to the touch, almost seawater cold, but his heart hammered. She kissed him again. He tasted like seawater.

It wasn't until later, when he was inside her, his skin glistening in the sun, that Kate saw his tears. His breathing got rough, seawater rose up through his pores, then slid over the crest of his shoulders. When he came, he held her face between his hands.

"I loved her once," he said.

She nodded. She knew about that. "People change on you. They grow toward the person they were meant to be, with or without you. You stay as loyal as you can."

Afterward, she must have slept. She woke to his lips pressed to the curl of her shoulder, her body leaning toward him even in sleep. They made love again as a cool, northern wind blew in. By the end they were chilled and had to dress quickly. He wrapped his coat around her shoulders.

She put away her paints; he carried the canvas to her car. He was setting it carefully into the trunk when he stopped, touched a wet drop of oil. He put his nose right up to the canvas, then backed off. He turned to her.

"Mermaid," he said.

She blinked back tears, laid her head against his heart. "I love you," she said.

"You could have left after I hired Wayne," he said. "You didn't have to stay."

"I know."

"I'd like to tell myself you knew this would happen," he said, smiling, then he let it fade. "But that's not it. What are you really doing here?"

She pulled back, the words slipping out before she could stop them, before she even knew what they were. "What I shouldn't be doing anymore," she said. "I'm looking for my son."

— 7 —

Riptides

Before the deathbed, before the pain and numbness, years before they had any inkling of multiple sclerosis, Patti Frankins had another ailment—she loved her husband too much. Kate remembered the mornings, her mother crying, clinging, inventing new and elaborate pleas, all of which went unanswered. Kate's father would kiss her gently, pick up his sack lunch, and never make a promise he might not be able to keep. He never said, for example, "See you at eight" or "Everything's going to be all right." He'd tell her to try not to worry, to take a walk, maybe buy herself something pretty. After he had gone, her mother would sit by the window, her visions of disaster nearly tangible—cop killers and stray bullets Kate could reach out and touch.

Kate used to bring her tea, sit by her feet while she drank it. She used to rest her head in her mother's lap, and sometimes they talked about how her mother and father had met at Patti's sister's wedding, when her father was so shy she had to ask him to dance. Other times Patti absently braided her hair, tugging too tightly, and told her she would recognize true love when it began to make her sick. It would eat away at the liver and kidneys, leave her gaunt and slightly blue. A notion Kate found oddly comforting, until it turned out to be a lie.

By the time Kate hit her teens, her mother could not rise from her wheelchair without help, but she'd also found distraction and solace in the garden. Apparently, Patti stopped worrying that her husband would not come back. She no longer hugged him when Gerald left for duty; on a good day, she went straight to the garden to gather rose petals for her potpourris. She lost track of time and seemed startled, perhaps even put out, when he came home unexpectedly, wanting a home-cooked lunch. She was in pain all the time, yet she laughed at the exuberance of robins. She twittered like a bird herself, and Kate grew disdainful. She wondered if it was possible to forget you were married. "I never expected to be happy with just myself," her mother said, when Kate finally voiced the question. "But I can tell you this for certain: Joy is in pursuit of us all."

By nineteen, many of Kate's friends had married the first man who asked rather than risk not being approached again, while Kate had gotten a reputation for cruelty. She looked young men in the eye and told them their kisses did no lasting damage. She debunked the purest declarations of love. She began to spice up her diet, gorging herself on deviled eggs and liver pate, foods she couldn't stand. She made herself sick on jalapeno jelly and crab cakes.

She believed she'd never met a single person who had fallen in love and stayed there.

Her father walked in on her one afternoon while she was devouring the last of his pickled pears and grabbed his wallet off the counter. He whisked her off to an unlikely spot, the betting booths at Santa Anita. A few years back, he'd cracked a coke ring among some of the trainers, and had struck up a friendship with the owner of the track. He took out a few twenties and put half on Devlin's Breed, a four-year-old gelding with twelve-to-one odds. He tried to stuff a twenty in her hand, but Kate refused to touch it.

"I'll stick to boy trouble," she said.

"The boys are not the problem. Exactly who are you looking for?"

Kate shrugged, although she knew. She was looking for the one who would make her cry when he left.

They walked to the Turf Club, where he seemed to know everyone. Kate drifted into a corner, refused a drink, stewed. Her father knew she was a PETA member at UCLA, that she had a soft spot for anything with fur. At dinner, he was always bringing up touchy subjects—abortion and capital punishment—anything that might spark a fight. He seemed to think, and maybe he was right, that at nineteen she was most at risk for apathy, she was in danger of losing interest in everything except falling in love.

With his attention focused on the race, she walked out. She asked a concessionaire the way to the Paddock Gardens, where the jockeys readied their horses. She considered it a lapse that the daughter of a detective hadn't found a way to get arrested yet.

She made her way down near the track, took advantage of a family with two crying children to slip past the ticket master. All it took was a glimpse of foam on a horse's mouth to make her livid. She darted around a security guard, charged the first trainer she saw.

He must have suffered that kind of assault before, because he evaded her easily. He ducked left, suffered no more than three fingernail scratches on his arm, and brutishly grabbed her wrist.

"Hey lady," he said. "Ease up, will you? You're spooking Matilda."

Kate had another free hand and might have hit him again if she hadn't noticed the filly's eyes were electric. The horse pawed the ground each time she heard the rumbling on the track.

"One of those animal rights protesters, right?" the man asked. "Gotta love 'em."

The horse pressed her head against his shoulder. He released Kate to stroke the white spot between the filly's eyes. The security guard was just about on her, but the man waved him off. "It's my girlfriend," he said. "Lover's spat."

He turned to Kate and smiled. He had a killer smile, the whitest teeth she'd ever seen. "Matilda Weatherspoon," he said, gesturing to the horse. "Known on the track as Lightning Speed. That's kind of a joke around here. She hasn't won in a year."

"Will you kill her if she doesn't?"

The man burst out laughing. "Jeez, lady, what do you think we are? Gangsters? Matilda's owned by Devon Jentz, of Jentz Steel. She'll go out to a three-hundred-acre farm outside Philly. She'll live better than me, I can tell you that."

The man had a deep voice that never broke, but when she looked into his eyes, colored a blue too dark to believe, she had the feeling everything he said was potentially a lie.

"Ray Vegas," he said, extending his hand. "Lois Lane, I presume?"

Kate ignored him. She ran her hand down the horse's muscled flank, surprised by the silkiness of her coat. "Don't think I believe a word you're saying," she said.

He laughed again. He looked like a giant compared to the jockeys, though he was probably under six feet. He might have been a boxer, a welterweight, lean and well-muscled, with way too much shiny black hair.

"Smart woman," he said.

He let her stay. In fact, he seemed to delight in debunking her theories of abuse. The horses he showed her were sleek, pampered, and eager to run, and when she finally went to find her father, it was only to tell him she was going home with someone else. He gave her his detective's stare—hard, long, and a little too knowing.

"You sure you know what you're doing?"

She had no idea, which explained why her stomach rolled as she ran back to Ray Vegas, why, long before she kissed him, she knew Ray was the one.

They stopped at the grocery store, bought cheap cheese and a fifty dollar bottle of wine, then drove up the coast to Will Rogers State Beach. Ray put down his jacket for a blanket and, like magic, pulled a moon up over the sea. No ordinary moon either, but one unnaturally large, bigger than both her hands held in front of her face, rimmed with a shimmering silver ring.

"Means snow," he said. "See how thick the ring is? Bet you a hundred dollars there's snow by morning."

"How long have you lived here? It never snows in L.A."

He smiled at her. "A hundred bucks."

"You're on."

They took off their shoes, dug their feet deep into the cold sand. He said he'd loved horses since he was a kid, had hung out at the track for three years before he was finally given a job cleaning the stables. He'd worked his way up to trainer, and he was never going to leave. It was the job of a lifetime. It was what he'd been made to do.

"What about you, Kate Frankins?" he asked. "What were you made for?"

She almost said "you," but managed to take a sip of wine instead. "I'm going to UCLA," she said finally. "I'm a sophomore, sociology major."

"Yikes," Ray said. "Saving people."

"Don't you think people can be saved?"

He shrugged, ran a finger over the veins below her knuckles. "Let's just say I know a thing or two about human nature. Mine, anyway. Don't waste your time, Kate. You'd have more luck saving horses."

There'd been an alert about riptides that night, but she put down her wine, walked toward the water. She gasped when the fluorescent foam nipped her feet, but that didn't stop her from peeling off her clothes in pure darkness and diving into the black sea.

She heard him shouting at her, so she dove deeper. The water was so cold her muscles revolted, then she shot back to the surface, whooped with exhilaration. She was a good swimmer, had been on the freestyle and breaststroke team in high school, and more important, she wasn't afraid of sharks. She could feel the warring currents yanking at her, but she sliced right through them. She dove again and surfaced on the other side of the breakers, in an icy, calm sea.

She looked at him standing onshore, and knew right then that it didn't matter how many hearts shattered around her, she was going to marry him, and fast. It wasn't his smile that did it, or the fact that it had begun to snow, but rather the sight of him taking off his clothes to come in after her, even while he anxiously scanned the surface of the sea for sharks. It was the idea that she could raise him to bravery, she could make him more than he'd ever intended to be.

In the weeks that followed, she should have believed her father when he talked about people who can't be changed. She should have valued her mother's middle-aged happiness more than her newlywed tears. But it wasn't until three days into her honeymoon that Kate knew she'd married the wrong man. Ray stood on the black sand of Waianapanapa Beach on Maui and let himself sink. Pretty soon his toes were gone, then his sunburnt ankles, then the freckles at the base of his shins. The sand was more like razor-backed gravel, and he would emerge eventually with bloody soles, but still he stood there, his back to the turquoise surf, his arms helpless at his sides. He was dead weight and he knew it, and in his eyes was a disturbing gleam, as if he imagined the legend that would grow around him when he washed up on Molokai, bloated and blue. That warm January afternoon, Kate realized her husband was already sunk, and if she wasn't careful, he was going to take her down with him.

The next morning, though, she forgot her reservations. They left the bamboo forests of Hana and drove to the desert side of Maui, where scrub gave way to emerald golf courses and mosque-like hotels, where it was too hot and beautiful to worry about anything. Ray pulled up in front of The Four Seasons in Makena and ordered them a deluxe oceanfront room. They had turndown service and white bathrobes, a never-ending supply of strawberry piña coladas. Kate sat on a lounge chair by the pool and fell into a fiery, dreamless sleep. She woke to a hotel employee spraying her with mist.

Ray took her hand, clasped it tightly. He flashed a sixty-megawatt smile. "Can you believe this?" he said. "Are we made for this, or what?"

He lifted her arm and kissed the underside of her wrist. He rolled his tongue over the oiled lines of her palm. Maui had to be in a trough in the Pacific because her head felt dense, confused, sublimely heavy. She closed her eyes, didn't know how people lived inland, without the danger of tidal waves, or the off chance that they'd be swept away.

"Let's build us a shack and never go back," Ray said.

Kate laughed and stretched her long, tanned legs. Her skin had darkened to the color of coconut shells, her fingers smelled of seawater and hibiscus. They had gone whale watching two days ago and spotted huge grays breaching in front of the boat; they'd taken scuba lessons and dived down where the rainbow fish gave way to electric eels. This place wasn't real, that was the trouble. It was someone's moist dream, an exhalation of palm trees and silk water and all the time in the world. It was almost painful, knowing they'd have to go back to California.

"I wish," she said.

Ray took her hand and hoisted her to her feet. He looked straight into her eyes and she knew then, if she hadn't before, that it was pointless to try to fight him. There were men you would love whether you wanted to or not.

"Don't wish," he said. "That's not gonna get you anywhere. From now on, we're just gonna act. You got it? We're going to make every last goddamn wish come true."

At that moment, a man with a bodybuilder physique took a wide path around him. Two women on nearby lounge chairs refused to look up over the pages of their novels. Ray Vegas had scars across his knuckles and stones for muscles, and Kate would never again feel as brave as she did in that moment, just standing there, loving him.

She kissed him and couldn't stop. She wanted to lie in his bed and make love to him until she was sore, which she did for the next three days. On the flight back to Los Angeles, they hit turbulence. There was a quick change in air pressure and the plane took a startling drop. Passengers screamed and the flight attendants strapped themselves in, but Kate merely grabbed Ray's hand and vowed this was what she would always feel—at risk and electrified, conscious of all she had to lose.

As an employee of the track, Ray wasn't allowed to bet on the races, but just before their wedding, a friend had done it for him. He'd won six thousand undeclared dollars on a hundred-to-one shot named Maneater. That win gave Ray and Kate their ten-day honeymoon in Maui and the worst kind of luxury—the kind that can be taken away. It gave them illusions of grandeur, and the ridiculous notion that everything was going to turn out fine.

By the time they got back to their new apartment in Santa Monica, Maneater wouldn't leave the box, he was slated to be put out to pasture, and Ray lay stiff and awake on the edge of the bed. Night after night, whenever she reached for him, a shield of icy air stopped her. She realized she had married a man she hardly knew.

On their one-month anniversary, she opened her apartment door and saw the champagne and diamond necklace Ray had laid out.

"Ray," she said, and he came out of the bedroom laughing, in nothing but a towel wrapped around his waist. She breathed in deeply. No man should look that good, a comma of curly dark hair down his chest, the face of a fallen angel. Kate had a 4.0 GPA, but around Ray she just felt dumb. She couldn't remember half the things she'd meant to say, and usually she didn't want to talk anyway.

She looked at the necklace, dripping with half-carat diamonds. "We can't afford this," she said.

He snaked his arms around her waist, bent his head to kiss her neck, and she breathed in the grassy scent of all that dark hair. She fell for him all over again.

"You don't make this much," she went on.

"I'm lucky," he said. "Let's leave it at that."

She didn't want to argue, not then or when he bought her a four-poster bed and a new stereo system. She wanted to believe luck like that was possible. She wanted to believe in Ray.

The black BMW appeared in their designated parking spot in March, the old Toyota carelessly relocated to the curb. Ray sat on the hood, smiling wickedly.

"Another hundred-to-one shot?" she asked, but behind her she crossed and uncrossed her fingers.

"Sure, babe," he said. "Let's go for a ride."

He took her to Sunset Boulevard, then headed inland. They drove past a new-age mosque and picture-perfect houses, lawns lit so extravagantly they could be theaters.

"Is everything all right with us?" she asked Ray suddenly.

He was going to laugh; she could see the beginnings of the smile. Then he turned the car around in a skid, pulled to the side of the road, cut the engine. Over the green hills lay the greener, flat Pacific, seemingly the edge of the world.

Ray gripped the steering wheel. He held on until the blood left his fingers, until they were pure white, then he released it. When he breathed out, there were little rumblings in his chest, as if something old and crusty was cracking, but he just turned to her and smiled.

"Everything's going to be fine," he said. Kate nodded, but later she would remember how his voice shook right at the end.

One month later, she grabbed her books for an abnormal psychology class, walked down to the parking garage, and saw nothing in their spot but an oil stain. She ran back to the apartment, found Ray taking a shower. She shouted through the frosted glass, but he went on washing his hair.

"I'm calling the police," she yelled over the roar of the faucet.

He opened the door and looked at her. "The car wasn't stolen, Kate," he said.

She stared at him, waited for more, but he just shook his head and stepped back beneath the water.

A week later, when her diamond necklace disappeared from the jewelry box, she found Ray on the balcony, lighting one cigarette from the butt of another. He didn't turn when she called his name.

During the next two weeks, Ray stayed later and later at the track. When he came home, he did not make love to her like he used to. Sometimes he just held on to her. Sometimes he just barely held on.

She searched the apartment daily to find what was missing—silverware, the last of her grandmother's turquoise jewelry, the speakers then the stereo itself. As expected, Ray's best days were the ones when nothing was lost. Her grades began to slip, she sometimes forgot class entirely, then in April she realized she hadn't had a period since her wedding. She'd always been irregular, but she bought a pregnancy test. When the line turned pink, she sat on her bathroom floor and pulled her knees to her chest.

Ray had been losing more than money. He'd dropped ten pounds and couldn't eat anything but the blandest foods—potatoes, pure bran cereal, oatmeal. He'd turned an unhealthy shade of yellow, and there were bruises on his ribs he tried to hide. Yet sometimes, if she said just the right thing, he threw back his head and laughed. Sometimes he took her hand, turned it right and left, ran his fingers over every knuckle. He put his head in her lap and cried.

She waited until he'd gone to sleep, then she took off all her clothes. Of course, now that she knew, the mound below her navel was obvious. It was small and tight, the size of a tangerine, but still big enough to ruin them. Her mother had not gotten love right until the end. Kate knew hundreds of people who cared for each other without ruining themselves. She and Ray hardly managed to love each other; there wasn't enough left over to start fresh with someone else. But even as she thought that, even as she considered women's clinics in the area, she got into bed beside her husband and picked up his hand. It was strong and callused, and she kissed the palm. Everything he said was probably lies, but she still placed his hand over her belly.

When he opened his eyes, she saw how scared he was. She saw how his life had stopped being a game and, to him, that was the harshest sentence, worse than losing all the money in the world. She leaned her head against his.

"If I have to choose," she said, "I'll choose you."

She pressed his hand firmly against her skin, where he could not yet feel even a bubble of life. Ray ran his thumb over it, then she felt him tremble all over, just once.

"God, Kate," he said. "I'm not a monster. You don't have to choose."

For a while, whatever financial problems he'd been having seemed to stop. What was left of her jewelry remained in the box. Ray went to work in the morning and came home at six; he would have seemed perfectly normal, if he hadn't been turning a deeper shade of yellow, the color that rises up at the end of a bruise. He made love to her gently, afraid to hurt the baby, and sometimes she woke in the middle of the night to find him standing over her.

"What?" she whispered. "What is it?"

"I love you," he said, as if he were pronouncing a sentence, as if it were just about killing him.

She couldn't find him the day she went into labor. She called the horse track, but Norman Catilla, Ray's boss, hadn't seen him for weeks. "He quit a month ago, Kate," he said quietly. "Jesus, I thought you knew."

Kate didn't know anything, obviously, except that if you crave the kind of love that eats you up inside, that's the kind you get. She packed her bag and went alone to the hospital. Ray found her in the labor room three hours later.

"Honey," he said, wiping the sweat off her face.

"You quit your job."

He didn't even turn away, that's how comfortable he'd become with lying. "I got something better. Holtzman's Arabians called me. I've been going to their farm in Arcadia."

"And you didn't bother to tell me."

"Didn't want to worry you. It's kind of a spec deal, to see how I do. I didn't want you to think I wouldn't be able to support you and the baby."

The contraction came on hard and strong, and she dug her fingernails into Ray's skin. Even when the pain passed, she kept her fingernails down deep.

"You've got to stop this, Ray."

"Don't look at me that way," he whispered. "Don't hate me."

She pushed him away. Of course she couldn't hate him, that was just the trouble.

The baby was born after sixteen hours of labor, and they named him William David Vegas. From the moment they brought him home, Kate realized how naïve she'd been. A mother never has a choice who she loves best. At two in the morning, dazed with devotion and lack of sleep, she held William to her breast and couldn't remember what had mattered to her before. Her days filled with the thousand tasks of baby care; her dreams swelled with everything William would eventually be to her. She lost half her memories and desires making room for all she promised him.

Those first few weeks were a blur, but later on Kate would remember one thing: Ray was happy again. She thought it the glow of fatherhood, the rapture of holding his son in his arms. Early one morning, while Willie slept between them, Kate woke to find Ray raised on his elbow staring at her. There were tears in his eyes.

"Why can't it always be like this?" he asked.

She reached out and touched his cheek. "Maybe it will be."

She fell back asleep, and when she woke up, both Ray and William were gone.

Sometime during her story, Kate's gaze had gotten stuck on Ben's face, on the flecks of brown in his green eyes. Every once in a while, she had stopped talking, and he'd taken her hand, pushed a strand of hair behind her ear, hair that had gone straight again now that they were away from the sea. The sun had disappeared behind the hills, and they'd climbed into the car to talk.

"I thought they'd gone for a walk," she said, almost able to smile at her naïveté now, almost, but not quite, able to stop blaming herself for those few seconds when she'd considered an abortion, as if the God she did not believe in had existed just long enough to condemn her. "Ray took the infant seat and diaper bag. I was actually relieved to have some time alone."

Ben pulled her against his chest, pressed his lips to her hair. "Kate," he said.

"I took a shower. Can you imagine what might have happened if I'd looked for them right then? Maybe Ray had just left. Maybe I would have caught him."

She remembered she'd been washing the soap from her hair when she'd gotten the chill along her spine. She'd left the suds in and jumped out without bothering to turn off the water. She ran dripping into the bedroom, opened the drawer where she kept Willie's clothes, and laughed shakily. Everything was still there—his onesies, the tiny socks, and the cotton gowns with the pull-cords at the bottom.

She finished her shower, got dressed, made scrambled eggs. She sat at the kitchen table and didn't eat a thing. She walked to the living room window and looked out at a perfect November day: seventy-five degrees and smelling of orange blossoms. Ray could walk for miles, and he probably would. She clutched the edge of the windowsill.

It was an hour later, maybe two, when she knew. While walking to the bathroom, her legs abruptly gave out. One minute she was standing, the next she was on the floor, rocking steadily. Her breasts were heavy, wet and achy, and the tips of her fingers went numb.

She might have sat there forever, except she heard the voice of the single mother down the hall getting more and more hysterical. "Now. I said now. What are you doing? Don't take them off. Adam, *put on your shoes*."

She tried to call her parents. When no one answered at home, she called her father's department. He was out on assignment, but she talked to Henry Freidrich, a detective she knew well. From the start, he sounded suspicious. "Now, Katie," he said, "you've been listening to too many of your dad's stories. Who's to say Ray didn't just take the baby to the park? What makes you so certain he's not coming back?"

"I'm telling you . . ."

"I'll come over, okay? But I guarantee you, by the time I get there, Ray and William will be back."

Kate slammed down the phone and grabbed her keys. She got in her car and drove to the track.

"Try one of the bars around Melrose," Norman told her. "That's where he used to go after hours."

Kate went from bar to bar, with no success. She drove to Holtzman's Arabians, but the owner had never heard of Ray, had certainly never hired him. In between, she called home, but Ray never answered. It was midnight by the time she got back, and there was a note taped to her door.

"Call me. Henry."

Kate yanked the paper off the door and went inside. She didn't turn on a light, but right away she knew Ray was there. The devil had a particular smell, moist and rank, worse than sulfur.

She ran into the bedroom, but the baby's bassinet was empty. She threw on the light and whirled around. Ray sat on the floor in the living room, his head in his hands. She leapt across the room and grabbed him by the collar. She fell to her knees and shook him as hard as she could, but he didn't cry out. He didn't even try to stop her.

"Where is he?"

Ray said nothing. His blue eyes were black, and the hands she'd once thought could hold her forever were curled into tiny, sallow fists.

"How much did you get?" she screamed at him. "How much was he worth to you?"

Ray finally focused on her. "Fifty thousand," he said, his voice no more than a whisper. "Enough to pay off Patterson. I swear, Kate, he was going to kill me."

She felt tears on her cheeks but couldn't hear herself crying. She held Ray's shirt without feeling the fabric. *Like ghosts,* she thought. *Both of us.* Fifty thousand. Fifty thousand they could have borrowed from her parents, or taken out on a loan. Fifty measly thousand dollars, the price of her heart.

She slapped him, but he didn't budge. She did it again and again, until she saw some effect. A welt rose up, her fingernails broke the skin, and he still remained motionless.

"Where is he?" Her voice got high-pitched; it wound up like a siren. "You've got to tell me where he is." She could hear the blood rushing between her ears, her heartbeat ripping like machine-gun fire. When he didn't respond, she stumbled to her feet and threw her head back. She was deaf to everything but the pandemonium in her chest, but whatever emerged from her throat must have been awful, because it moved Ray from the floor to her side. He held her firmly by the shoulders. "Hush," he said. "Hush, Katie."

She looked right at him. It would haunt her for years, the soulless look in his eyes. "Please, Ray," she begged.

He said nothing. He'd gone from yellow to slightly blue. He was hardly breathing. Neither of them were.

She pushed him away, made her way unsteadily to the phone to call her dad. It took her three tries to push the right buttons. He answered the phone immediately, as he always did in the middle of night. "Ray sold William," she said.

There was silence, then the sound of him whipping back the sheets. "Jesus," he said. "I'll be right over."

Kate couldn't turn around. Every muscle had stiffened and it was never going to get any better. Not without William.

She leaned against the wall, heard the window slide open. By the time she got her body working, Ray had shimmied down the balcony and was gone.

She didn't run after him. She could track him by scent now; she'd kill him after she'd found William. Besides, she'd already let the evil through. Worse than that, she had welcomed it.

Now, eighteen years later, Ben pulled away to look at her. "You never found him," he said.

Kate leaned against the car door. "No. I tried everything I could think of. Wanted posters, hotlines, psychics. It's amazing the things you can do even when you're dead inside. How your body just keeps working."

Ben touched his forehead to hers; she had no idea when he'd started crying, but there were tears all down his cheeks.

"My God," he said.

"I'm all right. You have to go on, you know. No matter what it is, you have to go on. It's your duty."

Ben kept touching her, her hair, her shoulder, the crease above her chin. She closed her eyes, concentrated on his fingers. "A few years after, I had trouble staying in the house so much. It felt like I'd been in the same room for twenty years. I was stiff and sore, but I couldn't stay there, either. I took up walking. I'd head to the beach every morning. You wouldn't believe Santa Monica. It's so tame, the water a balmy fifty-eight degrees, the breezes warm and mild. I started noticing the kids—the oiled-up preteens who were vulgar-mouthed but harmless, still sweet enough to drink

Mountain Dew instead of Coors. I had already begun painting. I'd made a few dollars, could support myself again. I saw this boy every day, about eight. He'd beg the fishermen on the pier for cigarettes, the fish they might have thrown back. He slept on the sand. I finally called the child welfare office. He was my first foster child. I had him for six months."

"Kate."

"I never wanted to replace William. It wasn't that. I couldn't help but love them individually. They shouted their uniqueness, each demanded a specific kind of care. We were what each other needed. Then the day I decided to bring Wayne here, I got a picture in the mail. A photo of William. I got another one after I got here. He's baiting me. As if he can't stand my happiness, the fact that I've survived."

"Ray?"

"I called all the R. Vegases I found in the Boston phone book. None panned out. He must be here. Watching me."

"But why? He must know he's got nothing more to hurt you with."

She looked at him, saw that she had two choices. She could tell more of the story, go on all night, or she could pull him into the backseat, make love to him like a teenager. She could cry or she could kiss him, and at last, she fell silent. She chose the one that would do her good.

— 8 —

The Rapture

Larry Salamano knew the truth about superstitions: The only people who needed them were the ones with no control over their lives. Salaried engineers didn't cling to lucky pennies. Only girls waiting to fall in love strained their eyes looking for falling stars. Only people who needed someone else to make their wishes come true bothered making wishes in the first place.

Larry was a short-order cook and damn good at it whether the moon was full or not. He had a flair for bacon-and-tomato sandwiches, and on a good Saturday afternoon packed Trudy's Kitchen with customers salivating over his onion rings. He'd introduced curly fries last year, and got up every morning at five to make his hamburger buns fresh. He didn't need a rabbit's foot or salt shaker to bring him luck. That had happened all on its own, the day he met Dominic Allen.

Fate was nothing more than a lucky break. If he'd left five minutes earlier that morning, if he hadn't had The Fight with his father the night before, if he'd decided to walk uptown rather than through Central Park the rest of his life would have been different. He might have married Sandra Liebowitz and had five kids by now. He might have been what everybody hoped he'd be; he might have been miserable.

Destiny took root in the most seemingly insignificant places, for him in an off-off-Broadway theater. One night he looked into the sparse audience and saw his father's smoldering face. Warren Salamano, a short, stout bricklayer, a whiskey drinker, a man's man, had so far ignored Larry's love of theater, but that night Larry discovered the cure for blindness. When he kissed the actor who played his homosexual lover, he did it with a passion he'd never shown before, he did it so that everything would be clear.

When he got home, his father beat him until his own hands were bloody. Warren Salamano would rather be considered a brute than a man who'd produced a soft son, and though Larry could have fought back, knowing his father had to live with that loathsome self-knowledge seemed retribution enough.

"No son of mine is gonna be a faggot," his father spat between punches.

Larry wiped the blood from his eyes. "I'm no son of yours."

He bandaged one eye and iced his ribs, but by morning the pain had intensified. He sought distraction in Central Park, walking for hours until he stumbled into a bicycle left along the path. He cursed loudly when he fell on his bruised left elbow. A huge, beefy man suddenly stood at his side.

"Jesus," the man said. "Don't tell me my bike did that to you."

Larry stood up. He was short, five-eight, put together with bricks. Unbreakable, no matter what his father might think. The man in front of him was a giant, a titan who might have terrified small children if he hadn't been sporting a goofy, lopsided grin.

Pale and freckled, his orange frosting hair defied gravity, fluffing magnificently in spirals from his scalp and chin. And just like that, in the time it took to realize he was no longer in any pain, Larry Salamano admitted there was such a thing as destiny, because he'd run smack dab into his.

They sat on the grass, shared one of the biker's Power Bars. Larry lay back and listened to the sweet tenor of the giant's voice.

"I'm Dominic Allen," he said. "A fisherman out of Seal Bay. Northern California. Like my dad and grandpa before me. Got started when I was fifteen, was first mate on a trolling boat for years, then last month Dodson named me captain of the *Jeannie,* his trawler. Can you beat that? I'm making more than I ever dreamed of, just for doing the only thing I'd ever do."

Larry smiled. It should have hurt his split lip to do it, but instead he felt the opposite, his first totally pain-free moment in years. Believe it or not, he had no desire to rattle people. He wanted an easy life, like everybody else. He'd taken girls to school dances, felt them up, played soccer, and was considered a real demon on the field. But on the night of his eighteenth birthday, he'd gotten loaded and ended up with his best friend in a hotel room in Brooklyn. He'd woken up *peaceful,* but Josh never looked him in the eye again, never spoke another word except to say that if he told anyone, he would fucking kill him, he would yank his lying heart right out of his throat.

Larry went straight to his father's church that morning, laid his head against the wall of the confession booth and could not speak. Father Thomas was a patient man, but after twenty minutes of silence, he snapped, "You must have something to confess."

Larry had a million things—he'd once stolen a Mars bar from the Roosevelt Market, had started smoking Camels when he was nine. He cussed too much, hid his father's car keys whenever the old man was drunk, and had, on occasion, wished him dead. But if he had to confess what had happened with Josh, if God had made him one way only to expect him to act another, the Big Guy was both weaker and more perverse than a dutiful Brooklyn priest would ever believe.

"No," he told Father Thomas, rapping his knuckles against the screen that divided them. "I'm clean."

Eight years later, in Central Park, Larry ran his fingers through Dominic Allen's amazing beard. He stroked the weathered skin of his cheek and neither of them moved. The wind swooped under Larry's hand and paused in the gap between them, then rushed out again, so that nothing stopped them.

At the end of Dominic's vacation, they sat on the edge of the bed in Dominic's hotel room, both looking down at their thick, sunburnt hands.

"I never thought this would happen," Dominic said, stretching out the leg that always cramped up on him, the one that had taken a monster fish hook a few years back. "I thought I had it under control."

As if you could pick who you loved, or contort yourself into a more acceptable form. Larry massaged his lover's leg. Back when he'd woken up aching for Josh, he'd forced himself to believe that desire was just another thing to be controlled and eventually lost, like those sudden outbursts of screaming he'd had as a kid, like giggles. But what kind of fool doesn't love being in love, perhaps loving it even more when it will be his undoing?

"Your father will kill you," Dominic went on. "The fishermen will drown me at sea."

There was nothing funny about it, but Larry threw back his head and laughed. For six days, he'd been as happy as he'd ever been in his life and now he knew why. Not because he'd finally given in to who he was, but because love had cured him of guilt. He no longer gave a damn what anyone else thought; he didn't even care what they did about it. Having enemies only proved he had something worth fighting for; he felt high on all the risks he was willing to take. If his father went crazy with a machine gun, if some Bible-thumping, family-values touting congressman came after him with a torch-wielding mob, it might be too much joy to bear.

He reached for Dominic's hand and held it tightly. "Don't be so sure about people," he said. "They might surprise you."

But, of course, Dominic was right.

Larry told his father he'd fallen in love with a man and Warren Salamano closed the door in his face. When Larry tried to call his mother, his father got on the phone and said, "Just go now. Both your parents are dead."

Larry moved in with Dominic in Seal Bay and within a week Dominic's crew went to Ben Dodson to demand another captain. Rocks sailed through their windows and kept breaking mirrors and televisions until they boarded up the panes with plywood and removed everything made of glass. Twice their laundry on the back line was replaced with unrecognizable shreds of fabric, stained with a poor imitation of blood. The crank calls and death threats started almost immediately, forcing them to go unlisted, and to maintain a post office box an hour south, in Sausalito.

Two weeks after they returned from New York, Ben Dodson asked Dominic to meet him at the docks. Dominic had so much trouble getting dressed, Larry buttoned his shirt for him. He held the collar tightly in his hands.

"They can't touch us," he said. "That's the beauty of it. We are impenetrable."

Dominic kissed him on the mouth. He walked out stiffly, his bad leg trailing behind him, and Larry followed. If there was going to be a fight, he wanted to be in the middle of it. He'd been quiet and tame for Dominic's sake, but now he itched to throw a punch, to show he was a better fighter than his father would ever believe. He'd been a boy in the theater, for God's sake. These fishermen were nothing. He could take them all, easy. He had so much more to lose.

Ben waited in front of the *Jeannie,* his men lined up behind him. From his place on the street, Larry laughed at their puffed out chests, their three-day beards, their attempts to prove they had never thought the same thing, hadn't even dreamed it, not even once.

Ben Dodson buttoned his jacket. "I've heard the sand bass are exploding around Catalina," he said. "It'll be a two-week trip. Anyone who wants a job will come with us. Anyone who doesn't do exactly what you say will swim home."

He stepped onto the *Jeannie*. Dominic searched the docks for him and when their gazes locked, Larry's heart slowed to the beat of a ballad. Nothing would ever be as clear as this: He would do anything for that man.

For a few minutes after Dominic boarded, the men stood there, proud, stupid, and stumped. One of them finally grumbled a curse and climbed up after him. Another tried to follow, but Harvey Pinkerton, who'd been fishing strictly heterosexually for forty-eight years, grabbed him around the wrist. The fisherman pried off his fingers, shook himself as if he'd been tainted. He walked stiffly up to the boat.

In the end, three remained on the pier, though it might have been less if Harvey Pinkerton hadn't been holding his sons by the arms. Harvey was an elder of the Church of Sea, Sky, and Salvation, the one who left fliers on the windshields of cars parked in front of the Merc, condemning gays, purple children's characters, working women, and other assorted miscreants. He frequented Eaton's Bar, where he delivered such an astounding abundance of information on hell, Larry assumed he had first-hand knowledge. No one had ever seen him smile, and who could blame him? He worshipped a spiteful, cranky God.

The Pinkertons walked up beside him, their faces crusty as barnacles, as hard as their squished-up little hearts.

"You're perverts, you understand me?" Harvey Pinkerton said. "I'm telling my grandson to take cover. I'm going to be watching you every day of my life."

"That'll make for a sorry life," Larry said.

"There's no ladder out of hell."

"Well, thank God," Larry said. "Otherwise you people would be climbing out."

He headed home. When he got to Fahrenheit Hill, Dominic blew the horn on the *Jeannie* twice, his trademark, and Larry turned back to watch him pass the breakwater. He saw Dominic in the wheelhouse, Ben beside him, both stiff and wary. They could take a stand and force the men to take one, too, but that wouldn't stop the inevitable from happening—a man or two turning mean so he wouldn't appear weak.

For the past year, Harvey Pinkerton had watched him. When Larry got the job at Trudy's, Harvey became a regular, though he never touched the food Larry prepared. He taped fliers to the windows when Trudy wasn't looking, first just the usual "God will punish the sinners," and "Sodumy (too zealous, apparently, to pause for a dictionary) is a sin." Trudy took them down and flashed Larry a sheepish grin. Then came the wanted posters, complete with blurry photos of Larry and Dominic stepping out their front door and the headline: "Kill the faggots." Trudy banned Harvey from the restaurant, and pretty soon he was not welcome anywhere except at his church and Eaton's Bar, where he wasn't any worse than the other drunks, none of whom got the attention they thought they deserved.

The biggest surprise was not the relentlessness of Harvey's hatred, but how little it mattered. It took some effort on the man's part to be so stupid, and Larry liked to watch the toll it was taking, the slow pull on his jowls, the sagging of his shoulders after a day of shouting the most un-Christian things Larry, a reformed, guilt-free Catholic, had ever heard. Besides, he had what he wanted. Only Dominic concerned him. As long as Dominic walked in the door every night with that goofy smile, the world could fill up with Harvey Pinkertons and it would still be the world of his dreams.

Then that smile began to sag. One night, the giant lay beside him and couldn't stop his tears, and Larry put his arms around him and decided love like this was too much to bear. Forget those comic strips of lovers dancing on air; love was heavier than blood or water. It was the actual, physical weight of a person on top of you, and Dominic was over two hundred fifty pounds and crushing him fast.

"You think Harvey's right?" Dominic asked.

"I think Harvey is a mental patient waiting to happen."

That's when Larry got the idea for the sea monster. He'd heard Keith's story, and the other whiskey-induced serpent sightings, so the next morning he drove to Marin to stock up on supplies. He hid everything in their basement, waited for a clear night when Harvey would be out on the water in his one-man gill-netter now that Ben Dodson wouldn't let him on the fleet. When the night finally came—the sky a rich, velvety black, a half-moon stabbing the water—he sneaked down to Sea Lion Cove and put together a monster of PVC pipe and green glow-in-the-dark stars. He waited to hear the one-of-a-kind complaint of Harvey's outboard, then waded into the shallows and let the beast loose. He crept into one of the seaweed-strewn caves to wait.

He didn't know if Harvey would see it, or if the man was at all susceptible to flights of fancy. Then the motor stopped with a clank and Larry heard the distinct sound of Harvey Pinkerton dropping to his bony knees and crying "Holy Jesus!" Harvey whooped and hallelujahed until the pipes of the serpent filled with water and sank, until the glow-in-the-dark stars flickered just beneath the waves, then sputtered out.

Harvey woke every member of the Church of Sea, Sky, and Salvation and forced them onto their boats. Twenty-eight skiffs cruised the shore until dawn. Though no one saw another monster, and a few of the elders wondered out loud how much time Harvey had been spending at Eaton's Bar, the man was not to be deterred. At dawn Harvey announced that the rapture had been revealed to him, and it wasn't coming from heaven at all. When Jesus finally returned for them, he'd arise from the depths of the sea.

After that, Harvey sometimes forgot to put up his Kill the Faggots fliers. He spent his money on fancy underwater cameras and his afternoons adding sea monsters to the church paintings of the Last Supper—beastly eyes staring up from Jesus' soup. The elders were horrified, the congregation titillated, and Larry fairly content. So after work one November evening, when he went for a hard jog up Fahrenheit Hill and saw the sap running down the trunk of the laurel, he didn't immediately understand its import. He'd heard the legend of the weeping tree, of course, along with every other far-fetched fisherman's superstition, but had never paid it any mind. He dipped a finger into the sap, was surprised when it stung. He lifted his hand and smelled gasoline, and from out of the blue he began to feel afraid.

Dominic was fishing, not due back until Friday. The skies were gray and threatening, the winds already gale force, up to forty knots, certainly more out at sea. It struck him that every pleasure—every view of the sunset, every belly laugh, every sip of a well-aged Merlot—was dependent upon Dominic sharing it with him. It wasn't happiness at all but cruel devotion, the kind that can crack at any time.

He ran down the hill and straight into Mary Lemming's kitchen. He found the old woman and Kate Vegas sitting at the table, sipping tea.

"The tree's weeping," he said. Mary followed his voice, her blurred blue eyes bouncing over him and beyond.

"The tree's weeping," he said again, and this time his voice broke.

"Well then," Mary said, laying her old, blue-veined hands flat on the table, "you'd better go wait for Dominic. Kate, you'll need to help me gather my supplies. People are going to start showing up."

Nicole stood just inside the front door while Jenny threw her things in the back of her Honda. Her sister had already cleared out the CDs, dumped every book in the house into three paper bags. She came back for the last of the suitcases, and Nicole drew back, careful not to get in the way or stop her sister's momentum.

"Don't look so pleased," Jenny said. "I'm not going far. Not yet."

Nicole didn't trust herself not to dance across the room. Jenny had been moving out excruciatingly slowly, a suitcase and trinket a day. Nicole hadn't wanted to celebrate until the very end. The whole bathroom to herself, no one perfect to look at over a bowl of Cheerios, no more boys passing her door on the way to Jenny's room. Really, how much more could she ask?

"You could have been nicer to me," she said. Her breathing was shallow. She'd barely gotten the words out, but they stung just the same.

Jenny lifted the suitcase, and Nicole wondered if she'd been crying. There were unsightly blotches on her cheeks, one eye looked particularly swollen. "I think, if I had, you would have hated me more."

She drove off in a puff of gray smoke, and Nicole ate half a carton of French vanilla ice cream in splendid solitude. Later, she walked into Jenny's room and sat in the middle of the bed. Jenny had not changed her furnishings since childhood, and Nicole considered this the one piece of the Jenny puzzle that did not fit. How did her sister invite boys into that canopied bed, pull a lace coverlet their mother had sewn over the two of them? How did she not feel the ghost of Jeanne Dodson in every fiber of that room?

Nicole closed her eyes, prayed for her mother to materialize, to rise up out of a stitch of pink wallpaper and flutter over to the vanity. But when she opened them she was alone.

She went into the bathroom, tossed the perfume Jenny had left behind in the trash. When she opened the medicine cabinet, she felt dizzy, a little weak. All the pills were gone. Jenny had even confiscated Lucky's arthritis tablets. She'd taped a note to the toothpaste.

Don't be an idiot, it read.

Nicole slammed the glass door, heard an answering crash of dental floss and hair spray. She stomped back to her bedroom, but the idea that Jenny had known all along, that she might even have been watching out for her, made her too antsy to lie down. She walked to the window, rapped her fingers against the slick glass. She stumbled upon the absurd notion that she had confused who was good and who was bad.

When her father finally came home, she slipped under the covers and feigned sleep. She concentrated on maintaining her even breathing when he eased himself down on the edge of her bed and brushed her hair from her forehead. She heard the rumble of his stomach, a swallow, thought for sure he knew she was faking because he continued to sit. He whispered something she couldn't make out, pressed his lips to her cheek. Then finally he left. He shuffled down the hall, went into Jenny's empty room. She opened her eyes, heard him closing the window, pulling the blinds.

She tiptoed to her window and quietly slid it open. She looked back, half expecting her father to stop her, or Jenny to return home in time to foil her plans and laugh at her pathetic attempt at daring. But no one came. She panicked when she first clung to the rain gutter, then found her balance, shimmied to the ground.

She walked without any idea where she was headed. Before she knew it, she stood outside Jenny's old hangout, the Dairy Queen on Landlock Street where the popular crowd hung out. David Collins, who had never said two words to her, who could have had anyone he wanted, including her older sister, was there, along with a very pregnant Kiki Modean. Every booth was taken, and though a week ago Nicole would have turned and headed back home, tonight some alien force took hold of her arm and pushed open the door.

Conversation stopped for a split second, then David Collins got up. Nicole could not believe it when he smiled the smile that made girls go weak in the knees and put his hand on her arm.

"Hey," he said and, interestingly, she did not go breathless. He was six feet two inches of a body to die for, but she was more intrigued by how quickly she was losing her appetite for ice cream and anyone blond. She knew what she wanted now, and it wasn't on the menu or in one of the red vinyl booths. It wasn't in this town at all. It had materialized on Crazy Mary's window. Her destiny. Something else.

"Excuse me," she said, walking out.

David came after her and grabbed her arm again. Girls looked out the Dairy Queen windows in open, murderous envy.

"Slow down," he said. "What's your rush?"

She almost told him the truth, that she had somewhere to go now, someone to get to. She was going to find that dream man, one way or the other. No one would be able to stop her until she did.

"David," she said, extricating her arm. "I've got to go."

"There's something different about you," David said, oblivious. "Your hair, or something. You been hanging out with your sister?"

Nicole flinched, found the suggestion an insult. She left him standing there and raced up the hill, past a man pressed to the glass of Trudy's Kitchen, past Carol Cannelini and Jack Woo making out in the doorway of Jim's Tackle, clear up to Crazy Mary's. She would have knocked on the door right then, demanded another vision of her dream man, except that when she looked up at the laurel tree he was standing right there.

He was eighteen or nineteen, with brown hair parted on the left side. He wore blue jeans, a long-sleeved white shirt with the cuffs rolled halfway to his elbow. She couldn't possibly see this, but she knew he had a dozen dark hairs looped around his wrists like a bracelet.

She took a step, froze. She had never given his picture to Kate. She kept it in the top drawer of her desk, knew the boy he'd been as well as if she'd grown up beside him. He ran his hand along the trunk of the laurel tree, yanked his fingers back, sniffed them. Then he looked toward her.

She sucked in her breath, held it. Extended her neck, rose up on the balls of her feet. His gaze slid right by. He wandered around the back of the tree. He hadn't even seen her.

She might have cried out, except that she was sick of crying. She was through with being overlooked. She marched up the hill, caught him on the back side of the laurel tree. He jumped when he saw her, then smiled a smile that would last her for weeks.

"Hey," he said. "Spooky up here."

He had deep blue eyes, but what held her was the line of his chin, the freckles across his nose, the rise of his cheekbones. He looked so much like Kate Vegas, Nicole's breath left her in a rush. Fate swished past her haughtily like a debutante in a dress.

But he smiled again. Touched her arm. "Smell this," he said.

He lifted his fingers and she smelled gasoline. He touched her right above the elbow. The skin beneath his fingers turned pink.

"Gas," she managed to say.

"Exactly."

He let go, circled the tree again, came up beside her and grazed her shoulder with his. Her heart began to pound. She prayed Kate Vegas would not come out of the house. She wished her fast asleep, dreaming of anything else. Even Nicole's father.

"I almost went into botany," he said. "Thought about it. But the counselors kept telling me how few jobs there were, how little I'd make. Sad to say, it got to me. When I started at BC, I picked economics. But it's not a thing you fall in love with, you know?"

Her heart hammered. She knew if she said anything, she

would ruin it. He would realize he was talking to the ugly duckling, some frizzy-haired, plump little girl.

"Hey," he said. "You must live around here. This is a California laurel, right?"

She chanced it. "Yes."

He nodded. "*Umbellularia californica*. This one's gotta be as big as the one in Santa Barbara. But that one doesn't have a wound like this. Look at it."

She flinched. She looked at the sap, the large gash in the V of the trunk. She felt woozy and he reached out, caught her before she stumbled.

"I know," he said. "That smell."

But it wasn't the smell. A man would soon die at sea, and it might very well be her father.

"Oh," she said. "I've got to go."

She started down the slope, was nearly to Mary's driveway before the young man overtook her and caught her by the arm. She'd almost forgotten about him, but when she met his gaze, she knew that would never happen again. It would be days, maybe only minutes, before her father's welfare wouldn't mean as much, when she'd start trusting him to his own devices. When someone else's future would matter more.

"Hold on," he said. "I'm going crazy, holed up in that hotel. My mom's freaking out, I've already missed a week of labs and two economics lectures, and now the first person I talk to runs away like a ghost. Give me a break, will you? Tell me your name, at least."

She looked down at his hand on her arm. "Nicole Dodson," she said.

He smiled again, and she realized there was no rush to get home. Her father wouldn't leave until morning. He could be convinced before then. "Jacob Shulman."

"What are you doing here?" she asked.

He didn't let go. "My mom's looking up an old friend."

She glanced at Mary's, didn't trust the dark windows. She thought it entirely possible someone was peering out.

"How long are you staying?"

"I don't know. Not much longer, I hope."

She stepped back, and his hand came loose. "Sorry," he said. "That didn't sound right. I'm just eager to get home. Get back to my life."

"I've got to go," Nicole said. "That sap . . . that means a man will go to sea and not return."

Jacob looked at her, then laughed. He ran his fingers through his hair. "You're not serious."

She raised her chin. "I am. It's happened before. My dad's a fisherman."

She was not crying, but he stared at her eyes. "Hey," he said. "Really?"

"Yes, really. The tree is never wrong."

He studied the laurel. "It did give me the creeps. That'd be cool, though, don't you think? Not anything bad happening to your dad, but something magical like that. Something magical coming true."

She looked for signs of mockery. She looked until his earnestness was imprinted on her brain, until no other face would do. "Have you seen the rest of the town?"

He shook his head. "Not really. My mom . . . she can get pretty psycho. She's been sick. She can't get around too well, so she needed me with her. But she told me to stay in the hotel."

"Who's her old friend? Maybe I can help."

"I don't ask. She looks at me too closely when I ask. Gives me the willies."

"Oh," Nicole said.

"My girlfriend's probably freaking. I told her I'd be back in a couple days."

Nicole stepped back. The wind must have switched directions because she smelled the gasoline. It overpowered her, quickly reached the point when every second standing there became excruciating.

"Come on," he said. "That tree's making me sick. If you're on the way to the motel, I'll walk with you."

They started down Fahrenheit Hill. The Surfside Motel had never been so close, less than two minutes away. They reached it before she'd figured out a single thing to say. He put his hand on the door, she turned toward home. Then she felt his fingers on her shoulder, the strength of him, turning her around.

"You be okay?" he asked. "Walking home?"

Nicole felt every one of his fingers. He had a girlfriend in Boston and he was very likely Kate Vegas's son, but she didn't think about any of that. From here on out, she decided, she would believe whatever she wanted, despite all evidence to the contrary.

"I'll be fine," she said.

She ran the rest of the way home, found her father asleep in a chair by the front door. She looked up the stairs and saw her bedroom door standing open. She knelt beside him, rested her chin on his knee. The touch woke him, and she readied herself for the tirade, to be grounded for weeks.

But all he did was lean forward, grab her around the waist, pull her into his lap. She was not ready for his tears, or the watery rumble in his chest. She was not prepared for the smell of him, musty, unused, or for the fact that he was old and somehow they had missed the best years, the ones when a girl falls in love with her father. The years when she insists he's invincible and, for a while, he feels like he is.

"Don't ever do that again," he said, his voice strained, little more than a whisper.

"The tree is weeping."

He stared at her. "I know."

Nicole could not believe how calm he was, and how quickly she began to *hate* him for that. She wanted to see some sign of panic in his eyes. She wanted one little hair on the back of his neck to stand on end, and then perhaps she wouldn't feel like an absolute fool, believing in things that made no logical sense.

"You can't go out then," she said. "Until the tree stops. You can't go."

He carried her up to bed, tucked her in like he used to, like she was a little girl, and this was something she would never say to another soul: She wished she had never grown up. She wished for a world where everyone was taken care of.

"The sea is more proud than that," he said. "It's not taking direction from some tree."

He kissed her forehead and she blinked back tears, made more wishes. She wanted to be small enough to be carried everywhere, the size of a quarter so she could be tucked inside his shirt pocket. She wished she had never met Jacob Shulman, because now what she wanted most was no longer in this house.

"I wish you would listen to me," she said.

He smiled, brushed the hair from her eyes. "Go to sleep now, baby."

She wished she had parents she could count on to survive.

— 9 —

The Princess

On the day the news came that there was a fire aboard Dominic Allen's trawler, still twenty miles out, Trudy Casson stumbled upon a man in her apartment. She opened the door above her diner and found him standing near the window, his gray, shaggy hair obscuring his face, her only satin dress in his hands. She screamed, but instead of bolting or raising a weapon, the man held out his arms. The dress across his fingers undulated like molten gold.

She ran down to the kitchen, thrust a meat cleaver into Larry Salamano's hands. By the time they returned, the man and the dress were gone, and though she expected to feel relief, Trudy fell into Larry's arms and wept. She'd bought that dress two sizes too small after a particularly optimistic bonfire on New Year's Eve, and had yet to wear it. She breathed in Larry's mesmerizing scent of onion rings and Calvin Klein cologne, and wondered for the hundredth time why she'd waited all these years to fall in love, then did so with a homosexual. She granted herself one moment of dreaming she could change him, she alone could lure him back to the lush pleasures of women, then she set her hands on her hips.

"I'm closing the diner until that tree stops," she said.

She didn't dare look in a mirror, or right in his eyes. She was fifty-two years old, her hair had gone gray at forty, her waist and hips had widened despite never giving birth to children, and the truth was she had never been whistled at in her life. Not once. She'd built this restaurant herself, with a little financial help from her brothers who farmed artichokes in Salinas. She'd run wire, fixed shingles, and occasionally decked a fisherman with too much alcohol and crudeness in his blood, but she'd never been loved. Never married or had children, nor had she cared, until Larry Salamano came to town with Dominic Allen. Until Larry took his lover's calls with a desperation she'd thought unique to teenagers and aging single women. Until he cooked up grilled cheese for the Stottenmeir boy, cutting off his crust and hiding a jelly bean inside the melted cheese, and she decided her heart stopped right there.

Larry took her arm, led her down the stairs. "You can't stop living," he said, but of course he was wrong.

She put up the closed sign, walked with Larry to the pier. The crowd that should have been gathering at church swarmed the docks as soon as they heard about the fire on Dominic's boat. Trudy and Larry didn't have a clear view of the slip where the *Jeannie* ought to have been, but they could see the empty bay. Only the children talked, and their parents shushed them. Ben Dodson's office door stood open, so they heard when the giant's radio went out and Ben called the Coast Guard instead.

Trudy took Larry's hand and held on tightly. In her younger

days she might have been crueler, perhaps even hoping for some kind of disaster, some sudden gap in Larry's heart that she could slip into. But now she only wished for the things he wanted. For Dominic safely home and more liberal parameters of true love.

Ben Dodson finally set down the radio, letting in an ominous quiet. Then above it they heard the double horn blast from Dominic's boat.

Larry looked to the murky heavens a moment, then fell to his knees in relief. The women dispersed first, talking of relief but looking mildly disappointed. The fishermen turned away from Larry in disgust. Since their leader, Harvey Pinkerton, had been branded a raving lunatic, the fishermen continued putting saltwater in Dominic's coffee and calling him a perverted faggot, but all the joy had gone out of it. Their girlfriends remarked that they'd never been kissed so much in their lives.

Trudy retreated to her closed diner as Dominic headed into the harbor, smelling of smoke from a fire that had started out of nowhere. One minute he was ordering in the trawl net, the next his loran was spitting cinders and his radio was smoldering. He'd put out the fire within seconds, but not before his equipment had been scorched, the bottom hairs on his beard singed clear off. Not before he'd begun to think about the weeping tree and curses that actually came true.

He docked the trawler, uneasy about the large crowd, the kind of reception he might receive. He stepped onto the pier, dragging his left leg, and stopped short of doing what he really wanted to do, which was kiss Larry until they both gasped for air. He stopped two feet away, full of more yearning than he ought to be able to stand, and saw the tears in his lover's eyes.

"Are you all right?" Larry asked.

Ben Dodson came up beside him, and Dominic turned to his boss. "Lost the loran," he said. "Damnedest thing. Just getting coordinates and all of a sudden it starts shooting flames."

Ben looked toward the *Jeannie.* "No one hurt?"

"Nah. Guys a little spooked though."

"I'll get Andy to take a look at your haul."

After Ben left, Larry touched his arm. "It's a joke, right? That tree? A crazy superstition."

Dominic actually began to smile. He'd known a sailor or two who'd dreamed of death only to wash overboard soon after. He'd watched fate, and a stubborn husband, trap his adventurous mother in her own home. He'd felt destiny's fingers manipulating even him, undermining his spartan, solitary existence no one could despise. Since he'd met Larry, he'd craved all sorts of unfisherman-like things—soft beds, good wine, nights at home, truth.

He thought at any moment fate might take away what he'd been given. He thought knowing this was the secret of joy. He looked at Larry, thought of their boarded up, glassless house as heaven on earth. "I adore you," he said, loud enough to be heard across the dock. "Let's go home."

On the way to their house near the woods, they passed Gwen Marmosett in her gray church dress closing up the Emporium.

"You hear about the tree, Gwen?" Dominic asked. "You gonna be nicer to me now, sell me my magazines at half price?"

"Oh, for God's sake," she snapped at him. "Someone ought to cut that damn thing down."

Gwen locked her door with a vengeance. She was sick of that tree. Sick, sick, sick. Sick of a silly superstition and the unlucky coincidence that its curse came true every time. Sick that a little tree sap made a death at sea seem worse than a landlocked one, than, say, a car crash with a young husband inside. Like there were gradients of human death, certain souls weighing more than others, and fishermen's souls weighing the most, saturated as they were with seawater and their dark, gray lives.

Gwen walked up the hill toward Crazy Mary's, just as dozens of women had in the last few days. Mary's stock in town had gone through the roof since the laurel tree had started weeping; within hours, women had forgotten every name they'd ever called her and had shown up, desperate and trembling, at her door. They took anything Mary would give them—a stash of copper bells, which Mary swore would ensure safe travel if held under moonlight for an hour, and a tablespoon of mint, a talisman against storms. Believing in magic was a lot like believing in God, Gwen decided. Sometimes people did it just so they'd be covered.

Gwen didn't take her eyes from the laurel tree, didn't blink once. She walked right up to that damn laurel, regardless of the scent that would have made a lesser woman faint, and kicked a soft spot in the trunk. She grabbed hold of a skinny, gnarled branch and snapped it.

"Knock it off," she said.

She breathed so heavily, she didn't hear footsteps, didn't notice she wasn't alone until Gerald Frankins stepped up beside her, whistling what sounded suspiciously like a rock song. He was her age or older, well over six feet, with arms as thick as tree trunks protruding from his Venice Beach T-shirt. He wore blue Bermuda shorts, though the day was cold, under fifty, and flat, dark clouds were halfway across the horizon already, on the march to blot out everything.

He grinned at her sheepishly, ran a hand over his balding head, and Gwen told herself to just forget it. Forget the sudden palpitations of her heart, the sweat that bubbled up on her palms and the back of her neck. Forget that, in the time it took for him to smile at her, she shed thirty years in her mind; her tongue suddenly tasted of orange soda pop, her hair felt as if it was growing past her shoulders and returning to the gorgeous shade of amber it had once been. Forget the whirlwind in her stomach and the girlish hope that threatened to erupt as the kind of giggling she hadn't let loose in years.

Olsen had died when she was twenty-eight, the year they'd decided to start having children. When the men had come to tell her it wasn't a drowning death at all, but a one-car collision—he'd rammed himself into a tree on the way home from the Sparrow—she'd been standing behind the counter, surrounded by seashells and coconut suntan lotion, and she knew what had happened before they said a single word. She knew because they brought the scent of the sea in with them, and for the first time in her life she recognized the smell for what it was—saltwater and dead things. The very air around her began to make her sick.

Sometime between that moment and Olsen's funeral, she decided to leave town. She ordered maps of every state in the union, and for some reason her heart got stuck on New Hampshire, a state with only a notch of coastline. She began to dream of white mountains and trees painted with crayons.

She called a realtor and made an appointment to put the store up for sale. Thinking she'd never have to ring up another box of condoms for men whose wives were sterile but whose girlfriends were not, or hemorrhoid cream for Jim Galley, or sympathy cards for one more wife, got her through the afternoon when she had to identify what was left of Olsen's wrecked body. Imagining herself in a small cabin, two feet of snow outside and still falling, got her through his funeral, when the fishermen's wives kept giving her those pitiful glances that, translated, meant they were thanking God it hadn't happened to them. Yet. While they buried Olsen in the fishermen's graveyard on Rockcod Spit, using jack-hammers to dig into solid rock, she planned the long drive east. But during the eulogy, the fog kept entangling itself in her visions of white churches and fiery maple trees. Whenever she opened her mouth to tell someone she was leaving, the icy mist slipped down the back of her throat until all she did was cry.

The nastiest fog of the season crept in during the funeral and did not let up for seventeen days, in which time she seemed to lose her way. She did not answer the realtor's phone calls or remember her craving for someplace else. She forgot, also, that she'd ever been loved, that Olsen had picked her out of a gymnasium of fifteen-year-olds at Seal Bay High's Valentine dance, and that his first words to her were, "Thank God. Now I can stop looking."

Now Gerald Frankins smiled, and Gwen thought not only of what it would be like for a man that large to kiss her, but also what he would look like on a granite mountain, the trees behind him the color of fire.

"Hiya, Gwen," he said.

Gwen turned away before he thought her pathetic, crying over a man she hardly knew, crying over everything.

"Gerald," she said.

"Beautiful," he said, looking right at her. "Beautiful day."

"You coming to church?" she asked. "Harvey Pinkerton's shenanigans are fodder for a week."

He glanced at the house, the studio beyond. "Like to," he said. "But Katie won't go."

He headed around back with a young man's gait, impatient and agile, as Gwen let herself into Mary's house and slowly climbed the stairs. She'd done the same thing every Sunday since the night Mary had been released by the sheriff. No one but Gwen had the guts to do it, but then no one but Gwen had known the kind of man Sam Lemming had been when he wasn't pretending to be charming. No one else had seen him coming down Fahrenheit Hill, whistling gaily, while his new wife sat on her porch and sobbed.

Mary stood in her bedroom already dressed in a black dress and hat. She'd positioned a veil to obscure the mischievous look in her eye. Whenever Mary entered the Church of Sea, Sky, and Salvation, the teenagers who had been dragged out of bed on a cold Sunday morning perked up. If a candle so much as dipped, the elders crossed themselves, thinking it the work of Mary and the devil.

Mary picked up a teacup, but Gwen wouldn't take it. "Oh, no," Gwen said.

Mary shook her head. "You're as bad as the men."

From the corner of her eye, Gwen saw the leaves swirling in the cup, forming patterns that would be left behind on the bottom. "Come on, Mary. You're as bad as a reporter, always sniffing for disaster."

They left the cups behind and headed out. The air was cold and still, the fog pressing down like a hat of ice.

"You've been busy," Gwen said.

Mary shrugged. "Just the women. The men enjoy their sense of doom."

Gwen wondered if that was so, or if they simply couldn't bear to be disappointed. If they'd rather ridicule Mary's magic than prove it didn't work.

"I keep telling them the tree might take me," Mary went on. "This body is getting too old to keep battling these cold nights."

"You can't die, Mary," Gwen said shortly. "What would this town do for entertainment?"

Mary smiled, her blind eyes sweeping the bay, the steeple of the First Presbyterian Church, which suffered from a lack of membership, despite the meticulously researched and ardently delivered sermons of young Pastor Clark, and the nearly empty parking lot of St. Mary's. The women, who decided what happened on Sundays at least, would not sit for an hour and a half being told they hadn't been punished enough. The First Baptist Church of Seal Bay had had a run for a while, after they'd switched from grape juice to Gallo for communion, but that was before the sea monsters. Ever since the sea serpent had been spotted in the bay, the Church of Sea, Sky, and Salvation had been resurgent. On Sundays, the pews were packed, the congregation boisterous, and old Reverend Hollyhock literally trembling from the exertion of trying to outshine Harvey Pinkerton's latest masterpiece. Every week, Harvey somehow outmaneuvered the elders and sneaked another work of art into the vestibule and stained glass, once even into the painting of the Last Supper on the pulpit. A green-spotted monster now floated in Jesus' wine glass. On one of the intricate tapestries, a particularly sly-looking beast hid behind a yew tree, apparently trying to creep up on the apostles. The children, who had once begged to be released to the playroom, would no longer leave the chapel. During the hymns, they ran up and down the aisles with toy swords, spearing imaginary beasts.

Harvey Pinkerton had typed up a newsletter on the intricacies of the impending rapture. Gwen thought Harvey a fool, but she had to admit she had not been this committed to attending church since Olsen had died.

For weeks after the car crash, Sunday services had been the

only things that had gotten her out of the house. Trudy Casson had brought casseroles for a month, Doris Singletary had phoned daily for six weeks, then they had all expected her to get on with things, to open up the Emporium again so they could pick up their aspirin bottles and half-priced toilet paper. Only Mary Lemming had sat beside her for as long as it took, which turned out to be every afternoon for six months. Only Mary knew Gwen just had to sit there and find out what it meant to be truly alone.

"You know what I'd like to do?" Gwen said, as they turned the corner and spotted the crowd in front of the church, gawking at Harvey's latest creation—a full-size serpent spray-painted onto the sandstone. "I'd like to take Olsen's boat out tomorrow morning and jump overboard. That way I wouldn't have to face another goddamn foggy day, and everyone in town would stop worrying about disaster."

Mary took her hand. "Don't you dare. Believe it or not, that tree weeping is a good thing. People are starting to live now."

Gwen eyed the serpent. It had a face remarkably similar to Harvey's first wife, the one who had left him for a forest ranger in Flagstaff. Lisa Stottenmeir, with that continuously screaming baby of hers, detached herself from the crowd and walked over.

"What do you think?" she asked, gesturing to the picture.

"I think Harvey's days as an elder are numbered," Gwen said.

Lisa laughed. The baby in her arms calmed for a moment then started up again with a shriek.

"You ought to let me make up some of my chamomile tea," Mary said.

Lisa looked down at her baby. "Nothing soothes her. I think she's the only one around here who isn't afraid to say what she thinks."

Mary turned her blind eyes on her. "What does she think?

That you could just pack up and go somewhere else? Leave Ron and suddenly become an independent woman? How would you support her and Jack?"

Lisa stiffened and her boy, Jack, raced from the crowd. "Mom!" he shouted. "Mom, you've gotta see this. There's people in the monster's stomach, and I swear one of them is Reverend Hollyhock. Come on, Mom. This is so cool."

He tugged her arm, showering her with sand. Grains sprayed from his little fingers, appeared permanently lodged beneath his nails. His paraphernalia was piled up by the church door—plastic buckets and shovels, sifters and starfish-shaped molds. Lisa ignored him. "Ron's out for three weeks again," she said. "He takes the longest routes, stays out until the hold is full no matter what. He doesn't care what it does to me, or the fact that Jack is scared of him every time he comes home."

"Mom!" Jack yelled.

Lisa's baby exhausted herself and fell asleep with a final, furious whimper. "Tell Kate I got her message," Lisa said. "I'd love to help her paint. In fact, I've got gallons of interesting colors in my garage that didn't look right on my place."

Mary watched her go, a swish of blue in her dress, the bright dashes of her boy darting around her.

"Kate's going to take up where Jeanne left off?" Gwen asked.

"In a manner of speaking."

"What do you think that will do to Ben?"

The crowd studied the bodies in the serpent's belly, finding neighbors, Abby Grange's bark-happy dachshund, and Larry and Dominic, bit in half and tossed to opposite ends. Mary took the opportunity to walk past them into the church. She glanced at herself in one of the gilt mirrors, was glad she couldn't see clearly. In order, she hated first her weak, blue-veined legs, then her loose-skinned arms, then the hair that fell out in clumps on her pillow. She hated the pain in her wrists and elbows, her bladder that could not hold more than an ounce of fluid, and her worn-out, floppy breasts, now the size and shape of sweet pickles. She had always known she'd live to be old, but sometimes she wondered what she'd been kept around for. She'd outlived two husbands and two children. When she slipped into the front pew, a position that always made Reverend Hollyhock garble his sermon, confuse Paul with Luke, she realized she'd run out of people to scare.

"If it does anything to Ben," Mary said, "this whole town should be grateful."

"You want to hear something alarming?" Gwen said. "I've been staring at one of those paintings I took on from Kate. Call me crazy, but I swear I've seen something underneath, a rather coquettish lavender sea monster rising up out of the swirls."

Mary turned to her. "You see. It's not just Harvey. You're coming alive, too. They all are."

She waved her hand at the congregation now excitedly filling the pews. Mary knew all about the state of living, or nonliving, in this town. After Sam's boat had washed up without him, and people stopped muttering about a murder trial despite the lack of a corpse, her sister in Massachusetts had invited her east. "Come to the city, Mary," she'd said. "We'll be the merry widows of Boston."

It would have been so easy to escape the gray skies and grayer moods, but at the last minute, she'd known she couldn't go. She owed something to the fishermen she'd listened to all these years. They'd given up their secrets and she liked to think that, in return, they'd felt her presence—an unexplained weight that stabilized the boat in rough seas. She liked to think it all balanced out—they both gave up a little privacy, but in the end, neither of them was alone.

Things would have been different, lonelier and perhaps happier, if she'd become a pilot as she'd intended. A mere two weeks before flight school, she'd fallen in love with Wally Felder, a fisherman, and moved to Seal Bay where the only officially recognized form of transportation was boating. She had every intention of carrying on with her own plans, but World War II intervened. Wally enlisted and, instead of flying, she took up the paralyzing task of waiting for the man she loved to come back. When he finally did, all in one piece, thank God, she had twins before she could blink, and with Ron and Lacy came an unanticipated, paralyzing fear of heights. Suddenly, she couldn't stand on the roof of anything taller than a single-story building. When the jets came along, and people started taking joyrides to Chicago or New York, she went inside her house and locked the door.

She got scared after she started loving people. She focused not on the things she wanted, but on what, and who, she could potentially lose. She never let Wally take the children on his boat, and if a storm was rolling in and he went out fishing anyway, she slid the bureau against the front door and locked him out. Night after night, Wally pounded on his own front door, demanding (once with a shotgun that, fortuitously, no longer shot) she let him in, and night after night she sang lullabies to the children to drown him out. If he was going to risk himself, fine, but she sure as hell wasn't going to continue loving a man who might leave her. She slept in her children's rooms, where she could still regulate exactly how many chances they took—whether or not they slept with the window open, which of their friends were allowed to enter. She watched them sleep and thought, *Take anything you want, God, except them.*

Turned out God was a better mind reader than she was, as well as a sucker for a dare. On Ron and Lacy's twelfth birthday, Mary planned a treasure hunt around the laurel tree that had yet to start weeping and mutilating people's lives. She strung the tree with yellow ribbons and on every branch taped pictures of the twins as babies and toddlers and gangly preteens. The twins were obnoxious with excitement, so when they asked Mary for the sixty-eighth time when their friends would show up and if they could eat some cake beforehand, she sent them down to the Merc to buy extra frosting.

That was all it took. Twelve years of avoiding airplanes and floating deathtraps, then a tourist in a rush rounded a corner and couldn't hit the brakes in time. Mary had been listening in on them—if anyone bought Ron clothes, he'd permanently end their friendship, and if gorgeous Skip Werner showed up, Lacy would *die*—so she knew the exact moment the impact came. They didn't have time to be shocked, they didn't feel a thing. Then Mary dropped the cake on the floor.

She got a case of macular degeneration two months later, and not a single doctor believed she'd brought it on herself. Even when she told them outright she didn't want to see anyone but her babies, they laid out the rules and regulations of disease. She waved her hand and told them, within a month, she would be legally blind.

By the time she'd proved herself right, she was aware that, blind or not, she was never going to be left alone with the memories of her children. She locked herself in her bedroom, refused to talk to Wally, but he might as well have been lying beside her, shouting that he could have saved them. His thoughts never stopped, day or night. If he'd just put up a Stop sign on that corner, or been home more, or watched over them every second, they would be alive today. Her neighbors' panic, too, found holes in the floorboards and attic, deluged her with visions of sudden, improbable deaths and an almost suffocating love for the children they hadn't been able to stand a week ago. After Ethel Nyad, mother of three teenagers, brought out a hose to clean up the bloodstains, it was all Mary could do to keep the woman's subsequent nightmares out of her head.

Mary wanted to stay in her bedroom forever, but what good would it do when her husband and neighbors could get in through her head? After two days, she flung open the door and told Wally he could damn well go get them some fresh halibut. She walked down the hill, paused just a moment where her children had been killed, then followed the trails of dread thoughts to every parents' door. She looked them in the eye so they'd have to hide their trembling hands behind them and force down their hysteria. She sat at their kitchen tables and drank what they offered; she talked about fishing and her sister coming for Christmas. She sat until she made them see that sorrow doesn't kill you, no matter how much you wished it would. Until the little hand marched resolutely on, their healthy children got an hour older, and their minds hushed enough to give them all some relief.

A woman doesn't *get over* the death of her children. She hoards their photographs, stops caring about dirty floors and other minutiae, and, if she's lucky, learns to talk to their ghosts. Mary conjured up Ron and Lacy nightly, told them to sleep well, stay out of trouble, keep their voices down. Maybe it was all in her head, and really, who cared, as long as she got to see them? As long as she took more care this time, and walked them everywhere.

When Wally died a few years later, she couldn't mourn him right. God had wiped out her family in three years, which even for Harvey Pinkerton's kind of deity seemed like overkill. Though the more imaginative people in town said she'd sold her soul to the devil, the truth was Mary had made a deal with God. She would not say the things she knew about him as long as he stayed out of her way. She took up witchcraft to solve her own problems, attended church as a neutral, gossip-hungry third party. She told anyone who would listen that she would never love again.

Then she met Sam Lemming. He boarded with her for six months and, from the start, outwitted her. He yearned to touch her, but recoiled from kissing. He loved fishing, scorned fishermen, and laughed when people called her psychic. He sat across from her at the dinner table and bet her a hundred dollars she couldn't read his mind. It was years before he lost the bet. The first time she let him into her bed, his mind was absolutely blank, and that's what convinced her to marry him—not love, but the idea that it might take the rest of her life to know him, that he would give her something to do. It wasn't until after the wedding that she stopped to wonder why he'd married *her,* then realized it was simply to prove it could be done. He'd won over the woman who had vowed not to love again, and more than that, he'd done it without revealing an inch of himself, without giving up a single thing. By the time she finally won that bet at the dinner table, she'd already decided to puncture the trunk of the laurel tree with one of Sam's own knives. By the time she finally figured him out, she was no longer interested in his secrets. Sam Lemming was a man who lied about everything. Sam Lemming was *mean.*

Now, Mary looked at Gwen, at the desire that had turned her middle-aged cheeks a girlish pink. She thought of the way Ben Dodson had stood beside Kate Vegas yesterday, his back to the ocean, his fingers spread over her hip to cover as much surface area as possible. How he'd leaned down, stopped just short of kissing her, which was better than a kiss, to Mary's mind—his breath riding up and over the ridge of her cheek. She thought of that sweet Nicole Dodson she'd seen talking to the strange boy beneath the laurel tree, leaning so far toward him it was a wonder she didn't fall right into his arms.

Oh, she was glad she was old. She was delighted to be too tired to ever get worked up over another man. She'd rather get one of those lovely books on tape and curl up in bed to listen to somebody else's story. As a woman who'd lost two mediocre husbands, she had a pearl of wisdom to pass on to any woman who would listen, a list that was shockingly short: With very few exceptions, she believed men were more trouble than they were worth.

She looked up as Reverend Hollyhock took the pulpit. She couldn't see his face, but she felt him eyeing her. She sensed the vibrations of his fingers, the sweat sliding down his neck. She sat back and smiled as half the congregation gasped, and Harvey Pinkerton escaped from the choir room, crying, "Hallelujah! The rapture is upon us!"

Miles Stavers, who had never been to church before, was the first to clap.

Kate and Lisa Stottenmeir put the last touches of paint on the exterior of Trudy's Kitchen. The waitress smoked a cigarette, squinted at the moss green she'd allowed Kate and Lisa to test on the siding. Lisa's baby was quiet for once, sleeping in a pack on her back.

Kate had chosen the color herself, thinking of new leaves, wood spirits, meadows.

"It looks like puke," Trudy said.

Kate stretched her neck side to side. She'd faced the same story at nearly every house in town. Women who, ten years ago, had agreed to paint their walls crimson and mustard were now scoffing at tangerine and lime. They'd done it once, they told her, and what had changed? Nothing. If anything, their lives had gotten worse.

"I think—"

"Kate, let me tell you something," Trudy said, taking one last puff of cigarette, then tossing it on the ground. She didn't bother to stomp it out; the mist snuffed it soon enough. "You know what it means, don't you? The laurel tree weeping like that?"

Kate squared her shoulders. "It means there's a chance of anything happening."

Trudy squinted at the green paint. "You let your son go on that weeklong trip," she said. "That was foolish."

"I also let him drive. I cooked him a steak dinner the night before he left even though, down the road, it'll probably clog his arteries and kill him."

"You have to take things seriously. Men die out there."

Kate looked over Lisa's remaining colors, found a pink nearly the color of Trudy's nails. She found a small brush, moved to Trudy's front door and began painting a butterfly with elongated wings, a tail like a dragon's. She painted for a good ten minutes, pausing every few seconds in case Trudy wanted to tell her to stop.

But Trudy just breathed deeply. She came up behind her and put a hand on Kate's shoulder. "I painted those stars on my ceiling," she said. "You would not believe the amount of ribbing I've taken for that."

Lisa offered Kate sunflower yellow for the spots along the tail. "I could paint all kinds of elves and sprites along your walls. It would be something. A fairyland."

"It would be just right," Lisa added. "This town hasn't been the same since you closed the diner. I'm telling you, Trudy, yours is the one place in town that takes in all of us. The one magical place."

Trudy leaned back, blinked. Kate finished the butterfly, moved down to paint a mushroom garden.

"I'll put in the queen of the fairies," Kate said. "Maybe . . ."

She stopped when the man emerged from the alley. She dropped the paintbrush, jumped to her feet.

"Oh my God," Trudy said. "That's—"

Kate didn't listen for the rest. She sprinted toward him, might not have caught him if he hadn't tripped over a trash can. He got to his feet, but she already had a handful of tattered coat.

He was not Ray. A wrinkled, smudge-faced old man emerged beneath her fingers, terrified, his shoulder-length gray hair matted with pine needles and dirt. Kate released him, recoiled from the stench. He curled down within his coat like a turtle.

"I just . . . I just wanted to see her."

"Her?"

"I've been making something for her. It's almost done."

"Pardon me?"

"I know the secrets of the ancients. Weight and leverage, that's all it is."

Trudy came around the corner, and the man darted away. Kate felt such an absence of air in her lungs, such an *absence,* she didn't bother to go after him when he headed toward the woods. Trudy reached her, touched her arm.

"That was the man in my house," she said. "He took my dress."

Kate could hardly concentrate. If Ray wasn't sending the pictures, then it had to be William. William must have been here all along.

Trudy looked up toward the woods. "That man's after me," she said. "Imagine that."

"I thought—"

"Crazy things are happening. You be careful of Mary."

Kate would have laughed if she'd had the energy. If the look on Trudy's face hadn't been so deadly serious.

"Please," Kate said.

"I don't get involved in other people's business. I'm just warning you. That woman's old, but there's no telling what she's still capable of. You know she reads thoughts?"

"So she says."

"Oh, she can do it. She knew the day I started thinking about going to Italy. It was just this harebrained idea, this girlish fantasy I'd always had. I'd never said a word about it to anybody. Then, out of the blue, Mary brought me a brochure of Tuscany. Scared me so much, I decided to stay home. Thought maybe she'd make the plane crash, or send terrorists to Rome. What was I thinking anyway? That I'd snare some Latin lover? Who was I kidding?"

"You might have," Kate said softly.

Trudy shook her head vehemently, her platinum-dyed hair slapping her eyes. "That's not even the worst she can do. It almost went to trial, you know. If that sheriff hadn't been so soft . . ."

"What almost went to trial?"

"Never mind. Just watch your back. Beware of the butter knives."

Kate laughed. "Trudy, you can't expect me to take this seriously."

"Fine. Laugh. But remember I warned you. You'll hear the story eventually, and then you'll wonder why you didn't turn and run first chance you got."

"She's eighty-eight years old."

Trudy squinted at her. "You think age has got anything to do with it? You think you stop fuming once you hit sixty? You think you ever stop loving the wrong people, or hating the people who don't love you right?"

It wasn't out of the realm of possibility that, on the day Trudy would have shown up in Tuscany, a sweet-natured man had stood in a quiet plaza for hours, lost in the smoke of his cigarettes, unsettled and on edge because he'd woken up thinking his life was about to change. He might have waited until sunset, then flirted with a woman not of his dreams but who had a nice smile, a woman who was now living in a sunny villa overlooking the sea, where other people waited on *her.*

They walked back to the diner, where Lisa Stottenmeir was feeding her baby and staring at her son down on the beach, digging, digging. The young wife and mother had shown her own flair for painting by outlining Queen Mab herself. She'd used only the boldest reds and painted the head and body of a siren—a woman with power over men's lives, not the other way around.

There were a couple of friends Jenny could have gone to. Alice Gwynn, for one, had been her best friend in high school until The Incident with her boyfriend. Kayla Leone, despite what Jenny had said about the way she looked in hats, might have taken her in. But for a week she stayed in a motel out on 86, slept most of the time and used up far too much of her cash. When she went back to the Aerie, she told her boss she was crashing with friends in Mendocino. As she'd predicted, this information was spirited all over town within hours. Then she showed up on Kate Vegas's doorstep hardly knowing what she was doing. Resentful and wary, too, as if beginning to need someone was a trick.

"I've got nowhere to go," she said.

Kate studied her a moment, then walked around back. Jenny had felt like crying a dozen times since she'd packed her bags, but she hadn't given in once. This time she flattened her hands against the door jamb to still herself. Her fingers were white by the time Kate returned with a can of paint in each hand.

"Aquamarine and salmon," Kate said. "Come on."

Kate was halfway down Fahrenheit Hill by the time Jenny followed. She stayed two steps behind so she wouldn't have to make conversation or hide her eyes. Kate took the alley between Summerset Drive and Whale Watch Lane, already familiar with the shortcuts through town. She led them straight to the Sea Cliff apartments, a condemned building slowly sliding down a cliff into Sea Lion Cove.

"You can't mean for me to stay here," Jenny said.

Kate shrugged, stepped onto the rotting porch. There was a hole in the center, under which sand crabs rustled, and an old sofa shoved precariously to one side, eroded to wires. "I've had a few kids," she said. "Two dozen unique histories, all with one thing in common. They were never sure they could survive until they had."

Jenny stared at her. "Nothing's going to change. It doesn't matter if you paint every house in town. The men will keep on fishing. My dad will still be the man whose wife killed herself."

Kate's face fell and Jenny felt a charge of victory, followed by the knowledge that she was no longer a person she even liked. "Maybe so," Kate said. "But I'm not painting for the men."

She tried the front door, found it locked, then walked around the side to a broken window. Jenny had been inside before with boys she hadn't called back afterward. Kate hoisted herself up, disappeared inside. In a few seconds, she unlocked the front door and let Jenny in.

The floor was sloping downhill, littered with beer cans and cigarette butts. There were mice droppings in the corners, a moldy brown velour sofa hoisted onto its side, but for a building that was sinking, it was surprisingly airtight. A pretty, amber light streamed through the dirty windows that hadn't been broken or boarded up.

"It's not that bad," Kate said.

Jenny looked at her, aghast, and caught her smiling. Then suddenly Jenny laughed, and a few tears spilled out with it. All she had to do was get through the next few months, save every penny she made at the Aerie, then she'd be out. All she had to do was get through.

"You're crazy," Jenny said.

They went to the Emporium for candles and duct tape. Gwen Marmosett was not as gossipy as some of the others, but even she raised her eyebrows when Kate bought a cooler, a camp stove with propane, and a knife the size of a small dog.

"Security," Kate said.

Next they went to the Merc, where Kate bought Jenny so many groceries, Abby Grange asked where the party was. By the time they got back to the apartment, the sun had set, and Jenny quickly lit candles in every room. She taped up the broken windows, felt sick to her stomach and also exhilarated.

Kate put the groceries in the cooler and cupboards, then handed Jenny her cell phone. "The number's on the back," she said. "Feel free to use it as much as you want. Call your dad or me if you hear anything. You've got that knife, but I don't want you to have to use it."

"Kate—"

"Let me make you dinner before I go. I happen to be a whiz at a camp stove."

Jenny sat on the tilted floor, listened to Kate humming in the next room. In a few minutes, the intoxicating smell of pan-fried pork chops wafted through the apartment. She closed her eyes and the song came to her whole, its rhythm slow and folksy. The lyrics took shape in her mind in a Joan Baez voice, accompanied by a single acoustic guitar. She grabbed one of the notebooks she'd bought from the Emporium and wrote quickly.

The princess lived in a golden wood,
did all the things princesses should.
Pretended to be interested
in gowns and fancy pearls,
while plotting an escape route
to a perfect, princess-less world.
The princess lived in a golden wood,
did all the things princesses should.
Let men have only what they could reach,
locked her heart away in a vault beneath.
Wrapped her soul in sheets of ice,
melted it under cover of night.
The princess lived in a golden wood,
did all the things princesses should.
Flew like an eagle,
raised herself strong,
proved anyone who thought her just beautiful
wrong.

Her handwriting was jittery, and halfway through she had to put down her pen and clasp her hands tightly in her lap. By the time she wrote her name at the bottom of the page, she'd decided to stay.

They ate pork chops and applesauce, drank Pepsis that had never tasted so good. It was almost perfect, then Jenny heard them coming.

They opened the front door, saw Gwen Marmosett with a basket in hand, Lisa Stottenmeir with her wailing baby on her back and books chin-high in her arms. Alice Gwynn toted blankets, Trudy Casson carried casseroles and onion rings. Even Crazy Mary Lemming trudged along behind, a velvet pouch clanking against her cane.

Jenny stared at them in disbelief. Didn't these people have *lives*? She whirled around, but Kate had turned her back on her, stood on the teetering porch looking out over the bay.

Gwen reached her first. "Well, we figured it out. Mary did, mostly. Heard you a mile away. These are toiletries. Soap, shampoo. I threw in some magazines. *The New Yorker, The Atlantic.* Mary said you like poetry. I think they've got some artsy-fartsy stuff."

Alice Gwynn stepped up with the blankets her mother knitted while her father fished. Alice, whose boyfriend had come on to Jenny and taken a knee to the groin for it, though Jenny had never told Alice this. She'd never dignified Alice's accusations with a defense.

"You should have come to me," Alice said. "I thought we were friends."

They walked up to the apartment one by one, dropped off food and suggestions. Don't sleep on the floor. Mint will get rid of mice. Call if you need anything. Then that crazy witch touched her with bony fingers, stared at her with those freaky blind eyes.

"There are things to run from, and things to keep. You need to learn to tell the difference." She opened the pouch, took out a brooch of diamonds and tiger's eyes. She snatched Jenny's hand, pressed the jewel into it. "It was my mother's. Diamonds symbolize strength and bravery. When you wear this on your left side, it will protect you from enemies. Tiger's eye signals independence. It almost always indicates change for the better."

Jenny looked down at the brooch, could not believe Crazy Mary would give her something that meant so much. She was stunned that she'd been loved all the time.

"Don't be a ninny," Mary said, then all those tears Jenny had stashed came out at once.

Kate stood on the edge of Jenny's porch, as far as she could go. She tested herself against the wind and her own fear of heights. She could see down to the rough sand of the cove, past a hundred feet of sheer, painful cliffs.

"She should have jumped," Jenny said.

Kate flinched, stepped back from the edge. Jenny stood in her doorway, which Kate had already painted blue with salmon trim. The women had swept out the shack, left more food in the pantry. A half dozen more had come down with flashlights and baked goods. Kate had gotten a few to agree to a new coat of paint for their own houses. Ethel Nyad had even asked for orange.

"Your mom?"

Jenny looked out to sea. "She should have jumped, or thrown herself overboard on one of my dad's long hauls. She could have at least made herself a legend. That was the one thing she had within herself to do."

While she'd been painting, Kate had imagined braiding Jenny's long, fine hair. The whole day, she'd had to consciously instruct herself not to touch her, not to go too far.

"I'm sure she loved you the best she could."

Jenny yanked her chin up. "Oh, she loved me. She loved me more than a person even should."

"Jenny—"

The girl walked into the house, returned a moment later with a pink envelope. Kate's heart slowed, then started up again with a vengeance.

"Some woman gave it to me," she said. "I'm sorry. I forgot until now."

Kate took the envelope, turned back toward the ocean so Jenny wouldn't see her tears. She ran a fingernail under the seal, got it only halfway open before she yanked the letter out. There was no photograph this time, just a few words, an even more unsteady script.

Jacob Shulman
462 Ambrose Lane
Cambridge, Massachusetts

Kate stepped up to the very edge of the cliff, looked over once more. Jenny touched her shoulder.

"Are you all right?"

She whirled around, took Jenny in her arms. The girl stiffened at first, then let her shoulders sag, the steel in her spine relax. Kate led her away from the cliff, back into the dilapidated apartment. She set her down on the floor and pulled one of Alice Gwynn's blankets up over her knees.

She wanted *this* family. She did.

"When Wayne and your dad come home," she said, "tell them I had to go."

— 10 —

The Keeper of Fishermen's Souls

It was easy to find. 462 Ambrose Lane. Cambridge, Massachusetts. A wide, woodsy street, a big white clapboard colonial on the corner. A sweeping lawn, covered in snow this time of year. Two leafless maples, one with a tire swing still hanging from a strong limb, the rubber well worn in the center, where a boy had sat, and swung, and probably fell a time or two, and someone in a blue dress came running.

Kate sat in the rental car, her coffee cup cold on the dash. She stared so hard it all blurred, and she was the one who had lived there, the one who had pushed the boy in that swing and made sure he *never* fell, while a casserole with all the healthy stuff hidden inside simmered in the oven. In winter, she decorated the house with twinkling white lights and took her boy to the woods, where they chopped down a perfect fifteen-foot tree. She set it up by the living room window and adorned it with William's cardboard snowflakes.

She bought him far too many presents, but how could she resist? Each toy equaled a moment's bliss. She lived to watch his face light up. She made him hot chocolate, laughed as he lunged at the foil-wrapped boxes. They spent Christmas day playing with his long-craved Brio train, his LEGOs. They built a castle taller than he was, then attacked it with plastic dinosaurs.

Kate leaned back against the seat. She did not imagine Ray, could not even bring his face to mind. For Christmas dinner, she and William feasted not on a twenty-pound turkey, but on a small duck. She couldn't picture side dishes, or what they said to each other between mouthfuls. She could imagine activities—graduations, bike rides, trips to the zoo—but not William's voice, his inflections. She could never decide if he'd have been gregarious or restrained. Whether he'd concentrate on athletics and his own popularity or larger issues—global warming and the homeless men in the park. In her imaginings, they sat at the dinner table, eating duck, two strangers. Her shoulders even tensed at the clanking of utensils.

After Christmas morning, all her fantasies turned fuzzy, undefined. As if she'd lost the point of the movie and walked out, complaining it was too hard to believe.

William would have grown up in an apartment in Santa Monica. He would have had a liar for a father, a man who, at best, merely disappointed him at every turn. A father she had to believe she would have divorced in time, if he hadn't left her. But she swore this: William would have been happy anyway. She would have seen to it.

The house was lovely, easily four thousand square feet, exquisitely cared for. It brought tears to her eyes, those pruned roses piercing the snow, the black shutters around sparkling paned windows. She tried to guess which second-story window was

William's, finally picking the one on the right with a view of the towering maple. She decorated it for him, taped up Dodgers pennants instead of the Red Sox. She was envisioning dark blue walls when an old man knocked on her window.

She jumped, knocking over her latte, staining the rental car's console and floor. She used her Cambridge street map to soak up the spill, then rolled down the window. The man wore a linty sweater. His hair was sparse and white, horseshoeing from ear to ear.

"You got business here?" he asked.

Kate opened her mouth, but nothing came out. She didn't exist here, didn't think she could speak in this world.

"I said, you got business here?"

Kate's father had begged to come. All the way to the airport in San Francisco, he'd squeezed her knee too hard. She'd made him drop her at the curb.

"I don't like this," he'd said. "It feels like a mean trick."

But it wasn't. Some things you just knew. She got out of the car, met the old man in the eye.

"I'm looking for a boy, eighteen. I was given this address."

The man squinted. "What do you mean, looking for a boy? What's Jacob got to do with this? He's not into drugs, is he? I told Sheila the other day, someone on this street is into drugs. They keep playing their music. Day and night. Trying to drown out their drug deals."

Kate leaned back against the rental car. "No. He's not into drugs."

"There's things going on," the man said, revealing brownish teeth. "Drive by at two in the morning. You'll see what I mean. Cruising up and down like lunatics. It never used to be that kind of neighborhood. When I first—"

"I'm just looking for Jacob."

She swallowed after she said it, then it was all right. She looked back at the house, thought she saw a figure in that upstairs window, but when she blinked it was gone. It was impossible anyway; blinds blocked her view of the room.

"You ought to be looking at BC. That's what surprises me about this drug thing. That boy's got too much brains for his own good. Can't even talk English to me anymore, he's fluent in economeese."

"BC," Kate said. "Boston College."

The man stepped back, squinted so hard she could no longer see his eyes. "Who did you say you were?"

The tears were long gone, snuffed like one more memory lost. She touched the man's sweater that was the color of old fish. "I'm a friend of the family," she said. "I knew his father."

The man scoffed, tossed off her hand. "Well then, no one will have anything to do with you. No one around here will speak Bob Shulman's name, I can tell you that."

He walked down the street to another white colonial, slightly less sparkling, in need of fresh paint. He went inside and shut the door.

Kate steadied herself, turned back to the house. She couldn't take it all in now, couldn't think of anything but making it to the front door. She forced her legs to move, stepped on the sidewalk, felt one flip in her chest that was easily steadied. She thought, with more sadness than relief, *It won't kill me either way.*

She walked the frozen path, saw a porch that was not as spotless as the rest, covered in dried leaves. Half a dozen newspapers had piled up near the door, a flyer for carpet cleaning had been strung through the door handle. She knew before she lifted her hand that no one was home.

For a good five minutes, she knocked anyway. She leaned her head against the door, rapped her knuckles until they ached. She might have gone longer, except she felt a hand on her shoulder and, expecting the old neighbor, turned.

It was Ray Vegas, in blue jeans and a black shirt, still gorgeous except that he was worn out, almost skeletal. She'd remembered him taller, at least six feet, but now it was obvious that he'd never been more than five-nine.

He squeezed her shoulder, blinked those eerie blue eyes once, then faded right before her eyes.

Somehow she got to her car, pressed her head to the steering wheel. It was her father's voice she imagined. "Breathe, Katie," he'd once told her. "For some things, all you can do is take a deep breath and live through it."

Kate squeezed her eyes shut. She'd seen pinpricks of light through Ray's skin, a crack in the concrete beneath his feet. A mediocre ghost, even less of a man. The devil wasn't frightening, he was pitiful. He was a man who couldn't do anything right.

She lifted her head, looked back at the house. She could have picked the wrong bedroom. Jacob's room might be at the back of the house, facing the woods. He could be a good kid or a troublemaker like Ray. The only certainty was that he would not be who she imagined.

She drove back to her hotel, unwilling, for the moment, to prowl through Boston College or downtown Cambridge looking for a stranger. She ordered room service, hardly ate when the salad came. She sat looking over the Charles, craving a different view—lemon-yellow walls, Mary's exotically aged face, the sight of Ben's boat clearing the breakwater, safely home. She fell asleep in the chair by the window, and knew the moment she started dreaming—her hands curled into fists, the back of the chair began to pinch, yet nothing in the real world could force her to wake.

Ray snatched William from his bassinet before dawn. She lay in bed, curled up, too exhausted to wake even when William whimpered and Ray soothed him with his pacifier. She didn't twitch when Ray dropped the diaper bag and stood over her, when he whispered, "Kate." He even touched her arm, offered them both a last chance, but she merely swatted him as if he were an annoying but harmless fly in her dream.

He turned, picked up the diaper bag, slipped out with two bottles. Almost free, which to him must have been better than free, because it was all anticipation and grandiose dreams. There wasn't a hint of mundane reality in it, not one single regret.

He drove over the hill to Encino, met a man at a crowded Denny's. The place was stuffed with businessmen and twenty roped-together day care toddlers, so no one noticed a couple of men in the back booth, with a baby sleeping in his carseat on the table between them. Ray stayed for fifteen minutes, enough time for a cash exchange, and for a woefully short list of instructions.

"He's not sleeping through the night yet," Ray said with a voice that wouldn't begin to break for another two hours, when it would get so bad he'd stoop to nothing but whispers. "He takes six ounces of formula at a time. And be sure to tell them it's soy. He's allergic to cow milk."

"They'll figure all this out," said the man who hadn't once looked at the baby. He jerked when William began to cry.

Ray grabbed the bottle from the diaper bag. He reached for William, the way he had at two in the morning when Kate had begged him to take a turn. Then he stopped, dropped his arm, merely stuck the nipple in his son's mouth. William stared up at him without blinking. Ray must have noticed his son was exactly the length of his arm from fingertip to elbow.

"He's already smiled," Ray said. "And not for Kate either. I was giving him a bath."

The man looked at him straight on. "This is a one-way ticket," he said. "You want to give me back that fifty right now?"

William sucked greedily, and Ray seemed to be mimicking him, taking in too much air. He put his hand over his mouth, looked out the window at the peach stucco facades lining Ventura Boulevard. "No," he said finally, then got up quickly, letting the bottle fall out of William's mouth. William shrieked in outrage, revved himself up to hysteria by the time Ray left the restaurant. The man never put the bottle back in his mouth.

Kate awoke the way she always had to William's cries, her heart thundering as if she'd just been jolted by a minor electrocution.

She woke to dawn over the river, a team of rowers already out, the interstate filling with commuters. She uncurled her fists, noticed how, with every second, her heartbeat calmed, sought normalcy. Her body, apparently, could take only so much euphoria or panic. Even ghosts, she thought, eventually wore themselves out.

She showered and drove to Boston College. She walked the campus, studied a hundred faces, though she didn't know whether to look for Ray's eyes or hers. She spent an hour outside the cafeteria, feeling like exactly what she was—a woman who did not know a soul in Boston. Finally, she walked into the administration building and asked for directions to the economics department.

She found the building, stood in the long, hushed hall. She looked through the first classroom window at nothing but a professor behind his desk, grading papers. In the next two rooms, men stood and lectured, students sat in stacked seats taking notes or staring off into space, their faces slack with boredom. Then suddenly one of the lectures broke, and the students filtered out. Kate examined every face, would have grasped at the vaguest familiarity, but there were none. He could walk right past her and she wouldn't know him.

She walked into the classroom. "Excuse me," she said, and the professor, a man in his fifties, bearded, looked up testily from his desk. "Sorry to bother you. I'm looking for Jacob Shulman."

The annoyed expression changed. The man smiled, became a new person. "So am I," he said. "My class has been in a stupor since he's been gone."

Her chest suffered that shock again, a sudden acceleration of her heart. "Gone? I was told he went to school here."

"He does. He'd better. He's the only student I'd trust to leave two weeks before midterms and still ace my tests. A phenomenal feat, really, when you consider all that trouble with his mother."

Kate looked up at the stadium-style seating, tried to picture a boy in the first row talking animatedly, turning economics into rousing debate. But that kind of effervescence would have been the other parents' doing.

"His mother," she said.

"Jacob is one of the few students I know who's never touched a cigarette. How can you blame him, after the things he's seen?"

"When did he say he'd be back?" she asked.

"Tomorrow, I think. Thursday at the latest. Midterms are Friday, and I'm sure he won't miss those."

He returned to his papers. Kate had very little recollection of her drive back to the hotel, or of getting into bed, slipping down deep within the sheets without bothering to untuck the tight edges. In the morning, she called Wayne, was so grateful to hear his voice she bit her lip to keep from crying.

"When will you be back?" he asked.

"Thursday at the latest," she said. "How are you?"

Wayne hesitated, and a prickle started on the back of Kate's neck. "You ever do something . . . You ever feel like any happiness you get is borrowed or stolen? Like you've done something horrible and you're being *rewarded*? You know what that feels like? You know how many times I've wished . . . I mean, I didn't think . . . Shit. Forget it."

Kate took a deep breath, enough time to swallow all the words he'd resent—questions, accusations, too quick or simple an answer. "I think each person has a chance for a good life. I also think things go wrong, and sometimes you have to start over. You have to do everything differently."

Wayne was silent, and Kate forced herself to look around the hotel room, at her suitcase, the used tissues, the pictures laid out on the desk—evidence of all she kept doing the same. She believed what she told him, and also what she didn't: People clung to habit, struggled to make the slightest change.

"How's Jenny?" she asked at last.

"Talk about doing things differently," he said, his voice immediately lighter, happier whether he believed he deserved it or not. "Lisa Stottenmeir helped her paint that whole apartment. She loves it. She's, like, enraptured with rot and sleeping on the floor, if you can believe that. When Ben found out she was there, he went ballistic."

Kate wrapped the cord around her finger. "Tell Ben . . . Tell him I'll be home Thursday."

She spent the morning at Boston College, waiting to see if Jacob would show up for class. When the lecture came and went, and no one new arrived to spark conversation, she returned to Cambridge. She walked for hours along the Charles, worrying not about what she would say to her son when she finally saw him, but about whether or not Jenny was being careful with that propane stove, if Nicole was sleeping well, if she'd sacrificed the man for his daughters.

That night, she slept for fourteen hours straight. The phone woke her, though it shouldn't have. It was already nine o'clock.

"Hello?" she said, groggy until she heard the strained breath at the other end, a hacking cough. She sat up.

The cough got uglier, a cough that hurt Kate just to listen to it. After a groan, it subsided. A woman said, "You saw the house then."

Kate closed her eyes. "Yes. And Boston College. A professor wants him back."

The woman chuckled then coughed again, worse this time, rumbly and dirty and wet. Kate curled her toes, wondered how much more she could be expected to endure. "He's popular with all of them," the woman said. "He participates, you know? He likes discussion."

So they would have talked politics at Christmas dinners. Equal rights and capital punishment. Global economics and theories on the extinction of the dinosaurs.

"Did you know Ray?" Kate asked.

The woman inhaled something, quieted her coughs. "Almost from the beginning. He died two years ago. He suffered, if that makes you feel any better."

"It doesn't," Kate said. "Can you please—"

The one thing she truly wanted she could not say. *Go away.*

"I wanted to make sure you'd go to the ends of the earth for him," the woman said. "I wanted to be sure."

"Who are you?" Kate asked.

The woman coughed once more, not as deeply. Just a surface

cough, as if she were merely offering Kate another moment of uncertainty.

"I'm calling from Mary Lemming's kitchen," the woman said. "I'm Shirley Shulman."

Kate tilted her head back, until the tears retreated. "The other mother," she said.

Ben had assumed he knew everything about Seal Bay. Its old man rhythm—up at dawn and asleep by noon, awake all night, prey to insomnia. Its routine complaints—the creaking of the underpinnings beneath the pier, the stern bellow of the foghorn, each crewmember's particular string of curses after he tore his hand on a hook. He even knew, on those few occasions when he stayed on land, what followed after all his men had gone: A sudden, pervasive hush, while the fog unceremoniously plugged the gaps where the men had stood, followed by a collective, female sigh.

Or at least, they used to sigh. He came around Pacifica Lane and stared at his own house, repainted purple in his absence. He stopped short when he found Nicole humming and painting lemon yellow curlicues on the railing. He thought, with a hint of panic, that the men had better return to land.

"I don't believe this," he said, grabbing the porch column and hearing a threatening crack. The porch roof sagged a little more to the right. "That woman . . . She can't come in here and take over my life. *My* family. If she thinks—"

"Kate's still gone," Nicole said. "I picked out the color. I thought it was nice."

He looked at her, saw she'd been crying. She'd been crying while he'd been fishing, and while this may have happened a hundred times before, he vowed it would never happen again. He took her in his arms, realized she'd lost weight. She was nearly as slender as Jenny.

"I'll fish until the end of the year," he said. "I'll do the Baja trip the first of January, then I'm done. I'm done with this, Nicole. We'll go someplace else."

She pulled back, dried her tears with her sleeve. He saw she did not believe him. At some point, she'd stopped taking his words on faith.

"Come on," he said. "Let's go see your sister."

They headed toward the Sea Cliff apartments, where sand crabs now scuttled across the abandoned living room floors, where his daughter closed her eyes at night. He reached the last derelict building, the one painted deep blue and sinking fast toward the cove. A basket of apples and cheese had been propped by the door.

They stepped onto the porch. It was two feet lower than it had been twenty years ago, with an ominous looking sink hole in the center. The broken windows had been patched with duct tape, the sofa on the porch covered with an air mattress and an old flannel blanket.

"She's lost her mind," Nicole said.

Ben knocked on the door, though he knew Jenny would not answer. Since he'd learned what Kate had done, since he'd been broadsided by her nerve and her sudden disappearance, he'd come here every day. He'd sat on the porch and asked Jenny to come home, and was answered only by silence. He wondered if Jenny had really thought he'd just let her go and forget about her. He felt ill when he imagined her thinking of him like that.

"We had a great haul," he said loudly. Behind the door, Jenny would be rolling her eyes. He imagined her yawning, everything as it should be. "Wayne's a great worker, when he's not talking about this girl."

He walked to the shoddy couch, sat down gingerly on the decayed arm. Nicole leaned against him and he closed his eyes, realized his dreams had never been fair. The month Jenny was born, he dreamt her full grown, happily married, staring out a window at a razor-flat expanse of sagebrush. Over the years, the same dream returned, so real that when Jenny was five, he talked Jeanne into a trip to Texas. He found a two-acre parcel outside Austin with the same view as his dream. Jeanne had laughed—one of the last times, he remembered—but she also went with him to the realtor's office and signed her name on the dotted line. She told him he was crazy, but on the flight home there were tears in her eyes.

He'd never pictured Nicole anywhere but with him, had never been able to stomach the thought of life without her. Which now seemed the worst curse a father could bestow upon his child. A singularly selfish act.

He released his youngest daughter and stood. "You shouldn't be waiting at home for me," he said. "I don't want you waiting at home."

Nicole leaned back, stung, and though he wanted to pull her back to him, he forced himself to turn, put a hand on the one exposed pane of glass. It was cold to the touch and dewy. Everything inside, he was sure, had a fine coating of mildew. It was almost too much to bear, the thought of Jenny lifting a soggy blanket to her chin, not being able to get warm, not ever.

"Wayne won't last," he said. "I can always tell. A fisherman can't let himself dream of anything or anywhere else, but Wayne's got these outlandish visions of Jenny changing, just like that. Falling in love so fast she won't have time to back out. He's already found himself a reason to quit."

He swore he heard a deep intake of breath, and he wasn't

sure if it was from the daughter behind him or the one inside the shack. He leaned his head against the glass, took his voice down to a whisper. "You're the keeper of fishermen's souls, Jenny Dodson."

If she heard him, she gave no sign, but Nicole was already off the porch, at a dead run down the street. Ben hunched forward, thought nothing had ever hurt this much—not Jeanne dying nor the aftermath he'd had to witness his daughters suffer through. Nothing but this—the moment when he had to stop needing his daughters.

Gerald Frankins had a thing about wood. Eighteen years ago, his sergeant noticed his skill with a saw and asked him to make a rocking horse for his youngest grandson. Up until then, Gerald had crafted only bookcases and a baker's rack for Patti, but somehow he crafted a magnificent three-foot-high Arabian stallion. He routed it out of pine instead of oak, because it was cheaper, and used twine for the mane instead of real horse hair, but when he saw what even that small effort did to the face of a boy coming off chemotherapy, Gerald decided to never skimp on anything again. From then on, he built his horses from nothing but oak or cherry or, when he was feeling especially exuberant, plantation teak. He used real emeralds for eyes, took classes on oils so he could make a palomino look like a palomino, and a black Stallion look like the sleekest, fastest animal in the world.

He insisted on unblemished wood, straight, unknotted, unscarred, so when he stood in front of the laurel tree of Seal Bay, it wasn't its curse that bothered him, but its total lack of worth as timber. Close to fifty roots poked up through the ground and not one of them was fit for anything but tripping people. The branches coiled and twisted, and Gerald couldn't find a single section worthy of being routed down to a wooden ear or muzzle.

He walked back down the hill, disgusted. He sat beside Mary Lemming on her porch swing, still in the shadow of that ugly tree. Mary had been huddled inside her kitchen most of the morning, talking to one of the women from town. Now she braved the cold and fog, haphazardly sewing in the final stitches of a flannel quilt. She took no care at all with the seams; there were giant holes between patches, gaps in her stitches half an inch wide.

"Nice work," he said.

Mary cackled and held up the quilt as if she could see it. "It's ugly and you know it."

"What's it for?"

Her pale eyes flashed. "Saying good-bye. Did you ever say good-bye to your wife?"

Gerald put a hand over his shrinking stomach. Since he'd come to Seal Bay, he'd been jogging like crazy. Up and down the beach, three or four times a day, though up until now he'd hated to run. Those skinny girls who ran on the bike paths of Santa Monica in sports bras and lycras were just plain ridiculous—they were beautiful enough as it was, any more and they'd do him in. But Mary had been feeding him too many pot roasts. He'd felt the need to expend some energy. In three weeks, he'd lost twelve pounds, and sometimes he looked in a mirror and didn't know himself. Sometimes he reached for skin that was no longer there.

"I had plenty of time to do that," he said. "Patti died slowly."

Mary patted his hand. "Yes, but did you say *good-bye*? Did you let her go?"

Gerald looked down Fahrenheit Hill. There was absolutely no reason for him to remain here. Kate did not need him; she hadn't for years. She'd lost William long ago, but never let go of his potential. Whether she returned with him from Boston or not, her boy's promise would remain exactly the same. Now if it had been *him,* if he'd lost Katie that way, well, he'd have been like any man. He'd have turned on a band saw to drown out the other ringing in his ears; he'd have retreated into a garage and, in some ways, never come out.

"Help me up," Mary said suddenly, biting off the last thread. She grabbed hold of his hand, stood shakily. She jammed the blanket roughly under her arm. "Come on then."

For a blind, eighty-eight-year-old woman, she kept up a good pace down Fahrenheit Hill. "I'll tell you this story," she said, as they neared the docks. "You might appreciate it, having met so many crazies in your time."

Gerald took her arm, led her around a child's skateboard left in the sidewalk.

"Sam Lemming was out to drive me crazy," she said. "We were married only a few weeks when he started rearranging the furniture so I'd bump into it during the night. He'd transplant my flowers to different locations, tell me he'd be home from sea one night, then not show up for another month. Oh, he'd swear up and down I was just forgetful, losing my mind, whatever. He'd pull out what he said was proof in notes he'd made, messages he'd left but I'd never gotten. But that was the one part of his mind I could always read. He was laughing inside. *Laughing.* He thought it was funny. Making me look stupid."

"Why did you marry him? You must have seen something in him in the beginning."

"He was tricky. Gentle one minute, mean the next. He kept me on my toes, and that was interesting for a while. Then he started cheating."

"I'm sorry, Mary."

"Oh, I didn't care about the adultery. Really, by then I had refused to touch him. What I hated was the fact that I couldn't read him right. I was a woman in a fisherman's town. Reading a few minds here and there was all I had, and I've always considered it a *privilege* to know what I know. I've never lived alone in my house. They've been with me all the time."

She waved her arm toward the little houses by the bay that, day by day, were getting brighter, as if someone was walking door to door, turning on the lights. Gerald reached over and took her hand.

"So I decided to get even," she went on. "I took the butter knife down to the docks. Sam followed me and was right there when I punctured his boat. He laughed the whole time and, I have to admit, I wasn't nearly as menacing as I wanted to be. It took me an hour to make six tiny slits in that boat. Afterward, I tried to stab the laurel tree, and Sam was hysterical by then. Rolling on the grass, laughing. I could have stabbed him to death with the butter knife, let me tell you."

Mary took a deep breath. "He left that night," she said. "Said the holes in his boat wouldn't have sunk a rubber raft. I was so furious, I spent the whole night at the laurel tree, trying to stab it through. I didn't even see the men when they came up in the morning. It wasn't until they told me Sam's boat had washed up without him that I saw the sap on my hands."

They'd reached the docks now, but Mary gestured toward Sea Lion Cove. They made their way along the wet sand, where the footing was easier, and the waves lapped up to Mary's black boots.

"What happened then?" Gerald asked. "The police must have been involved."

"Sure, they brought me to the station. I told my story to that nice Duncan Fritz, who had just been named sheriff. People had heard me screaming at Sam. They knew there was something bad between us. But it was tough on them. One little woman with a butter knife, an empty boat with no body ever found. There was water in the bottom of Sam's skiff, but it was still seaworthy."

She paused, looked out to sea. "If you ask me, Sam got off somewhere south," she said at last. "Santa Barbara probably, so he could breathe in bougainvillea every morning. He's going to waltz back up here someday and say it was all one big hallucination of mine."

Gerald looked at her and did not doubt it. Real life was exactly that strange. People fell in love with dead movie stars, faked their own deaths in order to live another type of life.

"What's the quilt for?" he asked.

She smoothed the edges. "Just witchy stuff. Throw scraps of a man's shirts into a strong southern current and he'll start falling apart. He'll confuse his head with his heart, his right hand with his left. If I sewed those pieces of Sam's shirts badly enough, one lovely evening, he won't even remember his own name." Mary smiled beatifically.

"I think your husband was a damn fool to cross you. I'd better make sure I toe the line around here."

Mary laughed. "Don't worry. I had you pegged the moment you walked in the door. You're a good man. That's why Trudy and Gwen are all gaga over you. They haven't seen your kind before."

She started into the water, waded out past the small breakers. Gerald rushed after her, reached her before the water splashed clear to her neck. It was ice cold, but Mary Lemming didn't notice. She laughed out loud as she and Gerald tossed the quilt over the farthest breaker and it got caught in the current going south.

Mary walked back to dry ground. "Now," she said, wiping her palms on her soaked skirt as if completing some dirty chore, "I think you ought to get yourself a cup of coffee at Trudy's. Yes, sir, I think you're dying for a cup of Trudy's famous, gritty blend."

His feet were freezing, but his mouth had already begun to water. Come to think of it, he did feel a little lethargic. He squinted at Mary, but she was watching the quilt float south.

"I'm going to stay here awhile," she said. "Make sure it really gets going. I'll be fine."

"Mary—"

She smiled, shooed him away. He left her on the beach, crossed the sand quickly, but when he got to Trudy's, he didn't go in. He saw the waitress hustling to bring out an order of Larry's new spicy home fries, an addition to the menu once Trudy reopened the diner and Dominic returned safely to port. He turned and headed up the rest of the hill. At the newly painted, fire-engine red Emporium, he looked past oyster ornaments and Santa in a lobster-shell suit to the woman sitting behind the counter, reading a book. Gwen Marmosett dragged her finger slowly across the page, occasionally stumbling and going back again, and Gerald heard a crackle in his stomach like something finally coming loose.

He pushed open the door and a shell windchime jingled. Gwen Marmosett lifted her gray head and set down her book. She smoothed back her hair, looked out the window, and when she turned back to him, he knew he had not stayed in town for Kate.

"I wanted to talk to you about rocking horses," he said, though he hadn't wanted to talk to her about anything. He'd just wanted to stand beside the counter and take a good long look at her eyes. Her face and hair blended together, the way the sea and sky do on a gray December day. Her skin was camel-like, pleated, stiff, and dry. But when he got close enough to smell the scent of baby powder she'd dusted herself with that morning, he planted his feet on the floor and refused to budge.

"Rocking horses?" she said. Her voice was deep and husky, the way he liked it in a woman. He found himself smiling for no reason at all.

"I make them," he said. "I've been selling them at craft shows for three hundred apiece. Maybe you'd be interested in commissioning some?"

He didn't know what had gotten into him. He had no interest in making money anymore. He went to the shows to talk to people. To get a few four-year-olds up on his varnished teak horses. He used whatever money he made to buy more wood.

But when Gwen rolled up a sleeve, revealing a luminous stretch of skin on the underside of her wrist, a pulsing blue vein, he suddenly did want a few bucks to spare. He had a desire to buy something nicer than his usual Venice Beach T-shirts. Maybe a white cotton Oxford and some fancy gabardine pants. One of those new, spicy colognes.

She walked around the counter, revealing an ankle-length skirt of gray wool and weathered leather sandals. He was mesmerized by her toes, which she'd painted red to match her store.

"I doubt there's a market here," she said.

That made him snap his head up. "What? No market for rocking horses? You've got to be kidding."

She shook her head. "Wood goes bad so quickly here."

Gerald stared at her. She was not that gray, actually. There was a surprising flush of pink along her collarbone, a hint of deep, exotic red behind her ear. He stepped forward just as the door flew open behind him.

"Gwen, thank goodness." Trudy Casson rushed in, then leaned against the wall to catch her breath. Gwen took her iridescent toes back behind the counter. "My head is on fire. I'm desperate for aspirin."

Trudy spoke to Gwen, but she looked at Gerald and smiled. She showed no signs of being in pain.

"You know where the Advil is, Trudy," Gwen said.

Trudy nodded, then took the long route around Gerald to the second aisle. She actually grazed his chest with her shoulder, releasing a rush of floral cologne. In her wake, Gerald breathed in deeply. He'd always been a sucker for Patti's gardenia perfume.

"You could have called," Gwen said. "You know I'd run it down."

"Oh, couldn't put you to that trouble," Trudy said, coming out beaming with a fifty-tablet bottle of Advil. She fished a ten-dollar bill out of her pocket. When Gwen was done ringing her up, she put the ibuprofen in her pocket.

"Don't you want one now?" Gwen asked.

"I'll wait a minute. Maybe I just needed some fresh air."

She turned to Gerald. She seemed to be waiting for him to say something, but he was speechless. She came only to his chest, the way his wife Patti had. She was not gray at all, but fully painted—eyelids blue, lips crimson, nails cotton-candy pink.

He felt dizzy, nearly in a swoon, the way he had every day when he'd come home to Patti. He'd never tired of walking through the door and seeing her pretty face, putting his arms around her and feeling safe again. She always smelled of flowers. He could count on her to overcook the roast. When she had first been diagnosed with multiple sclerosis, the full import of the disease hadn't sunk in. She'd felt only a little tingling in her hand, after all. It wasn't until years later, when she was wheelchair-bound, that they both realized what had been stolen from them—not only time together, but the sound of their footsteps, the matching shuffling steps of an old couple who had been in sync for half a century.

Now he turned from Trudy to Gwen and imagined what a new woman's hand might feel like in his. He wondered if that quilt had really been a spell for Mary, or a secret one for him. He thought, *I'm becoming single again.*

He wanted to go jogging, smack his feet into the sand, take a little nasty sea spray in his eyes. He pulled himself up to his full height, which, with two woman staring at him, felt like a good seven feet. He hadn't been this happy in a long time.

"Well," Trudy said, when the silence lengthened and she saw that, though he tried to be fair, he kept looking at Gwen. "I'd better go."

"Trudy," he said. She paused at the door, gave him ample time to come up with something smooth and kind. He wished he could tell her she was beautiful, Gwen was beautiful, every woman in this place had a streak of beauty in her somewhere, and then he'd be a man to reckon with. He'd be a whole new man.

He managed nothing but the awkward smile of a widower who'd slept with one woman his whole life.

"Okay then," Trudy said. "Bye."

He watched her walk away, shoulders stiff, her steps short and careful in those high heels. He ought to run to the door and call out that he'd been lonely, too. Now that possibilities were rushing back at him, he felt clueless how to react. He didn't know how to deal with desire, or if he could bear to let any woman see him with his clothes off, see what had become of his stomach and the mostly flaccid thing between his legs.

He wondered how any woman could possibly find him attractive, but behind him Gwen Marmosett pressed the palm of her hand against his back. He felt the heat of her fingers through his shirt—he'd have felt it through Gore-Tex—and he slowly straightened.

He turned around quickly, and Gwen met his gaze. "I'll take two," she said. "Rocking horses."

She had more guts than he did, a notion that, surprisingly, he didn't mind. When he walked out, he was whistling "Dixie." By the time he finished the first horse he'd present to her, all of Fahrenheit Hill could hear him singing out loud.

— 11 —

The Stone Castle

The first thing Kate noticed when she pulled into Mary Lemming's driveway was the broken ax on the sidewalk, then the wales along the laurel tree's trunk. The attack had been brutal, but ultimately unsuccessful. The tree stood defiant and mutilated, a dozen fresh wounds oozing with sap. Kate opened the door to the smell of gasoline, a crackle of panic in the air.

She didn't bother to retrieve her suitcase from the trunk. She reached the porch in three strides, had her hand on the door when a shadow removed itself from the corner. She braced herself, felt for William's picture in her pocket, then heard the thud of boots, smelled Ben's unique scent of sea and soap.

She took a step toward him and opened her arms. "I'm sorry I didn't—"

"Jenny told me you encouraged her to stay there," he said. *"You."*

Kate dropped her arms, listening to the sounds coming from

Mary's house—water running, a shuffle, a brutal cough. She had wanted a drink on the plane, but had restrained herself. She'd wanted to be completely sober for this moment, an idea which now seemed ludicrous.

"I thought she needed—"

"She is not one of your foster children. She is not some *experiment.*"

She flinched, the dryness in her mouth turning bitter. She reached for a peppermint in her pocket, then realized she'd left the candy in the car. "I care about her," she said.

"No. You do not. You placed her in an unsafe building. You filled her head with adventure when she needs to be getting herself together, deciding what she's going to do with her life. You brought that boy here, and now she's destined for the same life as her mother. And don't tell me she doesn't know that. Don't tell me that isn't what's driving this whole thing."

Kate heard the cough inside the house. It went on and on while she stood there, as if she was destined to keep losing time, wasting precious seconds.

She crossed the porch, laid her head against Ben's chest. He stiffened but she concentrated on the sound of his heartbeat, a rhythm like the surf. These were not wasted seconds. Her life, anyone's life, seemed little more than a series of reactions to unforeseen circumstances, one response leading to another, leading away, yet she'd ended up where she belonged. Miraculously leading a life she would not trade.

She leaned back, smiled at him despite the fury in his eyes. "I would never take chances with your daughter," she said. "I knew it the moment I saw her. Jenny is going to be fine."

He stepped off the porch, jammed his hands in his pockets. He reached the Emporium within seconds, disappeared into the fog by Jim's Tackle a moment later. She blinked back tears, craved Scotch now, what her father had drunk after his roughest days. She squared her shoulders, opened the door.

She found the woman seated on a fold-out chair in Mary's otherwise empty parlor. She'd seen her before—entering Gwen's shop, sipping soup at Trudy's. The other mother was not thin but shrunken, concave and hardly more substantial than fog. Her hair was thin, uniformly gray. A lit cigarette dangled from her fingers, an inch-long tail of gray ashes clinging to the stub. Beside her, on the floor, was a shoe box and a large photo album, wrapped in white satin and lace.

"Hello, Kate," she said. "I'm Shirley Shulman."

By seven, the temperature was as close to freezing as it ever got in Seal Bay, though Larry thought it felt colder. The rain came in sideways and penetrated everything—plastic, wood, his zipped parka. The wet sand had crystallized, so that every step he and Dominic took shattered the ground, crackled like pop guns going off.

Larry did not care if anyone heard them. He didn't care who looked. He took Dominic's large hand in his and vowed he wouldn't let go until someone else, someone's not-so-true love, satisfied that damn laurel tree. Until they were safe.

Dominic squeezed him back, although beyond that he'd been silent on the subject of the weeping tree. He'd refused to acknowledge the chance he was taking just getting into the wheelhouse of his trawler every dawn. He refused to speak, but at night he rested his head of curly hair in Larry's lap, wrapped his arms around Larry's waist and held on.

They reached the docks. A few men stood on the pier drinking Coors Lights and casting lines into the bay.

"We could go to New York," Larry said. "I've got friends there. That curse cannot extend to the Atlantic. I'll move to Nova Scotia, if that's what you want."

He began to cry. More than anything, he regretted choosing the route through Central Park that had led him to Dominic. He wished, before he'd met the giant's gentle gaze, that he'd considered the price of joy. For every minute of ecstasy with Dominic, the payment was exactly sixty seconds of fear. For every kiss, he'd have to face one mean, drunken fishermen, for every touch, the curse of one tiny spot of sap. The price of joy was always eventual loss, a cost that, now, seemed too steep.

Dominic turned to him. His Dominic, who never offended, who refused to rock anyone's tame world, kissed him unchastely on the mouth. He opened his lips, slid his tongue inside, cupped his hand around Larry's neck.

The men on the pier went silent. Larry counted to seven before one of them charged. He smiled beneath the kiss, slipped his arms around Dominic's waist and held on tighter. He heard the muffled thump as the man jumped off the pier to the sand. Larry let go of Dominic and whirled around, fists raised.

It was Ron Stottenmeir, whose wife, Lisa, had come into the diner last night with paint in her hair and a map of New York state in her hands. She'd unfolded it on his cutting board, over an assortment of chopped vegetables.

"You're from New York," she'd said. "You ever been here?" She pointed to a tiny town upstate, one he'd never heard of. "I've got a cousin there, a real nice girl from what I can remember, though it's been years since we've seen each other. It's a long shot that she'd help me now."

That baby of hers kept crying. Larry took one of his soft cookies from the jar and broke off a crumb. He pressed it into the baby's open mouth and she suddenly quieted, moaned in pleasure as if a little sugar was all she'd been asking for.

"Upstate is nice. Beautiful. A whole different feel than the city."

"A good place for kids then?"

Larry looked at her, noticed flecks of gold and maroon above her scalp, cobalt and fuchsia in the hair that hung near her eyes. He wondered if she'd stopped washing the paint out, if she no longer bothered with mirrors. "A good place," he agreed.

Now Ron pointed a finger at his face, and if Dominic hadn't been holding his hand, he might have bitten the calluses right off Ron's palms.

"I'm not prejudiced," Ron said, and Larry rose up on his toes, recognizing this opening as a precursor to the worst kind of bigotry. "I don't give a damn what men do in private. But, hell, keep it out of my face, you know? Take a good look at the human body. Things fit, if you know what I'm saying, between a man and a woman. Two men, hell." He grimaced. Larry thought he might actually be curling his toes.

Larry glanced up at Ron's elaborately painted house on the bluff, then back to the man who abhorred color in any form. "Your wife is going to leave you," he said.

Dominic sucked in his breath, turned to Larry as if he could not believe this of him, a nice man's ability to be cruel.

Larry dropped his hand. He not only believed it of himself, he'd seen it coming all along. Spite was contagious. Their only hope for goodness, as he saw it, was to move away from everybody else.

Dominic retook his hand, tucked it between his own, forgave anything. Larry leaned his head against his shoulder.

"You goddamn faggots," Ron said. "You perverted little—"

The rest never came. Ron's gaze slid past them to the water, to the men running and pointing at the bay. Larry turned. It was there for only a second, riding over the breakers, but long enough to realize he didn't really want to hide. Not when, beneath the surface, there were wonders he hadn't dared to imagine.

"You see that?" Dominic whispered, pointing where the blunt head and mammoth body rose out of the water. An enormous, oddly pointed tail followed, its green spots glowing, a splash rising thirty feet in the air.

"Yes," Larry said. "I do."

Ron Stottenmeir followed the other fishermen to the water. Two of the bravest even waded into the surf.

"Probably a whale," Dominic said.

Larry nodded, but his head hurt. He actually yearned for Manhattan, where people had a stronger grip on the world, where the bay was too polluted to support alien forms of life. He wanted to believe in one thing, the only thing that mattered—that Dominic would be all right. Sea monsters and magic only muddied the issue and, frankly, downgraded the value of his love. All of a sudden, devotion didn't seem much different than a green-spotted serpent, or anything else that couldn't be explained.

"Ben asked me to head with him to Baja on the first of January," Dominic said. "It will be a twenty-one day trip."

Larry said nothing. The men, even Ron Stottenmeir, huddled together on the sand, nervously lighting cigarettes.

"I'll come back," Dominic went on, but Larry wished he hadn't. Because at the very end, his voice rose, then broke. "I'll come back and we'll take another vacation. Inland, I swear it. New Mexico, like you've been talking about."

"I'd like to see Santa Fe, find out what all the fuss is about."

Dominic nodded. He nodded until his neck must have hurt, until it must have taken all he had to just stand there and pretend. "Santa Fe it is then. After the trip."

Kate pulled in a chair from the kitchen and sat down opposite her. She pressed her hands in her lap, then slid them behind her, clasped them so tightly she lost feeling in her fingertips.

Shirley Shulman never once smoked her cigarette. She let it burn all the way down, then lit another one from the end. She coughed every two minutes. She lifted her hand to her mouth, came away with blood in the palm of her hand. Finally, she said, "I stopped smoking three years back, but I still like the feel of a cigarette between my fingers. The secondhand smoke is probably just as bad, but even my doctors say it's not going to make much difference at this point."

She coughed again, and her whole body shuddered. Kate began to rock. She knew Shirley must once have been healthy, vibrant, and perhaps even quick, but she had visions of her too weak and slow to stop William from running into traffic. Too tired to cook him a healthy dinner or help with homework. So sick, the best she could do was watch him while he lay sleeping, then stumble into the yard so he would not hear her cry.

Shirley struggled to stop coughing and squinted at her. "You probably think I'm going to hell."

Kate could not speak. One word would start an avalanche of others. She'd have to know everything, and what would that get her? Cold images, someone else's memories.

"I don't care if I am," Shirley went on. "I got to have him all these years. He was my boy. He was meant for me."

Kate could have hit her, but she heard Wayne rummaging around upstairs. She longed for the sound of his voice. A time-out, a pause in all these compulsions, so she could hold him, make sure he was all right, calm her breathing.

"It was my pleading that did it," Shirley said. "Robert couldn't take it anymore. I told him I didn't care how he did it, as long as he got me a child. He had a record, you know. He was in jail for a time, for embezzlement. That's why the agencies denied us. Maybe we could have gone overseas, but I wanted a boy who could pass for my own."

Kate turned away. One tear and that was all. She was drying up.

"I was there when your husband died," Shirley went on.

Kate must have twitched because Shirley smiled, seemed delighted to have finally broken through. "Ironic, isn't it? I was the last one holding Ray Vegas's hand."

"Was he—"

"He showed up three years after we got Jacob. Not directly, you understand. He'd come at night and leave candies. These caramels he'd discovered Jacob loved. Every night, I'd look through my window and see him there, bent over, leaving foils on the stoop."

Kate's throat swelled. Shirley dumped ashes, whirled the cigarette around. "I knew who he was. I knew it the first time I saw him. I never told Robert. I thought . . . I don't know. It was between Ray and me. This weight. The things we knew, what we carried. I could have killed him, but once I saw his eyes I knew it was pointless thinking. He was already dead."

Kate leaned back, closed her eyes. Wayne had turned on the water, let it run. She pictured him shaving, turning his face right and left, trying to determine his best side. She imagined him lying down on his bed, dreaming of Jenny, plotting ways to charm her.

"I never saw Ray after that morning," Kate said hoarsely, opening her eyes. "I never heard another word."

Shirley nodded. "He left without a trace. That's what he told me. He went to Mexico right after he sold us Jacob. He drank tequila and was, ironically, lucky with money."

Kate stood. "Please," she said, and she didn't know if she was pleading with Shirley to stop the story or finish it. If she wanted to see William more than anything in this world, or if she wanted him to leave without a trace as well.

Shirley waited. She put out her cigarette in one of Mary's china bowls and did not light another one.

"You stole him," Kate said. "Snatched him out from under me. You could have killed me and it would have done less damage."

Shirley looked over her shoulder, looked at all the things Kate couldn't see. She was crying; Kate didn't know how she'd missed this the whole time. Tears coated the woman's sunken cheeks, the collar of her jacket, her lap. She thought, with some panic, that she was running out of people to blame.

"Imagine knowing all that," Shirley said. "Imagine knowing it and putting on a smile every morning so your son won't see."

"Where is William?"

Shirley reached down, grimacing, and picked up the photo album. She hugged it tightly against her chest. "His name is *Jacob.* He's always been popular. Exceptional in math. He played soccer for a while, then turned to track. He doesn't like to let anyone down but himself."

Shirley coughed, opened the book to the first page. Kate looked at the photo that had come in the mail, the one she'd taken of one-month-old William, with spots still on his nose.

"Ray gave this one to me," Shirley said. "I started the scrapbook almost immediately. I thought of you, even then. I didn't know I'd be dying this early, but I knew I owed you this."

She turned the pages. William as a toddler, a young boy, a preteen riding a skateboard. With his friends at the beach, camping, his arm slung around a pretty girl. "That's Rebecca," Shirley said. "They've been dating about six months. A sweet girl, but I don't think it's as serious on Jacob's part."

A young man's lifetime, a good life. He'd been in the wrong place, but he'd been happy. As if nothing—not even who he became devoted to—was sacrosanct.

Kate walked out of the room and up the narrow staircase. She knocked on Wayne's door, waited for him to invite her in.

"Enter," he said, his voice deep, sweet. She couldn't turn the knob. She leaned her head against the wall and sobbed. When he finally opened the door, he seemed horrified. He looked past her down the hall, obviously praying for aid.

"Kate?" he said. "Jeez, Kate. It's all right. God."

He held her, patted her back awkwardly, smelling of aftershave and a clove cigarette he must have recently smoked. She wanted to squeeze him so tightly he melted into her skin, but she leaned back, smiled, made herself laugh.

"I'm home," she said.

"Don't go away again if this is what it does to you." He stepped back, eyed her warily, tenderly. "You find him?"

She had thought the same thing about each of her children, somehow swollen to make it truth: She couldn't love anyone more than this.

"No," she said. "You have a good trip?"

He studied her a moment longer, then walked back to his bed. A dozen fishing magazines lay tangled in his sheets.

"We kicked ass. Dodson wants me to come with him to Baja after the first. A long haul, Kate. Twenty-one days."

His voice faded at the end. Kate thought of the tree, the woman downstairs. She thought of a dozen endings, then wrapped her mind around the only acceptable one—Wayne stepping off the boat safe and sound.

"I'll miss you," she said. "Jenny will, too."

"Yeah, right."

She smiled because his voice was not that incredulous. Because he looked toward the window, as if he'd already begun to hope. She turned to go, but he came back to her, untucked a hair from her collar the way her father might. "You okay?" he asked.

"Fine," she said, smiling the way Shirley Shulman had. The way all mothers did when their hearts broke in clear view of their children.

She walked downstairs, found Shirley still sitting on the chair in the parlor. "What do you want from me?"

"Two things," Shirley said. She turned to the last page of the scrapbook, a photo of William at his high school graduation—all smile, deep blue eyes. She picked up the shoe box, laid it on top. "This is from Ray."

Kate probably imagined the smell of sulfur. She could imagine almost anything at this point. Shirley jabbed the box at her until she took it. She lifted the lid, saw the money inside, stacks of hundreds, neatly wrapped.

She looked at Shirley, but the woman was struggling to her feet. She leaned against the wall for support, breathed heavier every second. "Fifty thousand," Shirley said. "I told you he got good with money. The rest he left in a trust for Jacob. They met at the end, by the way. I told Jacob he was a friend of the family.

They talked sports, ranted about the Patriots. Ray died a week later."

Kate stared at the money, dropped it before she was sick.

"I'm dying," Shirley said. She pressed her head to the wall. "That must be obvious. The doctors say I've got a year, but they're just being kind. You asked me what I wanted from you. Here's the first thing: I want you to wait."

Kate looked at her and laughed harshly, tears sliding from the corners of her eyes. "You can't be serious."

Shirley met her gaze. "I am."

Kate shook her head, the laughter replaced by goose bumps, a relentless chill. "Why on earth would I give you more time?"

"Because you know what it feels like to be denied it."

Kate walked to the window, held on tightly to the sill. She felt hollowed out, exhausted.

"Robert left me six years ago," Shirley said, "before the cancer. Took up with some young thing from the office. Jacob visited them for a while, but the new wife had her own kids, told Robert it was awkward whenever Jacob was around. Robert gave him a check for thirty thousand dollars, as if that was what losing a father and becoming a man was worth."

Kate stiffened. She didn't want to know the bad things, would never be able to stomach the thought that she hadn't been there when her boy was sad.

"Robert was never any good to him. Just like Ray. I hung on. I swear to you, this body wanted to give out a year ago, but I hung on. Got Jacob into college. Got him started. He's a good boy. Came here with me when he should have been studying for midterms. I never told him why and he never asked. He takes care of me. When I'm . . . He'll tell you he'll be fine, but he's going to need family. Not Robert, but someone who will be loyal to him. Kate . . . *Kate—*"

She wouldn't go on until Kate turned around. Kate moved slowly, trying to dredge up hatred but managing only a hint of disgust, an overload of pity.

"I want you to wait," Shirley went on, "and I want you to be ready. I'll leave him a letter he can read after I'm gone. I'll tell him everything. I swear it. He'll find you when he needs to. He'll find the one person who will be devoted to him."

Kate suddenly sprang to life. She stomped across the room, took Shirley Shulman's papery arm between her fingers and squeezed. The woman had dark circles beneath her eyes, a yellowish cast to her skin. She grit her teeth but never cried out, not even when the bruise began to show.

"I'll never forgive you," Kate said.

Shirley didn't blink. She covered Kate's hand with her own. "As if forgiveness matters at this point. I'm here for Jacob. Maybe you should ask yourself this: Could you have loved him more than me? Do you think that's even possible?"

She extricated her arm, walked to the door. Kate listened to her shuffle across the porch, hobble down the street. She swore she heard her wheezing all the way down Fahrenheit Hill.

Then she realized she was going back to William.

Kate raced out the door. She didn't care what Shirley Shulman wanted. She spotted the dying woman easily, laboring to reach the Surfside Motel. She ran after her, concentrating on keeping her footing on the slick streets rather than the thought that would really rock her—the knowledge that she hadn't felt her own son's presence.

Shirley had gone inside the motel by the time she reached the entrance. She put her hand on the door just as Dominic blasted his horn twice in the harbor. Someone laughed as they came out of Eaton's. A baby cried, probably Lisa Stottenmeir's.

She owed Shirley Shulman nothing except revenge, but she hesitated, turned her attention to the docks, where Lucky was hobbling along beside Ben. Ben picked him up and carried him aboard the *Sarah Jane.* He set him down gently on the deck, paused to rub his belly while Lucky stretched out. A few minutes later, Ben disappeared in the wheelhouse, revved up his engine.

Kate stepped back, stared at the lit windows of the motel. There was a shadow in the corner room, a head behind the curtain. In her dreams, perhaps, Shirley Shulman suffered, but now she wondered how the woman would climb the stairs. The shadow left the window, perhaps opened the door, helped a dying woman inside.

She reached for the door, drew back. She paused, steadied her breathing, let urgency fade in one minute, and panic subside in the next. She would never care what Shirley Shulman wanted, but it would always matter that cruelty did not rub off. She'd had little or no control over most of her son's life, but she could guarantee this: Her first act would not cause him pain. Would not deny him the chance to say good-bye to his mother.

She watched two shadows slowly pass the window then she turned her back, stared at the docks. She didn't care what Ben Dodson wanted either. She headed toward the *Sarah Jane,* whether he'd let her on or not.

Wayne went two days without sleep. Forty-eight hours, then he started hallucinating. He saw a beast in the bay, Jenny walking stealthily along the foot of his bed in flannel pajamas. He'd never been afraid in his life and suddenly rainstorms and the smallest swell beneath the *Sarah Jane* terrified him. Today he hadn't been able to do his work and ended up in the wheelhouse, huddled on the floor beside Lucky. The dog licked his face, stretched out on his back for a belly rub.

Ben Dodson found him there. He handed him a cup of coffee, which Wayne took with shaking hands. Ben noted the coordinates from the loran, plotted their next course now that these fishing grounds had proved worthless.

Wayne spilt his coffee, set the cup down beside him. He thought he might be sick. "The long haul in January," he said. "I was thinking we might not want . . ."

"Don't think."

Wayne could not meet his gaze. His father had left the family when Wayne was two and Wayne had no recollection of him. Nor had he suffered from the loss. His mother had worked twelve hour days as a computer chip assembler, then worked another four cooking and cutting the grass. She dated men who were smart enough to see her value, but too stupid to offer to help.

The year he'd dropped out of high school, two sixteen-year-old boys had shot each other to death over the colors of their shirts. The men he'd known, even the boys, had been expendable. They risked themselves and attacked each other because it didn't matter. Because they weren't scholars or athletes or even the meanest. A flair for recklessness was the best they could do.

He stumbled to his feet, scrambled out of the wheelhouse and was sick over the side. Ben found him there a few minutes later.

"You can't think too much," Ben said, touching his shoulder. "It'll drive you crazy."

"I'm the one who burnt a hole in the laurel tree. If anything happens to us, it'll be my fault."

Ben dropped his hand, squinted out to sea. They rode a four-foot swell, came down the other side. The sea was nearly calm, but Wayne was sick again. He vomited up water and a thin vein of blood. He wished he had the guts to jump overboard, to stop struggling and let the ocean take him, but what had really kept him up the last two days was his sudden desire to be well. A yearning even more perverse than his former craving to defy everyone. He suddenly wanted to be whole, calm, and beyond reproach.

"I'll tell you something you won't want to hear," Ben said finally. Wayne steadied himself, squared his shoulders. "You don't have that kind of power. You never will."

When Wayne turned, he found Ben smiling, rapping his knuckles along the railing and looking toward home. "Mr. Dodson—"

"Come on the long haul," Ben said. "Spend ten days without sighting land and see for yourself how small a man really is."

"I'm sorry."

Ben touched his arm, right above the elbow, and for the first time in a year, Wayne recalled the faces of those boys who had shot themselves. One black, one white, both with smiles that, on another day, might have defused the tension. Hands that might have softened up over time. For the first time in years, he scorned his father for not having the guts to come back.

"Go ready the net," Ben said. "You've got a lot of work to do."

Once the fishermen saw the sea monster, the frigid, seaweed-strewn beach gained a new allure. There was hardly room for a blanket. Teenagers came straight from school and stayed until dinner, young mothers brought their children down to play. Station KSOS sent a reporter. The sand quickly became littered with brown bottles and empty film canisters, and one man, Gil Dexter, set out in his skiff only to have a fatal heart attack not thirty yards from shore—from fear or from what he had seen, no one could be sure.

The Christmas season took on an alien cast. Ron Stottenmeir denied his family a Christmas tree so he could spend the money on thirty pounds of meat he dropped from his boat as bait. Harvey Pinkerton made papier-mâché sea monsters instead of wise men for his front lawn nativity scene. The McDermott boys—now over forty, but still sleeping in bunk beds in their mother's house—chopped down a fifty-foot cypress tree and set it on the corner of Fahrenheit and Main. They decorated it with green bubble lights that the moist air and near constant drizzle kept blowing out.

Trudy paid little attention now that her own body had started to defy her. She'd given up on Gerald after catching him gawking at Gwen, and was the first to spot the wedding ring on Larry's finger. Yet she could not feel depressed. She'd woken up breathless every morning for the last week, as if her dreams knew something she didn't. As if she was on the cusp of the best season of her life.

She was certain something was going to happen, but when the shadow slipped past the back door of the diner, she had no idea that foul-smelling, dirty stranger would be it.

"Get out!" Larry Salamano shouted, slamming down his basket of onion rings. "For the last time, I'm telling you to get out."

Trudy saw a dark coat, long, matted hair, eyes like gems. She hardly realized she was running until she was across the alley. She didn't know how fast she could go until she darted into the woods. She ran after the stranger like the girl she'd been, the captain of the track team. A girl who ran just for the joy of it.

She followed him around pines, leapt over boulders, as springy as a teenager, a thought that made her run faster. She kept him in her sights the whole time. She ran until she couldn't hear the surf, until the fog thinned and then disappeared completely. Until she was out of breath but energized, thinking, absurdly enough, that she was never going back again.

She emerged in a clearing and stopped. She was already winded, but what she saw took her breath away. What she saw changed everything the way she imagined the child she'd never had would have. One look, and a thousand new possibilities arose.

Before her was a stone castle. Sea serpent–sized boulders, chiseled to a smooth finish out of dense, unwieldy basalt, had been stacked into improbable walls and towers. One circular structure rose a good thirty feet to the tops of the pines, and was connected to the castle with an elaborate parapet. The entire perimeter was smooth, shiny stone, but one twenty-by-twenty-foot rock had been fashioned with some kind of bolt or pinion and was swinging shut like a revolving door. She pressed her hand to the rock and, with very little effort, got the massive boulder to swing open again. She looked back once, let loose an uncharacteristic giggle. She followed the door to the inside.

The center of the castle was open to sky. She walked along the wall, running her hands across smooth flanks, sanded ridges, perfectly formed archways with no apparent nails or braces of any kind. Hallways led both north and south; the rest of the castle appeared to be roofed with boulders.

She spotted the circular tower to her left, wanted to see what he'd done for stairs. She ducked beneath an archway and nearly stumbled upon him in the sudden darkness. He stood like a shadow in the corner, trembling beneath his tattered coat.

She stopped, felt her heart racing again. He was foul—long, matted hair, dirt on his cheeks and beneath his nails, clothes made of rags. He smelled of Dumpsters and God knows what else. They stared at each other for what seemed like an eternity, while Trudy contemplated the danger she was in, which way led home, and whether or not anyone would believe her if she told them what she'd found. Then she noticed he'd taken something from his pocket. An old letter, now nearly worn through, yellowed and soft.

He held it out. She took it with the tips of her fingers, careful not to touch him. She stepped back into the light of the entry, saw that the paper had been fingered so much, the creases had torn through. She recognized her own writing.

Dear Zachary,

I'm taking the coward's way out and writing you this letter. I think we ought to be just friends. I'm sorry, but I just don't feel that way about you. I'm sure one day you'll find some girl who does.

Best regards,

Trudy

She looked up, saw him cowering against the four-foot-deep walls of his castle, hiding behind matted hair that might once have been dark brown. Beneath the dirt and void of wrinkles, his skin could have been prone to sunburn and acne. His eyes, she remembered now, had reminded her of amber gems.

"Zachary Levine?" she said.

He stepped beneath the archway into the light. She'd given him that letter during their junior year of high school, after Trent Ackerman had come to Seal Bay High. Like every other girl in town, she'd fallen in love with Trent's golden-boy looks, his easy smile, his foreignness, being from a landlocked town in Florida.

Trent had lasted only two months, his father having thought fishing would be more glamorous, a little more Hemingwayesque. The Ackermans had left for a commune in Oregon about the same time Zachary Levine started fishing. She'd been heartbroken about Trent, and had not shown much sympathy when Zachary developed that problem with vertigo and could no longer earn his keep on the water. She remembered he'd called every day for a month, until she sent the letter. People said he vanished. Crept away in the dead of night when even the sound of the sea began to make him dizzy.

Now, Trudy dared to touch a hole in his coat, run a finger over the rough wool. She had to hold her breath, he stank so bad, and when she finally let it out she had trouble getting the rhythm of normal breathing again. Even when she stepped back, away from the stench of him, she couldn't breathe right, as if the problem was not air at all but yearning. Wanting something a little too late.

"Zachary," she said.

He took back the letter, folded it gently, placed it in the pocket of what passed for trousers—moldy blankets, apparently, someone's garbage, sewn together. He stuffed his hands in after it, walked across the sunlit expanse of his grand foyer. He paused at an open arch leading to a spectacular room, a perfectly round cathedral. A madman's work of art.

"How?" she asked. "How did you do all this without anyone knowing?"

He disappeared through the arch. She followed him a moment later, but by then he'd disappeared. She stared at the rounded walls, the boulders too large for a single man, or even a dozen men, to lift. She saw no signs of equipment, no evidence of a crane. But she did see what had eluded her before, the name that had been carved into every stone.

Trudy. Trudy. Trudy. Trudy.

She raised her hand to her hammering heart, curled her fingers into a fist. "Oh," she said. "Oh, my."

— 12 —

The Sea Monster

Nicole stood alone in the kitchen when the air suddenly filled with the scent of elderberry pie. She reached for the counter only to yank her hand away. The tile was frigid, the grout lines turning to ice. She felt a prickle along her spine. She swore a figure shimmered in front of the kitchen sink, a remnant of blond hair and concave shoulders, a blue cardigan buttoned clear to the top.

She held her breath, not believing it, not daring to think it had come for her. She took a step toward it and the vision turned, showed its face. Nicole screamed, then covered her mouth. The face had shrunk to nothing but eyes. Swollen, liquidy, *hungry* eyes that absorbed everything—light, joy, other people's dreams. She had forgotten an important fact since she'd found her mother's body. For months beforehand, she had avoided Jeanne's gazes. She'd been afraid of getting too close.

The spells Mary had been teaching her were worthless now—charms to make her frizz disappear, amulets to guard against acne. She stepped forward until the hairs on her forearms rose. She met her mother's unhappy gaze and did not flinch.

"Go away," she said.

The vision shimmered and sank, like the phosphorescent fish her father spoke of, chased off by the wake of his boat.

She caught her breath, disappointed once more in her mother's lack of effort. She went upstairs to the bathroom, spent a solid ten minutes on her hair. The frizz had definitely subsided. She set down the brush, put her hand on the medicine cabinet, which she'd restocked with aspirin and Sominex. She paused, looked at herself in the mirror.

"Flick, fleck, skittle, twirl, I see a pretty girl."

She studied her eyes, which *did* seem less dingy since she'd been going to Mary's. Every day, the old woman said the same thing. "Not the pretty spells again." But Nicole was adamant. If Jenny was any indication, as long as you started out beautiful, everything else came easy.

She closed the medicine cabinet without looking inside.

She left the house, made her way to Sea Lion Cove. The beach was packed with teenagers who had taken to swimming, hoping to emerge with a green cast to their skin or, even better, to suffer a beast bite that would brand them a legend for life.

She maneuvered around video cameras and buried beer, past David Collins, who had been calling for days now, begging her to go out with him. She kept her eyes on the pier and, as she got closer, made out a glint of fair hair and stiff shoulders. Jenny sat on the edge of the docks, her feet dangling over the water, her back to the crowd. Nicole had left a basket of Jenny's things on her doorstep—her Australian shampoo, paperback novels, CDs. The empty basket had been returned this morning by an obvious impostor. Nicole had stared dubiously at the note left inside.

I miss you.
Jen

Nicole took a step toward her, then felt a warm hand on her arm, smelled Polo cologne. She turned to find Jacob Shulman smiling at her.

"Hey," he said. "I've been looking for you."

Someone shouted from down the beach. The camera crew ran toward the waves, but Nicole didn't turn. She stood perfectly still, the way she might if she were staring at a sea monster, afraid to do anything to startle it. Afraid the slightest movement would make it bolt.

But Jacob only smiled, encircled her arm above the elbow with his thumb and forefinger. She thought this was what the women's movement was up against, this intoxicating feeling of being enveloped. The idea that she was the heart, protected by muscle and bone.

"I'm leaving," he said, his smile fading. "My mom . . . We've got to go back."

She blinked. She'd been told over and over by her dad and various teachers that these were the years that would define her future, determine the kind of woman she would become. *These* years, the ones when everything was done to her, when she could not even act on her own behalf.

"Oh," she said.

"I wanted you to know. I wanted—"

He ignored the shouts, a man flinging himself into the sea. He leaned forward, kissed her on the corner of the mouth. Hardly grazed her at all, yet she felt the warmth of his lips through her skin to the tender insides of her mouth. Felt the heat tingle across her tongue, down her throat, into a secure hold somewhere between her ribs.

"I had to do that," he said.

He pressed a folded piece of paper into her palm, then backed away. He walked backward, watching her until he reached the pier. Then he turned and ran up the hill.

She unfolded the paper, saw the address. She ran a finger across the block letters—he had that improbable architect's script, angular and perfect. She would imagine, for as long as possible, that he had no flaws.

She turned to see Mary Lemming walking down the hill, a crowd of teenagers parting before her like a skittish Red Sea. As the old woman passed Sandy Orvis's blanket, the girl's radio turned to static. Mary must have been able to tell how close she was to the water by the sound of the waves and the density of the sand, but it was still amazing to see her stop right before the foam. Water never touched the tips of her high-top black boots.

No one had the guts to either taunt the old woman or say hello. Nicole respected her friends less every day; she really did. She walked up to the old woman and put her hand on Mary's bony arm.

"Hello, dear," Mary said, without looking. "That boy's been with you again."

Mary was ancient, more skeletal than human, but out here, her edges blurred by a fresh sea fog, she looked almost youthful. Like one of Jenny's anorexic friends.

"It really is like falling," Nicole said. "Once you start there's no going back."

"Grab a piece of driftwood," the old woman said. "Make sure it's at least three feet long."

Nicole didn't hesitate. She scoured the beach, found two bat-length sticks she handed to Mary. The old woman ran her hand over the smooth gray grain, decided on the longest of the two.

"This'll do," she said. "Draw a circle in the sand around us. Don't let any of those busybodies cross it."

Nicole was surprised to see a few of her classmates inching closer. Sandy Orvis stood in front, David Collins and his harem right behind her. The shouts by the water had stopped now that the sea monster had turned out to be nothing more than a thick swarm of seaweed. Nicole drew a line in the sand.

"Cross it and I'll hex you," she said to the crowd. She was surprised when they all drew back. Mary smiled at her like a proud mother.

"Sit here," the old woman said, positioning Nicole in the center of the circle, her back to the sea.

Mary touched the top of her head and, after a while, the hair there grew warm. In front of her, the crowd was now up to thirty, so Nicole closed her eyes. Right away, she conjured Jacob.

"That's right," Mary said. "Let him come. He's persistent, that one." Mary let go of her, started dropping things in the sand. Nicole concentrated on Jacob's eyes, colored them a deep ocean blue. She parted his hair on the left.

She blocked out the sound of the ocean once it no longer fit her vision. She drew in buildings around Jacob—not skyscrapers, but older buildings, square and mortared with redbrick. Jacob stood in the middle of a congested square, books beneath his arm, students jostling him. Behind him the trees were bare, but she could make out a few red leaves trapped in the melting snow. The smell of apple smoke was thick and already familiar, as if destiny lived its own secret life and merely waited for her to catch up.

She opened her eyes, surprised to find herself still on the beach, with thirty faces hushed and awestruck staring past her, the closest belonging to Jenny. Mary sat behind her, staring out to sea where the last of an enormous blunt head rose out of the water, then sunk just as fast. There was a shared intake of breath as they made out the wings along the beast's flanks, the eerie green spots.

Nicole looked down at the sand. The inner circle was littered with pennies, her own hands clenched into fists. She leaned against Mary's shoulder and the old woman put an arm around her.

"They're going to blame us for that," she said, gesturing out to sea, but Nicole had already left her neighbors behind. She considered what to pack, how she would get to Massachusetts, exactly how much she was willing to lose in order to gain the one thing that mattered.

"What about Kate?" Mary asked, and Nicole went still. The old woman was a mind reader, and sometimes that was flat-out annoying.

"What about her?"

"That boy was hers first."

Before either of them could say more, the crowd pushed forward. David Collins stepped on the circle Nicole had drawn, breaking her concentration. She felt a pinprick of pain behind her eyes.

"How'd you do that?" he asked.

Half the kids ran toward the water, swam out as far as they dared, but Jenny was not one of them. By the time Nicole got to her feet, Jenny was halfway to the Sea Lion apartments, to a home that was sinking fast.

Nicole helped Mary to her feet, though she was well on her way to hating her. Her and Kate and her father and Jen. All the ones she couldn't bear to hurt.

"I know," Mary said. "Go on."

Nicole turned her back on the kids hamming it up in the water for the news cameras, pretending to be tugged under. She started up Fahrenheit Hill, didn't stop until she was standing in Mary Lemming's kitchen. Until she saw Kate Vegas sipping coffee with a face full of eyes like her mother's. Swollen and hungry and sad.

"Jacob Shulman," Nicole said. She reached into her pocket, took out the address he'd given her and tossed it on the table. "I have a picture, too. I'll bring it up later. He's all yours."

Kate stared at the address, and Nicole's eyes filled with tears. The room was blurry by the time Kate reached her, but Nicole shrugged off her hand.

"He doesn't have to be only one woman's destiny," Kate said.

Nicole started crying in earnest. She turned into Kate's arms, realized the smell of elderberries permeated not just her house, but this one, perhaps the entire town. It had come off the hills and flooded the air. It had been here the whole time.

Kate insisted on making dinner, an elaborate wild mushroom quiche for which she had to drive an hour to find the right mushrooms. She refilled Mary's cocktail three times, until the woman fell asleep in her chair. She tried to keep her father in the house, but he wanted to prowl the beach with the other men, the self-appointed sea monster patrol. Alone, she paced the living room floor, then grabbed her jacket and headed toward the woods.

She tried to clear her mind, but it played tricks. She imagined she saw Trudy Casson emerging from the trees, unlikely bluebells woven through her hair. She thought she heard a man's laughter, but it had to be coming from town, from the Sparrow. She thought of going there herself, but by then what she craved was lucidity, cold-hearted sense. She walked back to her studio, slid out the scrapbook she'd tried to hide beneath some canvases. She took it with her to bed, laid the book on her lap.

She turned the first page, felt her heart race then slow to a weary beat. The last drop of sweat on her neck cooled.

Jacob Harrison Shulman
born William David Vegas
October 5, 1984
8lbs. 4oz. 21 inches tall

And for the first time, she felt she was there. Everything was familiar, as if she'd dreamed his whole life from pudgy, good-natured infant to bowlegged toddler to gangly young man. She knew the color of his room—blue—and the exuberant way he threw his arms around the dogs he loved. The daring glint in his eye when standing on the edge of a diving board, the sticky summer days when he and his friends lounged on the grass, too languid to talk. The clutter in his closet, the racy magazines stashed beneath his bed, tests he'd aced, a book report he'd failed to write and had to copy from a friend, an act that still shamed him.

Perhaps she jumbled a few elements, but the theme was dead on. He would have been happy either way. Any mourning left in her was for herself. For what *she* had lost. Not for William.

She left the scrapbook on the bed and walked to the pier. She looked for her father, but he must have headed up to Trudy's or to Eaton's, along with most of the sea monster patrol. Only a few diehards remained on the sand, chugging down beers and eating the ham sandwiches Larry Salamano had started preparing to go. She went to stand by them, took a few sips of a beer that was offered.

"It's out there," she said, suddenly certain. Harvey Pinkerton, who had brought down an old recliner, accounting for the labored tracks in the sand behind him, looked up. His eyes were red, but he'd stopped drinking beer. There was a pile of Perrier bottles beside him.

"Of course it is," he said.

She walked along the sand to Sea Lion Cove, to the base of the tall cliffs beneath Jenny's rickety apartment. She leaned back, tried to see the building, but there were no stars, no lights on overhead. Only the fluorescent foam on the waves gave off any glow at all. She leaned her head back, called up: "Jenny."

"Right here," a voice said behind her.

Kate jumped, found the girl inches away, hands slung in the pockets of her jeans, bare-shouldered in a tank top. She had to be shivering but it was too dark to tell. Kate reached out to touch her shoulder, but Jenny jerked back.

"You probably heard," Jenny said. "Nicole's the witch's apprentice now."

"She's got a flair for magic."

Jenny stepped back until she was lost in darkness. Kate followed, but after a few steps felt disoriented. The sound of the surf echoed around the cove, so she could not be sure where the water was, if she was stepping right into it.

"It was a fucking whale," Jenny said, her voice on the left instead of the right. "A fucking whale, and all those lunatics think Nicole pulled up some sea monster."

"Jenny—" Kate reached out, hoping to grab hold of her. Instead her hand struck rock. She was stunned to realize she hadn't gone farther than a few steps, in the wrong direction entirely, back to the base of the cliffs.

"There was this guy," Jenny said. "Some new guy. He kissed her."

"Kissed who?"

Jenny took her arm, turned her toward the one bit of light in the sky, a sliver of moon. Kate breathed out, realized she'd been sweating despite the cold.

"Nicole. It was some out-of-towner. Some gorgeous out-of-towner."

In the light of that slim moon, Kate saw the tears on Jenny's face. "Honey," Kate said. "You need to go home."

Jenny let go, vanished in an instant. Kate heard the slapping of her feet on the sand, the sound of a body hitting water.

For a moment, Kate felt an invigorating chill of liberation. She'd reached a milestone, had seen her last child into adulthood. She had the chance now to rediscover a penchant for lazy mornings, the spontaneity of a walk that went on right through dinner. She might even regain a looseness to her shoulders, the flexibility of a body that took care of nothing but itself.

For a moment, she celebrated her freedom. Then she thought of sharks and hypothermia. She thought a girl like Jenny was itching to do something dramatic, and she peeled off her own clothes to go after her.

When she first dove in the water, her legs and arms locked up. She floated just beneath the surface, swore shards of ice in the water drew blood that was quickly absorbed by the sea.

After a few seconds, she broke to the surface, forced her arms to move. She swam tentatively up and over the small breakers, then out into the sheltered swells of the bay. She called for Jenny, heard nothing in response. She imagined her nearly to Seal Rock by now and, in the darkness, didn't know which way to head. She put down her head and swam anyway, paused only long enough to call for Jenny again. She heard a distant reply, out to the right. She aimed past the gentle sighs of the bay straight into the mouth of the ocean.

She called her after every breath, heard the replies getting closer. She was stunned when she lifted her head and saw Seal Rock dead ahead of her. The rock seemed to be giving off a light of its own, steaming as if it was heated from within. Sitting naked on a crusty rock, watching her, was Jenny. And Kate realized this chase had been for nothing, that guilt was ludicrous. Loving this girl was one thing, but in the end even children were responsible for their own happiness.

Kate treaded water, her legs dangling like lead weights, her arms unable to rise past her waist. She tried to turn back toward shore, but her limbs would not cooperate. She was no longer cold, just completely exhausted. She couldn't kick her feet above the surface and even if Jenny had shouted for her, she wouldn't have heard it once she slipped beneath the water.

She wanted to struggle for the surface, but her fingers would not respond to her commands. She opened her eyes underwater and saw only blackness. Her chest tightened until it felt like she would explode, then all at once the pressure lifted. She started to feel warm and amazingly calm. She thought, as she sank, that Shirley Shulman had been wrong. All mothers were wrong. Children don't need us as much as we think they do. Children are better swimmers than we are.

For nearly twenty years, Ben had dreamt of little but fishing. Tuna runs, trolling for salmon, gill-netting, and the occasional nightmare filled with nothing but loading ice. The retired psychologist up the road had told him he'd really been dreaming about all the chances in his life that had slipped away, but Ben didn't delve too deep. Sometimes a dream was just a dream, and in the one he'd just woken from, he'd dreamed he'd been netting for rockcod when his lines went slack. He pulled them out empty and knew there wasn't a single creature left in the whole vast ocean. In the dream he panicked, but when he woke, he wondered why.

He opened his eyes, found himself alone on the sofa in his living room. He thought he smelled peppermint, the kind Kate always ate, then he saw the candy on the coffee table, wrapped in clear cellophane. He stared at it trying to figure how it had gotten there. Kate had tried to board the *Sarah Jane* the other night, but he'd told her he was busy. Nicole had been dieting, whittling herself down to Jenny's size. That left only one other explanation: He had acted out of character and put it there himself.

He stared at the candy, conceded the odds: It was safer to put to sea in a storm than to love someone. The sea, at least, would give him a fighting chance to survive, while love was going to hurt him regardless. Either she'd die or leave or stop caring, but one way or another, he'd have to live with the loss. For a moment, he stayed where he was, safe and sound. Then his mouth started watering for candy.

He picked up the mint, hurriedly unwrapped it, popped it into his mouth. He tried to savor it, but he'd been so long without sweets, he merely bit it in two. He devoured the peppermint in seconds, then had an awesome craving for more.

He checked on Nicole, then walked out onto the brittle lawn. He headed across the street toward the bay, spotted Harvey Pinkerton and his posse turning spotlights on the waves. Usually, Ben didn't give their shouting a second thought. Usually, he only wondered what he'd done to deserve a life with these people, but tonight their yelling had a higher, more alarming pitch, and suddenly Ben went cold all over.

It took forever to run to the beach, then another eternity to reach the pier where they stood pointing their lights on the bay. By then, Kate was barely above water, with Jenny struggling to keep them both afloat. Ben screamed their names, but they couldn't have heard him. He ran to his father's skiff. Someone was already there to untie the boat and push him off. Ben gunned the motor and headed toward the mouth of the bay.

The men kept their lights on the women; otherwise, he never would have seen Kate slip through Jenny's hands. Jenny barely treaded water. She cried so hard she forgot to swim. For every second it took to reach her, Ben offered up something else. First fishing, then his home, his health, any future happiness. By the time he cut the engine and pulled his daughter in, God had him down for all he owned, everything he'd ever wanted.

Jenny kept screaming, pointing at the water. Ben could only hug her once, hard, then dive overboard. His eyes burst open at the sting of the icy water, but right away he knew he'd never find her. Beneath the surface spotlight, the sea was blank. He swiped his hands, caught nothing but seaweed, and surfaced for another gulp of air. Jenny was crouched over, hysterical. He made another blind dive.

He swam down as far as he could, spreading his arms through the darkness but grasping nothing. The cold was sharp as knives and, worse than that, it stole his senses. He spun around, but in that black soup it was impossible to tell which way was up. His chest began to tighten and Kate's had to have given out long ago. Later, he would say it was his oxygen-deprived mind that brought on the hallucination of the sea monster.

The creature swam up from the depths, the phosphorescent green spots on its winged back illuminating it in the darkness. It was a full sixty feet long, wide as two gray whales, and its momentum sucked lazy fish and a woman up in its wake. Ben fought the pain in his chest and swam for her, latched on to Kate's arm just as the beast dove again, and the sea around them went black.

He guessed where the surface was and raced for it. By the time he broke through, there were four skiffs idling near his. Someone had jumped in his boat, wrapped a blanket around Jenny. He wasn't even aware of who pulled him and Kate in, but suddenly there was a blanket around him, a barnacle-like hand touching his cheek. Someone bent over Kate and breathed into her mouth.

She was lifeless long enough for Ben to begin despising the sound of idling skiffs and strong breaths. Ben pushed the man away, bent over Kate himself. He pinched her nose, tilted back her head, breathed into her mouth. He lost track of time, heard nothing but his daughter crying in the boat across from him. Then, finally, Kate came alive with a gush of water from her mouth. He turned her over while she retched it all out. Ben shivered so badly, his father put one arm around him while he guided the hushed fleet back to the docks.

They pulled up against the pier, where the sea monster patrol stood in a silent, sober line. Patrick Dodson jumped onto the pier, held out his arms for Kate. He picked her up and tucked her against him as if she were as easy to carry as one of his granddaughters. He smiled at Ben over the top of her head.

"You notice how good that skiff was running?" he asked.

Ben stepped out of the boat. Patrick Dodson might have been sixty-five, but when Ben leaned against him, he still bore his child's weight. He paused a moment, then carried Kate up to the office.

Ben found Jenny emerging from another skiff, huddled beneath a blanket Dominic Allen had wrapped around her. She started crying all over again when Ben touched her arm. She stumbled on her own words, but he understood her. She blamed herself for this. She blamed herself for everything.

He took her in his arms, was amazed at how light she was. How light and how strong. He held her so tightly she had to hush if only to breathe. He pressed his face into her hair, smelled Jeanne and himself and the sea and the scent that was all her own.

"You saved her," he said. "You kept her up long enough to survive."

She cried harder, tucked her face sideways against his heart the way she had as a little girl.

Kate was beyond cold. If she could have stopped shaking long enough to speak, she would have told Ben her blood had frozen solid. She couldn't raise a single finger beneath the blanket he'd wrapped around her, and she didn't want to. Just breathing was agony.

Her hearing was shot, too, because Jenny's sobbing sounded like it was coming from miles away. Yet she could see her, kneeling on the floor right in front of her, sobbing until Kate thought she might die from it.

"Don't," she tried to say.

Jenny curled forward, tucked herself into a ball no bigger than the pile of her wet clothes by the door. Kate couldn't move to comfort her; when she blinked, ice crystals formed on her lashes. Ben must have turned the heater up to ninety, but she was never going to feel warm again.

She couldn't feel her hands or her legs. Her toes seemed like some other entity, and were the blue of a new bruise. Despite all that water she'd taken in, she was parched. She had a craving for, of all things, Mountain Dew, slightly warm.

Jenny sat back on her heels and, if she could have, Kate would have gasped at what she saw—the face of an old woman. Jenny's eyes were swollen and, sometime tonight, one lock of her hair had turned completely white.

"I told her we're leaving," Ben said. He must have been standing by the door, but her vision was blurry, as if there was a film of saltwater over her corneas. "I've got that last trip January first, then we're heading out."

"Where?" Kate managed to say.

She didn't care about the answer. It no longer mattered what he said. If he went to Phoenix, she'd go to Phoenix. If he went to Alaska, she'd go there, too. She wasn't going to choose between William and Ben's family. She was done with intolerable choices. Somehow she'd have both.

"Boston, maybe?" he said.

Kate found him in the gloom. He was almost unrecognizable—wet, slouched, arms hanging loosely at his sides, like a man who'd been cut free and didn't know how to hold himself. Yet.

"Did you see . . ."

She saw the sparkle in his eye, the smile. She saw a flash at the window, Wayne's face pressed up to the glass.

"Ben," she said, "take me home."

He marched across the room, lifted her gently. She felt a sting where he touched her, then a thrilling warm pulse. Jenny still crouched on the floor when Wayne let himself in.

"I just heard," he said.

His gaze fell on Kate, his sweet, tender gaze, then she closed her eyes and cut him loose. Ben carried her out, but not before they heard a fisherman's promises and, a few seconds later, a young woman's cry of surrender and relief.

— 13 —

Dead Water

Jenny moved home gradually—a book a day, a jacket or pair of boots at night. She slept fitfully, sometimes waking Nicole in the dead of night with her pacing, her ultimate shuffling down the stairs and out the front door. Nicole looked out her window sometimes and saw her running down Pacifica Lane in nothing but a nightgown and flip-flops, her pale hair riding the wind like a streamer.

She kept turning the heater up to eighty, and Nicole kept turning it down. Jenny put on Megadeth, and Nicole changed it to jazz whenever she left the room, and after a while Nicole realized that all those spells she'd been practicing at Mary's must have finally kicked in. Sometimes Jenny did not even fight her. More often than not, when the phone rang, it was for Nicole.

Christmas morning, before they'd gotten up, the phone rang again. Nicole heard Jenny answer it on the first ring, the sweetness of her voice turning almost instantly to sullenness. Her bed creaked as she got up. Jenny padded down the hall, opened Nicole's door.

"It's some guy," she said. "From Cambridge."

Nicole lunged at the phone beside her bed. She should have paused for a deep breath but couldn't. Her voice came out squeaky. "Jacob?"

"Merry Christmas."

She closed her eyes, ignored the tilt of the bed as Jenny got in beside her. She shimmied to the edge, out of her sister's reach. She thought of how easy it would be to feel sorry for Jenny, to try to stop her sister's slide. How much safer it had always been to worry about someone other than herself.

She gripped the phone. "How are you?"

"Better now. I had to call."

"I've missed you."

"Me, too."

She squeezed her eyes shut, saw him clearly in her mind. Her body literally ached—her legs throbbed, she curled her knees to her chest, the muscles on either side of her neck tensed and pulsed. She thought it entirely possible that people died from yearning, their hearts simply giving out when they did not get what they wanted.

"I don't know what's happening to me," she said.

He laughed. Jenny turned on her side, sucking down the mattress so far Nicole had to hold on to the edge. "That's easy. You're starting the rest of your life."

She smiled, loosened her grip on the phone. "How's your mom?"

As he told her about the decline, the Christmas breakfast he'd brought to Shirley on a tray, none of which she could eat, Nicole slowly turned around. She found Jenny on her side, staring right at her. She spotted the last remnant of her mother in the straight line of unhappiness across Jenny's mouth, a line that had no right to be there, considering how blessed Jenny's life had been.

"I'll call again," Jacob said. "Soon."

When she hung up, Nicole saw that Jenny had perfected the art of not crying. Her eyes swelled with water that wouldn't fall, the whites turning red from the effort of holding back tears. Nicole got out of bed, walked straight to the bathroom. She took all the pills—aspirin, Sominex, even the diet pills she'd hidden at the back—and lifted the lid on the toilet. She poured them into the bowl. Jenny came in while she was flushing. It took three tries to get them all down.

"Do you think she loved us?" Jenny asked.

Nicole tossed the empty vials into the trash, glanced at herself in the mirror. All the frizz was gone now. Her acne had cleared completely. On a good day, the fishermen turned to watch her pass the docks, but it was not Mary's spells that had done this. She'd simply never believed she was beautiful until someone else said that she was.

"I think she was utterly hopeless," Nicole said. She held her sister's gaze, took her hand, and squeezed it once, hard. "And I think she knew just how tiresome that was."

"Nicole—"

"Come on, let's wake Dad. I got him an atlas for Christmas."

Years ago, when boats stopped dead in the water, prey to some mysterious resistance, captains blamed it on sucker fish, or on a coating of freshwater sticking to the hull. They tried to break their vessels free by ordering their crews forward and aft, or by shooting bullets through the glassy surface, but generally speaking, they were as good as trapped, with no walls in sight, in the middle of the ocean.

Old mariners knew nothing about varying layers of water density and submarine waves that, while creating turbulence beneath the surface, increased resistance on top. They didn't know that if they had just speeded up before entering the still water, they would have coasted right through.

Ben had always had a fascination with these pockets of stillness. On this, the last night of the year, he turned the *Sarah Jane*'s floodlights on a circle of dead water midway between the breakwater and Seal Rock. Kate touched his shoulder just as he cut the engine and glided into it. She leaned against him and he marveled at his luck. For a moment, he could stop time. Despite the fact that a hundred yards ahead of them the swells rose and fell normally, they didn't move an inch.

"Is this the calm before the storm?" Kate asked.

Ben ran a hand down her arm. They hadn't left each other's sides since he'd pulled her from the water. Twelve days straight, but that didn't mean he'd gotten used to the feel of her. He'd covered every inch of her body with his, warming her, taking her in, but he did not make the same mistake he once had, assuming he knew a woman's mind. He acted on the slightest fall in her face, responded to the least trembling, until she told him she was only cold. Until she kissed him, took his face between her hands, and said, "I'm fine."

He had not been on the water until today, had not missed it. He'd seen what his life would be like once he finished this last trip. He'd replace starkness with hedonism. He'd spend nearly every waking moment exploring the contours of Kate's skin.

"That saying is actually untrue," he said. "You'll notice that right before thunderstorms roll in, the wind always picks up. The surface of the sea often looks calm, but there are surges and submarine waves rolling beneath us all the time."

Kate left the wheelhouse, walked down to the stern. Dominic had strung a line of multicolored lights over the rail, and though the crew had rolled their eyes and grumbled, they hadn't taken them down. In fact, last night Ron Stottenmeir had stunned everyone by getting a baby-sitter and taking his wife out on a pleasure cruise, to show her how prettily the lights glowed on the water. He'd bought her a corsage, which wilted by the time they came in, and which must have set off her allergies, because by then she was crying.

Kate held her hands over the lights, studied the blood illuminated through the skin. The boat was still, but Ben's legs were so attuned to the nuances of the ocean, he could feel the dead water beginning to break apart beneath them. The wind from the northwest picked up, the current drove in, and pretty soon they wouldn't be able to stand there without holding on to something more stable than another rickety human. He'd have to get into the wheelhouse to keep the boat from slamming against Seal Rock.

But for now he merely said, "The New Year's Eve bonfire is tonight. I'd like to take you."

Kate must have heard about Jeanne, about how she'd stunned him and the whole town by showing up at the bonfire two years ago in her best dress. She'd pulled her hair up, even dusted her cheeks with Jenny's blush, and danced with him until he thought his heart might not be able to withstand it—this unexpected gift, this reprieve. Later everyone slapped him on the back, as if he'd accomplished some great feat, as if a simple night out was a triumph. Andy Gullet, whose own wife had had a fit of the blues, whispered as he left, "The worst is behind you."

Six days after the bonfire, Jeanne took the pills, but Kate still smiled when she told him yes. The dead water broke, the stern rose up the wall of a ten-foot swell and raced down the other side. Ben got the engine running just as the current started taking them toward Seal Rock.

They cruised the shoreline, past the black semicircle of Sea Lion Cove and along the town's eerie display of green holiday lights. The bonfire was already fifteen feet high. Miles Stavers and his buddies kept shooting it with lighter fluid. A stereo pounded out rap music, which only the children danced to.

Kate stood beside him as he piloted the *Sarah Jane* around the buoys. They'd been drinking Jenny's triple-strength coffee and were jittery.

"You don't believe in that tree, do you?" she said.

He kept his gaze straight ahead. "I can't believe in it and still do what I do."

She nodded. He could feel her trembling, whether from the coffee or the cold he couldn't tell. He docked the boat and tied it off. When he took her hand, her palms were sweaty.

"One more trip?" she asked.

He looked away. "Yes. I'll leave before dawn. Be back before the end of the month. You won't even miss me."

It was only then that he started to believe in premonitions. His men suffered from an excess of them, refusing to step foot on a boat they'd dreamed would sink, trembling at the sight of a sky clear of everything but a single ominous crow. Fishermen were notorious for canceling trips at the last minute, then holing up in dark apartments while somebody else faced disaster, but Ben was known for common sense. So when he got a chill down his spine, when every single inch of him went cold to the bone, he only smiled.

"Come on," he said. "I want to dance with you."

He pulled her toward the bonfire. The beach was thick with revelers dressed in their new Christmas sweaters and hand-knitted scarves, Trudy Casson's legendary spiked cider in hand. The children skewered marshmallows on sharpened sticks of driftwood and held them at the edges of the fire. Ron Stottenmeir, as always, was in charge of the blaze. He had loaded his pickup with a cord of dried fir and backed onto the sand. His son, Jack, sat atop the wood and looked petrified every time his father came near him for another log.

Many of the teenagers had already paired off and headed to Sea Lion Cove, to one of the many damp caves deep enough to lie down in. Ben searched for his daughters, spotted Nicole sitting on a log beside Mary Lemming, the two of them scratching hieroglyphics into the sand. He did not find Jenny until someone handed him and Kate a glass of cider, and even then he wasn't sure. His older daughter leaned into Wayne Furrow's shoulder as if she couldn't support her own weight. Wayne stood with one arm around her, the other stiff at his side. Ben knew that stance, knew the weary look in Wayne's eye. He could only love her so much.

Kate sipped the cider and coughed immediately. "Good God," she said.

He laughed. "J.D., bourbon, Triple Sec, and rum. A splash of apple cider thrown in for color. Trudy's been making it for years." Kate looked around, saw that everyone was drinking it as if it were fruit juice. "You get used to it," he said.

He took her hand, led her close enough to the flames to feel the heat on their cheeks. He guarded her from flying embers. Jeanne had stayed in the shadows until someone turned on "It Had to Be You." He remembered thinking there was no way she would dance, then her hand slipped into his. He remembered the feel of her tiny fingers, the way she'd winced when he'd squeezed. He'd led her near the bonfire, ignored the hush that came over his neighbors. She laid her head on his shoulder, didn't once look up at Nicole and Jenny watching them, their yearning an almost physical presence, burning into their backs.

When he and Jeanne had gotten home, he stood in his bathroom for half an hour, afraid that she'd retreat to bed, petrified that nothing had changed. By the time he emerged, Jeanne had changed into her old nightgown, the one she wore for weeks on end, and sat in the chair in the corner of the bedroom, staring out at the bay.

"Promise me you'll look after the girls," she said without turning around.

He could have hit her, could have done it and given them both a way out, but he could still smell her on him, the perfume she rarely wore anymore sinking into his skin. He crossed the room, knelt at her feet.

"I will," he said, and for a moment their eyes met in understanding. For a moment, it was the way it had been in the beginning, when he would have done anything she asked.

Now he looked at Kate, thought men were most foolish when they pretended to know what the future held. When they dared to think happiness, once attained, would go on and on.

A few couples had paired off and were dancing near the dunes. Someone turned off the rap, changed it to something softer. A dozen pairs of eyes watched him while he asked Kate to dance.

She set down her cider, took his cup from his hands. He led her near the dance floor, a twenty-by-twenty-foot stretch of beach Gwen Marmosett had raked clean—the closest she ever came to attending the bonfire. He held Kate at arm's length, just to look at her, and heard a collective catching of breath behind him. Then he took her in his arms. She laughed when his hand grasped hers, slid her arm around his neck to hold him tighter. He closed his eyes and swayed.

Through the flames of the bonfire, Jenny caught glimpses of her father—his hand pressed to Kate's waist, his mouth near her ear, his head suddenly raised in a grin or thrown back, laughing. No one begrudged him his happiness, but Jenny thought they had all forgotten fairly quickly how undeserved her mother's sadness had been. That was the real tragedy, not the suicide itself but a life so underlived it could hardly be remembered.

She stepped backward into darkness, still waiting for the euphoria to set in now that she knew her father was serious about leaving Seal Bay. Away from the fire, though, she felt nothing but the cold. She could not react to anything, not to what she'd thought she wanted or her sister's popularity or the writer's block that had come on since she'd moved back home. Not even to the look in Wayne's eyes when he snapped, "That's enough."

Since they'd pulled her from the water, she'd been frozen both inside and out. She recalled little more than bits and pieces of that night—the surprising weight of Kate in the water, her slipperiness. It had been like trying to grip a struggling fish, and after a while she couldn't do it and hold herself up at the same time. What she did remember was that moment when she gave up, when she let Kate go so she could save herself. When she realized she'd been dreading the opposite of what was true: She was nothing like her mother.

Wayne stepped in front of her, blocking her view of the flames, the only warmth. She began to shiver all over.

"Stop," she said.

"No, you stop."

He dragged her toward Sea Lion Cove like a prisoner. It was a testament to how unpopular she had become that no one stopped him. No one even looked. He had her fifty yards down the beach before she found enough energy to jerk out of his grasp. "Who do you think you are?" she shouted.

He smoked his cigarette, looked out to sea. He was a goddamn thorn in her side, that's what he was. Needling her, pricking her when otherwise she would have been perfectly content. She'd *want* to leave, she'd be dying to go, if not for him.

"You can't keep blaming yourself for everything," he said. "Contrary to what you'd like to believe, you are not the center of the universe. Neither of us is."

She scoffed. She couldn't scoff enough, he was so full of himself. "Yeah, right. Mr. Shrink."

He smiled as he dropped his cigarette in the sand. He flicked back his hair and she caught her breath. She'd forgotten how attractive he could make himself, how he could fool her into thinking it wasn't the worst thing in the world, falling for a fisherman.

"I'm just saying," he said. "Kate's a big girl. If she made a mistake in the water, it was her own. If your mother couldn't take things, she couldn't take them. It had nothing to do with you. That's what's really eating you. None of this has anything to do with you."

Jenny stomped her foot, but the sound was lost beneath the surf and the drumbeat of a dance song. "What do you know," she said, then she started to cry.

She expected him to comfort her, wrap his arms around her, use the tears as an excuse to cop a feel. But he didn't. He took a step away, turned his shoulder until she couldn't see his eyes. She cried slower, cried without tears. "I hate you," she said.

He looked her over from head to toe, then shrugged. "Okay."

He headed back toward the bonfire. Jammed his hands in his pockets, left without another word. Jenny could not believe it. When he began whistling, heat rose to her cheeks. All the boys who had competed for her affections were paired up with less prickly girls, even strangers were now more interested in Nicole. *That* was her mother's true curse—a propensity toward underliving, an ability to disappear.

"Please." She could not believe she said it. *Please,* like a little girl.

He stopped, turned back. Her heart clamored so hard, the cold finally withdrew. Her skin stung with the nearly intolerable sensation of needing to be touched. They stood in silence for what seemed like an eternity. Two entire songs passed before he spoke.

"I'm going to stand here and imagine you talking sweet," he said. "Telling me you'll miss me, that you'll be waiting for me to come back."

He smiled at her, that killer smile, and she felt one last wave of sullenness come and go. She stood her ground as long as she could, which was only a couple of minutes now. Nothing, in the whole scheme of things. Then she went to him. She wrapped her arms around him, pressed her lips to his neck. He smelled of aftershave; the sea hadn't sunk that deep yet.

"The laurel tree," she said, squeezing him tighter, holding on until neither of them could breathe.

He was the one who trembled now, yet when he pulled away, he smiled rakishly. He touched her face, bringing tears with nothing but a quick stroke across the cheek. "I'm coming back for you," he said. "I swear it."

She couldn't speak, couldn't bear to diminish his promise. She kissed him instead, kissed him until she couldn't think straight. Kissed him the rest of the night, while the bonfire devoured two cords of wood and children were carried home, sooty and asleep. Kissed him until her lips were sore and the rest of her body hungry, while her friends turned their collars up over hickeys and the fishermen trudged home, grumbling about needing to rise at dawn. Until she no longer even noticed the thorn in her side, or had the energy to tell him no one can make a promise like that.

Gerald danced with seven women. Meredith Galley pretended to swoon in his arms during a Cole Porter song. Trudy Casson, in an unusually exuberant mood, extracted cheers when she taught him the tango. He danced with girls and grandmothers until his old bones ached, until he'd downed six glasses of hard cider and realized he could no longer get drunk. He managed nothing but a warm buzz and an unusual amount of courage. He put on his jacket when the party began to clear out and headed up the hill to the Emporium.

The closed sign was up, but Gwen sat behind the counter, reading a magazine. He opened the door to the shop, setting off the wind chimes. Gwen set down her magazine, folded her hands in her lap.

"Why didn't you come down?" he asked.

She said nothing, but he could see she'd been crying. She looked miserable—her eyes red, the skin beneath her lids swollen—and the little high he'd managed wore off. He'd danced with seven women, none of them the right one.

"I don't dance," Gwen said.

He reached the counter, laid his large hands on top of it. A surge of totally sober daring raced through his blood and he looked Gwen Marmosett over from top to bottom.

"Well, you should," he said. "You're a goddamn beauty."

He held his breath, wondering what had come over him, why he'd decided to court trouble. But Gwen merely blushed like a teenager and pressed a hand against her chest.

"Gerald," she said. "Don't."

"I'd like to take you to dinner," he went on, rising up on the balls of his feet, feeling reckless, like some of the men he used to arrest for drag racing or streaking across Dodger stadium. "Somewhere so fancy, we can't even read the menus. Then I'd like to come back here and make love to you with the lights on. I want to see every inch of you. If that's all right with you."

He had never talked this way in his life, and now he had no idea why not. Gwen's cheeks flamed, but when she stood, she had a teenager's sparkle in her eyes. She put a hand on her hip and checked him over, too. She bit her bottom lip and, by God, she looked marvelous. There were twenty gray buttons down the front of her sweater he'd like to spend an hour popping open with his teeth. He was not going to be able to think straight the rest of the night while he imagined pressing his mouth to the pink skin beneath.

She had every right to slap him, but all she did was smile. "Pick me up tomorrow at six," she said.

Gerald laughed. The best part about being an old man was that he could wait. He could savor it all day. By the time he got to Gwen's tomorrow, he'd be so full of wanting, he'd look ten years younger. He'd look fully capable of satisfying her every desire.

"Don't let Kate see the tree, if you can help it."

The euphoria evaporated before he reached the door. "Ben leaves tomorrow," he said. "He's taking Dominic and Wayne."

"I know it," she said. "Damn fools."

He walked out, stared at the laurel tree as he climbed the hill to Mary's. The scar was not only weeping now, the sap had gouged out a channel in the hill. A narrow river snaked clear to the sidewalk. It seemed to have every intention of winding its way to the sea.

Gerald Frankins left the Emporium as Trudy reached her diner. Larry and Dominic walked hand in hand up the hill when she turned the key. She knew, at that very moment, half a dozen young couples were making love in the caves of Sea Lion Cove, and the amazing thing was that this revelation did not make her cry. If anything, she felt a sort of kinship with the lovers, a surprising affinity, now that she had plans of her own.

She walked upstairs, slipped out of her clothes that now smelled of woodsmoke, and opened her top drawer. Beneath her usual flannel pajamas was the white satin gown she'd splurged on twelve years ago. She'd seen it in the Victoria's Secret catalog, had ordered it one night after hours. But Patrick Dodson and Harvey Pinkerton had been at the counter when the UPS man delivered her package, and they had hooted with laughter at the Victoria's Secret box. "Whoa now," Harvey Pinkerton had said. "You got yourself some secret life we don't know about, Trudy? You got yourself some reason for *lingerie*?"

She never wore the gown, never took it out of the box until Larry Salamano came to town, and even then she only ran it through her fingers to have a good cry. But tonight she slipped the spaghetti straps over her shoulders and, when she looked in the mirror, saw herself for the first time in twelve years. She saw Trudy Casson, who liked to tango. Who could be as much a fool in love as anyone else.

She got into bed, picked up her paperback, but couldn't read over the shouting and music coming from the beach. She set the book aside, tried to watch television, but for once she couldn't concentrate on the late night chitchat. She turned off the set and sat in silence, hands folded in her lap. She closed her eyes and thought, *Please.*

When the doorbell rang, it was almost as if she'd wished it. She took a deep breath, made her way downstairs to the front door of the diner. She didn't turn on the porch light, didn't want to startle him. She opened the door, blinked, let them both adjust to the light.

When she finally made him out, it was like rushing back in time. He must have soaked in a scalding bath for hours, scoured his skin until it was the color of cherries. He'd shaved the beard, cut his hair above the ears, wore a blue suit from another era but which fit him fine. He was still as thin as the boy she remembered, aged and weathered but otherwise the same at heart. He held out a white rose, all the thorns plucked.

"Well," he said, "look at you."

She glanced down at the nightgown and laughed. She held the rose to her nose and decided she'd never smelled anything so fine, that she was going to put in a rose garden around his castle, that she was moving in, whether he asked her to or not.

"It's finished," he said. "I put the roof on your study."

He offered his arm, and though it was frigid outside, she didn't bother with a coat. She was warm the second she touched him. He'd always blended into the night and now she was nearly invisible, too, mistaken for a low-lying fog, a pocket of mist. A phantom seen only by the hopeful.

— 14 —

Oannes the Fish-Man

Ben did not pack much. He'd made this voyage countless times, never took more bait and ice than was necessary so his speed would not be compromised. Each fisherman was allowed one dry bag for clothes and personal items. Clean shirts were often sacrificed in favor of videos and cartons of cigarettes.

He had studied the weather charts, plotted the *Sarah Jane*'s course through familiar waters. The mackerel swarmed around Cedros Island, turned to wahoo by Hurricane Bank. Three times he'd filled his hold with yellowfin at Revillagigedo. Three hundred pounders were not unheard of. If he was lucky, he'd be back in three weeks.

He stood over Nicole's bed, just as he'd stood over Jenny's half an hour earlier. It was not quite dawn, but he knew she was awake. She kept her eyes squeezed shut the way she had when she was five and a spider had come into the house. Until he lifted up the tiny beast, transferred it outside and, poof, order and safety returned.

He tucked the blanket beneath her chin. "You be good for your grandpa," he said.

She wrapped her arms around his neck and pulled him down. She cried a long time, and he wished he could tell her all this longing would spend itself. One day it wouldn't scare her so much to face loneliness. One day she might even embrace it. But he no longer believed this and, at fifteen, it would probably sound to her like a threat.

"Please don't go," she said. "It's Thursday."

He sighed deeply, brushed her hair out of her eyes. "I've got to get down there before the southern fleet to get the best sets, and you know the men won't leave port on a Friday. I'm surrounded by too much superstition. I try to ignore it. You've got to try."

She cried harder, soaked his shirt with her tears.

"Honey," he said, holding her away from him, by the shoulders. "This is a chance for me to train Dominic, to hand it all over to him. You've got to trust me, let me do this. By the time we get back, Dominic will be at the helm. Deal?"

Nicole swiped her cheeks, grit her teeth the way her mother had, when he kept promising things and Jeanne kept trying to believe him. "You're really quitting?"

He imagined one day he would stop flinching when he thought of his future. The things he missed would become as manageable as his craving for cigarettes, a weakness that could be overcome with willpower and time.

"I'm only sorry that, when your mom was here, I couldn't offer the same. I'm sorry about that, Nicole."

Nicole pulled her knees to her chest, turned her head in such a way that he saw what she would become—a beauty, not as perfectly drawn as Jenny, but more interesting, physically complicated. Hungry eyes, a child's smile, the lines of her cheekbones slightly offset. She'd grow into a woman you'd have to look at twice, three times, to truly take in.

"I think it would have been worse," she said, "if she'd woken up somewhere else and still felt the same way."

He stared at her, stunned by this offering, taken aback by how generous a person she had become. He remembered when this room had been the nursery—crib in the corner, rocking chair by the window, talcum powder floating in the air. She'd been nine pounds and colicky at birth, and Jenny had thrown tantrums when her little sister had cried, enraged that she'd somehow lost her position at the center of the world. With Jenny screaming and Nicole miserable unless she was rocked in one arm, sometimes all he'd wanted was to get away from them both, to walk out of that cloyingly sweet-smelling room and be alone. It horrified him now, how many minutes he'd wished away.

"Will you marry Kate?" she asked.

He drew himself up, did not feel the guilt that he'd steeled himself for all these years. At the bonfire, when Kate had slipped into his arms, he understood why Jeanne had danced, why she'd sometimes fought her depressions with an even more uncontrollable rage. He understood why she had suffered most: Deep down, she'd known it was a privilege to live.

"Yes," he said.

He took his bag to the *Sarah Jane,* then headed up to the Merc, which Abby Grange always opened early on sailing days. He bought two bags of peppermints and the rabbit's foot Abby stuffed into his hand. She told him about the typhoon warning in the western Pacific.

"I heard it, too," he said. "We'll be well out of range."

He walked up Fahrenheit Hill, passing Scott Merkowitz, one of the men who'd refused to take this trip. The fisherman hugged Ben fiercely, but wouldn't meet his eyes. "I'll be on the docks when you get back," Scott said, his voice wavering. "First ugly face you see will be mine."

Ben watched him hurry toward home, still stumbling from last night's excesses. He would not come out of his house for days, Ben knew, until whatever danger he'd smelled in the air had passed. Ben turned toward the Emporium, spotted Gwen standing in her doorway, trying to smile at him but not doing a very good job. "You be careful, you hear?" she said.

"Don't tell me you've succumbed to the paranoia, too."

"Of course not." But she glanced down at the river of sap that was now winding past her door.

He walked to the top of the hill and Mary Lemming's blood-red front door. Just once, he was going to accept the superstition that it was bad luck for fishermen to say good-bye. He left one bag of peppermints on the doorstep; the other he slipped into his jacket pocket. He didn't knock, though he felt Kate right inside, full of hope but not a fool. Pressing her hands against the door but not opening it. Not about to take any chances now.

Kate ate the peppermints within the hour, all thirty of them. She sat on the porch and stared at that awful tree, then finally went into the kitchen where her father and Mary were smothering their sausages with honey.

"Let's cut it down," she said.

Mary shook her head. "That'll only make it worse. It'll send up a hundred baby sucker trees. It'll drown the whole damn fleet."

This morning Wayne had tapped lightly on Kate's door. He'd stood in the mist, hat in hand, like a man used to leaving. But when he'd held her, she'd felt him shivering. He showed fear the way a man did, by smiling right over the top of it, by tending to her.

"I was thinking," he said. "You'd better concentrate on your paintings now. Really belt a few out. Once William comes for you, you'll probably be too distracted."

She'd squeezed him tightly and thought, *I won't let you go.* She'd thought it the whole time he'd walked away from her, down the hill and onto the *Sarah Jane.*

Now, she tapped her foot on Mary's kitchen floor. "I don't care," she said. "I'll take my chances."

She found her father's chain saw around back, but he'd taken the chain off to sharpen it. She had no idea how to put it back on. She shoved the saw aside, whirled around angrily. Her father stood there, chewing the last of Mary's sweet sausages.

"I'll have it ready for you by tomorrow," he said. "Won't be able to work on it tonight. I've got a date."

She found it hard to stay furious when he puffed his chest out that far. "I've got to do something," she said.

He nodded. "Go see the girls."

Ten minutes later, in the house on Pacifica Lane, Nicole led her upstairs. Ben was on the radio. "He's been at it for an hour," Nicole said.

Jenny sat wrapped in a blanket on Nicole's bed, the radio beside her clicking out mostly static. Ben's voice broke in and out, unintelligible until he caught a strong signal. The sudden strength of his voice seemed to suffuse the room with the scent of brine and fish.

". . . something you should see," he was saying. "You don't even need a moon. The fish light the way. Did I ever tell you there are fish that glow? Sailors used to mistake them for ghosts or their own waning minds, but that's all they are. Glow fish. Leading the way."

He went quiet, and Nicole curled up beside Jenny. When their mother had died, they'd lost a well-tended garden and a person who understood the necessity of brightening things up. When their mother had died, things had gotten uglier, and for years that must have seemed unbearable, but perhaps now they were realizing it was not. Perhaps now they saw the truth about their father, about Kate's father, about any man whose love was, ultimately, not enough. These men were gravity. Invisible and unaware of how essential they were, the last things to tie women to earth.

"It's so beautiful," he said now, static popping between the words. "I know what you girls see. What we look like when we come back, covered in fish blood, more like our fathers every day. You don't know how we stand it. But you want to know the truth about fishermen? We not only stand it, we live to stand it. It's a different world out here. There are rules, sure, but none a man can't break if he has a mind to. You know what I'm saying? This life is fierce, and there's no doubt that's alluring. That's a siren's song. But a fisherman, or anyone else, has to know when to plug his ears and sail on by. He has to remember he lives on land, like everybody else."

Jenny curled against her sister's back. "I'm drowning," she said.

Nicole threaded her fingers through hers. The static popped, a few muffled words came through, then more static. It was a good five minutes before Ben's voice broke clear again.

"Jenny, Nikki, you there?"

Jenny reached over and pressed down on the microphone. "We're here," she said.

"Jenny," he said. "Jen." He went quiet and they heard the hum of the motor. Kate thought she heard the distant rumble of thunder, the groan of the hull as it took a wave.

"I love you, Jenny," he said finally. "I'm so thankful you came back. I want you to know—"

Jenny got up and, for a moment, her hand hovered over the radio. A month ago, a week ago, she would have turned it off, she'd have been that cruel. But now she merely walked to the corner, looked out over the sea.

"I want you to know how proud your mother was of you both. How much she envied your strength. How much she wished she could have stayed."

When there was nothing but static, Kate said, "I'd like to stay here until your father gets home. If you'll have me."

Nicole looked up. "We're okay. We've got Grandpa."

Jenny turned in time for them to catch her rolling her eyes. "We don't need anyone to take care of us. Especially not Grandpa."

The static crackled so loudly, it hurt Kate's ears. She crossed the room, put a hand on Jenny's arm. "I'm sure he knows that," she said. "I'm sure that's one reason he stays out on the bay all day."

"We've always taken care of ourselves," Jenny said.

Nicole looked down at the lilac bedspread her mother must have helped her pick out. She looked at what a girl's life should be—a purple bedspread, flannel sheets, a safe, warm place to lie down.

Ben's voice came back suddenly, startling them. ". . . the end of the line. You know what I mean?" The channel crackled again.

"Girls? I pray you can hear this. It's calm as glass out here. Everything's going to be fine."

"Stay," Nicole whispered. "Please stay."

Ben might have been nervous when they'd launched the *Sarah Jane,* but a day into the journey, he knew he'd been feeding off other people's fear. Early on the morning of January second, the sky seemed to start over, debuting in a breathtaking blue. The only clouds were along the southern horizon, too far away to mean much. The wind swept up out of the southwest, orange-scented and balmy. They were sailing back down to summer, and everything was going to be all right.

Dominic slept while Wayne took the watch in the wheelhouse. He followed the course Ben had laid out, drinking cup after cup of his own bitter coffee, brewed to the same strength as Jenny's. As usual, Ben did not feel entirely comfortable leaving someone else at the helm. He tried to sleep but couldn't, and finally came into the wheelhouse to pet Lucky, massaging the hips that gave the dog so much trouble. He added an aspirin to Lucky's food, took the wheel from Wayne.

"We won't stop until we reach Cedros Island," he said. "We can do a sixteen-day turnaround, if we have any luck. It'll be the strangest feeling when I walk off this ship for good."

Wayne finished the last of his coffee, grinds and all. "I made this deal with myself," he said. "I swore I wouldn't go east of California. I wouldn't take a single step inland, no matter what. It would be a cop-out, you know?"

Ben nodded. He knew.

"I used to dream of being a fisherman," Wayne went on. "Night after night, the same dream. Now I dream of Jenny. Last night I dreamed we were on this ranch in Texas. *Texas.*" He laughed, shook his head. "Jenny sitting on this big, wide porch when a hot, thirsty wind starts lunging at her. Still, there isn't a thing in her eyes but happiness. Not one lick of discomfort or fear. Nothing. Like a tornado could blow through and it wouldn't touch her. Like she's safe now."

Ben squinted at the sun. "Texas," he said, taking a deep breath. "I've got a proposition for you."

The moon lingered while the sun came up, skimming the ocean for an impossible hour. Ben told Wayne about the property he'd bought near Austin. By seven, it was warm enough to peel down to short sleeves. After he sold the fleet to Dominic, he hoped Boston wouldn't be too cold. They were all due for a little fair weather.

"Ben?" Wayne asked, when he realized Ben had gone silent.

"Yeah?"

The swell picked up. He turned the boat to the wave, took it straight on, saw the clouds were closer now, a thick band of them blotting out the southern sky. A fin broke the surface ahead of him, then another, a pair of dolphins.

"You ever get scared?"

Ben turned to him. Dominic had come into the wheelhouse, his crazy hair even crazier, uncombed, flaring up and out in amazing orange coils. The giant looked ahead, where the swells were rising and all the seagulls had suddenly disappeared.

"Nah," Ben said, and they all laughed.

For two nights straight, Nicole dreamt a swarm of crows attacked the wharf. The birds flew beneath the docks and clawed at the pilings with such vengeance, the pier began to fall. Whenever anyone tried to stop them, they flew right for their eyes. They filled the sea with splinters, rode fallen planks into the mouth of the bay. When the last piece of wood had disappeared beneath the water, they flew inland, boisterously triumphant, and disappeared into the hills.

On the third morning, the dream dissolved to absolute silence. Nicole opened her eyes to dust motes hovering in the morning light, defying gravity itself.

The radio was quiet. Nicole jumped up and turned it back on. She prayed for her father's voice, but instead heard Andy Gullet's.

". . . you get the last coordinates, Jim. Coast Guard picked up the final transmission over channel sixteen at oh-five-hundred. National Weather Service says it's at typhoon levels. Their EPROM's out. Haven't got a signal."

Nicole leaned against the edge of her bed. The worst was not Andy Gullet's strained voice or even the knowledge that her worst fears had been realized. No, the worst was her own lack of surprise, the way her hands went still instead of starting to shake. It made her furious, that calmness. It made her want to pick her father up by the collar and shake him.

She snatched the microphone. "Andy, it's Nicole Dodson," she said. There was silence on the other end. Silence, then a deep, quivery voice. These big, gruff fishermen were babies, when it came right down to it.

"Nicole," Andy said. "Honey. Listen to me for a minute. We had a distress call from your father a couple hours ago. A low pressure system from the north crossed a moist flow coming up from the south Pacific. Mean conditions. Thirty-foot swells. They were trying to ride it out."

"Anyone near him?" she asked. It was her mother's voice.

Calm whenever anyone else was in danger, absolutely determined not to lose a husband to the sea. And Jeanne hadn't. She'd seen to that, at least.

"The *Candy Striper*'s headed that way, but it's slow going in those seas. We're trying to contact the *Sarah Jane* again. The storm might have knocked out their radio. Their EPROM isn't working either. I'm sure we'll get a hold of your dad soon."

For once, Nicole could not hear the surf from Sea Lion Cove. She couldn't hear anything except the beating of her own heart. She left the radio on and walked out of the room. Later, she would not recall getting dressed, or any surprise she might have felt at finding the house and herself deserted. She would not remember walking to the docks, or the people she passed, most of whom had radios, too, and had been listening since the first distress call came in. She would not recall the way they looked at her and patted her arm. "Hey, Nicole." "Hi, sweetheart."

She would not remember anything except the exquisiteness of the morning. The storms and fog had all gone south, leaving behind a post-dawn sky that looked like a child's painted ceiling—periwinkle, and dotted with stars. The moon had plummeted to the bottom of the horizon and was half full, pockmarked and so rickety looking, it appeared it might fall into the sea at any moment.

Jenny sat on the end of the pier, her legs dangling over the edge. Her slim shoulders bounced up and down and, even from twenty feet behind her, Nicole could hear her crying.

She had gotten what she'd sworn she'd always wanted, the goal of any fifteen-year-old: Everything had changed. Once their father's ship went down, they'd be the ones, rather than Crazy Mary, who were to be avoided. They'd be the girls new mothers couldn't look at without bursting into tears. They'd get casseroles at first, then sympathy cards, then people would wonder why they hadn't left for college yet. Their neighbors would stare at their broken fence and dead grass, that ever-sinking foundation, and get a little annoyed that nothing was being done.

She walked to the end of the pier and sat beside her sister. Jenny had picked all the polish from her fingernails, and Nicole couldn't tear her gaze away from her ugly hands. Jenny should have stopped crying by now, if only from exhaustion, but every time she let up, she took a deep breath and cried from somewhere further down.

Nicole picked splinters out of the decking and threw them into the calmest sea they'd had for weeks. She ought to be crying, too, but she was strangely, frighteningly calm. She tried to imagine what it looked like down south, swells rising thirty feet above the boat, waves crashing over the bow and washing away anything not tied down. She tried to picture her father shouting orders, even though every time he did so, his mouth filled with brackish water. She tried to imagine him making sure his men and Lucky were safe in the wheelhouse, then tying himself to the deck to secure the rigging, as the boat rode up the back of a huge, black monster.

She tried to imagine what terror felt like to her father, but she could not. He had made sure of that. He'd never taken her fishing, and when he'd come home through fifty-knot winds, he'd talked down all adventure. He'd never given Nicole any reason to doubt his ability to stay alive, and now he would expect her to trust him. He would demand no less than her last drop of faith.

Jenny had finally stopped crying. She swiped at the last tears on her cheeks with the hem of her shirt.

"When he gets back, I'm going to kill him," she said. "I'm not sitting on this goddamn pier waiting for *him*."

Nicole waited for her to get up, but Jenny just sat there and continued to stew. Then Nicole realized she was not talking about their father.

Jenny leaned against her. It was sudden and violent, all her sister's weight on her at once, and they tipped precariously toward the sea. Nicole put her hand down on the planks to steady them. She started humming, a torch song their mother had belted out whenever one of them had suffered a cut or bruise or broken heart, as if she could out-sing their sorrows but not her own.

"It's all right," she said. "You'll see."

"I'm so tired of this," Jenny said, turning her face into Nicole's neck. "It's too hard to love people. I don't know why anybody does it."

Nicole stroked her hair and thought of Jacob. If it was this easy to love someone she hardly knew, then they were all in for it.

"He promised he'd come back," Jenny whispered.

"Dad?"

"No. Wayne."

While Nicole rocked her, Larry Salamano ran down to the docks, his face ashen, his chef's apron still on. He looked not at the sea, but at each person who'd come to wait it out. He waved his arm, taking in all of them. "Murderers," he said.

Someone gasped, but Larry was right. They could have cried and pleaded until the men tied up the boats and waited out the weeping tree. They could have somehow convinced them it was better to be safe than satisfied, but the result would have been identical: A drowning was still a drowning, whether it occurred in air or in water.

Larry stared them all down, then climbed atop the breakwater. He headed out on the rocks, charging incautiously into the heart of the bay. Every once in a while the wind carried his voice their way, and they heard him calling Dominic's name.

"Make him stop," Jenny said.

Principal Harris canceled classes at the high school. Students gathered at the docks, as though it would do any good, as if everything was not happening six hundred miles south, in the middle of a Pacific typhoon. Andy Gullet stood guard over the radio and occasionally emerged with the news that there was no sign of them anywhere.

Nicole's grandfather got in his skiff and idled along the mouth of the bay. He smoked cigarettes and kept the boat facing south. Nicole squeezed Jenny once more, then let go.

"I better find Kate," she said.

Jenny's hair had come loose from her ponytail and kept slapping the corner of her eye. She didn't brush it away. She stared out at Larry Salamano, who had reached the end of the breakwater and couldn't go any farther.

Nicole left the docks, headed up Fahrenheit Hill. Because the morning was so clear, halfway up she spotted Mary Lemming beside the laurel tree, dressed in all her witchy glory—black dress, black boots, the bottom of her cane stabbed into a wound of the laurel tree. Then Nicole started to run. She reached the bloodred front door of Mary's house and threw it open. She stomped across the empty parlor and found Kate at the kitchen table sipping coffee spiked with peppermint, as if she didn't have a care in the world.

"What's wrong with you?" Nicole asked. "Why aren't you down there?"

Kate looked up. "Down where? I came to get a few more of my things."

Nicole leaned against the wall. The tears finally came when she realized Kate didn't know. She hadn't sunk to her knees the instant the *Sarah Jane* had lurched. Her father's fear hadn't crossed the miles and pierced her body the way it ought to, like a wound they both could share.

"At the docks," Nicole said. "Dad's boat is lost."

Kate went pale and the mug spun out of her hands. Nicole couldn't comfort her, couldn't even look at her. The last thing she would concede today was that, ultimately, love was not enough.

She walked out of the room, marched up the hill to the laurel tree. "Mary, you've got to help."

Mary held up her gnarled hand. She'd gotten into the butter knives again. In addition to the stab wound from her cane, she'd made an incision clear around the trunk. Behind it, a fresh stream of amber sap oozed out.

Kate had grabbed one of her father's jackets and ran up the hill behind them. Even wrapped in Polartec, she was shivering like crazy by the time she reached the tree. "Nicole, what happened?"

Nicole whirled on her. "The boat's lost, that's what happened. Their radio's out. There's a storm and no one can find them."

Crazy Mary tapped her on the shoulder with the sticky butter knife. "No talking," the old woman said. "I mean it."

She smeared the knife into the fresh line of sap, ran her hand around the back of the tree in search of an unharmed limb. When she found one, she wielded the sap-covered knife like a paintbrush, wrote Ben's name with a flourish. Then she went over it again. Beneath it, she did the same thing with Wayne's name, then Dominic's.

"It's just a superstition," Mary said. "Let me see if I can remember it." She cleared her throat, even gave them a shy smile.

Cut it deep,
Smear the knife,
unharmed canvas,
paint it twice.
Rise up Oannes,
awake the fish-man,
calm the rough oceans
return safe to land.

Mary must have felt the heat of their stares, because she shrugged. "It can't hurt. Certain women swore by that spell whenever the tree started weeping."

"You've got to do more than that," Nicole said. "It's my dad out there."

When Mary turned, she looked so much more like an old woman than a witch that Nicole put her head in her hands. There wasn't enough magic to go around, that was the trouble. Worse than that, she'd used up all of hers on Jacob. She hadn't given her father a second thought.

Mary cradled Nicole's chin with her bony hand. "This would have happened no matter what you'd done," she said. "Haven't you been watching this tree? Can't you recognize destiny when it's oozing out right in front of you?"

Mary pulled her close and, for once, the old woman didn't smell of must and mold, but of rainwater and the sea and, if they were lucky, a typhoon in the western Pacific that was finally winding down.

"He told me he'd run the route a dozen times," Kate said. "He told me, no matter what happened, not to worry."

If Jenny had been there, she would have scoffed, but Nicole just pressed her face against Mary's chest. She didn't want to know the last things her father had said. She wanted Mary to tell her what he would say when he came back.

Instead, the old woman gestured down the hill where a dozen women were gathering. Gwen Marmosett led the pack up the hill, bundled in a man's overcoat, with Trudy just behind her, a power walker in four-inch heels. Abby Grange, from the Merc, brought up the rear, stopping every few feet to let out a small sob.

When the women reached the tree, Gwen pressed her cheek quickly to Nicole's before taking the butter knife from Mary and poking it into the sap.

"Do you know what that Wayne did before he left?" Gwen said, standing on an exposed root to rise to a clean spot. She wrote an elaborate *W,* then went over it again with more sap. "He bought every last one of my CDs. Every one. Didn't matter which artist, he just wanted me to send one to Jenny every day. Said to tell her to listen to her future, whatever that means. Some secret code, I imagine."

She went over his name twice, then handed Trudy the knife. The waitress wrote Ben's name, then Harvey Pinkerton's wife herself took extra care inscribing Dominic's. They were all so intent on their work, they did not notice the man who came up behind them. Larry Salamano stood at the back of the line with a look on his face Nicole had seen too often. The look of someone who could not be trusted around cliffs or sharp objects, a person who was just barely holding on.

Mary let go of Nicole and held out her hand. "I can smell those magnificent onion rings on you, Larry," she said. The women cleared a path, and Larry stepped forward, never taking his gaze from the tree. When he got close enough, Mary clasped his hands tightly in hers.

"I heard Dominic thinking just the other day," Mary said. "You should have heard him going on. Something about the desert. An adobe house he thought he might build."

Gwen Marmosett held him steady, Trudy Casson pressed her hand to the small of his back. Mary handed him the knife, which he dipped deep into the sap. The women formed a wall around him while he wrote, with his finest script and twice over, *Dominic Allen, my love.*

— 15 —

Song of the Seals

The benign conditions lasted all morning. Not a hint of wind, the January sunlight meek but constant, the sky a creamy azure blue. Even the grass on the north side of the Merc lost its coating of frost, and Kate spotted Abby Grange standing in the center of the lawn chanting one of Mary's spells, squeezing her eyes shut as if darkness and desire could make wishes come true.

By the time Kate reached the Church of Sea, Sky, and Salvation, the sun had hit its low, winter peak, slanting sideways through bedroom windows, bouncing off the kaleidoscopic eyes of Harvey's sea serpent and shooting back a rainbow that landed at her feet. She stepped out of the reflection, discounted this as a trick.

The doors had been left open, the voices of the women inside drifted out. Most of the men had remained at Ben's office, listening to the conditions reported by the Coast Guard. Winds above sixty knots, seas to fifty feet, air filled with foam and spray, nearly no visibility. Typhoon weather.

"Kate," Harvey Pinkerton said.

He stood in the doorway, filled it almost completely. Since the sea monster had been spotted by less fanciful souls, he seemed to have risen another two inches. The fire in his eyes had dimmed to a slow-burning calm. Though no one could confirm this, rumor had it that he no longer slept at all but walked the beach from dusk till dawn, that his mumbled prayers were surprisingly generous, for neighbors he'd once scorned, souls he'd once branded as unsalvageable. As if he was beginning to wonder if certain heavens were lonely.

After services, he stood next to Reverend Hollyhock and took the hand of anyone he might once have offended, a task that, every Sunday, took a good hour and a half. He'd even knocked on Larry Salamano's door, though reportedly Larry had refused to open it.

"Would you like to come in?" he asked Kate.

In the last few days, his voice had gotten softer, as if he'd worn it away shouting. She wondered if he was peaceful, or just the tiniest bit afraid.

"For some reason, I can only remember going to church in summer," she said. "My mother taught Sunday school in the chapel and there was no air-conditioning. When the sunlight came through the stained glass, it just hung there, purple and dusty, like a weary angel."

Harvey smiled, revealing a surprisingly boyish grin. "My wife taught the six and unders until last year. You'd have been amazed at the simplicity and thoroughness of their prayers. They'd plead for world peace and a puppy in the same breath, for the souls of their friends who did not go to church."

"I stopped going to church years ago."

Harvey moved down the steps to her side, and she realized his size had been an illusion. He was trembling, his right hand flitting against his hip.

"Perhaps that doesn't matter," he said. "Have you ever wondered if there is nothing we can do to make Him hate us?"

Kate saw the tears in his eyes, the toll it was taking on him to rethink everything—haggardness, sleepless nights, and the fear that there was too much to make up for. But when he took her hand, squeezed it, she knew he was grateful for every struggle, because in the process he had fallen in love again with God.

"Come in," he said.

She followed him into the church, took a deep breath as she entered. Candles cluttered the altar, and apparently someone had opted for scented ones because the room was a mishmash of aromas—vanilla, cinnamon apple, and balsam fir. Mary and Gwen knelt beside Trudy and Lisa at the altar. Lisa's baby carrier was propped on the front pew, the baby for once cooing, having caught hold of her toes. Kate squeezed Harvey's hand once and let go. She made her way alone down the aisle, took her place on her knees beside Mary. The old woman must have known she was coming. She'd left one candle unlit, a book of matches beside it.

Mary smiled at her, then picked up her prayer again, one that sounded suspiciously like a spell.

Kate lit the candle, watched the rising smoke in case it turned into one of those angels she remembered. By the time it dissipated formlessly into the walls of the cathedral, she was already looking up.

An hour later, Kate walked to Sea Lion Cove. She needed to hear the surf, what Ben was hearing and nothing else. She took off her shoes and waded into the water, but something must have happened to her when she'd gone under, because even that little bit of cold was agony, like knife blades through her soles.

For the first time in her life, she was afraid of the water. Riptides, sharks, jellyfish that could poison a person to death before she could cry for help. Yet Ben and Wayne and Dominic were out there, colder than she was, so she stood in the waves. Her toes went numb, her ankles an unhealthy shade of blue, while she imagined them in the middle of the sea, fifty-foot swells knocking them to the deck if they were lucky, sweeping them over the side if they were not.

She backed up, picked a spot in the wet sand where the waves still lapped at her feet, and sat. The moon seemed out of sync, because once again it rose at noon. The swells roiled in response to the sudden anomaly, seemingly trying to hurl themselves to the sky.

Like any woman, she could imagine a thousand and one disaster scenarios. The ocean had probably been calm at first, winds less than three knots, the surface almost a mirror, then from out of nowhere came a stinging breeze that raised the seas to eight feet. First the men welcomed the change, anything to take the edge off the heat and boredom. Even as the seas roughened, they didn't feel fear exactly, but more a nibbling along their necks, a rush of adrenaline every time the floor of the boat dropped out beneath them.

They might have been laughing when the boat slammed against a monster wave and stalled.

By the time the winds rose to gale force, and the engine went out for good, they had long since realized they had put to sea one time too many. Even with all their high-tech equipment, they were at the mercy of the storm. There was one moment when the three of them looked at each other—maybe Ben even said how proud he was of this crew—but after that, words were pointless. They each stood on that ocean alone.

Then came the hours of trying to keep the boat head-on to the waves, tying themselves down while the *Sarah Jane* was tossed like a plastic toy in the bathtub, inconsequential against eight-story swells. Finally a rogue wave, a mountain of water, collapsed over the boat, sucking everything and everyone down with the force of a whirlpool. Fifty feet under, they knew it was hopeless to fight for the surface, but they struggled anyway. The wasted effort poured water into their lungs, and they gasped and took in more. A vise-like pressure clamped down on their chests until they felt like they were going to break apart. Perhaps then came that moment people talked about, when the pain eased and the drowning became almost pleasant, not a struggle at all, more like a liquid dream. But probably not. Probably it just hurt until it was over. Probably, once a man's veins and stomach filled with water, he simply sunk to the bottom and was devoured by sharks and bacteria in a matter of weeks.

Kate pictured every second of this, never deserted Ben and Wayne and Dominic for a moment, but she never believed a word. She drew their faces in the sand, Dominic's inspired hair, the smile Wayne shined on Jenny, the lines around Ben's eyes. She called them up from memory, and was surprised at all the details she remembered, as if they'd risen right to the surface of her eyes. As if will alone could keep them alive.

She was staring at their portraits when she heard the singing coming from Seal Rock. She raised her head, squinted, but she couldn't differentiate between sealskin and stone. The sound was terrible—human and poignant enough to send chills down her spine. A seal answered, then another, and the screeching slowly melded into music, into an eerie fugue.

Mary came up behind her, her cane leaving zigzags in the sand that children would later mistake for snake tracks. Kate stood and took her arm, swaying to the rhythm she heard within the squealing. A dozen seals were now singing on Seal Rock, their voices rising up in one breath, then falling in a rush, like a wave. Finally, one strong voice came through.

There was no listening to that song without shivering, without thinking that she was, finally, in the right place at the right time to hear something extraordinary, perhaps not even of this world. She let go of Mary, stepped forward into the waves. Joy had probably hoodwinked her, but nevertheless she took the singing as a sign.

"They're coming back," she said.

Kate forced the girls out of the house, tugging them down to Sea Lion Cove, then back up the beach again. They complained about the cold then lapsed into a more ominous silence. As they neared the pier, Kate spotted Jack Stottenmeir up on the bluff by his house, digging for treasure with a battery-powered shovel. Half a dozen mounds of sand were scattered through the Stottenmeir's yard, various broken shovels and pails discarded around him. From somewhere in the house, the baby wailed and Lisa turned on Mozart, something slow and sad, to soothe her. A chill inched its way from Kate's shoulders to her toes. She grabbed the girls' arms and smiled.

"Come on," she said, pulling them quickly back to the house.

She hadn't touched Ray's dirty money since Shirley had given it to her. She'd stuffed the shoe box in the closet, might have donated it to a charity for children if she hadn't gotten sick just looking at it. If there hadn't been so much talk about curses. Now she knew how to break one, the only fitting ending for

Ray's sad story: Find another desperate person and give her a way out.

She left the girls in the living room and ran up to Mary's. She took the box from the closet, divided the bills into stacks of twenty hundreds then tied them off with red rubber bands. She stuffed the money into three brown sacks, and brought them back to Pacifica Lane.

The girls were still on the couch, staring glumly at the television. Kate opened the bags so they could see the money. Fifty thousand dollars divided into lumps of two thousand each.

"Shit," Jenny said.

Kate laughed and forced them back into their coats. Once on the beach, she made sure Sea Lion Cove was deserted, then scrounged up three of Jack Stottenmeir's discarded plastic shovels. She handed them out then knelt in the sand, dug down a good two feet and set in a stack of twenty hundreds. She covered the stash with sand, marked it with an X, and by the time she stood up, she had the energy of a child. She saw the girls' astonished faces and smiled. "How often do you have the chance to make wishes come true?"

For a moment, Nicole forgot what horrors might come tomorrow and ran down the beach. She picked a spot and began to dig. Jenny remained where she was, the bag crushed under her arm. Kate touched her softly, the way she'd tend a butterfly who has lost a wing.

"Wayne adores you," she said. "He's out there right now wondering how he's going to make this up to you."

Jenny struggled against tears, managed a weak smile. She headed toward the dunes.

They crisscrossed the sand, drawing elaborate Xs and marking each spot with flags of seaweed. Kate imagined the boy's face when he finally struck treasure, and Lisa Stottenmeir's amazement that would, hopefully, turn quickly to resolve. When they were done, Nicole voiced a craving for hot dogs, and Jenny didn't want to go home. Kate brought hot dogs and blankets from the house, and after dinner, they lay amongst their buried treasure and slept soundly until dawn.

Kate woke achy and cold, her hair splattered with sand. She nudged the girls, wrapped the blankets around them when they stood. Up on the pier, a crowd had gathered. Nicole let loose a little cry.

"No," Kate said. "I'd know it if they were dead."

She put an arm around each of them and was surprised by what she saw in their faces. Fear, certainly, but more important strength. They were young; they could sleep on the beach for months without doing any lasting damage. They could go forty-eight hours without food and water and still rebound.

Suddenly, there was a burst of activity around Ben's office. Someone stood at Ben's door, then a baritone hum arose from the crowd, as if they'd all hit the same low note at once. A baby began to cry.

Kate ran first, but the girls were faster. They dropped their blankets, hardly let their feet sink into the sand. The crowd parted for them, and by the time Kate reached the office, they were already coming back out.

The last of Jenny's mascara ran down her cheeks. Nicole took one step, then hunched forward and put her head in her hands.

"What?" Kate said, though she decided right then that whatever had happened, she wouldn't believe it. She'd ignore the pain even if it swelled into every corner of her head. She'd go mad before she gave in to it.

Neither of the girls spoke as Larry Salamano came out of the office, his eyes dry and not hovering too long on anything, certainly not the sea.

"Larry," Kate said, grabbing his arm.

He turned to her. All the diner odor had dissipated from his skin. He smelled now of the sea and though he would scrub and scrub in the days to come, he would never get it off himself. None of them would.

"The *Candy Striper* reached the last known coordinates," he said dully. "They found only wreckage, pieces of the lifeboat, three life jackets that had not been used. They'll put out a search, but everyone knows they're dead."

Kate squeezed his arm. "No, Larry. Don't give up. We can't—"

He shrugged her off. He headed not toward the breakwater, but back up Main Street into Trudy Casson's arms. Trudy had closed the diner yesterday, knowing no one would be able to bear the sobs coming from the kitchen, the taste of tears in the soup.

Kate looked back at the girls. Nicole was inconsolable; Jenny walked to the end of the pier where the *Jeannie* was still tied up safe and sound.

"Please," Kate said. "Please, let's not give up."

Nicole looked at her with eyes so full of anguish, Kate pulled her into her arms. "I'm not leaving," she said. "I, for one, am not going anywhere. All right? Do you understand what I'm saying to you?"

Nicole cried against her. Jenny stood at the end of the pier, looking over the edge.

He tried to will himself to sleep. It was the only thing to do, floating in what seemed the middle of the ocean, beneath a cold, slate sky. It was past dawn, had to be, but there was very little change in atmosphere, just a slight thinning of night, perhaps a rise in the ceiling of storm clouds.

He kept expecting his body to give out. This was what he waited for. Where the hell was the hypothermia? The cruel southern current allowed a fit man in a weather suit and life jacket to bob for days if it rained and he drank the droplets. It had poured during the night, and he'd tried to close his mouth, to choose the quicker option, but he'd been as unable to do that as unbuckle his life jacket.

The freak storm had passed toward land and imploded. When it washed over San Diego Bay, it would be nothing but a nice cool rain. Probably, when this was all over, people would say they'd simply been careless, or drunk. If he did not survive, no one would ever know what had happened, and maybe it would be better that way. Maybe, if he did survive, he wouldn't tell the truth anyway.

Who would believe they'd ended up with only one life jacket, down from the four they'd started with? Could there really have been that much chaos pulling on the weather suits and leaping into the lifeboat before the *Sarah Jane* sunk, so much confusion that no one noticed they carried on only one jacket between the three of them? How did he convey this without crying, without going into what it was like, three men staring blankly at one jacket, while they rode out the roller-coaster swells, while the dog swam by, lost in waves then spotted again, a dot on a crest, a struggling, lost thing? How did he explain that all the tears he shed then had not made a bit of difference to the weight of the sea, to anything?

He couldn't explain this, and he wouldn't, and that's when he realized he was going to forget. Eventually, the sun would burn through and bleach out the memories of what he could not stand—like how each of them had argued vigorously why they ought to be the ones to die, spouting outrageous claims to prove they had the least to live for, and how they had started laughing, laughing with tears streaming down their cheeks that left white trails of salt behind. Over time, he would forget the awesome quiet that came after, when the two of them put the life jacket on him, and that moment, the lowest moment of his life, when Wayne stopped fighting and took up the burden of living for all of them.

He would never remember that last rogue wave, the one that pulverized the lifeboat and sent them all flying. Or what it was like when he bobbed to the surface and only Ben could be seen. He had gone to him, held him above water until a monster wave ripped him from his hands. Wayne had called out, "A ship will come. Hang on. Storm's almost done," even though he'd lost sight of the man to whom he owed everything and it didn't matter what the storm did. It was almost evening and they had drifted away from the last location of the ship, where it sank.

He would forget that last horrifying image, when he spotted Ben on a crest, eyes wide open, eyes burning, at the last moment, with the desire to be wearing that life jacket, wearing that life. And the moment when Ben squeezed them shut on that useless knowledge and swam down the other side, a strong man reduced to a plaything. A rag doll tossed between the teeth of waves.

He decided to forget everything, and this was already beginning to work. He had started with his name. He didn't want only one. He had to live for all of them, so he would be all of them, Benjamin Wayne Dominic Allen Dodson Furrow. He'd raise girls and love two women and one man.

When the clouds finally cleared, the sun was halfway up the sky. It blinded him, thank God, to the wreckage still floating about. He leaned back, kicked his feet, floated. In no time at all, though it might have been hours, even days, everything grew hazy. His arms blended into sky, the sky into horizon, so he didn't see the boat until it was nearly upon him. Until people he knew were shouting one of his names.

Jenny walked to the summit of Mt. George and back. Walked as far as the beach would take her, until the cliffs and high tide blocked her path. Walked up and down the streets of Seal Bay, then out to the woods, where she stumbled upon a castle, imagined laughter within its walls. She pressed her head to the cool boulders, against the intricately drawn *T* in Trudy's name, and decided she'd gone crazy. She prayed she'd gone crazy, so that nothing seen or told to her was guaranteed to be true.

She walked back to town, already dismissing the improbable visions. She plucked one of the yellow ribbons her neighbors had left on a lilac bush and twisted it around her ring finger. If she were braver, she'd wish for a life without love. That would be the smart request, so that twenty years from now she wouldn't find herself in Kate Vegas's position, clinging to memories and those five pounds she'd never lost after childbirth, clinging to the little she had left. If she were brave, she'd wish for loneliness, but when she neared her father's office, she slapped her pockets and wasted her wish on a cigarette, anything to take the edge off a relentless headache.

She eyed the gloomy crowd who pretty much lived outside her father's office now, then slunk around to the alley. She'd sneak in the back door and snatch some of Andy Gullet's Marlboros. She had the door halfway open when Andy spoiled even that meager plan. He stumbled into her path, trash bag in hand.

He took one look at her and dropped the bag. "Just hold on," he said, then ran inside.

They were all crazy, Jenny decided, as she leaned against the orange-and-green walls Kate had repainted. All she wanted was a cigarette. She swore that was all she was asking for. Andy came rushing back out, paper bag in hand. He held it up to her mouth.

"Now just breathe," he said. "Easy does it."

She stared at him incredulously. As if breathing could help her now. "I'm fine," she said. "Jeez."

"I understand," Andy said. "We all cried ourselves to sleep last night."

Jenny's eyes burned as she pushed away the bag. She stomped off without another word and was grateful, for once, for the sting of the sea breeze. It dried the last of her tears.

She walked toward the docks. Alice Gwynn stepped out of the crowd to try to hold her, but Jenny evaded her easily. Miles Stavers had the gall to call her sweetheart, and gesture her over. Jenny turned her back on him, spotted Nicole and Kate huddled together on a bench, the way they'd been huddled together ever since the wreckage had been found. Jenny stared at them with a mixture of longing and disgust. She could not bear to let anyone touch her now.

She was halfway down the pier when Andy Gullet flew out the front office door. She rolled her eyes, expecting another paper bag or fancy breathing apparatus, but he merely knelt down in front of Kate and Nicole. His hands flew as he talked, but the breeze blew his words the other way. Finally, he searched the crowd for her.

He started for her quickly, then slowed his pace. For the last couple of days, they'd all done that, like she was a deer who might bolt or die of shock. As if she was as fragile as that.

"They picked someone up from the water," he said. "There's some confusion which one. Some of the guys down south swore they knew him, but he's insisting they've got it wrong. Anyway, the point is they found one. And if they did, maybe we'll find the others. Maybe everything will be all right."

Jenny went still. Alice came up beside her and said something no doubt encouraging, but Jenny couldn't hear what it was. She looked down the pier at Kate, who was rocking Nicole from side to side. She took a good look at her face, then pushed Andy aside.

"You don't think it's Dad," she shouted.

Kate had been crying and now tried to hide it. She tilted her head back and forced a smile. "Of course I do. I think it's all of them."

"How can you even say that?" Nicole said to Jenny. "It's got to be Dad."

Jenny ignored her. "You're lying," she said to Kate. "I can see it in your eyes."

"Jenny—"

"Don't 'Jenny' me! Don't even talk to me." She stiffened, disgusted with all of them. She knew exactly how Kate and her father had talked before he'd left. Exactly the way she and Wayne had, when he'd said he was going and, despite the weeping tree, despite the fact that he was the first decent person to think her decent, too, she'd said, "Fine. Go." All fools, taking such chances with each other. So careless with the most important moments, so casual with good-byes.

"Jenny, no one blames you," Kate said softly.

Jenny whirled on her. Kate was the worst, already knowing, more than anyone, how much there was to lose. Knowing how quickly a person could slip right through your fingers.

"Shut up," she said.

She wanted to turn away, but Nicole had folded herself down to the size of a little girl, pressed her knees to her chest. Her throat was not working right—only weak, dry sobs came out.

"Goddammit, Nikki," Jenny said. She took her sister's hand, yanked her to her feet. She grabbed her shoulders, made her stand straight. She shook her until her crying turned to whimpers of pain. "Stop crying. You're a woman of Seal Bay."

Nicole's eyes widened, as if, with that realization, she might merely cry more. But she stilled herself, bit her bottom lip until it stopped trembling. She didn't say a word until she could meet their gazes directly, as stoic and silent as the rest of them.

"Okay?" Nicole said.

If she were braver, Jenny would wish to be sisterless. She'd walk away without a glimmer of admiration in her eyes.

But she stayed. She let men keep their bravery. She slid an arm around Nicole's waist and held on.

"Okay," she said. "Now we wait."

— 16 —

Flood Tide

Kate led Nicole to the end of the pier where the railing had broken off, another casualty of wet rot. The depth of the water below was fifteen feet, surely deep enough to drown a small child or a drunk, but Nicole told her no one had considered replacing the balustrade, or even hanging up a rope.

"People here don't die that close to shore," she said.

They took the precarious seat at the end of the pier, with a clear view to the southern horizon. Jenny had refused to join them; she'd silenced the crowd with her paleness and had gone back home to wait. For forty minutes, Kate listened for the hum of a ship's motor. Nicole had hardly blinked, hadn't rested her head on Kate's shoulder until the *Candy Striper* came into view. Then she whispered, "Please."

A crowd gathered behind them, talking loudly at first then tapering off to whispers when Larry Salamano took up a solitary position behind one of the storage boxes.

Nicole got to her feet as the *Candy Striper* passed the buoys, but Kate couldn't stand. She kept commanding her legs to function, but while the boat crawled maddeningly slowly toward the docks, she felt heavier, more like liquid, until she would have sworn pieces of her slid through the slats in the planks to the water below. She wondered what they were doing on board, why no one stood on deck to give them some indication of how much joy or sorrow they were in for. Finally, the ship docked, the men on the pier tied her to shore, and Andy Gullet hopped on board. A tense silence followed. Lisa Stottenmeir's baby cried and three ladies shushed her at once. Nicole worked her way through the crowd, hands clasped in front of her. It was taking far too long for Andy to bring the man out, and that was when Kate knew sorrow had neither boundaries nor mercy. When she was glad she was sitting, because otherwise her legs would have given out.

Finally, the door to the wheelhouse opened and a murmur raced through the crowd. Andy brought out a man wrapped in a brown blanket. There was a slow gasp from the crowd behind her, then Nicole sank to her knees and began to cry.

Wayne swayed in the face of so much disappointment. He set foot on dry land and met the eyes of the girl who would have traded him in a heartbeat for a father. He withstood the silence of the man who would always blame him for the quiet and the cold. He reached out a hand to Larry, who ignored him and walked away. Kate stumbled to her feet, pressed a hand to Nicole's heaving shoulder, then ran past. She took Wayne in her arms, clutched him tightly, and knew that somehow Ben had seen to this. He had made sure *this* child came home.

She kissed Wayne's icy cheek, broke off the slivers of ice clinging to the tips of his hair. "I love you," she said. "Jenny's at home."

"She'll hate me."

"No. She'll only wish that she could."

Nicole's sobs grew louder, and Kate had to let go of him. She knelt down beside Nicole, gathered her on her lap. She closed her eyes, but this time the world remained steady. She could move if she had to. She could still her own tears. She didn't love Ben any less, but twenty years ago she'd had no one left to be strong for. Back then, there'd been no one who was hurting more than she.

Half the town escorted Wayne to Jenny Dodson's doorstep. They held the blanket around his shoulders, shielded the wind from his face. After the initial surprise that he'd been the survivor, after they'd been chastised by the look in each other's eyes, they'd welcomed him home. Someone had jammed a cup of coffee in his hand, squeezed his shoulder, offered him one of the yellow ribbons that had been tied to the lilac bush. They'd bitten their lips to keep from asking too much about the others. They all took turns touching him, then, to a man, pulled back from the iciness of his skin.

They stood on the curb while he knocked. When Jenny answered the door, they stepped back and, without a word, returned to the docks.

Wayne Furrow stood on the porch, still cold as ice but not as amnesiac as he would have liked to be, well aware that he had nowhere else to go but here. It wasn't the gouging of the weeping tree that had given him the power to ruin lives, but love. If he'd felt anything less than total devotion, he'd have jumped ship and left Jenny to fend for herself. One less drop of commitment and he'd be a coward, his back turned to the things he'd done, indifferent to any pain but his own.

But he loved Jenny Dodson, and when she looked at him, when she saw who was alive and who was dead, he broke her heart. She didn't look behind him, to see who else might come up the path.

"Jennifer," he said, and she blinked. She turned and walked back inside. She wore a red flannel nightgown that fell past her knees and black wool socks. She sat on the couch and pulled her slim legs up beneath her.

He let himself in and sat down beside her. Sometime on the boat ride home, he'd started throwing up seawater. He hadn't taken in much, but he still heaved up a bucketful of green, foamy brine. He had gotten a pain in his left leg, just like the ones Dominic Allen used to complain about. He started to feel a little afraid.

Now that fear was making him delirious. Although he'd never entered this house before, he knew every object in the room. He recognized the portrait of the girls with their mother over the fireplace, and an old pipe, the end marred with teeth marks, on the mantel. He knew, if he got thirsty, he'd find only Tang and Diet Coke in the refrigerator, and that if he wanted to get drunk, all he had to do was go down to the basement, where there was a stash of vodka and two remaining bottles of the Robert Mondavi Merlot Jeanne had once enjoyed.

He knew everything about Jenny. Surprisingly, she'd been the shy one as a toddler, clinging to her mother's pants, refusing to meet the eyes of strangers. It was only when she'd been alone with her parents, the center of attention while Nicole slept in her crib, that she'd come to life, danced and preened and insisted she was a princess named Nambia. When they'd laughed, she'd put her hands on her hips and glared. "I am not pretending," she'd said. "This is not pretend."

In the early years, she had adored her mother, and Ben had been grateful for that. Grateful and ashamed that he did his best fathering while she lay sleeping, when he could explain about tides and currents to his heart's content, imagining he had something to offer her, too.

The last thing Ben had said before Wayne had let go of him was "Watch out for Jenny." As if that hadn't been his whole point since the moment he'd first seen her.

He reached over and took her hand. She struggled a little, but he didn't let go. There was no way he was letting go now.

Finally, her fingers went limp. She began to cry softly. He released her hand and put his arm around her shoulders. She fell into him and he sighed deeply, a different sigh than he'd ever made before, deeper, longer in coming, accompanied by the salty breath that comes from the mouths of longtime fishermen.

She cried for an hour straight. He patiently watched the clock, amazed at her depth of feeling, stunned that both of them had been able to keep so much hidden and not explode.

He held her and whispered in her ear, "I love you, Jennifer. I love you. Love you. You." And every time she heard it, she shuddered a little less, until by the end of the hour she took the words in quietly. She finally believed them.

Then she led him to her mother's garden, stark this time of year except for the elderberry bush that would not go dormant. The plant ran rampant even in winter, yielding copious amounts of blue berries that the neighbors and birds could not finish off.

"For a while," Jenny said, "my mom was really into gardening. She ordered rare seeds, bought only the hardiest stock, the plants that could take sea salt and relentless fog. She mixed her fertilizers herself, refused to ration water even when the well up on Fahrenheit Hill went dry."

Wayne looked at the unyielding ground, moist on top, solid rock an inch down. "She babied those plants," Jenny went on, "and almost all of them still died."

"I'll never forgive myself," he said.

She twisted off a fruit-laden branch, handed it to him. The scent was overpowering—sweet and fecund, as if it was still growing in the palm of his hand.

"Then almost casually one day, she bought this tiny, sickly looking elderberry. It was like she couldn't bear to invest herself in anything better. She didn't amend the soil when she planted it. Didn't water it once. Now look at it."

"I can't believe I hurt that tree," Wayne said. "Can't believe that was me."

Jenny closed her eyes, wrapped her arms around her waist. For a moment, there was nothing but the roar of the surf between them, a relentless rumble. Then she opened her eyes.

"That tree was cursed long before you arrived," she said.

"Jenny—"

"She wanted roses so badly, but only the elderberries would grow. She could never accept that the garden had a mind of its own. The things that survived were those that should be there."

Wayne looked at the vibrant bush, and at her. The scent of the elderberries made him unsteady. It seemed almost ghastly to feel such joy.

It was ironic and a bit frightening to give the girls sleeping pills, but otherwise it seemed they might stay awake forever, Nicole weeping, Jenny blank-faced, limp in Wayne's arms. Nicole looked horrified when Kate handed her a tiny red pill, until Kate told her it was just for the night, that she'd throw out the bottle tomorrow to prove the point.

Kate put them in their own beds, but when she went up to check on them, she found Jenny in Nicole's room. They were a heart shape on the bed, their heads tucked together, the comma curls of their bodies meeting in a tangle of feet. Despite the weight of sorrow in the house, she savored the look of them, slowly running her gaze over the tangle of hair on their pillows, the solidness of their limbs. She imagined that, even when she'd first gotten him, even at the height of her guilt, Shirley Shulman had done the same. When she'd seen William sleeping, something hot and painful must have struck at her heart, something she could not defend against and would have dared anyone not to call mother love.

Kate walked downstairs, where Wayne stood at the front window. His hair would not dry. There was no explanation other than the irrational—seawater was oozing from his pores.

"Hear that?" he asked.

She stepped up beside him, cocked her head to listen. She heard nothing but the pounding of surf.

"It's wind," he said. "Wind like you hear when you're just below the surface of the water. Kind of like muted screaming—someone shouting with their hand held over their mouth."

Kate slipped an arm around his waist. There were still search and rescue helicopters scouring the area around the wreckage, but they had not found any signs of Dominic or Ben. They had, unofficially and quietly, changed the goal of the mission to search and recovery. Kate understood that they had to remain reasonable, sending out the older, steadier men where they thought the bodies might be found. None of their efforts, however, took into account the lifelike dreams she had of Ben at night. The lingering sound of his voice when she opened her eyes—so real and tangible she felt his breath on her ear, the raising of gooseflesh.

No one had mentioned funerals, not after they'd seen the look in her eyes. Larry Salamano had driven south, where he'd been picked up by the Coast Guard and taken out to see the wreckage. No one expected him to come back. Patrick Dodson could not stay in the house for more than twenty minutes at a time. He spent most of his time on his skiff, going farther each trip and not fishing at all. Just looking out where his boy had been lost, just staring at the sea.

Wayne's shoulders curled forward and he ran a hand along the back of his neck.

"I keep seeing their eyes," he said.

He stiffened, but couldn't support it long. He slipped back down to his shell and kept staring south, back to that moment when their lives had to end so his could go on. He said nothing.

"Then I'm sure you saw what was in them," Kate said. "Courage and relief, I'll bet. They got the chance to save you."

He was crying now, the way fishermen always do, with tears that could pass as sea spray, with such subtlety no one could be sure. She tucked him into her as if he were six and had suffered little more than a skinned knee, a defeat in Little League.

Later, she found Ben's father in the kitchen, staring into his coffee. Patrick's fingers were red and cracked, and she wondered if it hurt him to use them, if everything hurt, and what it must be like to never tell another living soul you were in pain.

She put her hand on his arm. He was old and weather-beaten, and worse than that, he was not giving up. He looked exactly the way she had looked eighteen years ago, when she'd refused to believe she had lost her son for good. When she would rather have died than believe it.

"Can't drown at flood tide," he said. "Everybody knows that. Fishermen can't drown at flood tide."

He stood up abruptly, put on his cap. "If you're staying," he said, "I might head on south. Take the skiff down near the wreckage. You know about Fairweather Island?"

Kate shook her head, and Patrick began to smile. "Down current from the wreck."

"Patrick . . ."

"Don't tell me, little lady. You, of all people, should know better."

She squeezed his arm, made him a sandwich to go.

Later, when she climbed Fahrenheit Hill, she found her father and Gwen Marmosett on the porch, a variety of saws around them. "It may take a while," Gerald said. "The wood's surprisingly hard."

"I've always hated that tree," Gwen said. "Even before it got mean." She kissed Gerald good-bye, a shockingly lush kiss, one that got Kate's father humming.

Gerald picked up the chain saw and followed Kate to the laurel tree. He flicked on the ignition switch, checked the gas mix, pulled the cord three times before the saw revved up. As soon as the blade hit bark, the teeth stalled and the air ripened with the scent of spice and toxins. Kate imagined curses flying everywhere.

The trunk was hard as basalt. They went through the three blades they had just slicing halfway through, then there was nothing to do but go at it with an ax. Gerald hacked out a V, set his weight against the corkscrew trunk. Kate joined him, shoving with her shoulder, and at last there was an ominous pop, a crackling as joints were severed and the tree began to fall. Mary Lemming had come out on her porch to listen, and the tree fell less than a yard from her feet, sap rocketing as far off as the Emporium, where it splattered against the fire-truck trim.

All night long, Gerald cut rounds from the laurel tree and Kate split the logs. She was glad for the green wood, the hardness, the seven or eight swings of the maul it took to start a split in the wood. By morning, her arms were shaking and she could no longer lift the splitter. Ron Stottenmeir arrived in his long bed. He loaded the wood without a word, didn't show a hint of panic until Mary got into the cab beside him.

"I want this burned by nightfall," she said. "I want to make that clear."

Kate stood on the top of Fahrenheit Hill as Mary and Ron went door to door. They handed out half cords and instructions, and within the hour, the sky was the color of an oil spill, scented with gasoline. The few who ventured out did so with scarves across their noses and mouths.

Kate stood beside the stump of the laurel tree, fearing reprisals less than she feared fear itself. The stump, surprisingly, was clear of sap, and the width of two people. She sat down and finally let herself cry.

Nine-year-old Jack Stottenmeir glanced at the four women climbing into the outboard, then turned back to his digging. His mother sat up near the dunes, holding his perennially screaming baby sister, Melinda, who had turned out to not only have no interest in playing saber-toothed alien warriors with him, but who also drooled like a Saint Bernard and slept in a crib beside his bed and wailed all night. Sometimes he wanted to thump her with his lightsaber, and other times he wished he was big enough to pick her up and tell her it was all right, everything was all right, jeez louise.

His mother shackled the baby in blankets, and finally the screams turned to bearable whimpers. Jack grabbed his latest prize—the battery-operated shovel his mother had bought him a week ago, after she'd sworn he'd never hear those words again, the vicious things mommies and daddies sometimes called each other. After his father had squeezed his voice down to something more chilling, a cautious whisper, as if his mother was an explosive, and any sudden movement would set her off.

Not even mean Marvin Wench had a shovel like this. The Super Scooper could dig to a depth of six feet with the flip of a switch and—his mother had luckily overlooked this part—convert its handle into a pellet gun.

He'd gotten every kind of shovel imaginable since his parents had started fighting. One of them always found him in the closet, where he hid with the quivering dog, then took him to Hansen's Toys for restitution. He had real metal shovels and garden hoes, twenty-six pails, and a crinkly old treasure map, obviously fake, because the clues led him to the Merc instead of to buried treasure. He had books on Captain Cook and Treasure Island, and an awesome pirate costume he wore every Halloween, but what he really wanted and never got was quiet, a good night's sleep.

He turned off the switch and reached his hand into the pit. As Melinda's cries tapered off, his adrenaline raced. He hadn't walked more than fifty steps from his mother when he'd spotted this X. He couldn't believe it. How could he have overlooked something so obvious, so close to home? Wait till that butt-faced Marvin found out! Wait until he held out a handful of rubies and told his father he never had to sink a line again! *Then* they'd stop calling each other names. *Then* his mother would have what she wanted, and there would be peace in his house.

He'd already dug down two feet, but all he'd discovered was more sand and the empty shell of an ancient Pismo clam. He dug with his hands, finally tapped something more solid than sand. His heart jumped so abruptly he felt it, a bird's wing against the inside of his chest. A couple of years ago, his mother had banned him from watching television, even told him his fantasies weren't real. Bluebeard was a legend and Captain Hook a cartoon. Peter Pan had sprung from a man's imagination; *everyone,* she'd said emphatically, grew up. He'd cried so hard, she'd cried, too. She'd brought back the shovels and told him he could keep on digging for treasure as long as he got his schoolwork done.

She was wrong about Captain Hook. The pirate *was* real. Everything was real. They had a sea monster in their bay, didn't they? And before he'd outgrown that kind of stuff, he'd seen an angel perched outside his window in the shape of his grandfather, looking unusually fit and sporting a new crop of black hair. Why not buried treasure here and now? He reached into the hole and pulled up a stack of green bills, tied together with a rubber band. Then he sat back on his heels.

He was monumentally disappointed. This was treasure? A couple week's worth of allowances, a few zeros, a stack of bills? Jeesh. He was about to throw the wad back into the sand when he heard some commotion behind him. He looked over his shoulder and couldn't believe his eyes. His mother, who had never done more than a slow trudge through the aisles at the Merc, was flying down the hill, running like Michael Jordan, for crying out loud. Who knew she had such speed? Her hand flew to her throat, and her face for once was eager, not crumpled up like the old rag dolls he had *never* played with. He handed her the bills, and though they weren't rubies, it didn't matter, because he decided right then to give them all to her.

She fell to her knees. She stared at the treasure in her hands, then back at him, then she started to laugh. An incredible laugh, like nothing he'd ever heard before. Not a mother's forced chuckle, a pretend giggle at one of his jokes, but a laugh she might have belted out ten years ago, when things were more funny. A laugh he didn't doubt for a second, it was so boisterous and rich. She tilted her head back and he could see clear down her throat. Even when she stopped laughing, he kept on hearing it; laughs like that, he thought, last forever.

She got to her feet, lifted him into the air. She swung him around until they both might have been sick, but they were laughing too hard to care. "Lucky Jack," she sang. "My lucky, lucky Jack."

He felt lucky for the next hour while they searched the sand, finding more and more Xs, wads and wads of treasure. Until his mother finally perched herself on a dune with the baby to count her money. Until she glanced one last time at Fahrenheit Hill and wrinkled her nose at the awful stench still belching from people's chimneys. Until she caught him scanning the bay for his father's boat and forcibly turned him around.

"No more of that," she said, flicking the bills, getting a light in her eyes that transformed her, that took them away then and there. She took his hand and held on tight. "No more."

When the excited voices echoed off the sand, Mary Lemming smiled. At least someone was having fun. She'd tried spell after spell to pop the gloom of the last few days, but she had finally run out of jingles, and anyway none of them worked.

She leaned back against the uncomfortable lip of the skiff and closed her eyes. It had been years since she'd allowed herself a ride on the ocean. She'd always had a theory that the first time she stepped foot on a boat, she'd drift directly to the place where her no-good husband was hiding out. She'd land on some deserted island that was no longer deserted but populated by big-breasted, giggly girls who thought Sam Lemming was the greatest. She'd have to go about the process of pseudo-killing him all over again.

Oh, she knew that was crazy thinking, but it was also a pretty good story. She liked to think about it once in a while.

Kate steered them toward open sea, the way Mary had instructed her. The girls remained silent, huddled together in the front of the skiff. In time, they would let her wrap her arms around them, they would be comforted by wisdom. But for now, Mary knew, all they needed was someone strong to cling to. She had laughed at their stunned thoughts when this had turned out to be each other.

Mary opened her eyes, looked through the hazy darkness that contained what was left of her sight, and decided they were far enough. She saw nothing but gray sea, smoky sky, and the blurry faces of three sad women.

"All right," she said, rubbing her brittle hands together. She'd forgotten how much she loved this—taking center stage, announcing that something spectacular was about to happen before their very eyes. She might not be a true witch, she might make up every spell on the spot, but at least she wasn't sitting around letting life run a truck over her. The power had never been in her love potions of milkweed and honey, but in the fact that she wouldn't tolerate helplessness. No matter how desperate the situation, she could think up something for people to do.

She reached into her bag and pulled out the things she'd asked Kate to gather. One of Ben's shoelaces, to tie him to life, an old photograph of him and his daughters, to remind him of what he'd be missing. A piece of cloth from his favorite shirt, blue-and-black flannel, to lure him back to comfort.

She gave the lace to Jenny, the photo to Nicole, and the flannel to Kate. Kate was so dry-eyed it must have been killing her, but the girls had been crying the whole time.

"That's enough," Mary snapped at them. "Really, I'm ashamed of you. Don't you believe in anything?"

None of them dared to answer her. Mary closed her eyes again, dipped her hand into the water, and touched it to her lips.

"You do the same," she said. "That's Ben and Dominic in there. That's all of them in there."

She felt them hesitate, but she didn't open her eyes, didn't dare see their doubt. Of course this was ridiculous—part old wives' tale, part her own imagination. It was ridiculous, yet she'd done it for Wally. And what she'd never told anybody, what she never would, was that right before she went to sleep each night, she felt a weight sink into the bed beside her. She heard a slow intake of breath, a chuckle, and that was the only reason she'd ever been able to sleep.

"Go on," she said, and she heard them splashing, kissing the sea. "Now you have to lure him back."

She opened her eyes and gestured for them to toss their treasures overboard. Not one of them could do it.

Mary shook her head. "You're just girls. Even you, Kate. Just girls, thinking a man can be found in the things he left behind. Thinking you know everything, that death is some cliff, and at the bottom of it nothing. Don't they teach you anything in school anymore? Haven't you heard the world is round, there is no end to it, and the sky goes on forever? Haven't you been listening to Patrick Dodson? The man hardly says a word, so when he talks, you'd better listen. Men cannot drown at flood tide. It's a known fact."

"Mary, I don't know if this is right," Kate said. "I'm trying . . . I couldn't bear to give the girls false hope."

Mary glared at her. "Shame on you. There's no such thing. You think a person's got to let go. There's books on it, all those depressing stages. Well, let me tell you something: *I don't buy it*. To hell with acceptance. Love is not something you get over. Why would you even want to? Why wouldn't you want to cry your eyes out some nights, when you want him so badly it hurts? What's wrong with that, is what I want to know. Of course we have to go on. We're the women; that's what we do. But why can't we wake up in our beds at night, sure he came to us while we were sleeping? I'm telling you, life gets lonely fast enough. Why not share it with a ghost or two?"

She skimmed her fingers across the water. She was ancient by most standards, but not too old to imagine her children's hands suddenly grasping hers and pulling her down to some amazing world below the sea, as amazing as the one above it.

They watched her, then Kate, finally, kissed the flannel and dropped it overboard. Nicole tossed over the photo, then put her head in her hands to cry. Jenny snorted as she flung her father's shoelace as far as it would go. "That was, like, so stupid," she said.

Mary cackled. Later, when it happened, when Jenny felt a tickle along her cheek, or got a whiff of her father's scent on a crowded street, it would be all the more remarkable. It would prove what Mary had known all along: No one had the slightest clue what would happen next.

* * *

Larry Salamano came home late one night to pack. He'd seen the site where Dominic had gone down; he'd thrown a wreath on the sea. He'd dared every last man on that Coast Guard ship to talk to him about the kind of love that counted, but they'd kept their gazes averted every time they'd fished another shredded scrap of fiberglass or oilskin from the sea.

He packed his clothes in less than an hour, then grabbed a crowbar from the garage. He spent the rest of the night prying plywood off the windows. By dawn, light reached his bedroom for the first time in a year, and he was too exhausted to care. He put his suitcases on the front porch and, despite the frost on the grass, lay down right in the middle of his lawn to watch the sky change from black to blue.

When he saw the man's shadow, he didn't move. It fell right over his face, and with the sun so low in the sky, whoever it was appeared to have Dominic's giant proportions—tree trunks for arms, a mountain range for a torso. When the shadow held out its oversized hand, Larry began to cry.

The shadow knelt, and Larry looked into the haunted eyes of Wayne Furrow. He jumped to his feet, his tears stopping instantly. Suddenly, he couldn't get out of Seal Bay fast enough.

"I had this dream," Wayne said, following him to the porch. Larry grabbed his suitcases, lugged them to the trunk of his car.

"Larry," Wayne said, grabbing his arm. "You want to hear this."

Larry jerked him off, slammed the trunk. "Don't tell me what I want, because believe me, you have no idea."

"It was more than a dream. I could smell the acacia trees. Taste the dust in the air. More like getting stuck in a moment in time than a dream."

Larry shook his head. "You can keep your dreams and your weeping tree. What good is magic if it never does any good?"

He walked around the car and opened the door. He got in and started the engine, but Wayne had already lowered himself into the passenger side. He stretched out his left leg, massaged it above the knee.

"It was of Santa Fe," Wayne said.

Larry leaned his head back, gripped the steering wheel, then just let go. He turned off the engine. "Shit," he said.

"You're there," Wayne said. "Living in this tiny adobe house. It's on a quiet side street, a corkscrew willow in the front. It's got only two bedrooms, but these incredible foot-thick walls. You hardly ever come out. Then one day someone bangs on the door so loudly, it's like he's knocking with a giant's hand. And your heart starts to pound."

Larry didn't dare look at him. His heart was pounding *now*. How could any man resist a story like that? How could anyone, even a cynical, slighted, lost soul like himself go on living without believing in his own happy ending?

"Go to hell," he said, but Wayne only laughed.

"It's on Red Rock Lane," he said. "They'll be asking two-eighty, but offer them two. They're desperate. Some kind of business problem."

"You're cursed, man," Larry said, looking at him straight on for the first time since he had stepped off that boat, alive.

"Don't I know it."

But Wayne Furrow was also smiling, and the cramp in his leg appeared to have subsided, because he hopped right out of the car.

— 17 —

Fairweather Island

Ever drifting, drifting, drifting
On the shifting
Currents of the restless main;
Till in sheltered coves, and reaches
Of sandy beaches,
All have found repose again.
—Henry Wadsworth Longfellow

It rained every day for two weeks. Rained when Kate went to bed and when she got up. Rained as she sipped tea in Mary's kitchen and while talking to her father, who had surprised Gwen with a last-minute trip to snowy New Hampshire, on the phone. Rained so steadily and so hard she couldn't paint, couldn't find enough light to tell pink from lavender. Rain slid beneath the slanted front door on Pacifica Lane and sloshed its way clear to the fireplace. The basement flooded, and when Kate went down with the repairman, she found an elderberry bush ripped clear from its roots floating in the murky depths.

It rained when they packed Jenny's car. They filled the suitcases with soggy clothes, wrapped Jenny's many books and CDs in plastic. It rained when Jenny looked at her father's house one last time and Wayne caressed her neck. Thankfully it rained when Kate kissed them good-bye, so they could not accuse her of crying again.

"I'll call you as soon as we get settled in Austin. If anything . . ." Jenny let the rest drop. Nicole stood on the porch, a tiny thing in one of her father's sweaters. They'd already said their good-byes, with tears and then an argument. The rain got on their nerves.

It rained and thundered and on one particularly volatile afternoon, electrified Fahrenheit Hill with so many lightning strikes, the ground sizzled and produced a hum that drove the dogs in the area wild. One bolt hit the stump of the laurel tree and for the next week the smell of gasoline was so strong, no one but Ron Stottenmeir put to sea. Since his wife had taken the kids to New York to live with a cousin, Ron put out during all kinds of weather. He left on Fridays, left with bananas on board. No man in town would fish with him.

Then exactly three weeks after the boat had gone down, the rain stopped. Within an hour of dawn, there wasn't a single cloud left in the sky. Kate emerged warily from the house on Pacifica Lane, but when she squinted at the sun and felt the warmth on her cheeks, she knew the worst was over.

She and Nicole headed toward Seal Bay High, but halfway to the school it was clear no one else was going. The beach had been overrun by the senior class, buttered up with baby oil, playing football on the sand. A sun day, apparently. Trudy Casson had closed her diner for the third time in a week and, Kate thought, probably for good. Her regulars shuffled unhappily along the sand, grumbling about the tepid coffee they'd had to bring from home, the cold cereal their wives had slapped on the table before meeting in the park like a flock of sun-starved birds. Trudy herself lay on a dune, her head in Zachary Levine's lap. Zachary, who now gave tours through his castle, was something of a celebrity. He had sealed the leak in Kate's basement with little more than stones and handmade mortar, and was in demand all over town for rock walls and elaborate stonework, for flights of fancy the woman had decided they deserved.

Kate spotted Harvey Pinkerton at the end of the pier, still waiting. He'd closed his umbrella, traded his Bible at least temporarily for the sports page, the latest on the Giants' upcoming season. News crews still came to town occasionally, though nothing was ever caught on tape. Last week, a great white had taken a bite out of a surfer in San Francisco Bay and interest had shifted south, to a more credible danger.

"Can we go see Mary?" Nicole asked.

It was difficult to be stern in the face of so much fair weather. Kate stepped over a Garfield beach towel, turned toward Fahrenheit Hill. She'd climbed the street so often in the last three weeks, she'd developed muscles she never knew she had. She walked at a brisk pace, was a few steps ahead of Nicole when the sun hit the stump of the laurel tree and revealed what had been hidden by the rain. In a shallow pocket of earth between the dead roots, the unmistakable bristles of a cypress tree had sprouted. Kate ran to the tree, breathed in the scent not of bay leaves, but of something woodier, an aroma of pine. Then she noticed them all over, cypress seedlings shooting up everywhere, taking hold in the bare, winter soil.

She turned back to Nicole, but the girl wasn't looking at the tree. Kate followed her gaze to Mary's front porch, where a young man stood with the rigidness of someone who has been taking care of things, who only weeps after the day's arrangements have been made. A boy, a man now, with Ray's jaw and her cheekbones, eyes full of pain and incredulity, though the loaded backpack at his feet suggested he would, at the very least, give her time to explain.

Her hand fluttered, and she stilled it behind her. She slowed her breathing, decided there was no scent more delicious than cypress after a rain, nothing in the world that mattered as much as taking a few moments to savor it.

She turned to Nicole, who was standing on tiptoes, holding herself back. "Go on," she said.

Nicole's smile was brilliant. "Jacob."

The boy turned to Nicole, lost a year of care and torment from his face. Nicole began to run, her eyes seemingly startled at her own speed, as if she'd expected this to be like one of her dreams where she moved her legs but got nowhere. When Jacob wrapped his arms around her, she laughed out loud, astonished and delighted. As if, even though she'd expected it, the intensity of joy still took her by surprise.

Whenever he was in the water, it was the most amazing thing. Nothing hurt. His joints no longer ached. Even his back paw, the one with the awful arthritis, felt brand-new again. His muscles and bones went numb, he floated as if filled with air. He lay on his back and rode the swells and was never bothered by the occasional thunder, since he'd gone deaf long ago.

Once, he washed up on a pinnacle of rock the seagulls didn't want to share, then for a few days he got lodged in a crusty tide pool that tore up his belly. Finally he landed on a hot stretch of sand and went no farther. He lay still, probably from weakness though it felt curiously like euphoria. The sky was a mosaic of clouds and sky, an occasional rainbow, and he was content to drift off into wavy, wet dreams.

He came awake to a slow-moving shadow. He opened his eyes, saw a plane passing him like all the others, already a speck in the western sky. He tried to bark, but the cold had worn off and his throat was swollen shut. The pain was unbearable. He couldn't snap at the miserable seagulls who circled him. He could do nothing but watch as the plane abruptly swung around.

Lucky disregarded the improbable vision of the plane aiming right for him, heading lower and lower until it practically skimmed the beach. Its belly opened up and a man appeared in the aperture. Perhaps the plane was too heavy because the man began tossing things out—crates and boxes, a bright orange raft that began to inflate the moment it hit the air. Lucky found the whole scene dubious and a little ridiculous—a man leaning perilously out of a plane and waving joyously, the smile on his face as wide as the fishermen's after they'd filled the hold.

Lucky was so hungry he might be imagining the whole thing. He couldn't remember eating, couldn't judge the passage of time. The man signaled something and sealed the door of the plane. Instantly, the wings arced upward, the engine picked up speed like a swallow who has been flying all winter and has finally spotted land. Within seconds, the airplane had disappeared across the island to the east.

Lucky struggled to his feet, then limped up the sand. He sniffed for anything—mussels, bugs, even the crab remains he usually disdained. He found nothing and finally collapsed.

He prayed for the tide to come in and collect him. He wanted the numbness back. He rested his head on his paws and closed his eyes. He fell asleep and dreamed of food.

For a long time, he didn't believe he had woken, because the air smelled as savory as the backyard barbecues the man used to put on. Even when he opened his eyes, the mirage of home continued. Though he was still on the island and a hundred yards out to sea an unfamiliar ship sat anchored, not fifty feet from him the beloved crew of the *Sarah Jane* sat on crates beside an orange raft and a campfire, dining on bottled water and an assortment of skewered meat. Lucky closed his eyes on the spellbinding apparition and sniffed the air. The smell, at least, was real, exquisite, and though his legs no longer worked, his mouth still managed to water.

The sea lapped at his paws, and he moaned in relief. First his pads went numb, then his legs. The waves had reached his belly by the time he felt the vibration of running feet. Each step electrified him, masked his hunger, doused the pain. He disregarded everything except the familiar scent of rubber and fish and the man who had carried him whenever he couldn't find the strength to walk.

When he opened his eyes, he was blinded by the giant's flaming hair, then slowly the second man, the one he loved best, came into focus. Lucky thumped his tail into the waves, made out a dozen colors in the man's eyes he'd never been able to see before now. When strong, familiar arms slipped beneath him, he let out a joyous howl. Before the keeper of his heart could lift him, he leapt right out of his arms. Forgetting he'd ever been old and tired, Lucky began to run.